THE EAST END

THE EAST END

WEBB HUBBELL

BEAUFORT
BOOKS

THE EAST END

Hardcover: 9780825308970
Ebook: 9780825308079
Paperback: 9780825309977

For inquiries about volume orders, please contact:
Beaufort Books
info@beaufortbooks.com

Published in the United States by Beaufort Books
www.beaufortbooks.com

Distributed by Midpoint Trade Books,
a division of Independent Publishers Group
www.ipgbook.com

Cover Design by Michael Short
Interior design by Mark Karis

Printed in the United States of America

To:
Suzy and George

Author's Note

This story is set in Little Rock, Arkansas. I used to know the names of its streets, parks, buildings, and neighborhoods like the back of my hand, but no more. There is a health clinic in the East End of Little Rock, but it was built long after I left. There are "east ends" in most cities and towns throughout the United States. They can be known as "the other side of the tracks," "the west side," "the south end," or by countless other names. The East End is where poverty, crime, and municipal neglect are a way of life. All the characters, places, and events in this book come from my imagination. But the reality of the East End is very much a part of the landscape of America.

Prologue

Standing on the edge of the cliff, Jana Hall looked over the blue-green expanse of Lake Ouachita—forty thousand acres of clear water surrounded by twenty thousand acres of towering trees and unspoiled flora. She came to this bluff to meditate, to clear her head, and to dream. It was her place. She would sit on the bluff's edge, sometimes for hours, and always leave refreshed, ready to resume life.

Today would be different. No, a developer wasn't building a condominium or a casino on the site, at least not yet. The surrounding forest was part of an Arkansas state park, free from commercial development. But it was only a matter of time before the state sold Lake Ouachita's shoreline to help solve the next budget crisis.

Her bare toes curled over the lip of the bluff, and she leaned forward, ready to fall into the deep water to her death. But one hand held tight to a small sapling, and she couldn't let go. What was wrong with her? She closed her eyes and willed herself to jump, or at least to let go.

But nothing happened. She felt the crackle of old leaves, twigs, and warm earth against her toes, and her courage vanished. Her unruly mind turned to the memory of the boy who first brought her to this place so long ago, and she sank to the ground, defeated.

He wasn't tall or athletic, but he was intelligent, and his dark eyes made her weak at the knees. His confident grin had convinced her to go camping and surrender to his awkward attempts at seduction.

She wondered if he remembered her, ever thought of her. Their relationship had lasted only a year in college before she'd ended it.

She'd gone on to med school in Memphis, and he went to law school in Fayetteville. They both ended up in Little Rock, but traveled in different circles. You could do that in Little Rock now—it had become a big city.

She had married twice, first to an aspiring doctor while in med school. He was God's gift to medicine, and every nursing student in Memphis. The marriage ended before it began, and she met and married Judd Wilson not long after finishing med school and moving to Little Rock. Her friends worried she'd fallen for him on the rebound, but she knew better.

Judd was a successful Little Rock businessman whose wife had left him for a golf pro and the Florida sun and sand. He was older than Jana, but his strong sense of ethics and gentle soul won her over. He adored her and always supported her budding career. They had hoped for children, but it wasn't in the cards. Otherwise, their marriage was as close to perfect as it comes.

Six years ago, Judd's doctor discovered an inoperable melanoma in his brain. Judd chose not to tell a soul or undergo treatment that might extend his life a few weeks or months. Instead he spent his last weeks arranging his affairs and then told Jana he had to go to California to meet a client. The next evening, he enjoyed a wonderful dinner accompanied by a Pinot Noir from Oregon's Domaine Serene Vineyard at the Four Seasons Hotel in Santa Barbara. Then he went for a stroll on the beach, turned toward the ocean, and walked straight into the water.

Two days later, Jana received his letter: he couldn't bear the reality of becoming a burden to her, undergoing the treatments that would make little difference. He preferred to die with dignity where his life had begun. He left her in good shape financially, but emotionally bankrupt.

A sudden gust of wind rustled through the trees and caught Jana's hair, bringing her back to the present. Stretching her limbs with a sigh, she rose and walked away, knowing she would have to face the day.

1

Jack Patterson was relaxing by the pool in LA with his client and friend, Red Shaw, owner of the NFL's Los Angeles Lobos, when his cell phone rang. Maggie Matthews, his paralegal and best friend, picked it up with a sigh because she and the phone were in Washington, DC. Jack was a top-notch lawyer, conversant with contemporary technology, but he had a habit of leaving his cell phone at home or turned off.

"For once, why couldn't he remember his phone?" Maggie mumbled under her breath. She recognized the Arkansas number with a twinge of apprehension. Phone calls from Arkansas often came with bad news.

"Sam, it's Maggie. Jack's in LA and left his cell phone here at the office. Anything I can do to help?"

"Well, hey, Maggie. How are you? What a nice surprise—I'd rather talk to you, anyway. When's he due back? Do you think you could talk him into coming here for a golf weekend?" Sam Pagano knew Maggie was about the only person who could get Jack to Little Rock no questions asked.

Maggie paused, wondering if there was more to the invitation than golf. It had been a rough year for Sam. He'd run for a seat on the Arkansas Supreme Court and lost. Everyone thought the election would be a cakewalk for Little Rock's long-time prosecutor, but it had turned out to be a nasty dogfight. His well-funded conservative opponent, Judge Glenn Coleman, had won, carried into office thanks to the sweeping takeover of constitutional offices and court seats by

Republicans in the once Democratic state of Arkansas.

"I'm fine, Sam. He's due back on Friday, but maybe I can convince him to stop on his way back in Little Rock, if that's not too soon?"

"This weekend would be great."

"Let me try to reach him. I'll get back to you," she promised.

If there was something wrong with Sam, Maggie should have already known. Micki Lawrence, a Little Rock defense lawyer and Sam's good friend, spent a good bit of time in DC these days working out of Jack's office while her significant other, Larry Bradford, supervised the construction of Maggie's new home in eastern Maryland.

Sam's invitation couldn't have come at a better time. Jack's daughter, Beth, and Maggie were supervising the move from his home in Chevy Chase to a condominium in DC's Kalorama neighborhood. The condo was perfect. Within walking distance of the metro, the renovated building retained its mid-century charm, but now boasted a fitness center, concierge service, and pool.

The unit itself consisted of two large bedrooms, two-and-a-half baths, an office/library, a family room, and a modern kitchen. Its high ceilings and beautiful woodwork fit Jack's personality. Still, as the move approached, Jack had become irritable. No surprises there—the house in Chevy Chase had been home to Jack and his late wife, Angie, for over twenty years.

Ovarian cancer had taken Angie more than six years ago, and Jack still struggled with the loss. The decision to downsize had been his, but reality hit when Maggie handed him the schedule and the movers dropped a pile of boxes on his front porch. Beth had offered to spend a week doing the hard work of sorting and tossing, but Jack insisted he wanted to do it.

As deadlines passed and frustrations grew, Beth and Maggie came up with a plan to get him out of town while they finished the packing and handled the actual move. Maggie called Gina Halep, the Lobos' president, and asked her to schedule a meeting in Los Angeles the week of the move. Gina, an able accomplice, assured Maggie she would need at least a week of his time.

Like most well-laid plans, not everything had gone well with the move. She should have known the cable guy would fail to show for the long-scheduled appointment. There would be hell to pay if the new place didn't have Wi-Fi or ESPN when Jack got back. If she could convince Jack to spend a few extra days in Little Rock, she felt sure everything would be shipshape for his return.

Maggie had laughed when she found his cell phone on his office desk several days ago. She considered his forgetfulness a good sign. For a short while Jack had become addicted to his phone, always checking for emails or messages. He called that time his "millennial stage" and joked that he'd fallen in with a bad crowd. Maggie blamed his obsession on his former girlfriend, Carol Madison. Her opinion had never wavered: Carol was a "bad crowd" all by herself.

Maggie called Jack, but he didn't pick up the phone Gina had loaned him, so Maggie called Gina, who handed her phone to an embarrassed Jack.

"Don't say a word—I know where it is. What's up?"

"Well, you'll be glad to know the move is proceeding as scheduled. Beth and I have everything under control, so you needn't rush back. In fact, you have an invite from an unlikely source." Maggie told him about Sam's call.

"I should have already been to see him, but Micki and Clovis said he was all right. Hurt and disappointed, but doing okay seemed to be the consensus. You sure you don't need me?"

"No, you check on Sam. Your new home will be in perfect order by the time you come home. I'll let Clovis know you're coming, and I'll book you a room at the Armitage. Do I need to FedEx your clubs?" she asked.

Clovis Jones had been Jack's occasional bodyguard and investigator since the Cole case, and was now as good a friend as Jack could ever have. He'd saved Jack's life more than once, and kept him out of trouble more times than Jack could count.

"Please don't tell Clovis I'm coming. He never tells me when he comes to DC. I don't need protection to play golf, and it will be fun to surprise him. Sam's club pro can lend me a set of clubs. But call Micki. Ask her if there's anything I need to know about Sam."

They talked business—what was going on with Red Shaw and the Lobos, anything but the move. She knew no matter how the condo was arranged, the first few days would be rough. The new place would require adjustment, and change didn't come easy to Jack, The concept of seeking change sounded good, almost noble. But he was a creature of habit, and this move wouldn't be easy for him.

Jack had a little news: NFL management had encouraged Red to move the Lobos to San Antonio to avoid the possibility of three NFL franchises in Los Angeles. Jack was to negotiate with both the NFL and the city of San Antonio. He promised to find his temporary phone, and they hung up on a high note. She dropped his phone into her purse, turned out the lights, and was about to close the door when a little chill ran up her spine. She had learned to take the feeling seriously. She rummaged through her purse for her own phone and punched in a familiar number.

2

Flying from Los Angeles to Little Rock took forever. I endured changing planes and terminals at DFW, and arrived late after a long delay on the tarmac caused by a line of heavy thunderstorms. My cell phone with the Uber app was still in DC, so I jumped into a waiting cab. I was lucky to find one at this hour.

Both the driver and his cab needed a bath, so I didn't engage in conversation, but watched as the downtown skyline came into view. We had almost reached the exit for downtown when the driver made an unexpected turn onto a state road I remembered as Highway 365, or Confederate Boulevard, a road that went nowhere.

"Driver, you're going the wrong way. I'm staying at the Armitage Hotel. It's downtown. You need to turn around," I said with irritation.

The driver didn't respond, but nodded and slowed. I looked at the visor on the passenger side for the driver's name, but there were no credentials displayed. The driver made another quick turn down a road I remembered that led to the Fourche Bottoms, Little Rock's version of the Everglades. Was he crazy?

"Driver, you are going the wrong way. Turn around—*now*!" I demanded.

He mumbled something that sounded like "shortcut."

What the hell? I considered jumping out of the car, but we were now speeding down a dark, two-lane road, going way too fast for me to jump. Suddenly a pair of headlights shone out of the darkness.

"Stop, do you hear me? Stop the car!" I shouted.

He came to a screeching halt and pulled off to the side of the road about a hundred yards from the headlights.

"Have it your way," he snarled, and I was glad to oblige. Anything would be better than another moment in his fetid car.

He peeled off at breakneck speed until the only light left came from the waning moon and the looming headlights.

"Time to walk, Jack," I said to no one, for once wishing I had my cell phone. As I turned to pick up my bag I saw a man walking out from the woods. I felt a line of sweat trickle between my shoulder blades.

"You won't need that bag," he said, gesturing with some kind of handgun. A robbery. *Okay, don't panic,* I told myself.

"Here, go ahead, take my bag. And my wallet." I tried to sound compliant.

"Walk," he ordered, and motioned for me to follow a gravel path that wound through the swampy woods.

I thought about running, but before I could test my options, I realized we weren't alone—every twenty yards down the path another man joined our procession. No one said a word, but they each carried a gun. By the time we reached a clearing—surrounded by a swamp, thick underbrush, and trees—three more had joined the party. This was no robbery.

The man who'd first met me on the road spat and said, "You came home one too many times, Jack."

"Who are you? What's going on?" I figured I already knew.

He spat again and grinned. "This!" His heavy fist landed square on my jaw. "And this!" The toe of his boot struck right between my legs. A pain like fire coursed through my lower body, and I thought my brain would explode.

When I came to, two men were holding me upright by my arms. The pain emanating from my groin distracted me from feeling the pain in my jaw. I coughed and sputtered, trying to recover my wits. My assailant was dancing around me like a boxer, trying to decide where to strike next. The men holding me up were laughing and egging him on.

"Enough!" A voice came from the darkness, and my assailant backed off.

Any sense of relief was quickly dashed by his next order.

"Get the rope," the voice barked.

Before I could react, someone threw a hangman's noose around my neck, tied my hands behind my back, and covered my mouth with duct tape. Two men dragged me underneath what was sure to be the hanging tree.

Still dancing and grinning, the first guy threw the other end of the rope over a sturdy limb. It was useless to resist. There was no sense trying to remember faces or voices—where I was going, it wouldn't matter.

The voice from the dark spoke again. "People who die in these woods are seldom found. Most likely, critters will eat most of you."

The others had backed off a little, no longer laughing. The duct tape kept me quiet, but my eyes asked one question.

"Why? Sorry, Jack. You don't deserve the satisfaction of knowing why. But I will tell you how," the voice answered.

I wasn't sure I was interested, but given the circumstances I had little choice but to listen. Besides, my instincts told me to keep him talking—maybe a miracle would occur. If there ever were a time for the New Madrid Fault to shift, this was it.

The man's voice interrupted my prayers for an earthquake. "For a good lynching, we raise you high enough so your big toe touches the ground if you stretch. For the first few hours you'll tiptoe and jump, trying to keep your feet grounded. Every time your ankle relaxes, the rope cuts into your neck, and you choke and gasp for air. After a while, your ankle cramps and your toe *can't* touch the ground, and slowly you choke to death. Then again, you might get lucky. A bear might find you first.

"I know Clem was itchin' to give you the butt whippin' you deserve, but I want you wide awake. It's a shame Clovis didn't meet you at the airport. I've got another rope with his name on it."

Every inch of my body clenched. I squirmed and tried to fight, but it was useless. Before long the the noose tightened, and my body rose.

"String him up real careful, boys, like I showed you." I heard the words, but could only focus on breathing as the rope burned my throat and my feet searched for the ground. My mind was alive and working, but my body was in a panic.

Who was this guy, and how did he know I was coming to town?

3

At first, I wasn't sure if I was alive or dead. Everything was white, and I felt suspended in mid-air. My throat was on fire, and I couldn't think straight. As my eyes focused, I recognized Terry Collins standing by my bed. We'd been childhood friends, and she was now the trauma coordinator for the University of Arkansas for Medical Sciences.

"You'll be okay, Jack. Don't try to talk. We've given you strong pain meds and steroids for the swelling in your neck. Try to relax—Dr. Thomas will be here any minute."

I drifted back to sleep, at some point wakened by an insistent voice calling my name. I recognized the silhouette of a doctor.

"Mr. Patterson, I'm Charles Thomas. You're a lucky man. I'm told this isn't your first time here, but it could have been the last. Mr. Jones got to you in the nick of time. You've had a CAT scan and a CTA of your neck—looks like no permanent damage, but you'll be sore for a while. If all goes well, we'll let you out tomorrow. But you need to take it easy. No more cabs." He laughed and was gone.

I tried to focus—what did he say about Clovis? But my throat hurt, and nothing made sense. It wasn't long before I fell back into my drug-induced slumber. I woke to the sight of a nurse, more attractive than the doc.

"My name is Hazel. Terry told me to take special care of you," she said as she adjusted the IV.

Hazel told me to relax and proceeded to check the various needles and tubes that were attached to me. Her hands traced what I suspected were rope burn marks on my neck, and what I assumed was a lot of bruising where I'd taken the first blow.

"You look at lot worse than you are. The blow to your jaw broke nothing, but your face will look bad for a few days. The rope burn is tender, and you should be careful with your voice."

She punched a button, and the head of my bed sank down until I was lying parallel to the floor. She lifted the sheet covering my lower area and said, "Now don't get embarrassed. Hold still." Her probing fingers were gentle and impersonal.

"You took quite a blow, Jack," she remarked. "If you're in a lot of pain, it's okay to push the button for relief. You can't over-medicate."

My jaw hurt like hell, but what terrified me was that I could see her hands moving around my groin, but I couldn't feel a thing—the entire area was numb.

"Sometimes this kind of trauma results in loss of feeling, but don't worry, everything is intact—you'll be fine. If the feeling doesn't return in a few days, you should see someone."

That wasn't a possibility I wanted to consider.

I dozed off again. When I woke I saw a familiar figure standing at the foot of the bed. "They tell me you're not supposed to talk, so don't." Clovis must have come into the room while I was sleeping.

"Do you remember what you told me when I was here a year ago? You said I looked like shit. Well, my friend, you look worse, and I apologize." I saw tears welling in his eyes. "Do you want to know what happened?"

I nodded yes.

"Maggie called to let me know you were coming to town and wanted to surprise me. She was worried—said something about someone stepping over a grave. Anyway, she asked me to meet you at the airport and promised to take the heat for spoiling the surprise.

"I couldn't imagine any danger, figured you'd be fine if I let you take Uber or a cab. I would follow at a safe distance. You'd be none the wiser, and when you called I could feign surprise. I was so wrong."

Clovis choked up, so I reached out for his arm, shook my head no, and mouthed, "What happened?"

He collected himself and continued. "Your plane was late. I felt sure all the cabs would have left, but one pulled up just as you walked out of the terminal. I watched you get in and settled in behind as it pulled away.

"When your cabbie took the wrong exit, I knew something was wrong. I called for backup and tried to keep up without being noticed. When your cab stopped, I pulled off the road and came running but waited when I saw the men following you into the woods. There were four of them.

"I warned my backup what we were up against and followed you into the woods, knowing if I charged you wouldn't make it. I heard their sick plan to leave you dangling and was about to crash their party when the leader ordered everyone to scatter. It killed me to wait to cut you down. I'm so sorry, Jack." Clovis hung his head.

"Clovis, give it up. You saved my life." I felt like I'd swallowed a frog, but it was worth the effort.

Clovis looked up and said, "Yeah, maybe, but you're still here."

I whispered, "Better than being bear bait. A point in your favor, I believe."

We both knew we'd escaped—me, with my life, and Clovis without the guilt of losing a close friend. We sat in comfortable silence for a while.

I dozed off and woke to find Clovis still by my side. "Who knows I'm here?" I could barely hear my voice, and Clovis had to stoop to hear.

"Sam does, and Maggie, Beth, and Micki are on their way. Sam kept you out of the papers, but it's no secret you're in town."

"Okay," I sighed. "It is what it is. I want to see Sam."

4

I DREADED MAGGIE, BETH, AND MICKI'S ARRIVAL. Not that I didn't love them all, but I didn't look forward to being fussed over or answering endless questions. Maybe there was a benefit to not having a voice.

The downside was I couldn't pester Clovis with questions. I've had lone assassins try to kill me, but what in the world had caused four men to lay a trap for me at the airport and try to leave me to die in the worst way I could imagine? How had they known my travel plans? And what would they do when they found out I was still alive?

Clovis interrupted my thoughts. "Sam should be here any minute. Wild horses couldn't have kept Maggie and Beth away, but it makes protecting everyone a little difficult. Thank goodness Martin is sending Big Mike with Maggie."

Martin is Martin Wells, head of security for Walter Matthews's companies. Walter is my best friend, golfing buddy, and Maggie's husband. He's the president of one of the largest insurance companies in the U.S., Bridgeport Life. Big Mike Fendler is a former Iraq War veteran who works for Martin.

"Don't worry—my people are on full alert," he continued. "Paul will make sure Beth and Micki are safe until we can figure out what's happening. For the moment we're assuming everyone is a potential target, including spouses."

Before I could respond, Sam burst into the room, an agitated nurse in tow. He shooed her away, greeted Clovis, and looked at me with a frown.

"I've seen you look worse," he snickered, dropping into the chair

Clovis had vacated. He was the picture of health and vigor, a stark contrast to my sorry state. His mouth curled into a smile that implied he knew a secret and looked forward to using it—an effective tool for a prosecutor.

I tried to wave away his obligatory apologies for dragging me into this mess and whispered, "Who knew I was coming?"

"Only Maggie, as far as I know. I had something personal I wanted to talk to you about, so I didn't even tell Micki. I figured once we did our business you could decide whether you wanted to stick around for a few days."

Unless Maggie's phone had been bugged, someone at the Armitage Hotel must have tipped off the bad guys. Whoever wanted me dead had gone to a lot of trouble to keep tabs on me and had planned my abduction and murder on short notice. Not a reassuring thought.

Sam shifted his weight and cleared his throat, trying to get my attention. I struggled to focus.

"Clovis has filled in most of the gaps, but we'll need a statement. I'll set something up in a couple of days when you're up to talking. I know you want to get back to DC, but I can't let you leave town without a statement. Okay?"

I shook my head no. Both Clovis and Sam looked puzzled.

I took a deep breath, and with my voice still a whisper said, "I'm not leaving until you and I talk about what's bothering you, and I'm not about to let some asshole get away with trying to kill me."

Stringing the words together took more effort than I expected. I took a minute.

"Clovis, talk to the management at the Armitage. Some member of the staff's a rat. Until we find out who, I want everyone on full alert and protected. Who's meeting Maggie's plane?"

Sam raised his eyebrows and looked at Clovis, who said, "Paul and Jordan are meeting the plane when it lands at Hodges Air Center. Maggie's ahead of you about the Armitage. She gave the manager what for over the phone and has scheduled a come-to-Jesus meeting with him tomorrow. If it's okay with you, I think you and Sam could use some alone time. Sam, keep him quiet if you can." He left without waiting for an answer.

Paul, his number one assistant, had looked after Maggie and Beth during previous cases. Jordan, another of Clovis's men, had proved more than capable the last time I was in Little Rock. If Clovis had sent two of his best to pick up Maggie at the airport, he was worried.

We sat in silence for a few minutes, before I took pity on him. "Okay, Sam. Tell me about your sudden interest in my golf game." It was time to get whatever was bothering him off his chest.

"That obvious, huh?" he asked. I nodded.

"I guess it's two things. The supreme court race took more out of me than I expected, and not the way you might think. Sure, losing hurt, but the thought that more than half of this state's voters believe my opponent is better qualified makes me question why I've spent my entire professional life in public service."

Sam's opponent had served less than two years as a traffic court judge in Sebastian County, but that was enough to allow his name to appear on the ballot as "Judge" Glenn Coleman. The NRA endorsed him as the only candidate who had a hunting license and believed in the sanctity of the Second Amendment. "Judge" Coleman had accumulated a three-million dollar campaign war chest, mostly from conservative PACs, the gun lobby, and companies who did business in Arkansas, all hoping to influence the court's decisions.

Sam was endorsed by about every lawyer in the state, but the campaign turned ugly when Coleman attacked Sam's record as a prosecutor, calling him "soft on crime." He described Sam's program to expunge the records of youthful offenders as a "free pass from responsibility," claiming it had turned Little Rock into a sanctuary city for drug dealers and gangs. Coleman inundated the airwaves with ads warning that a vote for "free pass Pagano" would bring violent crime right to the doorsteps of innocent citizens.

It hurt that Sam was a well-known Democrat, and Coleman ran as a Republican. It will be a while before a Democrat gets elected to a major office in Arkansas. Hell, a mediocre former TV sports announcer had been elected governor by a landslide under the Republican banner. I'm not sure Tony White knows what a governor does, but his new wife, Kristine McElroy, does. She tried to lasso Sam last year, but he wised up, more than willing to allow the press and anyone else to think she had dumped him. She was a piece of work.

Sam continued. "Jack, I've decided to resign, sooner rather than later. Part of the reason I ran for judge was because I didn't want to get burned out, or even worse, hardened and cynical, as a prosecutor. It's time to move on. I've had a few offers, and if you've got the time, I thought maybe we could talk, well, about my future."

"Sure," I replied. "At least for now you've got a captive audience. But I know a red herring when I hear it. What else is going on?"

"Well, I had a favor to ask, but given what's happened…"

I had no idea what he was talking about. What could be so hard?

"Sam, my throat hurts and I can barely speak. Please just tell me what's bothering you."

He looked a little sheepish, but finally blurted out, "Jack, do you remember Jana Hall?"

5

Sure I did. Jana Hall had been Sam's girlfriend his junior year at Stafford State University. How could anyone forget Jana? She was tall and slender, but not fragile, with strong features and straight dark hair that reflected her Choctaw heritage. We all thought Sam had found the perfect girl, but the relationship didn't last.

"I do," I croaked. "But I haven't thought about her in years."

"Well, she's the real reason I asked you to come. She's a doctor, an internist, lives in Little Rock. I've seen her at an event or two, across the room, but that's it. We went our separate ways a long time ago. You could have knocked me over with a feather when her name came up in my office a few weeks ago."

"Is she in some kind of trouble?"

"Well, the answer is yes and no. That's why I wanted to talk. Don't worry—I won't prosecute her. I learned my lesson in Woody's case. If it comes to that, I'll recuse."

Sam was the prosecutor when our boyhood friend, Woody Cole, was arrested for killing U.S. Senator Russell Robinson. Sam's refusal to recuse had strained our relationship, but that was history. Still, I was glad to hear Sam wasn't ready to prosecute his former girlfriend.

"Because Little Rock is the state capital, my office has jurisdiction over misappropriation of state funds. Several times a year, a legislative audit turns up an irregularity and reports its findings to the Legislative Audit Committee. Sometimes the committee refers the matter to my office to determine if any criminal conduct occurred. Usually that's the end of the matter, but on rare occasion we've had to prosecute a specific individual if the conduct was egregious. Neither the state agency involved nor the legislature has ever pressured us. They refer the matter and let our office take it from there.

"About three weeks ago, I met with my deputies to review our pending cases. Nothing unusual, we do it every month. We were about to wrap up when my chief deputy, Kate Erwin, brought up a matter that had been referred to us from the Health Department rather than the Legislative Audit Committee. The department's auditors didn't think there was any criminal conduct involved—just poor bookkeeping by one of the department's contractors—but the director of the Health Department had demanded a full-scale criminal investigation.

"Kate said there was no evidence of criminal conduct, but the head of the Health Department had called several times to ask when to expect indictments. I told her to ignore his calls, and if the facts warranted no further investigation, to close the file. She agreed, but said she had also received calls from an aide to the governor and the chairwoman of the Senate Appropriations Committee. The political pressure made her nervous.

"Well, I admit to getting a little pissed. I wasn't about to let the executive or legislative branch pressure my office over a decision to pursue or not pursue a criminal case. Political pressure has no place in prosecutorial decisions."

When I worked at the Department of Justice, various congressmen and senators alike had tried with no success to use their political clout to influence individual cases. Janet Reno bit the head off of any congressman who tried to get in the middle of a pending matter at Justice. She listened politely, gave the offender a lecture on how the cow eats the cabbage, and closed the door firmly behind him. She was the epitome of integrity and politically tone deaf—I can't think of a better combination for the job. The memory made me smile.

I saw that Sam was watching me. He looked nervous, and I tried to reassure him with a go-ahead gesture. He let out a deep breath and continued. "Kate had no idea what was behind the Health Department's zeal to prosecute. The audit clarified that the money had been used for its intended purpose—providing health care services to Arkansas's poorest citizens in four public health clinics around the state. A few invoices were missing, but that was it. Otherwise everything was clean and above-board.

"At first, Kate thought it was a power play by the Health Department to gain control over the monies given to the clinics. The initial enabling legislation bypassed the department and sent money directly to the health clinics, but it didn't take long for the department to convince the legislature to move the money allocated to the clinics to the Health Department's general appropriation. It took even less time for the department to move those monies to a new program—a statewide obesity study—effectively defunding the clinics.

"Jana was both the founder and director of the four clinics. She's been at the forefront of health care for the disadvantaged in Arkansas for many years. The *Democrat-Gazette* has run several positive stories about the clinics and published what amounted to an obituary when she had to close them for lack of funds. Now it looks like the Health Department wants more than Jana's funds—they want her head."

I asked, "Does anyone in your office know about your former relationship?"

"Not that I know of. I've told no one. That's why I'm asking you. I need objective advice."

"Why not ask Micki?"

"I can't talk to Micki about this and neither can you," he said.

"Oh, come on, Sam. You and Jana dated thirty years ago. Micki couldn't care less about an old girlfriend."

Micki and Sam had enjoyed a short-lived romance a few years ago. Both had moved on.

"It's not what you think. Micki and I have been talking about my failed romances for as long as I can remember, but for some damn reason the state hired Micki as counsel for the obesity study. Why they need a lawyer, I don't know. Neither did Micki, but she wasn't about to turn down ten grand a month."

Micki is a criminal defense attorney, a damn good one in fact. But as far as I know she had no expertise in health law. I made a mental note to ask her about this mystery. But Sam was right—as long as Micki was working for the Health Department, even as a contract attorney, he couldn't consult with her about Jana.

Sam interrupted my musings. "Jack, there's something else."

"Don't tell me your deputy chose to prosecute."

"No, Kate closed the case, but the Health Department director blew a gasket. His exact words were 'we'll see about that.' Kate thinks the governor might intervene."

I raised my eyebrows. My throat hurt, and my voice was about gone.

Sam shook his head and said, "I think the guy was bluffing, but I could be wrong. No, that's not why I asked you to come."

I responded with a gesture that I hoped meant "okay, out with it."

"Jana called me a few days ago out of the blue. I was out of the office so we didn't talk, but I have to return the call."

6

Jana's call was surely not a coincidence. And there was no way Sam could return her call. The health clinics had been under investigation, and she had already retained counsel. Any communication should be through her lawyer. Besides, there are no secrets in politics—if Sam returned her call even to say he couldn't talk, a political enemy could make a mountain out of a molehill, and the press would have a heyday when someone leaked there had been a private conversation between Jana and Sam.

I whispered, "How does your office handle a direct call from someone under investigation?"

"Well, that doesn't happen often, but the lead prosecutor on the case, Kate, would call Jana's lawyer and ask him to advise the client that until the investigation was closed, I couldn't return her call."

"Then why not do that?" I asked, suspecting I knew the answer.

"Because my assistant sent me the message through our internal message system and noted that the subject was personal, not business."

Sam's problem was two-fold. He hadn't told Kate Erwin he knew Jana when the subject of her clinics came up at the staff meeting. There was no actual conflict of interest, but it was still awkward. On top of that, Donald Trump could be the only guy alive who wouldn't want to receive a phone call from an old girlfriend. Sam was dying to call Jana back, but he knew he couldn't.

If he asked Kate to call Jana's attorney, Kate would wonder why he hadn't disclosed their relationship at the staff meeting, and Jana would be embarrassed when Kate told her lawyer she had called. I could see only one solution to Sam's problem.

"Do you and Kate Erwin have a good relationship?" I asked.

"Absolutely. I don't think the governor will listen, but I'll recommend he appoint her as my replacement when I step down. She's been with me since our days at the public defender's office. Ask Micki about her—they're good friends. She's the best prosecutor I've got."

"Here's what you do. Tell Kate you didn't think there was any reason to mention you had dated Jana so long ago. Tell her Jana's phone call came out of the blue. Apologize, and tell her that with her approval, you'll ask a friend to return Jana's call—me. If the call has anything to do with the matter at hand, I'll let her know and she can call Jana's lawyer."

A slow smile was his only response.

"Sam, I'm okay with calling Jana, but I'd like to wait until they let me out of here. What day is it, anyway? I'll call her tomorrow afternoon, or the next day." I could barely hear my own voice. Oddly, it didn't hurt. It just wasn't there.

"It's Saturday," he replied, pushing back his chair and moving toward the door. "Jack, I'm sorry to involve you in all this. Take care of yourself, get some rest. I'll talk to Kate tomorrow. Why don't you hold off calling Jana until Monday? You'll have your hands full when Maggie and Beth get here. Maybe by then you'll have your voice back."

Tuckered out after our long conversation, I sank back into the meager hospital pillows, hoping to sleep, but my thoughts turned to Jana Hall.

Her parents had met at Oklahoma State, married, and moved to Bartlesville when her father took a job with Phillips Petroleum. When Jana was about five years old, the family moved to El Dorado, Arkansas. Her father worked for Murphy Oil, made good money, and they lived in a nice neighborhood. But her mother, a member of the Choctaw Nation, never felt comfortable with their neighbors. I remembered Jana railing about the clear lines drawn between the "haves" and "have-nots," determined by skin color.

She and Sam were thick as thieves in college, and she fit right in with our fivesome—Sam, Woody Cole, Marshall Fitzgerald, Angie, and myself. She and Angie were good friends, and we all enjoyed our time together. Then Sam developed a bad case of the dumb ass. The virus that infected him came in the form of a cute blonde, Margo Montgomery, a sophomore who drove a bright yellow Porsche.

On a Thursday, Sam told me Margo had asked him to go with her to Dallas. Her daddy was exchanging her Porsche for a different car—a dark green Jaguar—and he didn't think it was safe for her to drive all that way by herself. The temptation to drive both cars was too much for Sam, not to mention the prospect of a weekend with Margo. I reminded him we were supposed to spend Saturday at the lake. He waved off my protests, telling me not to worry, and that of course Jana would understand.

No surprise, Sam didn't say a word to Jana. I drew the short straw and had to explain his absence. I tried to cover for him, but failed miserably. Jana's reaction was sharp and to the point.

"You're a terrible liar, Jack Patterson. Margo cornered my roommate and told her all about her weekend plans. Sam made a poor choice. I hope the weekend is worth it."

Angie took out her frustration with Sam on me the whole weekend and refused to speak to Sam for weeks. To no one's surprise, Margo moved on to her next trophy, the football team's punter, a guy with long legs, a surfer's tan, and a Virginia accent. Sam tried his best to make amends, but Jana would have nothing to do with him. Sam's ego could only stand so much, and he took comfort in the arms of another bright-eyed coed and cheap beer at the Ship Ahoy, a local beer joint. None of us saw much of Jana afterwards, not even Angie—Sam's infidelity had tarnished us all.

The whoosh of the opening door and an incoming rush of women, including an indignant nurse, interrupted my memories. I smiled at the nurse and waved her away, submitting to careful hugs from Beth, Maggie, and Micki. I was glad to see them all, but it was a relief when Clovis walked in.

"Okay, ladies, let's give the patient some air. We've all seen him like this before." A gentle reminder that only a few years ago I'd been shot in the bar at the Armitage Hotel and spent several days in this same hospital. "And he's supposed to be resting his voice, so quit asking questions."

Maggie glared at him and took control.

"Beth will stay here tonight. I'll check in at the hotel and get things in order for your release. The doctor told me you should be able to go back to DC in a day or two."

"I won't be leaving for a few days," I rasped. "I can't leave until I give a statement to the police. And I need to spend a little more time with Sam."

"What could be so damned important?" Micki demanded. "Those guys are still on the loose. Shoot, they could be in the parking deck right now. The police can take a statement any time, and if Sam needs to talk, he can fly to DC. You need to get the hell out of here."

I reached up to take her hand. "Do you trust me?" I could barely hear my own voice. It didn't seem to belong to me.

"Most of the time, yes." Her frustration was clear, but at least she'd lost the scowl.

"I'm asking you. Trust me. I can't tell you why just yet, but I promise—"

"Okay, fine. Whatever you say. Maggie, let me know if you need anything." She leaned down and said, "Be careful, Jack. And try to remember who *you* can trust."

She gave Maggie and Beth quick hugs and was gone before I could say a word. I knew I'd hurt her feelings, but why did she have to be so prickly?

Maggie tried to cover Micki's awkward exit. "Well, I for one almost never trust you. Your new place is ready, but if you need to spend a few days here, I guess that's okay. I'll be back first thing tomorrow. Beth, call if you need me." She gave Beth a hug and left. I wondered if maybe…

I turned to Beth. "Sweetheart, go to the hotel with Maggie. Get a good night's sleep. I'll be fine."

"Sorry, but that decision is not yours to make. I'm going downstairs to get something to eat, but I'll be back in a few minutes." She closed the door before I could argue, and Clovis and I were alone.

I looked at my friend with tired eyes and asked, "Is everything under control?"

"I knew you wouldn't sleep until I reported. Yes. Big Mike and my people are a visible presence with Maggie and Beth at all times. The Wildcat didn't even object when I told her two of my guys would watch her ranch. Everyone's a little nervous. Martin's people in DC have increased Walter's protection, and I've notified our friends in St. Louis to be on alert."

Clovis had nicknamed Micki the "Wildcat" several years ago, and for good reason. Both her actions and temper could be swift and unforeseen. Beth and Jeff, my daughter's fiancé, live in St. Louis. It's a long story, but in the past few years I've taken on some cases out of the normal purview of an antitrust attorney. In return for a favor, some rather unsavory characters watch over my daughter and future son-in-law while Jeff finishes his residency and Beth gets her master's at Washington University. Only Clovis and I know of this arrangement.

I asked, "What about you and Stella?"

"Paul has my back and is in charge of Stella's protection. She threw a fit, but now that she knows what happened, she's being as cooperative as she can be."

"Fine mess we're in. Any idea who did this?" I could feel my concentration slipping.

"Not yet. Sam has the sheriff patrolling the area hoping someone will try something stupid—nothing so far. Speaking of Sam, anything you can tell me? Any possibility his problem relates to the attack?"

"Long story, we'll talk tomorrow. It's more personal than business."

Clovis raised his eyebrow at my confidence. He was a skeptic, but there was no way Sam's long-lost college girlfriend had anything to do with my near death. Of that I was sure.

7

I WOKE WITH A SHUDDER and a yelp to an almost blinding light and the touch of probing fingers. *Why don't they ever knock? They tell you to sleep....* Usually they're gone in a flash, but this one pulled up a chair and looked me in the eye.

"Mr. Patterson, my name is Henry Squire. I'm your attending physician. We'll let you out of here today, but listen to me. When you return to DC, I want you to have a complete physical, sooner rather than later. It's not about what happened the other day—I'm concerned about all the trauma you've experienced over the years. At some point it will take its toll. You need to pay better attention to your day-to-day health. Give me your internist's contact info, and I'll arrange for the hospital to send him a copy of our records."

"What do you mean, you're concerned?" I asked, now a little concerned myself.

"I can't put a finger on anything in particular. But Terry Collins told me that thirty years ago you received what we in trauma refer to as a 'fatal stomping.' I'm not sure how you survived that night, but in the last five years, you've had a broken bottle embedded in your leg, you were shot in the shoulder—the bullet barely missing your heart and lung—and now you've suffered severe trauma to your jaw and groin. Your internal organs have taken a beating. I hope you've lived a less stressful life in DC. I've signed your discharge papers, but I'm serious, Mr. Patterson. Don't procrastinate. Our bodies can only stand so much—one day yours might simply shut down."

Nothing like an optimistic prognosis. Thank heaven Beth and Maggie aren't here. They'd have me back to a doctor in DC in a New York minute.

"Thanks, I won't," I replied. He shrugged and left, ready for his next patient. I breathed a sigh of relief. He'd gotten my attention, and I promised myself not to procrastinate. But the last thing I needed right now was for him to keep me in the hospital for a week of tests.

I wondered where Beth had gone. The blankets were in the chair beside my bed, but her purse wasn't. I considered getting up, but the thought of dealing with the IVs wasn't appealing.

The door opened and in walked Micki. She had on runner's shorts and a tank top, and she carried two cups of Starbucks, a welcome change from weak hospital coffee. She was all business.

"Time for you to get up—the nurse told me you'll be discharged today. Beth's gone back to the hotel, so you're stuck with me." She gave me a quick kiss, deposited the coffee on the hospital tray, and sank into the chair Beth had vacated.

"Glad to have you back. Nice outfit," I teased.

"Don't get any ideas. From what I hear, your goods are damaged."

So much for light conversation. "Thanks for the coffee. Any idea when I can leave?" I asked. My throat was still sore and my voice was still raspy, but I felt better.

"You know hospitals. They wake you up early to say you can go home, but it's late afternoon before you see the light of day."

Micki and I had seen too many emergency rooms and hospitals in our history together. Both of us had learned how to sneak out of hospitals, but I needed someone to remove the IV, and I felt shaky. I couldn't help but remember the doctor's warning—I'd better leave the right way this time.

So I relaxed, and while we sipped our coffees, Micki caught me up on Little Rock friends.

"Ben has already called. There's a Jack's Special and a rack of ribs ready for you anytime you're up to coming to the restaurant."

Ben Jennings owned the best barbeque restaurant anywhere, and was sort of my second father. Micki and I had represented the family when his daughter was charged with stealing military secrets. No way I could leave town without dropping by for a meal and getting a case of barbeque sauce to take home. No way I would want to.

"Clovis had a tough time with Helen when she heard you were in the hospital. She wanted to come and camp out in the visitor's lounge. He promised you'd come see her as soon as you could."

Helen Cole is Woody Cole's mother. Micki and I defended Woody when he shot Arkansas Senator Russell Robinson. Helen believes in going to the hospital when a friend is ill and never misses a funeral.

Truth was, now I was here, I couldn't leave without checking in with old friends. These were people I've cared about, people I grew up with, people I've loved. I sure couldn't leave without seeing Helen and Ben. And I wanted to see Judge Marshall Fitzgerald, my daughter's godfather and one of my oldest friends.

Micki's voice roused me from my reverie, insistent and concerned. "Jack, what happened? Who could have done this? We're in Little Rock for God's sake—why…" Her voice trailed off as she thought. "Do you think it could be related to one of our old cases?"

I took a minute to think. "I have no idea. The leader wanted my death to be slow and painful. I can't imagine what could generate such hatred. In the past, physical attacks were related to the case. Now I don't see any rhyme or reason to it."

"You know Maggie will do everything she can to get you back to DC. She thinks you risk your life every time you come here. Maybe she's right."

"Well, that sure seems to be the case this time. But, Micki, I have to stay. This is my hometown. Clovis and I need to find out who or what is behind all this, and I need you to help me convince Maggie and Beth to leave."

"That's a tall order," she said, smiling. "Besides, what makes you think DC or St. Louis is any safer than Little Rock?"

"For starters, Martin and his team are on twenty-four hour watch for people trying to kidnap or harm Maggie. She's much safer in DC. As for Beth and Jeff, Clovis and I have a system in place for their protection."

"At some point, I will get either you or Clovis drunk enough to tell me what that system is. 'No secrets between us'—bullshit!"

Micki wouldn't understand or approve of my arrangement with the St. Louis organization protecting Beth and Jeff. I wasn't sure I did either, but it had worked so far. I kept quiet.

Micki knew when to give up. "Do you want to stay at the ranch while you're here?"

Micki lived on a couple hundred acres west of Little Rock. It was quite a place, and we had used it as a both a haven and work area during previous cases. But given the awkwardness of Sam's issues, I thought maybe not.

I dodged her offer. "Let me see what Clovis thinks. I bet he wants us to stay at the Armitage while Maggie and Beth are here."

"That make sense, but it's an open invitation."

Micki stepped outside when the nurse came in to remove the IV and help me put on the clothes that Clovis had brought.

When Micki returned, she got right to the point. "Jack, I've never seen either you or Clovis so undone. You and I have dodged a lot of bullets, so to speak, and they seem to bounce off you like rain off a duck's back. What makes this attack so different?"

"Well, getting lynched was something new." Her frown wiped the smirk off my face. "Sorry, but that's part of it. Another part is that the voice of the guy in charge was pure evil. It was personal, directed at me, and I'm sure I've heard it before. Who could hate me that much? Until we figure it out, I won't feel comfortable walking down any street here, in DC, or anywhere else."

She stared at me for a few minutes and then abruptly changed the subject. "I ran into your doctor in the hall. He gave me your discharge papers. You're free to go as soon as an orderly shows up with a wheelchair."

We knew how long *that* could be. It didn't take much to convince Micki to pretend we were going for a walk before slipping into an elevator and riding it to freedom.

Micki had already texted Clovis to meet us at the back exit, and before you could say "Jack Robinson," we were climbing into a waiting Suburban driven by Jordan, with Clovis riding shotgun. My grandmother used to use the "quick as Jack Robinson" phrase except she would say "Jack Patterson" instead. I loved my grandmother.

"You know, Jack, Dr. Squire told me he wants you to see an internist. If you need a recommendation, Clovis and I can give you a few names in Little Rock." Micki elbowed me.

Dr. Squire's recommendations were in the discharge orders that Micki stuck in her purse. I knew it wouldn't be long before both Maggie and Beth had read them.

"Thanks, but I've got it covered. I already have a doctor here in Little Rock. I'll make an appointment tomorrow. How is Larry?"

"Larry is fine, thank you. Don't try to change the subject. Who is this doctor? You haven't lived in Little Rock for thirty years. Do you keep him in reserve, just in case?"

My attempt at diversion hadn't worked.

"Well, no, but given the circumstances, maybe I should," I answered with a grin. "And I'm surprised at your assumption. The doctor I have in mind is female."

"Who? An old girlfriend?" she asked.

"No."

"Okay, so what's her name?"

"Doctor-patient confidentiality." My turn to act smug.

"Now you're messing with me," she said, pretending to sulk. We dropped her off at her office, and in a matter of minutes Clovis and I walked into one of my favorite hotels anywhere—The Armitage.

"You know Micki won't give up. She knows you're holding out on her about Sam," Clovis remarked.

"I know, but it's for her own damn good. Warn Paul not to spill any beans to Debbie."

Debbie Natrova is Micki's quirky office manager who lives with Paul. The two met during the Stewart case, and he fell head over heels for her. Micki isn't above suggesting Debbie engage in strategic pillow talk.

"Don't worry about Paul. But don't you think it's time you told me what's going on?"

"Yes, but not yet. Do you mind getting Maggie and Beth while I sit? Maybe the three of you can help me figure out how to keep Micki in the dark. You and Martin are worried about those guys in the swamp, but I'm more worried about Micki." I sunk into an armchair in a quiet corner of the lobby.

"One more thing—can you help me schedule a doctor's

appointment? I'd rather not involve Maggie," I asked.

"A doctor's appointment? In Little Rock?" He looked doubtful.

"Yes, in Little Rock."

"I thought you were just bullshitting Micki when you said you already had a doctor."

"No, I need to see a particular doctor, a Dr. Jana Hall. Can you call first thing tomorrow morning and see how soon I can get in?" I handed him the number Sam had given me with a straight face.

"Dr. Jana Hall. Why do I think this appointment is not about a physical?" He walked away laughing.

8

Clovis returned with Maggie and Beth. It didn't take long to agree on a spot for lunch. We headed to the Buffalo Grill at the foot of Cantrell Hill. The Sunday brunch at Crittenden's in the Armitage was as good as it gets, but that day I needed a cheeseburger with extra crispy fries. Between bites, I explained Sam's dilemma and his history with Jana.

"Why can't you tell Micki the truth?" Beth asked.

"Because if I tell her she might have a conflict, she'll quiz me about every case she's had with the prosecutor's office. Once she realizes the problem is her Health Department retainer, she might give it up. Sam wouldn't want her to lose that kind of money over a matter that's closed. Neither do I. She can stew for a few days." I dipped one of my french fries into Beth's cheese dip.

"So instead of seeing a real doctor, you're using the pretense of needing a physical to ask Sam's former girlfriend why she's calling him." Maggie had an uncanny ability to make me squirm.

"Maggie, the attending physician told me to see a doctor when I get back to DC, and I'll do that. But why not use his order as an opportunity to reconnect with Jana? She was a good friend a long time ago. She'll understand."

"If you say so." Maggie looked doubtful. "But tomorrow morning I'll make you an appointment with Mike Newman in DC. If you try to back out, either Beth or I will be glad to go with you." Beth nodded in agreement.

"And while you're taking a nap this afternoon," Maggie continued,

"I'll inquire about this Dr. Hall. For all you know, she might be a gynecologist, and then won't you feel like a fool."

She had a point.

"For your information, I'm not taking a nap. Beth and I are on our way to see Helen and Marshall."

No objections, as expected. She knew how much Beth loved Helen and Marshall. But I also knew my next announcement would go over like a lead balloon.

"As soon as you two decide I'll survive, I want you to go home. There's no case here."

I expected an explosion, but Beth remained silent and Maggie said stiffly, "We'll see."

No argument, no tears, just Maggie putting my suggestion on the back burner. We sat in silence until she cleared her throat.

"While you two see Helen and Marshall, I'll talk to Brian about next week's schedule. I don't think there's anything we can't push back. I hope you'll call Red and Gina tomorrow. You don't want them to read what happened in the papers before you tell them yourself. I'm surprised Sam has kept the press under wraps this long."

Brian Hattoy is the paralegal we hired less than a year ago to ease the burden on Maggie. He's a veteran of our country's never-ending wars in the Middle East, a hero in fact, awarded both a Silver Star and a Purple Heart. He's become a valuable member of our little team, a point his uncle, Red Shaw, reminds me every chance he gets.

I was more than a little tired after lunch, but I was determined to keep on schedule. After dropping Maggie at the hotel, Clovis drove us to Helen Cole's. Marshall was already there. I'd like to report more on the afternoon, but after hugs all around and evading questions about bruises and my still-raspy voice, I promptly fell asleep. The next thing I knew, Beth was shaking me, saying it was time to go.

Embarrassed beyond words, I tried to apologize. Marshall said to forget it—he was happy to spend time with Beth. Helen smiled and folded the old afghan she had laid over me.

Once in the car, I couldn't help myself. "I'm so sorry," I stammered.

"Quit apologizing. We all wondered when you'd crash," Beth said.

"Still, it's embarrassing."

"Helen said this wasn't the first time you've fallen asleep while she and Marshall talked." Helen's house had been a haven for all four boyhood friends: no judgments—no third degree.

Clovis took the front seat again, as our new driver, Sally, navigated the streets of Little Rock. He turned to speak to us.

"I took a chance and called the number Dr. Hall left for Sam. Turns out it was her personal number, and after some confusion over how I got it, she burst out laughing."

"Was it a good laugh?" I asked.

"She told me she's no longer seeing patients, but for you she'd make an exception. She'll meet us at Ben's tomorrow at eleven-thirty."

There weren't any private rooms at Ben's, but beggars can't be choosers. Besides, I could kill two birds with one stone. The prospect of a Jack's Special and reuniting with Jana filled me with nostalgia. I almost forgot what had happened Friday night.

Beth spoke up. "When we get to the hotel, Maggie wants you to meet her in the restaurant. You have an early dinner reservation."

"What about you? Aren't you joining us?" I asked.

"I'd rather order room service and finish a paper that's due. You know how much I love room service."

Angie and I had taken Beth with us on our travels when we could, and nothing pleased my daughter more than to order room service while Angie and I went downstairs for a cocktail and dinner. We never understood her affinity for room service, but enjoyed the time alone.

"Clovis, would you and Stella like to join us?" I asked.

"Thanks, but not tonight. Stella's had a long week, and, well, the last few days have been a little tough. I need a night off. Don't worry—Paul has security covered, and I'll be there tomorrow bright and early."

"I think I'll be okay at the Armitage," I said, ready for some peace and quiet.

"Have you forgotten the man with a knife?" Beth asked.

How could I forget a man with a knife lingering outside my hotel room, or Micki hearing the disturbance and breaking a wine bottle over his head?

"Okay, you're right. Please give Paul my thanks."

We arrived at the hotel, said goodbye to Clovis and Sally, and took the elevator to our rooms. As I used the key card, I realized I had no idea what had happened to my bag. For all I knew it was still somewhere in the Fourche Bottoms with my laptop. But there on the stand sat a suitcase full of clothes, my cell phone, and the old battered briefcase that Angie gave me when I left DOJ. A note from Maggie read, "You might need this."

I called Stella, who also managed our office's information technology, to tell her my laptop was gone. She told me not to worry. The computer had been fully backed up, and she would have a new one ready for me tomorrow afternoon. Except for all new passwords, I wouldn't notice any difference. "New passwords," I sighed. She'd installed an app that kept track of all my passwords, but of course the app had a password, too.

I shaved, took a shower, and felt better. Hot water on my sore bruises felt terrific, and I was able to shave around the rope burns. The lower half of my face was still purple, but I felt fairly presentable in a clean shirt and a pair of khakis.

As soon as I walked into the restaurant, I saw we had company. Beth was chatting with Maggie and her husband, Walter Matthews. They all rose, and Walter gave me a hug as Maggie and Beth giggled at my surprise. My good friend and golfing partner was surely a welcome sight.

Both Beth and Maggie had dressed for the occasion, and Walter wore a coat and tie. I felt underdressed, but couldn't imagine wrapping a tie around my swollen neck.

Maggie was tickled that she had pulled off the surprise. The last time the four of us had been together at this restaurant was during the middle of the Cole case. Walter had announced that Maggie had accepted his marriage proposal, and we spent the rest of the night celebrating.

"This brings back good memories," I said.

"I thought it might," Maggie said, smiling.

For the rest of the night we mirrored that evening—drinking good wine, enjoying scrumptious appetizers, and sampling each other's entrees. My favorite was Beth's bourbon grilled salmon with shallots. Avoiding the elephant in the room—the reason we were all here—we reminisced about their wedding and then turned to the plans for their new home in the Maryland countryside.

We were enjoying after-dinner drinks when Walter cleared his throat and said, "Jack, you haven't asked why I'm here."

"No, I haven't. Figured you'd tell me when you were ready." I tried to match his serious tone, but my voice refused to cooperate. We had a little laugh at my expense before he continued.

"I wanted to make sure you were okay. Now that I have, I'm here to drop Beth off in St. Louis and take my wife home. Home where I know she'll be safe. You've become a dangerous friend to have." His tone was light, but I knew he meant business.

I understood his concern, couldn't blame him one bit, but his remark still stung. It had never occurred to me that Maggie and Beth would leave without a fight.

"Surprised?" Maggie asked. "Well, Beth and I talked about it. There's no case involved, no legal matter. Sam's concerned about his future and wants you to help him with an old girlfriend. That's okay, you're good friends. But we think you're more likely to leave Little Rock if we leave first."

"Surprised, yes. Pleased, even more so."

Maggie wasn't through. "Don't get cocky, now. No one has any idea who was behind the attack on you, but Micki thinks it's about retribution for some former case. I wish you'd come back with us—get out of this place and never come back. But I understand why you need to stay for at least a few days. So, deal with whatever Sam needs and come home."

"I'll come home as soon as I can, Maggie, I promise. It shouldn't take long. Believe me—this time I'm ready to leave."

Our glasses were empty, but Walter showed no inclination to leave. Maggie and Beth excused themselves.

"Okay, Walter what's up?" I asked when they were out of earshot.

He took his time choosing his words. "Jack, if it weren't for you I'd never have met Maggie. You are my best friend, so what I have to say doesn't come easy."

"It's okay. I think I've got a good idea where you're headed," I responded.

He pinched his lip. "All right, here it is. This last attempt on your life is the tipping point. I can't keep you from putting yourself in harm's way, but I can stop you from including Maggie in your adventures. When I heard what happened, my stomach tied up in knots. But the next thing I thought was what might have happened if Maggie had been in that cab?"

"Good God, Walter. Don't you know I had the same thought? Thank heaven she wasn't."

"I know you did, and I know you love Maggie as much as I do. Bottom line, this has to end. I love my wife and I want to spend a long life with her."

"Take Maggie home, my friend, and thank you for taking Beth back to Jeff. I don't know who's behind this latest attack, but I know I'm the only one who can find the answers—and I need the answers or I'll never feel safe.

"Walter, I know I must have met the lead guy before—I've heard that voice before. I can't place it, but I don't want that voice anywhere near Maggie, Beth, or you. So, yes, please take Maggie home and keep her there. That assault wasn't about any case. It was about me, and it damn near killed me."

Walter sat in silence, watching his fingertips drumming on the table. I waited. We'd become close friends. This was tough for us.

"You know I'll have my hands full keeping Maggie away if you end up staying any length of time," he said at last.

"I don't envy your job," I replied with a grin.

"I've told Clovis that Martin and his people are at his disposal." He didn't return my smile.

"Thank you. I hope they're not needed."

Speak of the devil, I watched Clovis walk toward our table.

"Come join us," I offered, but Clovis wasn't here to share an after-dinner drink.

"The press found out what happened Friday night. Someone at the police department must have leaked, and they're all over the med center trying to verify the story and find out where you are. No telling what they'll report in the morning," he said.

"The story was bound to get out," I sighed. "Walter, wheels up early.

Clovis, get some rest tonight—tomorrow will be an interesting day." The dulling effect of the wine had evaporated in an instant.

Walter asked, "You worried about the press?"

I paused before I spoke. "No, the press I can handle. Tomorrow, the bad guys will learn a bear didn't tear my carcass to shreds. I'm worried they'll want to finish the job."

9

THE NEXT MORNING, I said early goodbyes to Beth, Maggie, and Walter, and sat down to read the local newspaper—*The Arkansas Democrat-Gazette*—over coffee. A brief article about the incident was buried in the middle of the paper and provided no details other than there was no obvious motive for the bizarre attack and I had been released from the hospital. My attackers would know I'd survived. Sam had used his influence to downplay what had happened, convincing the reporters that the more they wrote, the more difficult it would be for the police to run the bad guys to ground.

I wondered if I should hightail it out of Little Rock after lunch after all. Until I returned to help Woody Cole, I had avoided Little Rock like the plague for twenty-five years. Maybe it was time to reinstate my self-imposed exile.

Clovis joined me at the breakfast table, followed by a server offering more coffee.

"They're halfway to St. Louis by now. It's strange not to have Maggie here giving me orders," Clovis commented.

"It is strange, but I admit I feel a lot better knowing Beth and Maggie are gone. Are our friends in St. Louis on the job?" I asked.

"You bet. They take their obligation seriously. I worry about the day they'll want to settle the bill. You know at some point your friends in New Orleans will call and ask for an accommodation."

"No sense borrowing trouble. We'll cross that bridge when we come to it. For now, it's enough to know Beth and Jeff are safe."

Clovis nodded in agreement. The waiter arrived with coffee for

Clovis and a basket of fresh pastries, compliments of the hotel. I reached for a warm croissant while Clovis told me the manager was still reeling from Maggie's tongue-lashing. They'd yet to pinpoint the source of the leak.

Wishing I could go back to bed, I asked Clovis what was on tap for the day.

"A lot depends on what you're up to doing," he responded.

I tried to look resolute, and he responded in kind. "If you're up to it, Sam will be here at ten to tell you about his meeting with Kate Erwin. He's also volunteered to be here for the police interview. You have lunch with Dr. Hall at eleven-thirty. I don't know how long that will last, but so far your afternoon is open. Stella gave me a laptop for you to use with an instruction sheet on how to access your email and files, and Maggie gave me a list of people you need to call.

"Micki has invited you for dinner tonight. She promises not to ask about Sam. I know it's awkward, but she's concerned. She told me to tell you not to worry—Larry's cooking."

I laughed. Micki wasn't much of a cook. "Is there anything Larry can't do well?" I kidded.

"I'm sure there must be, but the last few times he's cooked the food has been swell."

"You know, he makes it hard not to like him." I'd had no use for Micki's past boyfriends, but Larry had become the exception.

"Not all is perfect in paradise," Clovis said. "Larry's mom thinks Micki isn't the right woman for her baby boy, makes Micki's life hell. I don't want to be around when that blows up."

"Me either," I laughed, "but my money's on Micki. Tell her I'll be there. How's she doing with full time protection?"

"Paul put the fear of God in Debbie, and his message rubbed off on Micki. She hasn't said a word."

I nibbled on a croissant while Clovis checked his phone for messages. I'd left my phone in the room, at least, I hoped so. Maggie would have my hide if I lost it.

"Okay, now how do we find out who wants me dead?" We'd dealt with the gnats—it was time to tackle the monster.

"Sam would tell you to let the police do their job. Give them a statement and go home," Clovis replied.

"Okay. And is that what you think?"

"It's the smart thing to do, but I heard the same voice you did, and that visceral hatred chilled me to the bone. So, no, I'm not ready to let it go."

******

Hotel management had reserved a small conference room for our meeting with the police. From my perspective, the interview didn't go well. The two detectives, Rick and Ted, were full of questions all right, but most of them were directed at my behavior rather than my abductors'.

"Why did you get in a cab with no credentials? Why didn't you call nine-one-one? Why did you come to town?"

When they asked why I hadn't offered more resistance, I said something rude—I'd had enough. Sam broke in and ended the interview.

After Rick and Ted left, I asked, "What the hell was that about? Do they think I came to town to be lynched for the fun of it?"

"No, they just can't figure out how anyone could generate that level of hatred. They don't know you like I do." Sam grinned.

"They didn't ask a single question designed to discover who the bad guys are, or why they wanted to kill me." I was hot, despite Sam's attempt at humor.

"Reality is, unless we catch a break, your assailants will be hard to catch. They didn't leave many clues. We hope one of them gets drunk and brags about their participation at a bar or in a lockup. That's how most cases are broken. It doesn't mean we aren't beating the bushes. We'll use every source we've got, but the assault on you fits no mold or pattern."

I knew Sam was right, but it didn't keep me from being both scared and pissed. I tried to let it go.

"Okay, how was the meeting with your deputy…? What's her name again?" I asked.

"Kate, Kate Erwin, and it went fine. No apology was necessary, and she admitted she knew something wasn't right the first time she mentioned Jana's name.

"She said, 'Sam, you should have seen your face. You looked like you'd seen a ghost, and you rushed out of the meeting as if you had a tee time at Augusta National.'

"She assured me there wasn't a prosecutor in the office who would recommend charging Dr. Hall with so much as a traffic ticket. Jana had done nothing wrong. She suggested that I could call Jana anytime I liked. I think she was teasing, but..."

Sam looked at me as if he was asking for permission.

"Don't go there, Sam. I know you. No, you can't show up at Ben's with me. Don't even think about it."

His face fell. I bet there's not a guy alive who doesn't think "what if" about at least one former girlfriend. But he knew I was right. It was too soon to tell whether Sam and his office would receive political heat for not pursuing a case against her. Better to let me find out what Jana wanted and let memories rest.

"I promise I'll tell you everything. For all we know she's calling to ask you to contribute to Stafford State's annual fund."

The door opened and I saw Clovis pointing at his watch. It was time to leave.

Ben's had just opened when I arrived. I stuck my head in the kitchen to say hello to Ben, only to find out he wasn't there. Ben Jr. told me his dad had a date with a largemouth bass.

"You watch. He'll be here before long. That old fish has outsmarted him for over a year."

I took a seat at a table in a corner. Jana walked through the screen door just as the waitress brought me a glass of sweet tea. Of course she was older, but she had changed very little, her dark hair still pulled back in a low ponytail, her confident, almost arrogant demeanor intact. White jeans and a light blue sweater complemented her tall frame. Her face lit up when she spotted me across the room, and I stood to greet her. I reached out to give her a hug, but she pulled back to take a closer look at me.

"Jack, your face looks awful. Does it hurt?"

"Not so much today, but I know the bruises look bad."

"That's an understatement." She smiled, and we sat down.

The waitress came over to take our orders. She had hardly turned away when Jana began.

"Before we spend the afternoon catching up, and you tell me why you're still running interference for Sam, I have something to say."

I hadn't expected such a direct approach, but I shouldn't have been surprised. Jana had always been forthright.

"I apologize. Not for missing Angie's funeral, but for never calling or writing. You had no way of knowing, but my husband died a few weeks after Angie. His death was sudden and unexpected, but that's no excuse. Angie was a special friend, and I was a poor one."

I knew Angie and Jana had stayed in touch after the Sam breakup, and they had remained long distance friends.

"Please don't apologize. For all I knew you could have been at the funeral. I was in such a fog I wouldn't have known and wouldn't have remembered. I should have known about your husband, but I didn't, and I'm sorry. So we're even."

I reached my hand out to hers and she squeezed it during an awkward and emotional silence. Thank goodness the waitress appeared with two chopped pork sandwiches and a side of onion rings.

Like most men, I polish off Ben's barbecue in three or four bites and then order another. But today I tried to eat slowly, glad for the opportunity to catch up with Jana. I learned she had been married twice, but never had children. After she finished her residency in internal medicine, she'd set up a health clinic in the East End of Little Rock.

"That's a tough neighborhood," I commented.

"It was where I saw the most need. It would have been easy to join a practice in West Little Rock and deal with a well-heeled clientele, but that's not why I went into medicine."

This was the same Jana I'd known long ago, but youthful good intentions and idealism seldom become the reality. I wondered why she hadn't returned to El Dorado, but decided it was none of my business.

"Okay, Jack, your turn. Tell me why in the hell Sam is afraid to return my phone call. Please tell me he's grown up by now. Tell me he's not the same jerk who relied on you to make excuses for him." Her voice held a hard edge and the smile was gone.

"That was a long time ago, Jana, and we've all changed, hopefully for the better. Believe me, Sam isn't afraid to call. In fact, I had to order him not to join us. He's champing at the bit to see you, but the timing of your call creates a problem."

"Timing?"

"Timing." I confirmed. "Let me explain."

I told her about the criminal referral from the Health Department, and that she appeared to have enemies there, and although Kate Erwin had closed the file, the Health Department's director was threatening to take it to the governor.

Jana remained silent, trying to absorb what I'd said. She looked at me with resignation.

"I had no idea about any of this when I called Sam. My lawyers have been handling the audit, and they assured me there was nothing to worry about. If they knew anything about a criminal referral, they didn't tell me. I'm sorry. Please tell Sam my call was innocent. I had no idea." Her eyes welled with unexpected tears.

"Please don't be upset. You did nothing wrong in calling. Sam will return your call before long. You two will have plenty of time to catch up. But I'm curious. Why did you call?"

"It was nothing. Just a whim." She looked away, trying to regain her composure.

Just a whim. I didn't think so.

"Who's the bad liar this time?" I asked.

"You have a good memory, Jack," she smiled. "You really want to know?"

"Yes, I do."

"It's a long story."

"I've got all day," I replied, and signaled the waitress for two beers. Jana didn't object. By now Ben's was noisy, busy with the lunch crowd, but it felt like we were speaking in a vacuum.

"Well, months ago I was ready to jump off a cliff." I couldn't hide my shock, and she took a deep breath. "Yes, a real cliff. I stood on the edge, willing myself to jump. But the memory of Sam and what we had shared on that very cliff walked me back from the edge. I know it was a long time ago, and maybe he doesn't even remember, but I didn't jump—I'm still here. I called to say thank you."

10

I COULDN'T IMAGINE this elegant, poised, successful woman on the edge of a cliff. "Oh, jeez, Jana, I…" I couldn't think what to say.

"Don't worry, Jack. And don't look so shocked. I felt overwhelmed by life for a time. I'm seeing a professional now, and I'm better—she's the one who suggested I call Sam. So, let me tell you a little about the director of the Arkansas Health Department, Brady Flowers, who wants way more than a pound of flesh."

"I'm all ears," I said, still wondering what could have caused her to even consider suicide.

"Opening the first health clinic in the East End made sense, but my dream was to set up clinics all over the state that would offer quality health care to anyone, regardless of their ability to pay. Arkansas has so many pockets of poverty—the Delta, the Ozarks, and many points in between. My husband subsidized the East End clinic while he was alive, but after his death, I knew that to make my dream a reality, I needed financial help from the state.

"I doubled my efforts, and with national attention on the Affordable Care Act and sympathy abounding for those who couldn't afford even the most basic health care, I got the governor and the legislature to help. They gave me funds to set up three more clinics, one in each congressional district in the state. The clinics supplemented other providers of health care in the poorest parts of the state and provided continuing medical care education to those working in the area. I worked with the university's med school to locate doctors and nurses who would live and work in these areas in return for forgiveness of student debt. Most days I ran the East End clinic, but whenever I could, I held training sessions at one of the other clinics. Good people took time off to help at these clinics and train the local professionals. My dream was becoming a reality.

"As an extra benefit, my work kept my mind off Judd. I bet you buried yourself in your work after Angie died."

I nodded.

"Anyway, my dream had critics. The funds for the clinics were funneled through the Arkansas Health Department, but no one there had any say over how the money was spent. That didn't sit well, and I spent many hours arguing with them about appropriations. To make matters worse, most of our doctors and nurses were from other countries, trained in the States, but only allowed to stay in the U.S. on visas. Some locals had a hard time trusting doctors from Asia and the Middle East and made life tough for the doctors and their families. Deep-rooted mindsets are hard to change."

I could only imagine how difficult it would be for a family from the Middle East to assimilate into rural Arkansas.

"To make matters worse, local healthcare providers weren't too keen on our clinics. Our doctors tried to be sensitive to local practices, but they spoke up if they thought the quality of care was below standard. Most of the providers called to task were long-time residents of these rural communities who enjoyed a close relationship with their political representatives in the Arkansas legislature.

"The emphasis on restricting immigration by the new administration dried up our source of doctors and nurses. It's become a problem everywhere, not just in Arkansas. Then the Health Department got the Legislative Audit Committee to audit all the clinics. The audit found a few missing invoices for equipment and some sloppy record keeping at our Mena clinic. Nothing serious, but enough to allow the Health Department to convince the legislature to make our appropriation part of the Health Department's overall budget so they could supervise our spending. At least, that was the excuse.

"It didn't take long, only a matter of months, before the money for the clinics was reauthorized to fund a bogus obesity study, and the director told me the clinics would never see another nickel. He told me our clinics would have to become more competitive or close up shop. My doctors and nurses were worried they were about to be deported, and now we had no money to subsidize those who have no ability to pay for health care, and no money to use for seminars and training sessions. I had no choice but to close the clinics, including the one in the East End.

"You know, Jack, the clinics provided health care for folks who had none otherwise. The training sessions were improving the delivery of services by both the locals and our doctors. We gathered statistics about the population that could have led to research on the link between poverty and health, but we had neither enough time nor money to begin such work. Now health care for those folks will revert to the way it was before, not much better than it was a hundred years ago."

Her story was another example of people gaming the system for financial benefit or their outsized egos while people trying to do the right thing were pushed aside. Not for the first time, it occurred to me that human greed might bring about the end of us all.

I managed to control my anger. "Any reason the director should have it in for you? From what I hear, he's the driving force behind the attempt to have you prosecuted."

Jana hesitated, folding and refolding her paper napkin.

"I'd rather not speculate. Do you mind? I have good lawyers at the Crockett firm representing my interests, and you tell me any prosecution is going nowhere. Let's talk about your daughter and catch up on the last twenty-five years. No good can come from discussing the clinics or the director, Brady Flowers. The clinics are closed, and I'm retired for the moment."

I don't know if I would have dropped the matter, but just then Ben Jennings burst through the swinging doors from the kitchen. He gave me a hug, gave Jana a hug that lingered, shouted at our waitress for a platter of ribs and three Buds, pulled up a chair, and sat down with us.

"When's the last time two of my favorite people have been at my place together?" Ben asked.

Jana answered, "Way too long. More than twenty-five years."

"I take it after Angie and I moved to DC, you continued to frequent Ben's?" I teased.

She laughed. "While you were in DC making the world safe for antitrust violators, my husband and I were eating barbeque, drinking cold beer, and shaming Ben into catering every fundraiser we had for the East End clinic."

Ben said, "I would have done anything for Jana and her husband—no shaming necessary. Judd Wilson was one of the most generous and gracious men I've ever come across. When I wanted to open this restaurant, not a single bank in town would lend me money. They were polite and all, but a Vietnam vet selling barbeque out of the back of his truck just wasn't a good credit risk. Then I got a call from Larry's father, Stan Bradford. He told me to come on over to his bank to sign the loan papers—my application was approved. Funny thing—it was the oldest and most conservative bank in town. I hadn't even bothered to apply there, but I wasn't about to object.

"Many years later, and I mean years, I learned that Mr. Wilson sat on the board of a bank that had turned me down. The bank's president bragged to his board about turning me down. Mr. Wilson left the board meeting and walked across the street to Larry's father's bank. He told Mr. Bradford he wanted the bank to make me a loan and he would guarantee it. The only condition was they couldn't tell me about his guarantee.

"After Larry's dad died and the original loan had been paid, the bank sent me the loan documents. Only then did I find out Mr. Wilson had guaranteed my loan. I tried to thank him, but he wouldn't hear of it. He said I would have done the same for him. Hell, when I applied for that loan I didn't have a plug nickel."

Blinking back tears, Jana whispered, "That was Judd. Ben, I never knew."

"I knew you didn't—neither did my wife. Mr. Wilson wasn't happy I knew about the guarantee, and made me promise not to tell a soul. I tried to give him free barbeque for life, but he insisted on paying full freight, telling me to be generous with everything in life except my product. I remember him shaking his head and saying, 'Ben, that's how you make your living.'"

I said, "I wish I'd known him."

Jana could only nod, trying to keep her emotions in check. But

Ben had more to say.

"Jack, your friend Jana is no slouch either. Her East End clinic was a godsend to this community. I can't tell you how many families owe their lives to this woman. Before she started the clinic, the only option available to the community was the emergency room."

"That's what I understand," I said.

Her voice husky, Jana broke in. "Okay, it's getting way too deep in here for this girl. Either we talk Razorback football or Cardinal baseball, or I'm out of here."

I was still trying to figure out what to say when the ribs arrived. We spent a few minutes giving them their due before turning to a much lighter subject—whether Ben Jr.'s dry rub ribs were better than Ben's original. We had to sample both.

11

Jana and I exchanged contact information and promised to stay in touch. I assured her she would hear from Sam soon. I hoped I might see her again, but given the distance between Little Rock and DC, the chances were slim.

My good mood was spoiled when I saw Clovis pacing the gravel driveway outside the Tahoe. He whisked me into the car and turned quickly onto Patterson Street. I waited in silence, and after a few blocks he relaxed and said, “Sorry, Jack, but we were followed to Ben’s. He didn’t stop, but I managed to get the plates, so maybe we caught a break. And Sam’s called three times, wants you to call him, wouldn’t say anything else.”

Well, that’s about par for the course, I thought and called Sam.

“You’re one lucky man, Sam Pagano. Jana doesn’t have a clue your office received a criminal referral. She was calling to thank you for something that happened a long time ago. I sure would like to be a fly on the wall when you two get together again. She’s as fantastic as ever, maybe more so.”

I expected some kind of strong reaction from Sam, at least his thanks. But he didn’t say a word. I had to break the silence.

“Something wrong?”

“Where are you headed?” he asked.

“Back to the hotel. I want to put my feet up. Clovis, Stella, and I are going to Micki’s ranch for supper. Larry is also a gourmet chef.” Sam and I enjoyed joking about Larry’s lack of faults, and I expected a wisecrack.

"I'll meet you there in thirty minutes," he said, and hung up.

I stared at my phone, wondering what was going on. "Sam's meeting us in thirty minutes. Did he sound upset when he called earlier?" I asked Clovis.

"No. He kept asking me what Dr. Hall looked like, and what was taking you so long. But no, he didn't sound troubled," Clovis responded.

We rode in silence. Then a thought hit me.

"Are we being followed now?"

"No. Once Dr. Hall walked into Ben's, the car left."

"Do me a favor. If you have a spare hand, get him to look after Jana. Nothing intrusive, just make sure no one's following her or watching her home."

"Wow, that comes out of the blue. You think she could be in some kind of danger?" Clovis asked.

"I hope not, but Sam is acting strange. Humor me. Check out Jana and her place. Nothing would please me more than for my instinct to be totally off base."

Sam was already in the bar by the time I arrived, slumped alone in a corner booth with a beer. I'd known Sam to throw back a few, but not at midday in a public place.

"Can I join you? You look like you could use a friend," I said mimicking the oldest pickup line in the business.

Sam managed a smile, and I motioned to the waiter to bring me a draft. "Thanks for coming. Have a seat. We've got big problems," he said.

"I'm all ears. What could be so bad?"

"The governor called. Said he hated to call, was sure my office had done nothing inappropriate, but he'd received complaints about our handling of the improprieties at the state's health clinics."

"I hope you told him where to shove it," I said.

"Well, I was about to do just that, but thought better of it. It didn't take him long to tell me he had consulted both the attorney general and the chief justice before he called. The AG had said that given the allegations during the campaign that I'd been soft on crime, she had the authority to investigate my office, and if she found improprieties she could bring removal proceedings.

"I don't have to tell you how devastating such an action would be for the office. I'd expect my entire staff to resign in protest, and given the attorney general's ability to manipulate the media and her animosity toward Democrats in general, my reputation wouldn't be worth a plug nickel. You can forget about advising me on career opportunities. There won't be any."

I had nothing to say—he was right.

"The chief justice was more cautious in his advice to the governor. He suggested the better solution would be for my office to recuse, making way for the governor to appoint a special prosecutor to investigate the clinics."

A special prosecutor would be a disaster for Jana. They operate under the technique developed by Beria, the infamous sidekick of Stalin, who said, "Show me the man, and I'll find you the crime."

On the other hand, an investigation by the attorney general's office would be even worse. The current AG was an ambitious woman who would like nothing better than to investigate Sam's office to make political hay at his expense. Not one employee in the prosecutor's office would escape the taint of scandal caused by such an investigation.

"The governor was generous, gave me an entire day to respond," Sam continued wih a grimace. "The chief justice is a friend, so I called him for advice. He didn't mince words—'Get the hell out while the getting is good.' He said both the chairwoman of the Senate Appropriations Committee and the House majority leader had called the governor. The gist of the conversation was that both the governor's budget and his highway expansion plans would be dead on arrival at the legislature if he didn't remove my office from the criminal investigation into the health clinics."

So much for separation of powers, I thought. The Health Department had already cut off Jana's funding—why go after her? There had to be more to this.

"Jack, what should I do?" Sam asked in frustration, running his hand backward along his scalp. "I could stand on principle, insisting that the case has been closed and my office will not recuse, but I'm convinced that Jana's enemies will find a way around me. In the meantime everything my office has worked for will be destroyed. It's a continuation of all the campaign crap, only much, much worse."

I couldn't think of anything helpful to say, so we drank in silence. The cold beer felt really good as it slid down my sore throat. I took a few minutes to respond.

"Well, Sam, it looks to me like Jana's enemies, whoever they are, are determined to destroy her, and they're happy for you go down with her. It's too bad, but your job is not to protect her. No matter how much you want to help her, you can't.

"She told me she has the best lawyers in Arkansas representing her—it's time to let them earn their fees. Right now both the auditors and Kate Erwin have determined that she's done nothing wrong. If another prosecutor thinks otherwise, her lawyers should be more than capable of dealing with the allegations." I took a healthy swallow. "Then again, you don't have to make things easy for her accusers."

Sam's face lit up. "I hear your devious mind at work. What do you have in mind?"

"First, by now someone has leaked your conversation with the governor. Get ready for a late-night call from a reporter."

"I've already thought of that," he sighed. "How should I handle it?"

"Well, you're better at dealing with the press than I am, but how about something like this? Yes, the governor called to say he was sure your office had done nothing wrong or inappropriate, but he had received complaints. Tell the reporter you asked for a day to consult with the lead prosecutor on this case. Your candor will amaze him.

"Meanwhile, tell Kate Erwin about the governor's call. Tell her you have her back and ask her to join us tomorrow morning to plan a strategy and response. I'll call Jana. I don't think she'll be surprised. Who knows—maybe you won't hear a word from the press, but I bet they've already gotten a full version of the story from Jana's naysayers."

Sam frowned, "You know part of me wants to tell the governor to stuff it, office reputation be damned."

"But that would hurt both your staff and Jana. Live to fight another day. Didn't someone famous say that?"

"Well, something like that," Sam growled as he stood to leave. But he knew I was right, and at least he was leaving with a plan.

12

Jana thanked me for the heads-up, although I didn't tell her much more than that the governor was considering appointing a special prosecutor and Sam was conferring with Kate about his response. She would call her attorney and told me not to worry, she wouldn't get depressed. But knowing the governor might appoint a special prosecutor had to be a downer for even the most upbeat person. I made a mental note to check on her tomorrow.

Clovis and Stella were waiting in the lobby. I remembered we were due at Micki's and asked for a few minutes to "freshen," as Angie used to say. The drive to her ranch gave me a chance to catch up with Stella, who had toned down her look since I'd last seen her. Her hair was still short, but all one color for a change, a deep black. She still sported tall heels and tight jeans, her standard uniform. She told me she'd gotten a new tattoo in honor of her marriage, but only Clovis had viewing rights. Clovis tried to keep a straight face.

Stella's computer skills had been a godsend during several of my high-profile cases. Walter Matthews had tried to hire her to manage his company's technology more than once, but she liked the independence of consulting, running the CrossFit gym she owned, and settling into her marriage.

Micki had tacked a note to the front door advising us to "come on in." Clovis took the wine he'd brought to the kitchen, and I found Larry on the patio tending the grill. He was cooking chicken thighs and drumsticks along with fresh vegetables over a low fire of hickory and cherry wood chips. He said Micki was still in the barn tending to her horses. Stella pulled an apple from her jacket pocket and left to join her.

After a few minutes of grill talk, Larry gave Clovis and me a quick tour of the furniture and woodworking shop he was building. He hoped to finish it in a month.

Curious, I mentioned my earlier conversation with Ben. "I was at Ben's today, and he told me a wonderful story about Judd Wilson guaranteeing his first loan from your dad's bank. Do you know the tale?"

Larry smiled. "Oh, yeah, Dad told me about it. Ben wasn't the only Vietnam vet or minority businessman Judd helped. Dad enjoyed telling me about the first day Judd walked into his bank and asked him to lend Ben whatever he needed. Thing was, Judd wasn't a customer of the bank, but my father knew him by reputation. He made the loan on the spot. 'A gentleman's handshake,' he called it. You couldn't do that these days. The regulators would have your head on a platter."

"You say he made other guarantees. Did Judd ever have to honor one of those guarantees? You know, did the borrower ever go into default?"

"Oh, yeah!" he chuckled, adding a pile of green beans to the root vegetables on the grill. "Let me tell you two stories about Judd Wilson. There are many, but these two will give you the flavor of the man. The first time a Vietnam vet's loan went into default, Dad agonized about calling Judd's guarantee, but he had no choice. He phoned Judd and told him the vet had run into hard times—her husband had developed health problems and the body shop they had started couldn't make a go of it. The loan was in default. Within thirty minutes, Judd Wilson sat across from my dad at his desk.

"Dad expected Judd to ask for time to honor the guarantee or to complain about lack of notice, but instead Judd pulled out his checkbook and wrote a check."

"Wow," Clovis and I responded in unison.

"Now let me tell you the rest of the story. After Judd handed Dad the check he said, 'I want you to call the vet and offer them another chance. I'll guarantee what they need.'"

"You mean after the vet defaulted, Mr. Wilson gave them a second chance? Did she come back?" Clovis asked.

Larry smiled. "Yes, and Dad lent her the money because Judd stood good for the loan. You may have heard of her: Rachel Brand, President and CEO of Brand's Body Shops, Inc. I think her company has about a thousand franchises now and is the bank's biggest customer."

"Did she ever know Mr. Wilson helped her?" I asked.

"Not that Dad ever mentioned. Judd insisted on anonymity. Not all of Judd's guarantees ended so well. But he never complained. He'd write a check, thank my dad, and in a matter of months return to ask Dad to make another loan, which leads to my second story."

We refreshed our drinks and waited while Larry adjusted his coals.

"After several years of this gentleman's arrangement, the regulators descended on the bank and insisted Dad get a financial statement from Judd. Dad told me it was the hardest call he ever had to make in the banking business. I doubt that, but he wasn't happy about the regulators' intrusion. He called Judd and asked him to lunch at the Little Rock Club. Back then, the club was on top of what was the old Union Bank building.

"Over lunch, Dad explained the problem and told Judd he needed a financial statement. He knew the request would offend Judd, but figured he would agree to the regulators' demands. Judd refused outright. He said, 'if my word isn't good enough, what good is a piece of paper?' Judd asked how much was outstanding on the loans he'd guaranteed. Dad didn't have the exact number on hand, but told him it amounted to over a hundred thousand dollars.

"Judd didn't flinch. He told Dad to call him with the precise number and he'd send over a cashier's check. Judd would buy the loans from Dad and find a different way to keep the loans confidential."

"There aren't many people who can come up with that kind of money in a day," I said. "Or many men willing to take the risk."

"That's what Dad thought, too. He decided on the spot 'regulators be damned.' Until the regulators closed the bank, Judd Wilson's guarantee was all the collateral a borrower ever needed. He and Dad had lunch at the Little Rock Club every Thursday after that day until Dad died. He told me he never asked Judd for any of his business but had something more important—Judd's respect and friendship.

They were old school southern gentlemen, if you know what I mean. I'll never forget Judd telling my mother after Dad died 'If you need anything, and I mean anything, you let me know.' He meant it."

Neither Clovis nor I said a word. I wondered how many Judd Wilsons were left in the world, people who give of themselves with no expectation of honor or return.

The sudden slam of the screen door broke the silence. "What are y'all talking about?" Micki asked as she tugged off her barn boots.

"Jack was asking about Judd Wilson," Larry replied.

"Judd Wilson? What about him? He must have died—oh, at least six years ago." Micki traded the boots for a pair of Toms slip-ons.

I didn't want to get into who I had lunch with or why, so I jumped in. "Ben told me at lunch today that Judd Wilson guaranteed his first loan. He seems to have been a very generous man. Larry was filling me in on some details."

Micki responded. "I didn't know him, but his wife is a saint. She ran a health clinic in the East End for years, took care of anyone who walked in the doors. Ask Debbie. When any of Novak's girls overdosed or were beaten up, they knew where to go. Too many of my clients owe their life and health to that woman."

Novak was a Russian ganster who dealt in the sex trade and ran gambling houses throughout the South for many years. He and I had developed a unique relationship during another case. I didn't trust him much farther than I could throw him, but sometimes our interests coincide, and so far he hasn't let me down.

"I thought you had a doctor's appointment today. How did that evolve into lunch at Ben's?" she asked.

"Well, turns out my doctor has retired, but for old time's sake she and I had lunch at Ben's."

"Name?" Micki was getting frustrated with my playing dodgeball.

"Dr. Jana Hall, the saint you told me about. That's why Larry and I were talking about her husband."

"How do you know her?"

"We were undergrads at Stafford State at the same time. She dated Sam for a while, and she and Angie were close. My recent flirtation with a hangman's noose gave me an excuse to reconnect."

Micki sighed in disgust. "She is attractive—I'll give you that. Why didn't you ask her to join us?" She knew there was more to the story, but decided to let it go, at least for now.

"Because I'm an idiot," I responded.

The spring on the screen door creaked again as Stella poked her head through to ask when dinner would be ready. I loved that sound. We spent the rest of the evening joking, reminiscing, and enjoying each other's company over a good meal and even better wine. Clovis, Micki, and I had become much more than colleagues, and Stella and Larry were now full participants. Who knew what tomorrow would bring, but spending such a fine evening with friends made me wish time could stand still.

13

I WOKE TO THE UNWELCOME BLARE of my phone. A sleepy glance at the alarm clock revealed it was only six in the morning, so I ignored it. I sunk back into my pillow, but the phone rang again. *What now?* I wondered. Still half asleep, I recognized Sam's number on the phone's face.

"No, I haven't read the papers yet," I said with a yawn as I picked up.

"Neither have I. Where were you last night?"

"I had dinner at Micki's—didn't get back to the hotel until close to midnight."

"Who else was there?"

"Larry, Clovis, Stella, and about a half a dozen horses." I didn't try to hide my irritation.

"I'm sorry to have to ask, Jack, but last night the police found a body in the Fourche Bottoms hanging from a tree, the same tree you were hanging from a few days ago. They don't know yet whether he was shot before or after someone strung him up. I'm glad you and Clovis have a good alibi."

"Why would anyone think I had anything to do with his death?" By now I was wide awake.

"We're sure the dead guy was the leader of the men who tried to kill you the other night. His name was Mace Cooper, but that's about all anyone knows. I was scared shitless you wouldn't have an alibi. You could have been suspect number one."

"So, you thought I'd figured out who the bad guy was and gone in for some kind of personal revenge. Thanks a lot, Sam." I was pissed.

"Come on, Jack. You know better. I'll explain the whole thing over breakfast. Ask Clovis to join us."

I called Clovis, then took a long shower. I couldn't seem to make sense out of this series of events that made no sense. Who was Mace Cooper? Why did he want me dead? Why had somebody hanged him from the same tree?

I picked up a copy of the *Arkansas Democrat-Gazette* on the way into the restaurant. To my surprise, I saw nothing in it about the health clinics or the governor's call. Sam must have called in a lot of favors to keep the story hidden. I asked for coffee, turned to the comics section, and relaxed while I waited.

I had just gotten a chuckle from *Pearls Before Swine* when Sam and Clovis walked into the restaurant together. They were both smiling, which I took as a good sign. After we ordered breakfast, Sam filled us in.

"The sheriff had a couple of his deputies patrolling the area down by Fourche Bottoms. Last night, they found Mace Cooper's body hanging from the same tree where Clovis found you. The only difference was he had a big hole in the middle of his forehead. His ID's were still in his pocket, a driver's license and his hunting license. The medical examiner thinks he was hanged first, then shot with a rifle. An autopsy will confirm."

The waiter brought our breakfast, and Sam and Clovis concentrated on their bacon and eggs. I took a few bites, put my fork down, and asked, "So why did you, or anyone else for that matter, think I did it?"

"That's bothering you, isn't it?" Sam sighed.

"Yeah, I guess it is."

"Well, the location and the similarities to your hanging. Few people know what happened or where. Stringing him up in the same spot has all the aspects of a revenge killing."

"Okay, I see that. But I don't even know Mace Cooper, don't have any idea who he was."

"Yes, you do," Sam responded.

"What are you talking about?"

"Remember back in college, the night Angie was attacked and you and I ended up in the hospital?" he asked.

"It was the worst night of my life."

"Remember getting your licks in on one of her attackers? I had to pull you off?" Sam asked.

"Vaguely." Truth was, I remembered every second.

"You busted his jaw and most of the rest of him—you could have killed him. Just as your baseball career ended that night, you ended the football career of one Mace Cooper. The big difference was that Mace had no one to turn to and nowhere to go. Football was all he had."

"Are you sure?" I asked.

"When the police went to his house off Kanis Road, they found an entire room dedicated to the glory days of his football career. They also found newspaper articles about how an automobile accident cut his career short, an accident which you and I know never occurred. The alleged auto accident was Stafford's cover story for what happened the night he and his buddies attacked Angie. Mace Cooper blamed you for destroying his football career and his future. Revenge became an obsession. He's been stalking you ever since you returned to Arkansas to help Woody. The police found a file drawer dedicated specifically to you. It's a good thing Clovis has been watching your back.

"They also found the bag full of clothes you left on the scene, except your laptop was missing."

Mace Cooper. I let out a deep breath. The voice from the other night in the Fourche Bottoms was the same one I heard on the night from hell. I never knew his name. No wonder I was the prime suspect in his killing.

"Good Lord, I had no idea. I'm sure glad Clovis and I had dinner at Micki's last night."

"Me, too," Clovis interjected.

"But, look—now that I'm off the official hook, we have a new mystery. Who murdered Mace? And why?"

None of us had the slightest idea.

When the server came to clear the plates, Clovis pushed his chair back and said, "You don't need me here, and I've got things to do. But remember, Mace may be dead, but somebody killed him—don't let your guard down. Don't go anywhere without one of my guys. I'll let the others know what happened."

The latter statement reminded me that I should call Maggie. While we waited for Kate Erwin to arrive, I asked Sam, "Did you call in a favor, or is it possible the governor didn't leak his phone call to the press?"

"I think he's nervous about my reaction. He's smart enough—correction, Kristine is smart enough—not to put me in a position where I have to come out swinging. I called him back after we talked and let him believe I would be cooperative. Was I right?"

I was about to say let's wait until Kate arrives when I saw a woman crossing the room toward our table. I thought it could be her, except she looked nothing like a hard-nosed prosecutor.

This was a tiny woman whose stylish glasses almost covered her face. She wore an attractive, pale-blue dress, and she carried an enormous leather bag over her shoulder.

Sam rose to introduce her and asked for more coffee and a basket of pastries from a passing waiter. After exchanging a few pleasantries with Kate, I turned to Sam.

"I assume you've told Kate about your conversations with the governor and the chief justice?"

Sam said he had and looked at Kate, who remained silent. She was trying, without success, to open one of those obnoxious little packets of creamer. We watched in silence as the cream spilled everywhere except into her coffee. To her credit, she didn't look the least bit embarrassed.

I gave her a glance and continued, "Sam, they have you in a box. The last thing you need is an ambitious attorney general investigating individual prosecutorial decisions and accusing you or your office of being soft on crime or worse. But I don't think that's what either the governor or the Health Department wants."

"Why do you say that?" Kate had removed her glasses and was looking at me, her coffee now under control.

"Because I think they're after Dr. Hall, not Sam. They just want your office out of the way. An investigation doesn't have to result in a prosecution in order to create havoc and suspicion. If the AG were to open an official investigation into your office, Sam would surely respond by calling it a partisan tactic meant to keep him from running for attorney general or governor. The governor doesn't need that kind of in-fighting or the press it would generate."

Sam interjected, "I have no intention of running for either AG or governor. I'm through with politics." I didn't believe a word of it.

Kate jumped in. "Maybe not, but they don't know that, and besides, Kristine isn't about to let the AG dominate the headlines for a week, much less for several months. Smart thinking, Jack."

"So are you still suggesting our office recuse?" Sam asked. "You know what that means for Jana?"

Kate answered for me. "They will dig through every record and find something to prosecute. No doctor could withstand the scrutiny of a special prosecutor. They will question every judgment call, every Medicaid claim, and every procedure. A prescription for pain medication or ordering extra bloodwork becomes potential fraud or worse."

I saw Sam cringe at the thought. I didn't like it either, but at least Jana had money and good lawyers to protect her interests. My job was to protect and advise Sam.

"True, but maybe we can make his job a little more difficult." I smiled.

"What do you have in mind?" Kate asked, reaching for more coffee.

"Are you confident there was nothing in the audit of the health clinics that gave you concern?"

"The auditors gave the clinics a clean bill of health. Sorry, bad pun," she answered with a smile. "There were a few missing invoices, and poor record-keeping at the Mena clinic, but no fraud or ill intent. Like I said, no health clinic or doctor's office is perfect, but there was nothing sinister, and no one lined their own pockets."

"Okay, then. Let's see how much of a box we can construct around the governor, his Health Department, and a special prosecutor." I was thinking as I spoke.

"Kate, as chief deputy, why don't you hold a press briefing, nothing too formal, a few remarks outside your office. You could say something to the effect of..." I trailed off and asked, "Shouldn't you take notes?"

She replied, "No."

I raised my eyebrows.

Sam clarified, "Don't worry, she has a remarkable memory. It's a little disconcerting."

"Okay, say the governor has asked your office to recuse so he can appoint a prosecutor to take a second look at the health clinics' financial records. That way you might be able to limit the special prosecutor's scope of inquiry to the financials rather than the clinics' health decisions or billings.

"Tell them your office has already conducted such a review and that relying on the state's auditors who also found no improprieties, you have closed the investigation. However, if the governor and the Health Department think a second look is a worthwhile allocation of the state's resources, so be it. The Pulaski County prosecutor's office will comply with the governor's request, but will continue to focus on prosecuting violent criminals rather than getting sidetracked by political pressure.

"While you're talking, your assistant can give them a press release. I bet you have good data on your success rate regarding violent offenders—I remember Sam running great ads about this issue last fall. Include data on your entire budget so every article about the cost of a special prosecutor can also emphasize the cost of going after Jana and your annual budget. Remind everyone the Health Department has already cut off all funding for the health clinics. A smart reporter might conclude the Health Department is beating a dead horse and wonder why. Try to avoid questions if you can."

Sam chimed in, "I like it, but I worry they could have something on Jana—a card they haven't played. They're waiting 'til we get out of the picture to play it."

"Well, they might, and we can only hope that Jana's lawyers are as good as she thinks. The audit report gives her a lot of cover. So does a career of more than twenty years treating the disadvantaged. Although you know what they say: 'no good deed goes unpunished'—one of my grandmother's favorite sayings."

"I think I can mock up a document with a few embellishments and run it by Sam before this afternoon. Do you want to see it, too?" Kate asked.

I smiled and didn't respond.

"I'm sorry. Did you not understand my question?" she asked, her smile changing into a frown.

"I did, and here comes the tough part. I don't want you to run it by Sam or me. If you believe this is the right way to go, I want you to sign off on it as the chief deputy and the lead prosecutor. Can you do that?"

Before she could answer, Sam stepped in.

"That's not the deal. I told Kate I had her back. I should be the one to handle this."

She turned to face him. "No, Sam, Jack is right. I know you always have my back, but no one is asking us to prosecute or not prosecute, only to recuse. I can do this. Not only is it my job—it protects the office from anyone nosing around about you and Jana thirty years ago. I'd bet a dollar to a donut that the Health Department director, Brady Flowers, knows you knew Jana then and planned to use the past to taint our handling of the case. He was too damn cocky. I knew he had something up his sleeve.

"I can say we are comfortable with our decision, but if the governor and the Health Department want to waste taxpayer dollars that's their business. We won't stand in the way, but we won't take part."

Kate questioned me about other issues that might arise. She was quick to catch on, and after we finished, I was comfortable with our strategy and her ability to handle just about anything.

She left to write her press release, but Sam lingered.

"You know, Jack, the governor didn't ask me to recuse. He told me what the attorney general and the chief justice suggested, but he didn't suggest I do anything."

I winked. "I know that. In fact, I bet Jana's adversaries hoped you would do nothing, or better yet tell the governor to go to hell. Then they would have had a field day about how your office was protecting Jana because of a past romantic involvement. Words like 'cover-up' would be on everyone's lips, and Jana's guilt would be presumed. Why else would your office be protecting her if she weren't guilty?

"The best thing you can do for Jana, given the political heat, is to let your office step out of the way in the manner we worked out this morning."

Sam shook his head. "I've got to get you out of DC. Only people who live inside the beltway are so devious."

"I wish that were true, but I'm afraid your old girlfriend is about to run up against some world-class devious bastards. I wonder what their real motivation is? Why go after a doctor who has dedicated her life to treating poor people? Makes no sense."

14

SAM AND I AGREED we needed to stay out of Kate's way, so why not do a little work this morning, then spend the afternoon on the golf course discussing Sam's life after public service? I went back to my room to make a few calls and check email on my new laptop.

Brian Hattoy was the only one in when I called the office. He explained that Maggie was meeting with the contractors out at the construction site. I'd forgotten that Larry had an early flight back to DC this morning for the same meeting. Maggie was not pleased with her new home's progress and had insisted on an all-hands-on-deck discussion. Sometimes you have to remind the contractors who works for whom. It rarely makes a difference, but it does makes you feel better for a while.

Maggie had given Brian a laundry list of phone calls I needed to make. She also wanted to know when I would return to DC.

"I'm meeting with Sam this afternoon, and since Mace Cooper is no longer with us, I can leave tomorrow. Can you get me a mid-morning flight?" I asked.

"Unnecessary. Maggie told me that when you were ready to return, she would send Walter's plane. She's anxious to get you out of Little Rock."

"Okay," I sighed. "Text me when I should be at Hodges Air tomorrow. I'm sure Clovis will insist on driving me to the hanger, so let him know, too. What else is on Maggie's list?"

Brian and I spent the next half hour going over my schedule, whom I needed to call, and what deadlines were coming up. My law practice hadn't disappeared because I had been strung up from a tree.

After finishing with Brian, the next item on my list was to call Jana.

"Wow, I haven't heard from you in thirty years and now two days in a row. To what do I owe this pleasure?" She sounded like she didn't have a care in the world.

"Jana, it's not good news. As I told you yesterday, the governor has asked Sam's office to recuse from the investigation into the health clinics. He wants to appoint a special prosecutor. Sam's office will send out a press release this afternoon saying they don't think the investigation has any substance, but they will step down." No sense in sugar-coating the message.

I heard a deep sigh. "That must be why my lawyer wants to see me. He called me before I could call him. I have an appointment with him tomorrow morning."

That couldn't be the reason her lawyer wanted to meet. The governor's call to Sam was not in the public domain, and Kate hadn't issued her press release. I wondered…but I didn't correct Jana.

"Would you like to come over for dinner tonight? I make a decent Bolognese."

The mention of her pasta brought back memories. How an American Indian from Oklahoma knew how to cook great Italian was a puzzle. I was tempted, but hesitated.

"Oh, come on, Jack! It's not a date—I won't try to seduce you. That would be too weird. It's only dinner and catching up with an old friend. I'd ask you to bring Sam if it would make you feel more comfortable, but I know I'm *persona non grata* for now."

She was right—my hesitancy was a guy thing. Jana had been Sam's girlfriend. What was I thinking? That was thirty years ago.

"Okay, sounds good. What time and what can I bring?" I asked.

"Six-thirty, and nothing, not even a bottle of wine. My husband had quite the wine collection, and I haven't put a dent in it since he passed."

I spent the next hour on the phone with Red Shaw and Gina Halep discussing the Lobos' potential move to San Antonio. Our first meeting with the NFL and city officials was in two weeks.

No surprise, Red had heard about my dance with death.

"Jack, get the hell out of Arkansas," he barked.

"I'm on my way back tomorrow." I chose not to tell him what had happened to Mace.

By the time I checked my emails and commented on a few documents Brian had prepared, it was time to meet Sam at the golf course. Sam had texted that Kate's press briefing was scheduled for three o'clock and would air on a local government channel. We would have time to get a quick bite at the club's grill, play nine holes, watch the briefing, and then play the back nine.

Larry had loaned me a set of clubs, and the ever-dependable Maggie had packed my cleats. I told Clovis about tonight's dinner plans as he drove me out to Sam's club. I said I'd take an Uber to her house.

He snorted. "Do you want to get me killed? Maggie Matthews would come out of her skin if I let you take public transportation."

"I need you alive, my friend, so forget I suggested it."

"Will do," he laughed. "Walter's plane will be at the airport tomorrow afternoon at two o'clock."

"I see no reason to stay, do you?" I mused.

"Can't say I do. But I am puzzled by the circumstances of Mace's death. His killer had to have known exactly where he tried to kill you, and then somehow lured him there, probably shot him, and strung him up from the same tree. He must have been one of the other men who were there that night. But why?" He shook his head in frustration.

"Wouldn't bother me if someone chopped down that tree," I joked.

He nodded and told me Jordan would pick me up after golf and run me by the hotel to change. I was glad to hear Jordan had duty tonight. I'd feel guilty about Clovis sitting out in a car while I was eating pasta.

After a bowl of excellent bean soup with hot cornbread at the grill, we teed off. Sam didn't play golf much anymore—he'd become more interested in running and cycling. But after a few rusty holes, Sam had no trouble beating his old roommate, who played golf every chance he got.

At the turn, we returned to the grill to watch Kate's press conference. She looked very professional in a charcoal suit and heels.

"Yesterday, the district's prosecutor, Sam Pagano, received a call from Governor White. The governor said he had received several calls from members of the legislature and the head of the state's Health Department complaining about our office's investigation into financial issues at the state's health clinics. The governor suggested that our office should step aside so he could appoint a special prosecutor to take over the investigation."

Kate paused for effect. "Sam asked the governor for time to consult with me, since I was the prosecutor in charge of the investigation. We spoke this morning and he asked me to respond.

"I have called the governor's chief of staff, Gloria Wright, to inform her of my response. You will receive copies of the press release when you leave the room. The crux of my conversation with Gloria was that our office had closed its investigation into any alleged irregularities at the health clinics. Our conclusion was that there was no basis for any charges, and I advised Mr. Flowers with the Health Department of my decision several days ago. I expect it was my call to Mr. Flowers that brought on the calls to the governor. Let me add the state's independent auditors also found no wrongdoing by anyone associated with the clinics."

I worried that Kate was going too far. Sam looked nervous and ordered two more beers.

"That said, as I explained to Ms. Wright, the governor has the constitutional authority to appoint a special prosecutor if he deems that action necessary. Our office will not stand in the way if he thinks this matter needs further investigation, or if either the governor or members of his administration have knowledge of wrongdoing they haven't shared. We will cooperate with a special prosecutor if the governor appoints one."

Sam was now smiling, enjoying the reference to knowledge that wasn't shared.

The press conference didn't last much longer, because Kate refused to speculate why the governor, Brady Flowers, and members of the state legislature were so interested in this matter or whether they had withheld evidence. She blandly repeated "you will have to ask them" or "I won't speculate."

Sam called Kate to congratulate her, and we spent the rest of the afternoon talking about Sam's future instead of returning to the back nine. Sam had received some intriguing offers, including an endowed chair at the law school and a general counsel's position with a growing bank holding company. I gave him some ideas, but the real question was whether Sam had gotten politics out of his system. Once the political bug bites, it's much like getting Lyme disease—it stays in your system for a long time and is almost impossible to cure.

We left the club promising to stay in touch about his prospects and his decision. Sam had suggested we meet with Kate and some other lawyers from his office for drinks and dinner, but I begged off. I thought it best not to tell him I was having dinner with his old girlfriend.

15

Maggie would be proud—I had ordered flowers for Jana from Cabbage Rose Florists this morning. While I was at it, I sent an arrangement to Helen with a note apologizing for falling asleep, and another to Micki to thank her for a wonderful evening. Maggie would say I was being excessive, but who knew when I'd get back to Little Rock. Maybe I'd run out of old friends who needed my help.

Jordan and I were on our way to Jana's when my phone rang. I hadn't lost the phone or left it back at the hotel—a miracle.

"Flowers?" Micki asked. "What's up, Jack? You must want something I'm not about to give you. What happened to your girlfriend on Pawleys Island?"

Right to the point as usual.

"Jo is a long story, but can't a man be grateful and show it for a change?"

"Hell, Larry did everything. That said, they're lovely, thank you."

"You're welcome."

"I hear you plan to sneak out of town without saying goodbye. Maggie told Larry you're flying back tomorrow."

"I would have called before I left. How about breakfast tomorrow?" I asked, expecting her to respond that she wasn't always available at the drop of a hat.

"That would be nice," she answered. "Can it be just the two of us, no Clovis, no Sam?" Something was bothering her.

"How about eight o'clock at the hotel restaurant? Does that work?"

"Perfect. Again, thanks for the flowers, Jack. They were a lovely surprise."

I had no idea what could be wrong, but we had just pulled up to Jana's house. The explanation would have to wait.

Jana lived on River Ridge Road, a single street traversing a high ridge overlooking the Arkansas River. Each river view lot falls off for hundreds of feet before reaching a steep cliff down to the river. This layout makes for wonderful gardens and breathtaking views of the expansive Arkansas River that splits the state from northwest to southeast. From the street, her home looked like it had been designed by Frank Lloyd Wright, or more likely, Arkansas's own Fay Jones.

She greeted me at the door with a kiss on the cheek. She wore a full bib apron over a silk blouse and white jeans, her hair held back and out of her face by an embroidered headband.

"You caught me running behind. Come into the kitchen and pour yourself a glass of wine while I put the finishing touches on the Bolognese sauce and the salad. I hope you're into simple."

"Simple sounds terrific." She led me through the foyer to an inviting kitchen.

"I've decanted the wine. Hope it's okay. I can offer something stronger if you prefer," she said as she picked up a spoon to stir the sauce.

"Wine is perfect."

I noticed she had a full glass, so I poured a glass for myself and watched her fuss in the kitchen for a few minutes. Before long she turned the stove off, placing a loose lid over the pot of simmering sauce. The apron came off, and she offered to show me her home.

She had chosen Southwest décor—I recognized an original Georgia O'Keefe above the fireplace and two Remington sculptures in the family room. But my eyes turned to the French doors leading to an expansive balcony overlooking the river. The view was breathtaking. We gravitated to comfortable chairs shaded by a canopy. A tug guided a large barge as it made its way down the river, avoiding the Interstate-430 bridge.

"If I woke up to this view every morning, I might never leave," I remarked.

"Judd and I used to take our coffee here most mornings, and we loved to begin our evenings with a glass of wine and the setting sun. I wish you could have known him."

"I do, too," I said, meaning every word. "Larry Bradford told me a little more about him last night. Sounds like he was quite a man."

"More than a few successful people in this town got their start with the help of Judd and Larry's dad," she said.

"From what I heard, all the risk was Judd's. Larry's dad always got his money back."

"That's the story Stan Bradford would have his family believe, including his uptight wife. Don't get me started on her. I could tell you..." She took a breath before continuing. "I didn't know about Ben, but yes, Judd was the guarantor for the first few loans. After they became friends, the two of them were equal partners." She raised her glass and laughed at the memory. "They'd sit on this porch many a night drinking scotch and strategizing about how to help some veteran without them ever knowing they had anonymous benefactors."

I wondered about Jana's opinion of Larry's mother—Micki had expressed a similar reaction. Our conversation turned to my family and old friends, including Marshall and Helen. When Jana and Sam were together during college, she had been a regular at our Sunday dinners at Helen's house.

"If I weren't leaving for home tomorrow, I'd arrange a reunion. I know Helen would love to see you. She's a special lady."

"My relationship with Sam ended long ago. There's no reason I shouldn't pick up the phone and call Helen myself. The same goes for Marshall. Maybe now, since I have all this time on my hands, I'll do what I should have done many years ago. You know, the worst part of my breakup with Sam was losing all of you. But, hey, life goes on."

"Speaking of time on your hands, why are you no longer practicing medicine? Why not keep the East End clinic open? I assume Judd left you in good shape. You're way too young to retire."

She smiled. "The East End clinic served a lot of families, but it's not practical to keep it going without state help. Even with Medicaid, Medicare, and the state's subsidy, we barely broke even—and that's with me never taking a dime. The clinic was so much a part of our lives. I know Judd wouldn't mind me using part of what he left to keep it open, but the estate is tied up in probate."

"Tied up in probate? It's been almost six years. What's the hang up?"

"Judd's two children from his first marriage are unhappy with the provisions he made for them in his will. And his no count brother from Oklahoma, Pickens Wilson, is contesting the will. He claims his brother would never have left him high and dry. Truth is, Judd repeatedly bailed his brother out of bad investments. I guess Pickens can't believe Judd won't continue to support him from his grave. Then there's his first wife, Doreen, who thinks a two-million-dollar life insurance policy and what she got in the divorce isn't enough. It's a mess.

"I get an allowance, and it's more than adequate to pay the bills, but until the estate settles, there's no money available to keep the clinic open even if I wanted."

Jana didn't seem bothered by the long delay, but I was. It wasn't my place to say, but I smelled lawyers slow-walking a file to earn a bigger fee. Then again, I knew nothing about her lawyers or the case. I held my tongue.

We watched the sun set in silence. After a few minutes she turned to me and said, "Let's eat. I'm hungry."

She put the water for the pasta on to boil, and I refreshed our wine. It wasn't long before I was sitting at a cozy table in her kitchen remembering how much I had enjoyed her cooking thirty years ago.

"This is even better than I remember, and I remember your pasta Bolognese being to die for," I said, enjoying every bite. "It's none of my business, in fact I'm sure it's not, but is there someone special in your life?"

"I should ask you the same question," she laughed. "Okay, I'll answer, but then you have to tell your story."

"Agreed."

"I've been out on a lot of first dates, but only a few seconds. I couldn't stop comparing every man to Judd. I tried to be more open-minded, but I wasn't interested.

"There was one man two years ago. At first he was a gentleman—respectful, attractive—we shared a lot of interests, I thought. The first few dates were fun, and I let myself believe we had a future. Turns out, I was wrong about both him and his intentions. That experience soured me, but I haven't become resigned to wearing widow's weeds quite yet." She took a sip of her wine. "How about you?"

"My story is much the same."

"That's not fair! You don't get to say 'me too' after I bare my soul."

"Okay, but it *is* much the same. I went through a period where I couldn't bear the thought of being with someone other than Angie. Then I went through a period where well-intentioned friends kept trying to introduce me to the perfect person, only she never was. I reconnected with an old high school flame. She's a wonderful woman, but lives in Vermont. Dynamite wouldn't move her, and I have no intention of moving to Vermont. I've had some wonderful short-term relationships, but nothing lasted. All my lovers become friends."

I looked across the table, wondering where this conversation was leading. Were we engaged in the dance we'd both expected from the moment I walked in the door? Her silence seemed to last forever. She looked at me and smiled.

"Oh, Jack, we're a fine pair. How about some pecan pie and ice cream?" she asked, breaking the tension with a pie knife.

After a generous helping of pie and a serious discussion about the state of health care for the underprivileged, I offered to help with the dishes. She brushed off my offer, and it was time to go. I texted Jordan, and we said goodbye at the front door.

16

JORDAN SPOKE UP as soon as I had closed the door of the big Suburban. "Clovis says your hunch was right. Dr. Hall is being followed and her house is being watched."

"Do you know who's behind it?"

"We're running the plates, but they're probably stolen. We have a few photographs. Clovis suggested you and he could talk about it tomorrow."

"Tell him I'm meeting with Micki at eight, but I should be free by ten."

I went down to breakfast early, hoping to read the paper before Micki joined me, but she was already waiting. She wore her usual "business casual" attire: a blue cotton work shirt, skinny jeans, and cowboy boots. She rose as I approached and greeted me with a kiss flush on the lips.

"Good morning!" she exclaimed.

"You're early, Ms. Lawrence."

"A little bird told me you didn't go to dinner with Sam last night. I thought I might catch you saying goodbye to someone."

"Wow, aren't you the little spy. May I inquire as to the identity of your little bird?" I asked.

"You may ask, but I'm not telling." She was in a good mood.

"Jealous?" I fired back.

"Not in the least. Larry Bradford has all my lovin' these days. You blew your chance."

"I'll have you know I slept by my lonesome last night. Now sit down and tell me what's up. You have my full attention. I told Clovis to stay away."

Micki slipped into her chair.

"First thing's first. I read about Sam's problem online last night, and I called Kate Erwin. Now I understand why you were so secretive the other night. You know I don't like being kept in the dark, but I was out of line suggesting you had a romantic interest in Dr. Hall."

Good thing Micki couldn't read my thoughts. She gave me a suspicious stare when I asked about Larry, but let it go.

We ordered breakfast, and Micki caught me up on a few friends and her office staff, for whom I had a special attachment. Conversation lagged; it was time to get to the point.

"Okay, I'm enjoying the heck out of breakfast, brings back great memories. But I suspect you have something specific on your mind."

She took a sip of coffee, her face pensive. "The last time you were in town, you asked if there was trouble in paradise."

"I did. You told me not between you and Larry, but you had a few in-law problems to work out."

"You have good memory. Well, things aren't any better. Larry's mother is still angry that Larry refused to become a banker like his father and grandfather. She won't accept that he's an artisan, a very good one. She refuses to use the word and substitutes 'common carpenter' instead. I hate it when she asks him when he'll put away those childish toys and get a real job."

"Those issues are between Larry and his mom. You can be supportive, but he's the one who has to deal with her."

"You're right, but she blames everything on me. Behind my back, I'm referred to as 'Larry's slut.' I'm not invited to family functions, which doesn't bother me, but it does bother Larry. He told her if I'm not welcome, he's not either, and she responds by asking, 'What kind of woman drives a wedge between a man and his family?' He says he doesn't care, but his family is important to him."

People say you don't marry into a family, but you do, for better or worse. Most of the time, all sides adjust, but it sounded like Mrs. Bradford wasn't the adjusting type. I remembered last night Jana had expressed a less than favorable opinion of her.

"How can I help, other than by being a sounding board?" I asked.

"Well, that helps, but can I ask a specific favor?"

"Sure, anything."

"Will you talk to Larry? He respects you. Don't give me that look. He knows all about our time together. I believe in honesty in a relationship. Jack, you were a wonderful lover, but you are a better friend. Talk to Larry, please."

"Next time Larry's in DC, I'll take him out for a beer, but don't underestimate him or how much he cares for you. A man doesn't move his power tools unless he plans on sticking around for a while."

"I know I'm being foolish, but…thank you, Jack."

"You know I'm a lawyer, not a therapist. I'll talk to him, but no guarantees."

After chatting about nothing for a few more minutes, we agreed to stay in touch and she was gone. I went back to the room to check email and return a few calls. I dreaded my return to DC. Maggie and Brian had tried to pick up the slack, but I had unhappy clients whose matters had been left hanging because of my unexpected stay in Little Rock. I was also returning to a new residence with no idea where Beth and Maggie had put my toothbrush.

I was packing my bag when Clovis texted to say he and Sam were on their way and would like to meet in the bar in five minutes. *Now what?* I wondered. The bar served as a coffee shop until lunch—I hoped I wouldn't need a drink this early.

Sam and Clovis were waiting when I arrived. No smiles.

"Why so glum, fellows? I'll be out of your hair in a few hours."

"Sit down, Jack. There's been a new development." Clovis sounded like my Uncle Ned, always the bearer of bad news.

Sam's voice sounded official. "The sheriff's office found another body in the Fourche Bottoms near the spot where Mace's body was discovered. The man's neck had been broken. Where were you last night?"

"Another body? You don't think I had anything to do with it, do you?"

"Just tell me where you were," said Sam.

I knew he wouldn't like my answer, but I had no choice.

"If you must know, I had dinner with Jana. I left her house around eleven o'clock, and Jordan brought me back to the hotel. I went directly to my room, where I remained, alone in my bed, until this morning."

Sam's face turned to stone, and I hastened to explain.

"Listen, Sam, I didn't tell you about dinner with Jana at the golf course for the very reason you're giving me that look. I called her after we met with Kate Erwin to warn her that your office would recuse. She invited me to come for dinner and to catch up on old times. She said she wished you could join us, but knew you couldn't." A slight exaggeration on my part.

"Oh, she did? Right."

"Yes, she did." I felt my face grow hot. "But let me say something I shouldn't have to say. Thirty years ago, you cheated on Jana, and you haven't seen her since. She was happily married for many years and had a successful career without you. So don't think you have some kind of claim on her. You don't."

Sam glowered, but remained silent.

"Now what in the hell does another body in the Fourche Bottoms have to do with me?"

Clovis intervened, "Jack, the dead man was the same guy who almost broke your jaw and kicked you in the balls. We'd gotten word that a man who fit his description has been frequenting bars in south Little Rock, bragging about kicking the shit out of you.

"Last night, Paul and I went bar-hopping. Several people had seen him the night before, but we struck out. We gave up around midnight. This morning, I got a call from the police chief. He told me a man who fit the description I'd given the police was dead and that his body was discovered close to where they found Mace. I went to the morgue, and he was the same man who attacked you. What do you think?"

"What do I think? You haven't given me time to think." I took a breath, trying not to lose my temper. "I can't say I'm heartbroken that the man who almost destroyed the family jewels is dead, but I'm more interested in who killed him and why. I'm assuming it's the same man who killed Mace.

"Sam, I get why you had to ask about last night. Surely it's not a coincidence that two of the men who attacked me have been murdered and were found at the same place where I was left to die."

"And I'm sorry that I acted like a spoiled kid. You were right to call me out," he responded.

I wasn't sure how sincere he was, but at least the air was clear. It wouldn't be long before Sam went knocking on Jana's door.

"Am I free to leave town? I'm supposed to fly back to DC this afternoon."

Sam flashed a grin. "Free to leave is one way to put it—'asked to leave' comes closer to the truth. If you didn't have a ride, I'd buy you a ticket and escort you onto the plane."

We laughed, both glad I was on the way home.

"Don't forget that your invitation was the reason I came."

"I won't make the same mistake again," he said with a wink, and pushed back his chair to leave.

I wondered whether or not Jana could ever be this possessive of an old boyfriend. Thirty years later, Sam's possessiveness didn't seem to make much sense. Maybe it only applied to *certain* old flames.

The waiter came to refill our coffee, and Clovis watched in silence as I fooled with the sugar and creamer. I'd had about enough.

"Okay, Clovis, explain this: I come to Little Rock as a favor to a friend and some nut tries to kill me, to hang me, for God's sake. The police are clueless, but happy to give me the third degree. Next, someone kills the guy who did it, and now his accomplice is dead. I can't blame the police or Sam for checking out my alibi or yours, but what the hell is going on?"

It would take a lot more than my little tirade to ruffle Clovis. "Jack, if Sam and the police chief didn't know us and if our alibis weren't ironclad, we'd be prime suspects, and rightfully so. I don't understand what's going on, but I can't say I'm comfortable with such a capable killer on the loose, whatever his motive. I'll let Martin know about this second killing and warn our friends in St. Louis. There has to be a logical explanation."

"Right. Now tell me what you know about Jana."

"Someone's watching her twenty-four seven. Nothing intrusive and there's no sign she's in danger, but someone is interested in her comings and goings. The plates are registered to another detective agency. As long as they do nothing more than watch, there's not much the police can do. I could tell Sam."

"No, Sam needs to stay away from anything related to Dr. Hall, at least for the moment. Jana is involved in a nasty probate fight. Maybe one of the other parties is tailing her to dig up dirt."

"Should you tell her?" Clovis asked.

"I don't want to scare her. Maybe I should let her lawyers know. What do you know about the Crockett firm?"

"They're one of those large international firms with offices all over the country. Most of their clients are Fortune 500 companies. I bet Jana is paying them a pretty penny to handle her probate case and to represent her in the state audit. If she becomes the target of a special prosecutor, there's no telling what that will cost."

"I can't help but wonder why it's taking so long to resolve the probate," I replied. "She seems to be comfortable with her lawyers, but I'm tempted to put in a call to Janis Harold."

I'd met Janis Harold during Woody Cole's case. She made up for her lack of height with a keen wit and an acid tongue. She and her husband were the two best tax and probate lawyers I'd run across, anywhere. Janis could give me the straight scoop on Jana's lawyers.

"Do you want me to pull back on watching Dr. Hall?" Clovis asked.

"Not yet. As you said, there's an accomplished killer on the loose, and we have no idea what he'll do next. Let's not drop our guard."

"Not a problem," he said. "Look, you've got two hours before we should be at the airport. Anyone else you need to see?"

"I forgot to pick up a case of barbeque sauce when I was at Ben's. How about some ribs and a beer before I leave town? I don't know when I'll be back."

17

Clovis pulled up in the gravel lot behind Ben's, and before long we were enjoying sandwiches, ribs, and beer while Ben embarrassed Clovis by telling stories. Clovis was an All-American linebacker at Tennessee State, guaranteed to be a first-round draft choice in the NFL, when a freak accident destroyed his football career. Ben knew a few stories about Clovis I hadn't heard, including the night that Clovis won the MVP trophy in the State High School Basketball Tournament. I was about to tackle my second pork sandwich when I felt my cell phone vibrate.

"Jack, it's Jana."

My internal radar kicked in. Something was wrong.

"Hey, what's up?"

"Last night you told me all your lovers became your best friends."

"Well, I may have exaggerated."

"Jack, we were never lovers, but I need a friend. Can we talk?"

She sounded nervous, almost frightened.

"What's wrong, Jana? What's happened?"

"Please, not over the phone. Can you come over? To my house?" she asked.

I sighed, but didn't think twice. "Sure," I said. "When?"

"Now!" she exclaimed. "Please, Jack, can you come right now?"

"Give me thirty minutes."

Clovis and Ben had overheard every word. "I'll call Walter's pilot and tell him to hold the plane," Clovis said.

"I've known Jana as long as you. She sounds upset. Let me know how I can help," Ben offered.

I had no idea what could have brought on the call, but I appreciated that both Clovis and Ben recognized this was not a call I could ignore. Ben pushed my wallet away, and Clovis and I were soon on our way to River Ridge.

Jana was pacing back and forth on her front porch and ran to meet me as I jumped out of the car.

"Oh, Jack, thank you!" She almost collapsed, and I held her for a few minutes. I noticed a dog walker staring and said, "Let's go inside."

Clovis stood next to the car, looking uncomfortable. "I'll stay with the car."

Jana responded immediately. "Don't be silly, Clovis. Please come in."

"You already know Clovis?" I asked.

"Clovis and I go way back." She had regained her composure. "I have nothing to say that Clovis can't hear. I feel better already with you here. I need to tell you what happened and get your advice. Why don't you go to the kitchen and get something to drink? I need to freshen up. I won't be a minute."

She disappeared, and Clovis and I wandered into the kitchen. I noticed a half-empty glass of scotch on the counter with lipstick on the rim. Something serious must have happened—I didn't picture Jana as a morning drinker. Clovis poured us each a glass of water from the fridge, and we sat at the kitchen table, wondering what would happen next.

Jana walked in after a few minutes looking calmer, more self-possessed. Every hair was in place, and her makeup and mascara looked fresh. I watched her pick up the glass of scotch and toss its contents into the sink.

"Drinking scotch at noon—what you must think!" She put the glass into the dishwasher, an automatic reaction.

"Jack, there's a bottle of Chablis in the fridge. Will you have a glass with me? I know how it looks, but this morning was awful."

Clovis came to her rescue. "Jana, why don't you take Jack into the den. I'll bring you both a glass in a few minutes. Have you had anything to eat?"

She shook her head no.

"I'll roust around your fridge and find something for you to nibble on. Jack can tell me what I need to know. I have lots of work to do, and I can't think of a nicer spot to do it than on your balcony. Now you two go on, I'll bring you wine and food in a few."

His voice had taken on a soothing tone. He walked away without a glance in my direction. I wondered....

Jana gave him a grateful smile and walked into a smaller room next to the dining room. The den was a cozy space, paneled in walnut with bookshelves lining one wall. It was furnished with a small sofa, a leather recliner, and two comfy side chairs. Jana turned to offer me a seat, and I saw tears sliding down her cheek.

"Hey, it can't be that bad," I said. "What's this about?"

She pulled a Kleenex from the box sitting on the desk, dabbed her eyes, and sat down on the sofa.

"Well, you know I had a meeting with my lawyers this morning. I assumed it was about the special prosecutor. When I arrived a little before nine, the receptionist guided me to a conference room full of people. Most of them were milling around a table of pastries, coffee, and soft drinks in the back of the room. The lawyer handling the audit case, Chet Dobbins, and the lawyer handling the probate of Judd's will, Kevin Toms, were sitting on both sides of the chair reserved for me at the head of the table.

"I took in the scene for a few minutes, then asked Chet who was paying for breakfast. He laughed and said, 'Well, I guess you are.'

"I said, 'In that case, do you think I could get a cup of coffee?' I was more than annoyed. A young woman seated at the end of the table brought me a mug. Not a man in the room moved a muscle, including Chet and Kevin.

"Then I asked him who all these people were and who was paying for their time. At least this time he didn't laugh. 'Well, your cases are very serious matters, and each person in this room has specific responsibilities either on the audit case or the probate of Mr. Wilson's will. We came prepared to answer any questions you may have.' I was irritated by this show of manpower at my expense, but I kept my cool. I said, 'Well since I'm paying for a meeting you organized, let's cut to the chase. Why am I here?'

"Chet said, and I'm trying to remember his exact words, 'We thought this would be a good time to provide you with an update on both matters. We also need to discuss a new development in the state audit matter—a problem presented by the appointment of a special prosecutor.'

"When I asked him what the problem was, he straightened the files on the table, and I knew something was up. So I said, 'Chet, look me in the eye. What problem?'"

Her story was interrupted by the sound of a knock. I jumped up to open the door for Clovis. He walked in carrying a large tray that held a bottle of wine, two glasses, bowls filled with vegetables and some kind of dip, and a plate of cheese and crackers.

"Jana, be sure to eat something, okay?" he said, placing the tray on the coffee table and closing the door behind him almost in a single motion.

She poured us each a glass of wine, picked up a carrot stick, and continued.

"Chet looked uncomfortable and asked, 'Wouldn't you like a status report first?' I just stared at him. He shrugged and said, 'Okay—the appointment of a special prosecutor required our firm to conduct a new conflicts check. Turns out we do have a conflict with another client. This conflict of interest means we can no longer represent you in the state audit case.' By now the room was silent.

"I was floored. After all this time, and all the money I've paid that firm, those jerks were bailing."

I held my tongue, but knew Chet had handed her a line of bull. They had called this meeting before news of a special prosecutor became public. Besides, the special prosecutor's appointment wouldn't require a conflicts check. No, the firm was covering something, probably its own ass.

"And that wasn't the worst of it," she continued. "Chet said they had contacted a criminal lawyer on my behalf to take over the case and had arranged for me to meet him this afternoon. When I asked about the conflict, Chet said they weren't at liberty to discuss it.

"I was mad. I *am* mad. Tens of thousands of dollars down the drain and they couldn't bother to tell me the nature of the conflict? I said things I shouldn't have. I asked if I was being charged for Chet to tell me his firm couldn't represent me. He said, 'Given the circumstances, there will be no fee for this meeting.'"

"How good of them."

"Yeah, they're so generous. I turned to Kevin and asked if he was withdrawing from the probate matter. He acted offended and said, 'No, the conflict doesn't extend to the probate matter. We're balls to the wall getting that case ready for trial.' I enjoyed telling him in front of three female lawyers that I found his language offensive and never wanted to hear the phrase again. That emptied the room in a hurry."

"Good for you. Who's the lawyer you're supposed to meet?" I asked, taking a sip of wine.

"His name is Les Butterman. Do you know him? Is he any good?"

I almost spit out my wine. Yes, I knew Les. He was a bottom feeder if there ever was one. My face betrayed my opinion.

"I take it you're familiar with his credentials? Chet said Les had a reputation for being able to negotiate favorable plea deals—that he was expensive, but worth the price. He wanted a hundred-thousand-dollar retainer. Kevin said that if I didn't have that kind of cash on hand he would seek an advance from the probate court. Jack, they already have me pleading guilty, and I don't even know the charge."

I took a deep breath, trying not to lose my cool.

"Why do they think you should plead guilty?"

"I asked the same question. Chet said a special prosecutor has one function, and that is to prosecute, much like a bomb's purpose is to explode. Then he said, 'Jana, the special prosecutor won't quit until he has a few scalps, and yours is the ultimate prize.' Do you realize how offensive such a remark is to an American Indian? I wish I had thrown my coffee at him. But I didn't. I cried."

"You were entitled," I said.

"You don't understand. I'm strong, and I'm smart. I don't cry. I'm not offended easily, and I don't let sexist, bigoted men get to me. But today, I did. I'm disappointed in myself and scared to death."

A million thoughts ran through my mind as she paused for another carrot stick.

"Jack, I'm sorry. I know you have to get back to DC. I appreciate your taking the time to listen. I'll be okay. I'll gather myself, meet with this lawyer and schedule an appointment with my psychiatrist." She rose and offered me her hand.

I can't sit back and watch while someone gets thrown under the bus, especially someone I care about.

"No, that's not what you'll do. Please sit down."

She looked surprised at my reaction, but she sat.

"Do you want my advice?" I asked.

"Of course. That's why I called."

"Cancel your appointment with Les. He'll try to talk you out of canceling, but say thank you and hang up. He's the last lawyer on earth you need."

"What about the special persecutor?" she asked, tripping a little over the title—special prosecutor.

"Jana, one hasn't even been appointed yet. You have plenty of time to find a competent lawyer. You should expect Chet to call, asking why you canceled the appointment. Don't tell him a thing—not that I'm involved or anything else. He has withdrawn from the case—he no longer represents you. Can you do that?"

"Yes, in fact I look forward to it." She perked up a bit.

"With your permission, I'd like to ask a lawyer friend of mine to do a little digging into the probate case. It shouldn't take this long to settle the estate, even with the brother, former wife, and children complaining."

"Go right ahead," she said. "At this point, I have no loyalty to or love for the Crockett firm. When Judd died, I asked the lawyer who drew up his will to probate the estate and he agreed. But he retired soon after Pickens filed his objection to probate. Then his old firm merged with the Crockett firm, and I got Kevin. I get a report and a bill once a quarter, regular as clockwork."

"My friend's name is Janis Harold. She's the best in the business. You can expect a call from her before long."

"Thank you, Jack. But does this mean you're my lawyer now?"

18

I WASN'T READY TO ANSWER HER, not yet. I knew nothing about what sort of case a special prosecutor might bring. Kate Erwin had declined to bring charges despite pressure from the state health director, and it was possible that a special prosecutor might reach the same conclusion. Possible, but not likely. I wished I could talk to Micki, but for now, that door was closed.

"I'm not sure I'm the right person to represent you," I began.

Her eyes flashed with disappointment, but I continued.

"What I can promise is I won't abandon you. We have time before anything happens. Let me ask Sam's deputy what the Health Department director claims you did. We also need to get the Crockett firm to return your records and files. And I'm worried that the press will hound you as soon as they get a whiff of what's going on.

"Jana, I want to hire Clovis on your behalf. He can keep the press away, and will contact Chet to arrange for the return of your files. He'll manage whatever else needs to be done before I return. Are the patients' records and the billing records stored in the same place?"

"Those files are in a warehouse in west Little Rock."

"Good. Clovis and his people will make sure the warehouse is secure and check out the security system here, too."

"I've had no problems with break-ins," she said.

"I know, but something smells fishy, so humor me. Clovis won't do anything without your approval."

"I trust Clovis—he and I go way back."

I was curious, but didn't want to get off track. I let it go. I also didn't want to put the cart before the horse.

"Jana, can you ask someone to stay with you, at least for the next few days?"

"You're worried about what I told you earlier, that I might jump off a cliff."

"Well, yes, I am."

"I won't, but okay," she sighed. "My sister lives in Russellville—she can be here in an hour or two. I need to tell her what's happened anyway."

"Good, you call her, and I'll get Clovis. We have a lot to talk about in a short time."

"Sounds like someone got to her lawyers," Clovis said when I told him what had happened.

"My guess is the firm doesn't want to get crosswise with the governor. They don't mind draining her husband's estate with legal fees, but to represent the target of the governor's special prosecutor is another matter.

"Listen, can you ask Stella to help? Whoever is watching Jana may have hacked her phone and her computer. Take a hard look at the warehouse where the clinics' records are stored. I don't know what's around the corner, but I don't want any of those records to go missing.

"And you know how to handle the press. As soon as the governor appoints a special prosecutor, they'll be all over Jana, satellite trucks in her driveway, the whole nine yards."

"Aren't you being a little dramatic? It will take weeks if not months for a special prosecutor to hire staff. Kate Erwin's statement was pretty strong—'no grounds for further investigation.' They might reach the same conclusion."

"It's better to be prepared. Everything that's happened in the last few days feels too neat, too packaged: the pressure from the Health Department and the legislature, the law firm's conflict, not to mention whoever's tailing Jana. It wouldn't surprise me if there's not already a special prosecutor and staff waiting in the wings."

"You know, Jack, I think you've been watching too much conspiracy TV. Jana embarrassed a lot of folks at the Health Department when she devised a plan to help care for the state's poor and got it funded.

She's not only an excellent doctor, she's also a whiz at analyzing data. She showed the legislature how education and preventative health care could save the state a lot of money. The Health Department and local health officials were left with egg on their faces. This attack is payback, pure and simple."

I was about to ask Clovis how he'd learned so much about the issues when Jana returned.

"Okay, my sister will be here in three hours, prepared to stay through the weekend. I also called Butterman's office and cancelled my appointment. The receptionist tried to get me to reschedule, but I put her off."

"It won't be long before he's on your doorstep, Clovis." I grinned.

"I'll be ready. Jana, I've got to take Jack to the airport, but my colleague, Jordan Ramsey, will stay until I get back. He's on his way now."

"I think I can deal with a lawyer knocking at my door," she said, frowning.

"I'm sure you can deal with Les and his minions. But he has a habit of bringing the press to help intimidate prospective clients. You shouldn't have to deal with the press right now—or ever, if I can help it," I said. I couldn't help overreacting to Les—the thought of him made my skin crawl.

"Okay, I'll mind Clovis and be quiet as a mouse. I know you need to leave, but when will you be back?"

"I'm not sure," I sighed. "But I will be back, by Monday at the latest. Listen, have a good time with your sister, catch a couple of movies and go out to dinner. But let Clovis be in charge of your logistics and security."

On the way to the airport, Clovis and I talked about her security plan. Neither of us had forgotten the Fourche Bottoms. We agreed that Jana wasn't in any immediate danger, but it was better to be safe than sorry. He assured me that Jordan could protect her from a respectful distance.

"Looks to me like you've taken on another client," Clovis commented.

"Oh, I hope not. Micki has a conflict, Walter won't let Maggie return to Little Rock, and I don't have any idea what's behind all this. I'll ask Janis Harold about criminal attorneys. You have any recommendations?"

"Well, the best firm is Lassiter and Cassinelli, but they're swamped with health care cases. The Justice Department has targeted about every doctor in the state for over-prescribing OxyContin. But any of the lawyers at that firm would be my choice after Micki."

"Thanks, Clovis," I said as he pulled up to Walter's plane. "I'll send you my return schedule as soon as I know it."

"That's fine, but this time I will make your hotel reservations, and I will pick you up at the airport, no deviations from the defined procedure." He grinned.

******

Clovis waited until Jack's plane was in the air before he left. He smiled as he drove away. Jack might say he wouldn't represent Dr. Hall, but he would, no doubt about it. Jack was loyal to his old friends, and that loyalty usually trumped practicality and good sense.

Clovis also knew he would have his hands full watching Jana. She was a beautiful woman inside and out, capable of compassion, sacrifice, and endurance, but a criminal prosecution would put her to the test. She had been fragile after Judd died, and only her work pulled her out of what could have been a dangerous downward spiral. The half-full glass of scotch on the counter at noon wasn't a good sign. Clovis hoped it wasn't an omen.

19

I SLEPT PRETTY WELL LAST NIGHT considering my new digs. Maggie and Beth had everything in order: the bed made, my clothes hung or arranged in drawers, the remote next to the TV, and the fridge well stocked. Maggie left a nice bottle of Cabernet along with a double sausage pizza ready to pop in the oven. She knew how to make me feel right at home.

Lisa Eckenrod, one of Martin's best, picked me up to go to the office, even though the metro stop was only a few blocks from my new place. When she met the plane last night, she told me that Martin wasn't ready to lower his guard. I knew Lisa from the Goodman case, and knew her skills were second to none. I thought this obsession with security was overkill, but kept my thoughts to myself. I wasn't about to incur Maggie's wrath by ignoring Martin's recommendations. Besides, I would definitely ruin Maggie's day when I told her about Jana's problems.

The ride to my office from Kalorama only took a few minutes. I opened the door to the office to find Brian sitting at the reception desk opening the morning's mail. In a small office like ours we don't worry about protocol—the first person in makes the coffee and opens the mail.

I poured a cup of coffee, and Brian joined me in my office to discuss what I'd missed. In the course of our conversation, I asked him if he was free to travel in the next week. I mentioned San Antonio, but was thinking of Little Rock.

I needed Brian to supervise the preservation and compilation of

Jana's records. Walter would veto Maggie going to Little Rock, but whether or not I represented Jana, someone had to preserve the clinics' records and organize them in a searchable format. Brian had worked on big document cases when he was with the Judge Advocate General's Corps—JAG Corps for short.

It wasn't long before Maggie flew into the office, made her tea, and joined us, ready to talk.

"I want to hear all about your first night in your new place. How are you feeling, and what happened in Little Rock—did you solve Sam's problem?"

"I felt right at home, and thanks for the pizza and wine. We have lots to talk about. Brian made lunch reservations at Bistrot Du Coin. But right now I need to get on the horn with Red about the move to San Antonio. We can talk about Little Rock at lunch."

She gave Brian a look, and they both left, neither looking happy. Lunch would be a challenge.

I spent most of the morning talking to Red. He wanted to go over some broad parameters for the negotiations. Red liked the idea of going home to Texas with an NFL franchise, that is if we could get at least half of the concessions he wanted. He was also talking about a possible link up with Mexico City.

I spent a good bit of time on the phone with Janis Harold, explaining Jana's probate problems.

She said, "I don't care how many heirs are contesting the will, this estate should have been closed years ago. Archie knew Judd's lawyer, and he's confident the will was ironclad. Judd Wilson is rolling over in his grave. I'll call Jana this afternoon. I'm sure we can do something."

Janis's husband, Archibald Morgan Harold, III, comes from an old Little Rock family with lots of connections. When he and Janis returned to Little Rock forty years ago, he discovered that the old line Little Rock law firms wanted him, but not his wife, although they were equally qualified. Disgusted, they started the firm Harold and Harold and have managed to both practice law and stay married for forty years.

"Any thoughts on a good criminal lawyer who can handle a complex document case?" I asked.

"Let me think about it. If the Crockett firm backed out because they didn't want to offend the governor, I expect the other big firms will have similar problems. I'll talk to Archie and get back to you."

It was a beautiful day. Big Mike Fendler, Maggie's primary bodyguard, joined us on the five-minute walk up Connecticut Ave to the restaurant. Big Mike had become part of our office family, so his presence wasn't awkward.

As we walked, I talked to Maggie about my new home. She and Beth had worked hard to make the move seamless. I showered her with compliments and thanks and kept the Little Rock news to myself. Maggie told me all about her frustrations with the progress on her new home construction.

"If it weren't for Larry, I'd have pulled my hair out by now. I don't understand why it's taking so long. At this pace, the contractor will finish the office complex and retreat center well before we can move into our new house."

Last year, Walter and Maggie had bought a large tract of land in eastern Maryland where they planned to build a new corporate headquarters for Walter's insurance company, a permanent home and retreat center for the Margaret and Walter Matthews Foundation, and a new personal residence.

"Why don't you follow my lead and leave town?" I joked as we entered the restaurant.

"That's what Walter wants to do. He's attending a conference in Zurich next week. He has arranged for us to spend two weeks on a river cruise through the Balkans after the conference."

"You should go. Larry can handle your contractors—you've been going non-stop for months. Take a break," I encouraged.

"What about the Lobos and the document production in the Butler case?" she countered.

"That's why we brought Brian on board. I've already asked him to go to San Antonio. He's doing most of the legwork in the Butler case. You can juggle more than one ball, right, Brian?"

"Sure," he said. I wished he sounded more confident.

"When are you going to tell him you need to spend a day or so in Little Rock on the way to San Antonio?" Maggie asked.

My jaw dropped, and Maggie flashed a wicked grin. Brian remained silent.

"What...what makes you think I'm going back to Little Rock?" I stammered.

"Because I know you better than you know yourself. Besides, I have my spies."

"I promised to tell you about Little Rock during lunch. I guess I should get to it."

We waited until the waiter finished serving our soup, then I launched into what had happened—the meeting with Jana, my advice to Sam, and the Crockett firm's recusal. I told them I'd engaged Janis Harold and that Clovis and Janis were looking for the right lawyer for Jana.

"Too bad Micki can't help her," Brian commented. Brian had worked with Micki on our last case together.

"I agree. Maggie, our trip to Little Rock only involves finding a lawyer for Dr. Hall and maybe helping her organize her medical records for a document production."

"Have you forgotten what happened the last time you flew to Little Rock?"

"I have not. Clovis has taken personal charge of my security and will meet me at the terminal. I'll be careful. No midnight cabs this time. Now, how did *you* know I had to return?"

"Before I tell you how I knew about your little surprise, I will impose a few conditions on this trip."

I thought about objecting, but had the good sense to just say, "Yes, ma'am."

"Please do not call me 'ma'am' ever again," she responded. "I intend to join Walter in Zurich after spending a few days with family in England. Brian, I'm counting on you to pick up the slack while I'm gone. Big Mike will accompany you to Little Rock and San Antonio. He's available because Martin and Walter's office security will be with us in Europe. It's not that I don't trust Clovis, but I'll feel more comfortable if Mike is with you, too. Don't argue with me, Jack."

I wasn't about to argue, and Clovis would be glad to have Big Mike's company.

"No problem. Brian can make the travel arrangements."

Maggie smiled. "That won't be necessary. They've already been made. Walter's plane is standing by. You leave this afternoon."

"Okay, Maggie, what's up?"

"Clovis called last night. You turned your cell phone off for the plane ride and forgot to turn it back on. The governor appointed a special prosecutor yesterday afternoon. I'm surprised Janis Harold didn't tell you. He called again this morning while you were talking to Red. The special prosecutor, someone named Reuben 'Dawg' Fletcher, held a press conference this morning. Why would anyone want to be called 'Dawg'? At any rate, he introduced his staff and confirmed that Dr. Jana Hall was a target, and that subpoenas will be served in a matter of days. He's convened a grand jury."

20

THE FOUR OF US WALKED BACK to my office in relative silence. Mike and Brian would meet me at the Montgomery County Airfield at four-thirty. Maggie had arranged for Lisa to drive the two of us to my new digs to pack and then to the airfield while Maggie returned to the office.

In a daze, I packed while Maggie reviewed the arrangements she had made with our other clients. I wondered how I would ever manage without her.

My brain came back online when I zipped up my bag. "Maggie, don't think about canceling your trip. I'll be fine."

"Don't worry. Walter is adamant. You understand why I'm not going, don't you?"

"I'll miss you, but yes, I understand. Walter is right—there's no reason to tempt fate. I'll get Jana a lawyer she can trust, then go straight to San Antonio."

"Jack, you'll never walk away from a friend. A friend in trouble is like catnip to you. I wouldn't try to change you if I could. But this time you must go it alone."

"You know, without you or Micki to keep me in check, who knows what kind of trouble I might get into."

"Or what woman might try to kill you," she teased.

"Ouch—I'll try to avoid that scenario," I laughed. There had been a few unfortunate incidents with women in Little Rock.

We hugged, and before either of us had time to get misty-eyed I said, "I'll miss you, Mags." If I ended up defending Jana, this would be the first time in my career since I left the DOJ that Maggie wouldn't sit next to me at the counsel table.

"I've emailed you the articles about the special prosecutor. He sounds like a real jerk. I also told Clovis to expect you, and he's made the hotel reservations," she said.

"Let's hope he's the only one who knows I'm coming," I responded.

******

Mike, Brian, and I climbed into Walter's jet and got comfortable. The pilot, Abe, and his copilot had filed a flight plan to Little Rock, and within a matter of minutes we were streaking across the skies. While Mike and Brian played gin rummy, I read what Maggie had sent me about thc special prosecutor.

Reuben D. Fletcher was better known as "Dawg." I couldn't help remembering a line from Top Gun: "Maverick? Did your mother not like you?" I felt sure Dawg looked nothing like Tom Cruise. He had been a prosecutor in Sebastian County, Arkansas for over thirty years. Sebastian County was famous for "Hanging Judge" Parker back in the late 1800s—his contemporary equivalent was "Dawg" Fletcher, who'd never met a defendant who didn't deserve the maximum punishment, guilty or not.

Dawg was famous for making folksy quips, wearing suspenders that kept his trousers from falling down, and donning overalls for press conferences. The good folks of Sebastian County loved him and reelected him time after time. That is, unless you or a member of your family was a target of his prosecutorial zeal. Then he was the biggest SOB in the county. His deputies were loyal to him and what they called the "rule of law," whatever that means. For them, it meant all means were justified if the end was a guilty verdict. Dawg and his deputies were notorious for withholding exculpatory evidence and were frequently held in contempt for unethical tactics.

What I read didn't bode well for Jana. He had already hired staff and was ready to convene a grand jury. The governor's call to Sam had been a sham. Someone had planned to destroy Jana and her reputation for a long time. Did the head of the Health Department, Brady Flowers, have that much clout?

One thing was certain: Jana was in a world of hurt, and we needed to find her the best criminal defense attorney in Arkansas. I wondered if we needed to cast a wider net. I closed my eyes, hoping a little nap would bring clarity to my thoughts.

A tap on the shoulder roused me. I woke to see Abe's worried face. Mike and Brian looked up from their card game.

"The FAA has diverted us to Dallas. I'll give it to you straight: we've got a problem. The front landing gear is acting up—it won't engage. I don't think it's a burned-out light on the instrument panel. One of Little Rock's runways is out for resurfacing, and DFW has more room and better crash equipment. We're dumping fuel—we've got about thirty minutes to go."

He gave me another pat on the shoulder and returned to the cockpit. Mike and Brian went back to their card game, although I don't know how. Now wide-awake, I tried not to panic. My mom's brother had piloted his own plane, and I remembered one time when I was about twelve we had to make an emergency landing. Uncle Jay kept his cool and put the plane on the ground without incident.

I settled down—Abe knew what he was doing, and there wasn't a single thing I could do. I adjusted my seat belt, and we all took the crash position when told. As the plane descended, I could see several fire trucks lining the runway. Abe spoke again over the intercom.

"Okay, the tower says all wheels are down, but the front wheel light shows the nose wheel isn't locked. We'll come in slow and try to set the plane down on our back wheels. We've all practiced this procedure—it should be fine. But it could get bumpy, so keep your heads down."

The approach was low and slow. It seemed like forever before I felt the familiar thud of the rear wheels hitting the ground. Then the nose dipped down, and I felt the initial touching of the front wheel. The plane leapt forward and down. Metal and concrete screeched for what seemed like an eternity as the plane spun.

I don't have any memory of the next few minutes—it all happened so fast. But the plane eventually slowed to a halt. Mike went to the emergency door, opened it, and activated the chute. Fire trucks were hosing the fuselage with foam. We were wrapped in fire retardant blankets and led to waiting ambulances.

Abe joined us later, looking forlorn, like he'd lost his favorite hunting dog.

"Abe," I said, reaching out to shake his hand. "I've heard it said that any landing you walk away from is a good landing. Well, I have to say that's the best damn landing I've ever experienced."

He smiled and gave me a melancholy thumbs-up.

No one needed an ambulance, so we thanked the firemen and EMTs, accepted a ride to the terminal, and took an Uber to a nearby Westin.

We agreed to clean up and meet in the hotel restaurant, the BlueFire Grille. Abe and the copilot remained with the plane, but they knew dinner was on me. Mike and Brian were already on their second beer, and after an excellent martini, I asked the waiter to open a bottle of a good Cabernet. We ordered steaks with the requisite baked potatoes and veggies, followed by a rich dessert. Our appetites had never been better.

I called Clovis, but decided not to call Beth. Why should she worry about an event that didn't occur? Abe had called Walter, so Maggie already knew. Clovis told me Paul and Jordan would be here in the morning to drive us to Little Rock. We tried to be cool, but appreciated that Clovis understood no one was ready to board a plane quite yet.

Our landing made the local news, but none of us watched. Both Mike and Brian had faced death in Iraq, but this wasn't the same. In Iraq they were armed and ready to defend themselves. Today, we'd had no control over the outcome. We like to think we have control over our lives, but the truth is, existence is fragile and can change in an instant.

I drank too much wine, ate too much food, and listened to Brian and Mike tell real war stories, as opposed to the kind lawyers tell over cocktails at bar association meetings. It felt really good just to be alive.

21

I DIDN'T HAVE A HANGOVER the next morning. In fact, I felt great. It pays to drink good wine. I was up early, ready for eggs and bacon, and maybe even biscuits and gravy. Neither Brian nor Mike felt quite as good. I suggested a little hair of the dog.

Mike answered, "No thanks. You forget I'm here to protect you."

"Well then, what you need is a real Coke over lots of ice and two fried eggs with sausage, hash browns, and toast. It'll either kill you or cure you. Either way, you'll feel better." My advice wasn't news, but we all had a good laugh.

I had just broken the yolks of my eggs when I saw the hostess lead Paul and Jordan to our table. Neither had bothered to hide their weapons. Paul had a black belt in martial arts—why did he need a gun to drive us back to Little Rock?

I motioned for them to sit down and asked the server to bring them coffee.

"Thanks, Jack," Paul said. "Don't let those eggs get cold. Eat while I fill you in. Last night, someone broke into Dr. Hall's house and tried to steal her computer. I say 'tried' because, thanks to you, we were watching the house and able to foil the attempt. The police have one guy in custody, but he isn't talking. The driver got away.

"Walter's folks and the NTSB will go over the plane from nose to tail, but the on-site mechanic has already given Abe the bad news: someone sabotaged your landing gear. Clovis laid down the law with Dr. Hall. She and her sister aren't to leave the house without our people. Stella's already been there to check out the phones and computers. I'll let Clovis tell you the rest when you get to Little Rock."

"Ask Clovis to make sure Dr. Hall's records at the warehouse are secure—and ask him to call Martin. Maggie and Walter are leaving the country on a private jet tomorrow." I felt a jolt of panic.

"He's ahead of you on all counts. Stella and Clovis went to Dr. Hall's warehouse first thing this morning. He's already talked to Martin—the Matthews' plane will be checked and double-checked. He told me to tell you that your friends in St. Louis are on full alert."

We missed the worst of the Dallas rush hour traffic, and before too long had crossed Lake Ray Hubbard and were headed to Little Rock on I-30. I leaned back and mused about the past week—two attempts on my life, two dead bodies in the Fourche Bottoms, and a break-in at Jana's. What next?

We stopped at Blalock's in Mt. Pleasant for lunch. When I lived in Little Rock, you couldn't drive to Dallas or back without an obligatory stop at Blalock's for barbeque. It was, and still is, a small, nondescript restaurant at the Mt. Pleasant exit. But it serves the best sandwich between Ben's and, well, about anywhere. No matter how many years have passed since my last visit, the owner always welcomes me with "Hey, Jack. You doin' okay?" I saw color return to big Mike's face after he went back for seconds. I'd had plenty of time to think. After I'd polished off my sandwich, I called Sam, getting straight to the point.

"Sam, if you try to contact Jana, you can bet the press will be all over you, and you might become part of the special prosecutor's investigation. As your lawyer, I'm telling you stay away."

He didn't say a word.

"But as your friend, I say you're a damn fool if you don't get over there right now."

"I like the advice, but why the change of heart?" he asked.

"My legal advice hasn't changed, but I'm convinced whoever is after Jana knows about your former relationship. They planned to use that connection to discredit Kate's decision not to prosecute. They'll still leak your old relationship to the press, but life is short. I say go for it. Besides, last night's attempted break-in gives you cover to interview her in an official capacity."

"You know, it's taken a lot of restraint not to call her," he responded.

"I had that impression. But if you ignore my advice, you have to be ready to take the heat for it."

He said nothing, so I continued.

"Do you think I could meet with Kate Erwin to get a better understanding of what Brady Flowers has against Jana?"

"I'll tell her to expect your call. I'm on the way to the office now. Thanks, Jack."

I called Clovis to tell him to expect Sam's knock on Jana's door before long.

"You sure that's a good idea?"

"I wouldn't stop him if I could. I hope he's discreet, but he was bound to break the leash at some point, and we've got bigger fish to fry. We should be in town in about two hours—what's the schedule?"

"I'll meet you at the Armitage. I've reserved a conference room for the next few days until we find office space. You and I have logistics to discuss, and I'd prefer to bring you up to date in person rather than over the phone."

So Clovis didn't trust my phone—great.

I stuck the phone back in my pocket and looked at Paul. "Why all the hardware?"

"Clovis told me to tell you this: a deputy sheriff discovered a third body early this morning in the Fourche Bottoms. He was the half-brother of the second guy. Sources report he had bragged he was going get even for his brother."

Another murder. I heard the words, but they didn't sink in. I felt like I was wading through Jell-O.

When we arrived, Brian offered to handle check-in, and Paul directed me to the conference room. Clovis had coffee waiting.

I poured myself a cup. "Clovis, I'm not comfortable with all this open carry nonsense. Nobody will shoot me in broad daylight. You know how I feel about guns."

"I agree," he responded.

"Wow, that was easy."

"I'll tone down your protection when you can tell me who knew you were flying to Little Rock and who sabotaged your plane's landing gear. Mace was after revenge for an event that happened thirty years ago, but Mace is dead. Unless you've ruined somebody else's sports career, you have a new enemy who's far more dangerous.

"To complicate matters, someone knows who was in the woods the night of your hanging and is killing them one by one. Got any idea who, or why?

"Then we come to your client, Dr. Hall. She's been followed, her house has been bugged, and there have been multiple attempts to hack into her computer. Stella can give you the details this evening.

"On top of that, the man who tried to break into her house refuses to talk. He'll make bail in a day or so and disappear."

"How is Jana?"

"She's okay. I'm glad her sister is with her. There are so many pieces to this puzzle I have no idea where to focus my attention, but my first priority is to keep you alive. If it takes a show of force, you'll have to put up with that for a while."

I understood his frustration. I had no objection to staying alive, so I dropped my objections and sat down.

"I apologize, my friend. I need to let you do your job, and stick to mine. Thanks to tampered landing gear, I'm already late to the party. I need to ask Kate Erwin what she knows about the case against Dr. Hall, get Brian out to the warehouse, and spend some time with Jana. We also have to locate a space where I can set up shop. We used a spare office at Tucker Bowie's insurance agency during Woody Cole's defense, remember? I'll see if I can call on his generosity again."

"Got it," Clovis responded. "I've asked Ms. Erwin to meet you at four-thirty. Jana is with Sam now, but she's set aside tomorrow morning for you. Brian and Jordan can check out the warehouse."

"Do you think Stella can figure out how to digitize the clinics' files? I don't know enough about computers to know what I need, but I have the feeling we'll need them sooner or later."

"You can ask her yourself. After you meet with Kate, we're off to Micki's for dinner."

"Do you think that's a good idea? I don't want to put her retainer at risk."

"She told me lawyers in Little Rock go toe to toe against each other in the courtroom every day and meet for drinks at five o'clock.

Socializing with an opposing lawyer is in the finest tradition of the Inns of Court. What's more, she said to remind you that you are advising Jana in a criminal matter. The fact that she is counsel for an obesity study does not present such a conflict of interest as to restrict her social life."

"She's right," I admitted. "And I don't think Brian and Mike have seen Larry, Micki, or Stella since Rachel's case." They had worked together to help me defend Ben's daughter, Rachel Goodman, who had been accused of selling military secrets to Israel.

"Larry cooking steaks again?" I asked.

"Nope, Ben Jr. is catering dinner. He came home with the idea of creating a spin-off catering business, and it's been a success—keeps him almost as busy as the restaurant, with an event almost every night. He rented space in the warehouse district, bought a new smoker, and talks about adding a food truck. Ben pretends to object, but he's tickled pink with Jr.'s success."

Brian walked into the room, and he and Clovis embraced, one of those military-man hugs. Brian was decorated for heroism in Iraq, but after two tours of duty, his superiors had suggested he should leave the JAG Corps because he was gay. I couldn't figure out how it mattered, but the Army's loss was my gain. What Brian did in his personal life was none of my business.

I told him I was meeting Kate in a few, and he was welcome to join us before we all went to Micki's for dinner. He thanked me, but said he and Mike would prefer to take a stroll downtown if it was okay with Clovis. They wanted to check out the exits and entrances to the hotel, and get a better feel for the neighborhood.

"Good idea," Clovis said. "I'm not worried about you and Mike. Jack is a different matter. Let me give you a key to this room. Stella has swept the room for bugs, but better not leave any electronics in here. The person who tipped Mace that Jack was coming to town may still work here."

I tried to listen as they talked about security issues, but finally had to interrupt.

"All this talk about security is driving me nuts. What time do we go to Micki's?"

"Jordan will meet you in the lobby at six-thirty. Dress casual."

I went to my room to clean up and change. I felt sticky from the long car ride, so I took a shower, shaved, and put on a golf shirt and jeans. The bruises had faded, but were still obvious, and shaving around the rope burns was still tricky. I walked into the hotel's bar exactly at four-thirty. I loved this place—the dark paneling and the comfortable chairs evoked a genteel atmosphere that has almost vanished. I had also been shot in this room once. I felt a twinge of apprehension as I approached the bar.

It was a little early for the after-work crowd, so I engaged the barkeep in a conversation about the Razorbacks' chances to reach the College World Series. I felt a tentative tap on my shoulder and turned with a visible start. Kate Erwin took a step back, her face reflecting my anxiety.

"Kate—I'm glad you could come," I blurted, trying to recover. "Can I get you something to drink? A glass of wine, maybe?"

"A glass of Pinot Grigio would be nice, thank you." She smiled and took my outstretched hand.

We took our drinks to a quiet table, and I congratulated her on how she had handled the press conference.

"Hmph—lot of good it did. A special prosecutor was in the works long before our office got involved. Just wait—Dawg will go after Dr. Hall for some separate, tangential matter—nothing the Health Department ever raised with us. Whatever the charge, if the grand jury indicts her, our office will look like incompetent saps.

"The Little Rock clinic got a clean bill of health. The auditors didn't find a thing wrong with the accounting for state funds or their use, but Brady Flowers insisted that we indict Dr. Hall. What were we supposed to indict her for? There has to be more to his obsession than a power struggle over state money."

"Why do you say that?" I asked.

"Well, Brady got what he wanted—the ability to control the dollars that went directly to the clinics. Last year the legislature amended the appropriation, placing it under the control of the Health Department. As soon as the legislation took effect, the department eliminated funding for the clinics, and put a bogus obesity study in its place.

Brady has hired three legislative spouses to work on the study, and God knows who else is sucking on its tit."

I smiled as Kate's face turned beet red.

"I can't believe I said that. Oh my God, what must you think?"

I couldn't help but laugh. "Micki must be rubbing off on you. Don't worry—I used the term 'chicken-shit.'"

"I'm still embarrassed, but you're right: salty language comes with the territory. But I can't believe I said it out loud."

"That aside, don't forget our friend Micki is reaping the fruits of this same obesity study," I added.

"I know, and I can't figure that one out either. Why does an obesity study need a criminal lawyer?"

I shook my head.

"Anyway, that's why I think there must be something more. Brady has already won. He has the money, he can hire his friends, and Dr. Hall's clinics no longer exist. Why on earth does he want to put her in jail?"

22

Kate had struck the nail on the head. Could the animosity between Jana and Brady Flowers be personal? I would raise that possibility with her tomorrow. But even if it were, the intensity made little sense. And how could a personal animus have generated such collective action? A state health director doesn't usually have the political clout to get the legislature and the governor to do his bidding at the snap of his fingers. I asked Kate what she knew about Flowers.

"I've never met him, only spoken with him on the phone—he wasn't very pleasant. His reputation is that of an ambitious man, a slick customer who gets what he wants. Rumor has it he's having an affair with the chairwoman of the Senate Appropriations Committee. Be that as it may, why on earth is Dr. Hall worth this effort—a special prosecutor, for God's sake?" She glanced at her watch.

"I'd like to order us another glass of wine and continue our conversation, but if you have plans…."

"I apologize. I didn't mean to be so obvious about the time. In fact, I'll see you later at Micki's. Larry had to leave town, and she's invited me to spend the weekend. My car is in the shop, so I'm hitching a ride with someone from the office. She lives out past Micki's ranch and is picking me up here at six."

"I'm leaving around six-thirty—why don't you ride with me? We can pick up whatever you need on the way out. I won't take no for an answer."

She smiled. "Thank you, I actually have my bag with me, and I'd love to let my friend go home early. Plus I'll catch hell from Micki if

I show up in work clothes. Let me find someplace to change. Another glass of wine sounds nice."

"Perfect. Feel free to use my room," I said without much thought, handing her the key card.

She smiled, said thanks, and left, promising she wouldn't be long. As she walked away, I realized she could quickly find herself in an unpleasant situation. I fished for my phone in the side pocket of my jacket.

"Paul, I've offered to give Kate Erwin a ride to Micki's tonight. She's with the local prosecutor's office. I told her she could use my room to change into casual clothes. Tell whoever's watching my room it's okay."

After a pause no longer than a heartbeat, he responded, "Not a problem."

I relaxed, relieved to know I'd prevented an awkward situation. I ordered two more wines and waited.

Our wine arrived just as Kate returned.

"Thanks. It feels so good to get out of work clothes," she said as she took the chair I pulled out. She had changed into jeans, a loose blouse, and sandals. "Where were we?"

I threw out various theories that might explain Flowers's animosity toward Jana, but nothing rang true. I decided to let it go for the time being.

"How did you decide to become a prosecutor?" I asked, trying to change the subject.

"I was one of hundreds of idealistic young lawyers, fresh out of law school. You know, ready to fight for the little guy, right the world's wrongs. But I got lucky. Your friend Sam hired me at the public defender's office. That job was a real eye-opener, nothing like what I expected. The hours were exhausting, the cases were hopeless, and the pay was miserable. I might have made more money selling shoes. That said, Sam was a terrific boss, and my colleagues kept me from going crazy or throwing in the towel. I learned more practical law in six months than I had in three years of law school.

"When Sam became the district's prosecutor, I had three choices: I could remain at the public defender's office, go into private practice, or go with Sam. By then, I'd seen enough to know a prosecutor, even at the local level, is a powerful person. I understand why Hillary Clinton said her dream job was to be a U.S. Attorney. A prosecutor can change a person's life, even end it. Good people need to fill those positions, not jerks like Dawg Fletcher."

"You're right, and if all prosecutors were like you and Sam, the world would be a better place. But they're not. If Sam leaves, will you stay?" I asked.

"Probably not. Working with Sam has been a terrific experience. But he's right: when you become jaded and cynical, it's time to move."

"You don't seem jaded or cynical."

"Thanks. But you don't know me very well—it's a constant worry. That's one reason I look forward to this weekend with Micki. She has a way of grounding me."

Swirling my wine, I considered the woman seated across the table. She was the lawyer Sam thought should replace him and one of Micki's best friends. Now her career was in danger, seemingly caught up in a mushrooming cloud of political intrigue. A text from Brian interrupted my thoughts. It was time to go. We walked out of the bar and met Brian at the door.

When we arrived at Micki's, Kate immediately left to find her and someone handed me a beer. It wasn't long before I noticed Clovis motioning to me and joined him at a patio table.

"Most people don't know what I'm about to tell you. Keep it under your hat," he said quietly. "Forensics has determined that the same rope was used in all three murders, but it wasn't the same rope used in your hanging."

"Well, I suppose that's something. But we already knew Mace and the other two were likely victims of the same killer," I said.

"They traced the rope to Kraftco, a local hardware store. The man who bought the rope paid cash. Nobody remembers him except his name and that he wore a Stafford State Cardinals baseball cap."

"He gave a name?"

"He told the clerk his name was Jack Patterson," Clovis laughed.

"My name? He gave *my name*?" I wasn't amused.

"Relax. You were meeting Sam when your imposter was buying the rope. You couldn't have a better alibi."

I let out a sigh. "Okay, so what's your theory?"

"I have too many questions right now and no answers. Maybe the killer was trying to frame you for the murders, or sending a signal. I don't have a clue, but don't ask me to ease up on your security."

"C'mon, Clovis—why would he want to send a signal? Why not shoot me and be done with it?" We both chuckled to eliminate the tension, but he was right—too many questions, and not enough answers.

I changed the subject. "Where is Stella? I'd like to hear what she discovered at Jana's."

"She went off with Micki and Kate to the horse barn. Larry leaves in the morning, and Micki's asked Kate and Stella to stay over this weekend. I think Micki wants to vent."

Larry emerged from his workshop as Paul and Debbie drove up. It was one of those glorious late April days when the air was fresh and cool, without a trace of humidity. Larry stirred up the embers in the fire pit, and Debbie entertained us with her bubbly personality and stories about Micki's receptionist-slash-investigator, Mongo Stankovich. That's right, Mongo, for the character in *Blazing Saddles* played by Alex Karras.

I pulled Paul aside to encourage him to look after Clovis and Stella. He nodded but didn't look too confident. Larry and I had a good conversation about how the construction was progressing on Maggie's house.

"Now that Maggie's out of the country there won't be any change orders, so we'll make good progress. My worry is she'll come home with a whole new set of ideas."

Micki, Kate, and Stella returned from the barn, laughing as Micki called out, "Okay, guys, we need a drink!"

Ben Jr. handed her a frozen margarita with a flourish before giving one to Kate and Stella. We congregated around Larry's fire pit, glad to enjoy its warmth in the chilly evening. I relaxed into the moment, determined not to let tampered landing gear and an unknown killer spoil the evening.

It wasn't long before Ben Jr. called us to dinner. Micki had arranged several tables on the patio that overlooked her fields. Votive candles filled the tables and lined the patio and walkways. I watched as my friends lined up to get their fill of pork, ribs, and all the fixings. It was nice to see them together without a care in the world, enjoying each other's company. Micki walked over, and I took her hand.

"Thank you for this," I said.

"It is nice, isn't it? I wish I had reason to entertain more often. On the other hand, who would I invite?" She laughed and pulled her hand from mine. "You made quite an impression on Kate."

"The feeling is mutual—she's got a good head on her shoulders. I haven't forgotten your predicament with Larry's mom. I might have a solution. Let me see what I can do."

"You pull that off, and I'll forever be in your debt. Now let's get some food and join the others."

I filled up my plate and sat down with Stella and Clovis.

"Stella, I hate to talk shop, but what did you find at Jana's?" I asked.

"You sure know how to spoil a pleasant evening," she responded.

"I'm sorry. It's just that...."

"It's okay," she smiled. "I know how hard it is for you to turn off the meter. Why don't we meet Monday morning? I can fill you in then. Dr. Hall's phones were compromised, and very sophisticated hackers tried to access her computer, but she had turned it off. She was lucky—people seldom turn off their computers."

"Thanks—it's nice to hear good news. See you first thing Monday morning. And you're right—I should turn off the clock. Let me get you another margarita."

23

We indulged in warm peach pie and ice cream, and after a few groans of pleasure, the party broke up. We thanked Micki and Larry and soon were on our way back to the city. I drifted off until Jordan's voice broke through my reverie.

"Jack, are you awake? We're being followed. Should I lose them?"

"No, call Clovis and let him know. It's not like our destination is a secret. Warn whoever is on duty at the hotel. You okay with that, Mike?"

"Yeah, sure. But why bother following us? Where else would we be going?"

Nothing made sense, not my attempted murder by a guy who'd held a grudge for thirty years, not the murder of his friends in a swamp on the wrong side of town, not the prosecution of Jana.

As we turned the corner onto Markham Street, satellite trucks lined the street and reporters and cameras blocked the front entrance. I didn't have to ask—they were waiting for me.

I asked Jordan to drive around the block and called Sam.

"The press is camped outside. Any idea why?"

"Nope. Unless—you've been up to no good again?" he said.

I took a breath and asked, "Are you still with Jana?"

"That's none of your business," he snapped.

"Dammit, Sam, I thought we were on the same side."

"Sorry, you're right. I'm in her driveway, was about to leave."

"My guess is that Dawg leaked to the press that Jana will be indicted."

"How can he have gotten an indictment? He's only had the case a few days," Sam asked.

"I have no idea, but it's obvious this has been in the works for some time. Your old girlfriend must have pissed someone off but good. Tell Jana I'll be there tomorrow morning at ten. Is her sister with her?"

"She went back to Russellville this afternoon."

"Sam, turn off the car and go back. You can't leave her alone."

"Um, do you think that's appropriate?" he asked.

"I don't know, Sam, and I don't care. She's fragile—someone tried to break into her house, and you're a friend. Sleep on the couch, but don't leave her alone."

I heard the front door open and the sound of muffled voices, followed by the slam of the front door closing.

"She says 'thank you,'" Sam said.

"Good—I'll see you tomorrow."

I spoke to Jordan. "Okay, go ahead and pull up to the front door. Mike and Brian, I feel lonesome. You two join me."

Makeshift press briefings had become commonplace during my recent run of high-profile cases—I had forged a good rapport with the fourth estate. For the most part, local reporters are hard working, poorly paid professionals who provide an invaluable service to their community. That said, a good defense lawyer never talks to the press. What did that say about me?

The three of us ambled toward the group of microphones set up outside the hotel's main entrance. I noted with some amusement that Jordan had left the Suburban running. I tapped the largest microphone a couple of times and was rewarded with complete silence.

"Please tell me you're here to interview Adele's agent about her upcoming concert in Little Rock," I opened, greeted by laughter. "No? Then what brings you out so late on this chilly night?"

The laughter died down, and I nodded to a young female reporter.

"Mr. Patterson, we've been told the special prosecutor will indict your client on Monday."

"I don't have a client in Little Rock."

A deep male voice interrupted. "C'mon, Patterson, we know you represent Dr. Hall."

"Dr. Jana Hall?" I responded. "She's a friend. What are the charges?"

The young woman regained control. "Sources have confirmed she is your client. Do you deny you're here to represent her?"

I thought about pursuing this bizarre back and forth, but at some point a more seasoned reporter would call me on my evasion.

"Ms., uh, Adams, is it? I have one rule with the press, I won't lie to you. Any of your colleagues will tell you that's true. So, let me say this: Dr. Hall and I were friends in college, and she was my late wife's good friend. I learned recently that the governor has appointed a special prosecutor, and that she is a target. I'm here as a friend to see how I can help. It's also been nice to reconnect with old friends, which I did tonight.

"I am meeting with Dr. Hall tomorrow morning, but I have not been hired to represent her. I hope she doesn't need me or any other lawyer. She is an outstanding member of this community who has provided health care for families in Arkansas for more twenty years. If that's a crime, God help us all."

The young woman looked uncomfortable, and I heard a few uneasy chuckles.

An older reporter I'd met before asked, "Are you saying you've had no contact with the special prosecutor's office?"

"Does he already have an office? Wasn't he appointed only a few days ago?" Now the uneasy chuckles turned to laughter.

I hoped they'd get my point. A special prosecutor should look into reputed criminal behavior, not specific people. They should investigate all the details surrounding the suspected crime before indicting or directing the investigation toward a specific person. At least, that's the way it *should* work. In reality, that's seldom how it works. Special prosecutors begin with a target in mind and search for a crime, or for friends of the target whom they can leverage and intimidate.

As the laughter died down, someone in the back raised a hand. "Mr. Patterson, any idea why Sam Pagano refused to prosecute Dr. Hall when the Health Department referred criminal activity to his office months ago? Do you know anything about a cover-up? Is that why the governor had to appoint a special prosecutor?"

The question was an obvious plant.

"Now where on earth did you get that idea?" I parried. "I know nothing about the detail of the referral to Mr. Pagano's office, but I happened to see deputy prosecutor Erwin's press conference and was impressed by two things she said: the state's auditors didn't find criminal conduct on anyone's part, and no reasonable prosecutor would indict based on the information being provided by the Health Department."

The reporter didn't back down. "But we have it on good authority the special prosecutor has found criminal conduct and will bring an indictment. How do you explain this inconsistency?"

I looked at this guy for a second, wondering if he was a regular shill for Dawg's office—he didn't have the look of a first-timer. Prosecutors love to feed lazy reporters their version of the facts, threatening to leave them out in the cold if they don't toe the line.

"I'm sorry, sir. I didn't catch your name?"

"Uh, well, it's Hugh, Hugh Houseman. I work for the local Fox affiliate."

"Well, Hugh, I can't explain your purported inconsistency because I don't know if it's true. If the special prosecutor claims to have discovered criminal conduct in the last couple of days, I'd want to know how he could have investigated the alleged misconduct in such a short time. A prosecutor should investigate allegations of misconduct before bringing an indictment. Maybe some new issue came to light, since the county prosecutor's office has already gone over the Health Department's stated allegations with a fine-toothed comb and found no basis for further action.

"So, here's a question for you, Hugh: who made Mr. Fletcher aware of an alleged new case of misconduct by Dr. Hall? The governor? The Health Department? And why wasn't it reported to the county prosecutor's office?"

Hugh had no answer, and the others remained quiet. I hoped at least a few realized there could be more to the story.

"It's been a long day. But let me add one more thing. The subject of this rumored indictment by a special prosecutor isn't a doctor whose practice caters to folks like you and me, folks who either have good insurance or deep pockets. Dr. Jana Hall has practiced medicine in the East End for more than twenty years and has said to this community, this city, and this state, one thing: she will care for those who have neither."

24

I WOKE THE NEXT MORNING with a dull headache and the lousy feeling that I'd blown it with the press. In trying to defend Jana, I'd attacked both Fletcher and the governor and given them insight into my strategy. I swallowed two Tylenol and dragged myself to the shower, sure I'd made Jana's situation worse.

The hot water loosened my aching joints and brought clarity to my thoughts. Fletcher was ready to indict Jana and had leaked at least that much to the press. But why?

As to revealing strategy, it didn't take a rocket scientist to figure out the way to defend Jana from the rash of bad publicity that would follow her indictment was to remind the potential jury pool of all the good Dr. Hall's clinics had done. A defendant often loses all credibility and their reputation is long gone before any trial, the victim of leaks and innuendo. My instincts last night told me all we might have in the way of a defense was Jana's reputation.

I texted Brian to meet me downstairs to review the growing list of things we needed to do over the next few days. Brian was efficient, but I wished Maggie were here—she seemed to know what we would need even before I did. I wondered how much we could accomplish over a weekend.

Brian and Big Mike were waiting for me in the restaurant. A copy of the *Democrat-Gazette* was on my chair. Brian and Mike sat quietly as I read the headline.

Local Doctor To Be Charged

Dr. Jana Hall Faces Multiple Count Indictment

The piece was based on innuendo and anonymous sources, and contained not a word about the substance of the predicted indictment or when she would be charged. There was no mention of the clinics or Jana's standing in the community. It did contain a brief report about last night's press briefing, noting that DC attorney Jack Patterson had arrived in town and would meet with Dr. Hall today. The article ended with this commentary from none other than Les Butterman:

> *"Patterson is notorious for courtroom tricks and obfuscation. He's a publicity hound who exposes his clients to unnecessary risks for the sake of his own ego. Dr. Hall should hire a local lawyer who can negotiate a minimal jail sentence for her crimes."*

I reached for my coffee and said, "If Les Butterman ever comes within a hundred yards of me, hold me back. Better yet, shoot him, and I'll defend you for free."

Brian laughed. "If you think you're upset with Butterman, you should have heard Maggie."

"Maggie? You've already spoken with Maggie?" I'd forgotten that she hadn't left the country yet.

"She called me. She's an hour ahead and was up early scanning the online issue of Little Rock's paper."

"What did she say?" I asked.

"She told me 'ole Les' should be glad she wasn't here. From what she suggested, I think a part of his anatomy would be in real danger of being whacked."

He glanced at his notes. "She gave me the name of the service you've used before to monitor the media and called your friend, Tucker Bowie, to arrange for offices. She sent me a huge file on Dr. Hall and her efforts over the years to help Arkansas's poor along with instructions on how to organize it the way you like. She'll call Stella to suggest how we should deal with the files in the warehouse. And she gave me specific instructions to send her a daily email."

That was Maggie, watching my back.

Brian continued, "I thought I'd check out the space at Mr. Bowie's while you meet with Dr. Hall."

"I'd rather you were there when we talk about the files at the warehouse. I wish Stella could be there, but I have orders to steer clear of Micki's. It's a women-only weekend, no interruptions."

Mike signaled the server for more coffee and asked about our schedule for the day.

"I'm meeting Dr. Hall at her home at ten," I replied. "I don't know how long that will take. I'll try to contact the special prosecutor—if he's in such an all-fired hurry, he'll be in his office this weekend. I'll need some time to strategize with Clovis. If we've got any time to spare, I'd like to see Marshall Fitzgerald.

"Neither of you have met him, but he is one of the great souls in this world. He was one of the original gang: Woody Cole, Sam Pagano, Marshall, and myself. We were best friends both in high school and at Stafford State. Marshall introduced me to my late wife, Angie, and is the godfather to my daughter. He's been a trial judge in Little Rock for years and was on the bench for the Cole case. I want to pick his brain about local courtroom procedure if we end up in court."

Brian asked, "So you'll agree to represent Dr. Hall?"

"I'd rather find her a good criminal lawyer. But if she's determined to have me, I'll take the job. I'd feel better if Micki could be co-counsel."

The server brought plates of eggs, pancakes, and bacon, and we dug in. I kept the conversation light, but my wheels were spinning with the many issues we faced. I needed an hour with a legal pad to organize my thoughts. We agreed to reconvene at nine-thirty.

I took a fresh cup of coffee back to my room and sat down with a pen and the long yellow pad, but I couldn't concentrate. After a few minutes, I gave up and called Maggie.

"Have you murdered Les Butterman yet?" she asked.

"I'll leave that to you."

"What a disgusting person!" Maggie usually kept her opinions to herself.

"When do you and Walter leave for Europe?" I had no desire to talk about Les Butterman.

"Late this afternoon. You should take a minute to call Red. I suspect he's heard about your rough landing."

"Good idea. Brian told me you've already given him marching

orders—thank you. Now turn off the meter and enjoy your trip."

"I'll feel better when you're back in DC. It doesn't feel right for you to take a case without me."

"No, it doesn't, but Walter was right. Little Rock isn't safe. Clovis and his people are smothering me with protection, so don't worry."

"You know I will, but tell me what's going on with the special prosecutor and Jana Hall."

We spent the next half hour talking over Jana's situation. Maggie wouldn't hesitate to let me know if she thought my conclusions were off base. I knew by keeping her in the loop she was less likely to cancel her trip. I also counted on our staying in touch by phone and email.

"Thanks, Maggie. Give Walter my best and y'all have a great trip." Then I called Red Shaw.

"Thank God you had an experienced pilot. I told you to stay away from Arkansas," Red began.

"That you did, but you know I'm stubborn."

"You are that. Do you need me to send my plane?" Red asked.

"Thanks, but no—I'm not ready to hop in a plane just yet. But don't worry, I'll be in San Antonio when you need me. I have all the files, and I'll be ready for the meetings."

"I'm not worried about that. Someone sabotaged your landing gear. You could have been killed." He sounded concerned.

"Red, I promise to be careful. Hell, I can't even take a piss without Clovis watching."

We spent the next hour going over a revised wish list of items Red wanted in the Lobos deal. I took notes, trying to rein him in when he got too zealous.

I glanced at my watch: almost nine-thirty. "Look, Red..." I began.

"That's okay—we're through, and I've got to take a shower. One last thing, and promise to forget this piece of news."

"I've already forgotten."

"Lucy received a call from one of her biggest Arkansas contributors suggesting she remain quiet about a special prosecutor and the indictment of your client."

"She's not my client, yet. Can you tell me who the contributor is?"

"C'mon, Jack, you know she will be. And Lucy didn't say who called, but she wanted you to know about the call."

Red was engaged to Senator Lucy Robinson of Arkansas. She's also the widow of Russell Robinson, the former governor and senator of Arkansas that my friend, Woody Cole, had shot and killed on national TV. I had defended him in court, which led to an awkward relationship with Lucy. I never quite know where I stand with her, but she and Red were cut from the same rough cloth, and I had a healthy respect for both of them.

25

WHY IN THE WORLD would a wealthy Arkansas business person give a hoot about Jana being indicted, much less call Lucy to make sure she stayed out of it? It was another piece of a puzzle that fit nowhere. I hurried downstairs where Brian, Mike, and Jordan were waiting.

When we turned onto the ridge at the top of the hill, I could see at least three satellite vans and a press tent set up in the street outside Jana's house. We pulled into the circular driveway, ignoring the shouts as we hurried inside.

Jana greeted us at the front door, and I saw Sam standing in the kitchen door.

"I followed your instructions and spent the night in the guest bedroom," he said. I was careful not to smile.

"I planned to leave bright and early, but the press had already set up. I called my driver and told him to stay away."

The county's prosecutor has twenty-four-hour protection, as well as a driver provided by the Pulaski County sheriff. Death threats were a part of his job, and a sad comment on the violence common in our society.

"Good decision. We don't want to explain why you were leaving the house at the crack of dawn. Mike, can you and Jordan work with the men watching the house to make sure none of the cameramen sneak around to look in the windows? Thanks."

They were out the door in a flash, glad to have something to do. I didn't think the press would be that intrusive, but once a high-profile antitrust client of mine discovered a cameraman trying to climb through his bedroom window while his wife was taking a shower.

Sam said, "I'll stay in the kitchen while you're talking to Jana. The press won't leave until you do."

"If it's okay with Jana, I'd rather have you sit in. You're an expert on local criminal procedure, and since Micki can't join me on this one, I could use your advice. I'll be careful to protect the privilege—my paralegal Brian will join us, too." I tapped Brian on the back, and he gave a bit of a wave.

"You okay with that, Jana?"

"Sure, no problem here," she said, managing a smile.

She poured fresh coffee, and we sat down in the study.

"Let's talk about the easy part first," I began. "Jana, when I first learned that the Health Department had sent a referral to Sam's office, I advised him to have no contact with you, and for good reason. Those reasons no longer exist, and it won't be long before some reporter discovers we were all friends a long time ago. In fact, I bet the special prosecutor and your enemies, whoever they are, already know."

"What are you trying to say, Jack?" Sam asked.

I hesitated, and Jana came to my rescue.

"Jack's trying to say is that it's okay for us to renew our friendship, but we should use discretion. Right, Jack?"

"Exactly," I said, relieved not to have to say anything more.

Jana continued. "And thank you for introducing me to Janis Harold. Turns out her husband and Judd were friends. I've already fired the Crockett firm and hired her to handle the probate."

"I thought you two would hit it off. I can't tell you how pleased I am—she will do a great job. I bet the fur's flying at the Crockett firm—they just lost a hefty chunk of change."

"Janis told me Kevin tried to argue with her. I already like her—she has a great evil-witch laugh. She wants you to call her when you have the time."

"I'll do it," I replied. Arguing with Janis was never a good strategy.

"Oh, here's something else. Both Sam and Janis warned me you will refuse to accept a fee, but, guess what?" She grinned. "I don't take refusals well. I've written you a check to get us started, but you are to let me know when it runs out. My husband taught me many things, and one of them was to hire the best, and to never select a professional based on what he or she charges."

I couldn't help but think she was one of the fortunate few. "Thank you, but—"

She interrupted. "Janis and Sam also warned me you would try to talk me into hiring someone else. You will tell me that your normal co-counsel isn't available to help and you're at a disadvantage because you're not familiar with Arkansas courts and procedure."

She paused and glanced at Sam. "Now you know what Sam and I were doing last night."

Brian shuffled papers on the table, and she continued before I could say a word.

"Yes, I want you to be my lawyer. I followed the way you handled the cases against Woody and Dr. Stewart. And Ben told me what you did for his family. You'd think that would be enough, but here's the real reason." She turned to face me. From my point of view, there was no one else in the room.

"This isn't only about me and going to prison. I've treated women in Arkansas's prisons for more than twenty years—I know how bad it is. But to lose my clinics, to never practice medicine again, and to know I've failed people who have no other options is a prospect almost impossible to fathom. I am retired for the moment, but I don't want to be retired forever.

"We knew each other a long time ago. You think you're helping an old friend. But, Jack, there's more at stake. With Judd's support, I've spent most of my adult life trying to make a difference for people who can't make it on their own. What is wrong with people like Brady Flowers? Why on earth do they oppose basic healthcare for folks who work at the Bi-Lo, McDonald's, farms, or in a nursing home?

"I've spent twenty years fighting jerks like Brady Flowers, people who don't believe in health care for folks who can't pay for it. Any decent defense attorney could represent Jana Hall. I'm hiring you to represent every person who has no one to represent them."

Neither Sam nor Brian seemed to be breathing. I cleared my throat to respond, but Jana stopped me with a raised hand.

"Sam, would you and Brian mind stepping into the kitchen? Jack and I need to have an attorney-client conversation. There's orange juice and soft drinks in the fridge, or you're welcome to make more coffee. This will only take a minute."

Brian jumped up to open the door, and an unhappy Sam followed him out.

She sighed. "I don't want to hurt his feelings, but I must tell you something that neither Sam nor anyone else needs to know."

"It's all right, go ahead," I responded.

"Remember the other night I told you that after Judd there was someone I thought might be Mr. Right, but it didn't work out?"

"I do."

"Well, that person was...Brady Flowers." She was barely able to get the name out.

"Brady Flowers," I repeated, trying to keep an even tone. "Do you think his animosity toward you is a result of the break-up?"

"No, I wish it were that," she said taking a deep breath. "Brady was very smooth. We were inseparable for almost two months, and he was the perfect gentleman—at first. He told me how much he admired my work and that he would be my advocate both with the legislature and inside the Health Department. But after a while, it became clear he only wanted two things—to get me in bed and my patients' records, and not in that order. I'll give you the details another time if you think they're relevant, but I don't want you to ask questions about him in front of Sam. Promise me you won't tell Sam or use that information in court. I'd rather go to prison than relive those last days."

"Was he abusive?"

"I didn't let it get that far. Let's just say when he didn't get his way, things got ugly."

"Since neither of us know what the charges will be, I have no idea whether or not it's relevant. I promise I won't use it or tell Sam unless you agree, but I can't promise I won't bring it up. Let's not cross that bridge unless we need to."

"You may have to get me drunk," she said with a laugh, which I took as a good sign.

"I'm more interested in why he wanted the patient records, although I'd like to deck him on principle. I really don't like this guy."

"Please don't. The issue of the records made little sense, but he was adamant that they belonged to the Health Department, and I had to turn them over or else. My refusal brought our relationship to an end."

26

I ASKED SAM AND BRIAN TO RETURN, and we spent a good bit of time educating Jana on the process of an indictment and arraignment. Sam knew how the booking process worked and would make sure that the head jailer treated Jana with respect. She wouldn't have to share a cell with an axe murderer or remain in one longer than necessary. But Sam hadn't dealt with Reuben "Dawg" Fletcher before. He had no idea whether Dawg would arrest and handcuff her in front of the press or wait to arrest her until late in the day when no judge could set bail.

I worried that Jana might get depressed with our discussion of strip searches, bail, and handcuffs, but she took it all in stride. When we finished, I turned to her.

"I'm sorry for all this, but the devil you know is easier to deal with than the one you don't." She didn't bat an eye.

"You forget that I'm a doctor. Most of my life I've worked in an atmosphere where the waiting room is overflowing and patients get forgotten, or worse, they wander off. And if you think a strip search is invasive, try going to a gynecologist. I have only one question."

"Angie made that same point more than once!" I laughed. "What's your question?"

"What does one wear to an arraignment? Are pearls appropriate?"

The rest of us broke into laughter. I knew she would do fine.

I charged Brian with trying to find out how to contact Dawg Fletcher and texted Jordan that it was time to run the gauntlet with the press. Jana hoped we would stay for lunch, but I declined, figuring Sam was ready for us to leave.

I walked straight to the bank of microphones the press had set up under a tent, Brian and Mike at my side.

"Good afternoon, this will be the last time I speak to you until the special prosecutor has completed his work.

"I have been engaged by Dr. Jana Hall to help her cooperate with Mr. Fletcher's investigation. She will not give interviews or speak to the press until this matter is over. I hope you will pack your tents and give the residents of River Ridge the privacy they deserve. Thank you."

A reporter shouted out. "Will you talk to Mr. Fletcher about a plea agreement?"

"We will cooperate with the special prosecutor's investigation. We are unaware of the substance or even existence of any charges against anyone. My client has done nothing wrong. That was the conclusion reached by the state's auditors and Deputy Prosecutor Erwin, and we hope Mr. Fletcher decides the same. Thank you."

Jordan pulled up and the three of us hopped in the car. I pulled out my cell phone and called Clovis. "Stella's out of town, and it's time for lunch. What're you hungry for?"

"How about a nice, fresh kale salad with iced tea?" he suggested. Stella was always after him to eat healthy.

"Perfect! Doe's it is. Brian and Mike want to check out the office at Tucker's. We'll drop them off and meet you there in thirty minutes."

Doe's was famous for its steaks, tamales, and great burgers. The original Doe's was in Greenville, Mississippi. Folks from all over the South and farther used to fly to Greenville to eat at a restaurant no bigger than a modern kitchen. George Eldridge—whose family was from Wynne, Arkansas—contracted with Doe's owners for the right to bring the menu and the name to Little Rock where it has maintained its no-frills tradition and great food since 1988.

I explained Doe's tradition to Mike and Brian, suggesting they wait until after lunch to look at Tucker's office. To my surprise, they declined—maybe they actually wanted kale salad and iced tea. I figured they might live twice as long as I would, but I'd be twice as happy.

I brought Clovis up to speed while we enjoyed our first course, a plate of homemade tamales and chili. Doe's is a place where you can see and be seen, or you can sit at a table in the back where no one will bother you except the waitress.

"Sounds like you have a new client, and you've made my job even tougher," he said.

"Looks that way. A lot depends on what I learn from Fletcher. You know, I have a hard time calling anyone Dawg. Hang on a minute."

My phone had vibrated, and I recognized Jana's number.

"Has the press left?" I asked.

I listened to her response and said, "Just a minute, Clovis is with me. Let me get his reaction.

"The press is gone, and Jana wants to know if she and Sam can spend the weekend at her cabin on the White River." I couldn't blame either one of them for wanting to get out of town.

"I don't have a problem with it, as long as my people drive them and stay close," he said.

"Jana, you're on speaker. Clovis wants one of his guys to drive you, but they won't be intrusive once you get there. I need you available in the event of an emergency. Otherwise, have a good weekend."

Jana said, "Clovis, I'm driving. If you want someone to go with us, they'd better get here soon. I'm supposed to pick up Sam in an hour. The trout are running." I could almost hear her smile.

"Don't worry—he'll be there. Be sure you don't lose him somewhere," he replied. "And bring me a string of trout." I hung up and we broke into laughter. Like they were going fishing.

We ate in silence for a few minutes, enjoying the last of the tamales.

"Clovis, I want Brian and Stella to focus on those patient files," I said as the waitress removed our plates.

"Why are those records so important?" he asked.

"I don't know, but the director of the Health Department has been after them from the get-go. You have to wonder why."

"Stella will be back tomorrow night. I'll set her up with Brian first thing Monday. If Dr. Hall is available, we'll include her, too. What else?"

"A lot depends on what Fletcher does. I don't know if he'll meet with me before an indictment or not. Hell, the truth is we have no idea what he's gonna do or when he's gonna do it. We're tilting at windmills. I'd like to have time to organize a response, but I'm flying by the seat of my pants."

The waitress came with hot burgers and extra-crispy fries. I could almost feel my arteries contracting. We took a break from business, pondering instead the disastrous beginning of the Washington Nationals' season and what it would take to get them back on track.

Clovis changed subjects. "Just curious, none of my business, but what happened to Jo McElroy? You haven't mentioned her once, and when I asked Maggie, she said I should ask you."

I had met Jo on Pawleys Island, South Carolina, at a low point in my life—a client had committed suicide. She helped me out of my depression and brought a sense of joy back into my life.

"Jo and I went to several Lobos games last fall. She loved watching a game from Red's skybox and meeting the coaches and players. She was a breath of fresh air among the corporate types."

Clovis smiled. "She would be that."

"Well, towards the end of the season I got busy trying to complete a merger and had to miss a few games. By that time, Jo had become a regular. She asked if she could go without me, and I said sure. Big mistake."

"I think I know what's coming," Clovis said.

"You guessed it. Another of Red's guests, the president of a computer software company in Greenville, picked up where I left off."

"How'd you find out?" he asked. "Did Red have to tell you?"

"Nope, Jo flew to DC and told me face-to-face. That's her style, and I love her for it. It hurt, but she was right. We were good for each other last fall, but didn't have much in common other than football and sex. She told me I had introduced her to a world beyond Pawleys and would be forever grateful. But where our relationship had been mostly physical, she was now in love."

"Ouch. What happened next?"

"Well, she asked me to walk her down the aisle. I had no idea what to say. Thank goodness she laughed and told me she was teasing, but she did expect me to come to the wedding. She wanted me to meet her girlfriends."

"That sounds like Jo," Clovis said.

"Doesn't it? I've met no one else like her. There isn't a phony bone in her body. I'm not the right person for her, or she for me. But I miss her. The rub is that I like her fiancé. And I'll have to get used to sitting at ball games with them. Red has made that clear."

He polished off his beer and grinned. "Jack, it's time for you get back on the horse."

I laughed and paid the bill. We were well on our way to see Marshall when Brian called.

"You're meeting Reuben Fletcher at nine o'clock tomorrow morning at the hotel."

27

Fletcher had told Brian he was pleased we'd sought him out and that meeting outside the eyes of the press was a good idea. The Armitage was an off-the-record zone. You were free to talk and meet with people inside its confines and would never read about it in the press or hear about it on the six o'clock news. Brian said the meeting would be just the four of us—Fletcher, his chief deputy, Brian, and me.

I didn't know what to expect from Fletcher, but it was better than going into court blind. I told Brian that Clovis and I were off to meet with Marshall Fitzgerald and I'd see him later at the hotel.

Marshall lived in a comfortable home in the Hillcrest neighborhood of Little Rock. He was a little taller than I am and had grown a little stouter in the last few years. His idea of casual was a golf shirt, grey slacks, and black loafers.

"Jack, it's great to see you. Come on in. Grace sends her apologies, but the altar guild has to ready the church, you understand."

"I'm sorry to have missed her. Be sure to give her my love," I replied, smiling.

We spent the requisite time catching up on the status of his boys and my daughter. He questioned me about my injuries—my face still showed some signs of the blow to my jaw. He and Grace had spent a week with Billy Hopper earlier in the month. Seemed Billy was getting serious about a young doctor who works near the Lobos practice facility, and he wanted the Fitzgeralds to meet her. Billy was the star wide receiver for the Lobos. For the longest time, Marshall and Grace were the closest thing to a family that Billy thought he had. Red had just finished locking Billy into a long-term contract that guaranteed he would play for the Lobos for years. For the first time in his life, Billy had real money.

"Jack, I read in the paper you're representing Dr. Jana Hall. I'm glad for her, but it gives me another reason to recuse if I were to draw the case. After what you did for Billy, there's no way I could be impartial. I suspect you already know this, or you wouldn't have taken the risk of seeing me before the clerk assigns the case to a judge."

"I do, but I'm curious about your other reason to recuse. If I weren't her lawyer, would you recuse because we were once good friends in college?"

"No, I didn't recuse in Woody's case when Sam was the prosecutor and you were defense counsel. I said then in a small state like Arkansas, college friendships are not grounds for recusal, and I was closer to Woody, Sam, and you than I ever was to Dr. Hall. If friendships with friends from college were grounds for recusal, no judge in Arkansas could hear a case. No, the recusal test is subjective."

I noticed that although Marshall knew Jana by her first name, he continued to refer to her as Dr. Hall. One of Marshall's quirks is his formal way of speaking. He still called Billy Hopper "William."

"Why would you have recused?"

"You haven't lived in Little Rock for a long time. If you had you would be aware of the work Jana has done for the least of the least in this city and state. Through her clinics, she treated many a poor family, regardless of their ability to pay. She's made sure her patients received the medical care they needed and always treated them with kindness and dignity. But for me, there's more to it. Seldom does a day go by that I'm not faced with the dilemma of what to do with an addicted young man or woman. The law dictates I must send them to prison, and to a life sentence as one of society's untouchables.

"Dr. Hall has been in my courtroom countless times to explain what the child has been through and to ask me to reduce the charge to a misdemeanor or put the child in an expungement program. She made sure that young person got the help they needed to turn their life around. Not all kids make it, but it was never for lack of effort on her part."

"It sounds like Jana is almost too good to be true. One has to wonder why she's the target of such an assault."

"What's the saying—to make an omelet you've got to break a few eggs? Dr. Hall has broken a lot of eggs and egos over the years. People who pay lip service to accessible healthcare for the poor, but don't really give a hoot nor a holler are the usual targets of her wrath. The list is long, Jack, from healthcare providers whom she's called to task, judges who refuse to listen to her pleas for mercy, and politicians who shortchange the poor come budget time, to name a few. You remember Jana as a young girl head over heels in love with Sam. Today, Dr. Hall is a force in health care for those who can't afford it."

Reserved in his opinions and his actions, I've never known Marshall to toss out casual praise. He'd make a terrific character witness, but I knew judicial ethics would prohibit him from testifying.

"Any idea who might agree to hear the case?" I asked.

"Well, yes, I do. But, Jack, you know I won't speak ill of fellow judges, no matter what I think."

His response came as no surprise. I turned the discussion to the procedural issues I might face, more of those little details I would need to know without Micki at my side. We talked about local courtroom customs until I noticed Clovis looking at his watch. I thanked Marshall and rose to leave, promising to come for dinner before I left town.

"I hope that Reuben Fletcher and I can work something out," I said to Clovis as we left.

He raised his eyebrows. "Jack, hold to that hope, but prepare for the worst."

"I need to go back to the hotel and organize my thoughts. Can you join me for dinner?" I asked, feeling the need for company.

"I have a stake-out tonight. When you come to town, I get shorthanded. With Stella gone, I took the evening shift. Give me a rain check."

Brian and I met at Bruno's for dinner, a short walk from the hotel. Mike insisted on sitting at a table outside. I turned to Brian after we had ordered beer, salads, and a pizza.

"Brian, I'd like you to ask Marshall, Ben, and Clovis for the names of people Dr. Hall has helped in extraordinary ways. Sam and Micki may know of a couple, too. I bet there are great stories out there."

Brian replied, "Paul suggested you talk with Debbie. He said Dr. Hall was a great help when she…well, when she was getting well." Novak had forced Debbie into prostitution and heroin addiction when she first came to Arkansas.

"That could be delicate because we don't want to put Micki's retainer at risk. Let me think about that for a while," I countered, raising my beer. "Okay, no more business. Can you believe the Caps finally won the Stanley Cup?"

We both ate more pizza than was good for us, and I insisted we walk back to the hotel. The fresh Arkansas air and the cool spring evening brought back memories of my Arkansas boyhood. Mike was nervous, glad to reach the hotel's lobby. Brian went upstairs, but my mind was racing. I settled into one of the empty seats at the bar and ordered a glass of wine.

I couldn't help thinking about Jana. What could she have done to warrant a special prosecutor? Why was I so worried? Why couldn't I hand her over to a good local attorney? Had I allowed my disdain for Les Butterman to cloud my judgment? My specialty was antitrust, not a minor criminal matter.

I remembered Micki advising a client to plead guilty to a misdemeanor and one year of supervised release. "It's a parking ticket—take the deal and get on with your life." Maybe Fletcher and I could come to a reasonable resolution tomorrow.

I was finishing my wine and waiting for the tab when an attractive woman who I guessed to be in her late thirties sat down next to me and ordered a martini. I noticed lots of long chestnut-colored hair and a short emerald-green dress.

She turned to me and said, "I'm sorry. I should have asked if this seat was taken."

Before I could do more than smile, she gasped and said, "Oh my God, you're Jack Patterson! I'm one of your biggest fans. I can't wait to tell my girlfriends where I am. They'll freak! I've had the biggest crush on you since the Cole case. I can't believe my luck!"

I watched, amused as she pulled out her iPhone and texted someone. The waiter brought her martini, gave me a knowing wink, and handed me a second glass of wine.

She picked up her glass, crossing shapely legs as she turned to face me. Her dress was tight.

"Please tell me what brings you to town? Oh, how stupid of me!" she gushed and extended her hand. "I'm Mimi Stephens."

There was little doubt in my mind where this conversation was going. She babbled about working for an advertising agency, and I felt sure if I gave her any encouragement at all, I would be in for a long and energetic evening. I almost took the bait, but between the memory of another woman in this bar and the sudden image of Maggie's scowling face, I reconsidered.

I moved her hand, which had traveled to my upper thigh, and said, "Mimi, I have to call it a night. I have a long day tomorrow. Please let me buy your drink. It's been a real pleasure."

She raised her hand to my face and asked, "Are you sure?" The bartender stared at me like I was crazy, and maybe I was.

28

Clovis and Brian were waiting in the hotel restaurant the next morning, no sign of Mike. I ordered coffee and asked Brian, "Where and what time are we meeting Fletcher?"

"Nine o'clock, at our conference room here at the hotel," he replied.

I turned to Clovis. "I thought you'd be home asleep after pulling the night shift."

"I'll find time for sleep later—first thing's first." His voice sounded tired, and I noticed dark circles under his eyes.

"Well, let's order breakfast before you give me the bad news," I sighed. We'd known each other too long to pretend.

I ordered scrambled eggs. In fact, we all did. Brian also asked for a pancake on the side and a Coke. I wondered where he'd been last night, but it was none of my business.

"The man we caught breaking into Dr. Hall's has disappeared," Clovis mumbled, sounding discouraged.

"I'm not surprised he made bail. Can we find out who posted his bond?" I asked.

"That's the funny part. He didn't post bond—he was released, allowed to just walk out the door. No one in the sheriff's office will say a word."

"Well, can't Sam find out what happened?"

"I'd be careful using Sam right now. His judgment is clouded, and he might say or do something he shouldn't."

"Okay. What else?"

"An attempted break-in at the warehouse. It was unsuccessful, but our guys didn't catch the guy either. He vamoosed as soon as he realized all the door codes had been changed."

"What on earth could be so valuable in there?" I asked. "Are the records made of gold or something?"

"I have no idea," he replied. "But Stella will be there first thing tomorrow morning to figure out how we can duplicate and preserve whatever records are there."

"Good thinking. Brian will meet her. He's had lots of experience in big document cases."

I was shaking my head at our latest puzzle when I noticed that Clovis still looked glum.

"Out with it, what haven't you told me?"

"Jack, the sheriff's department found another body in the Fourche Bottoms. The police say he was the last of the group that tried to kill you."

My face froze. This was a nightmare. "*Why*? Why do they think that? Was he hanged?"

"No. He took one slug in the head, but his body was leaning against your tree. There was a sign around his neck."

"A sign around his neck? Come on, Clovis, spit it out."

"The sign read, 'Revenge is mine says the Lord. Now it's your turn, Jack.'" His voice sounded gravelly, and he cleared his throat. "It was simple enough, magic marker on cardboard."

"The sign said what?" Brian asked.

"It said, 'Now it's your turn, Jack,'" Clovis repeated.

"I'm not sure about the revenge part, but whoever murdered those other guys is coming after me." My voice came from somewhere else.

Clovis puckered up his face and sighed. "Jack, I never thought I'd say this, but it's time you went home. The police had cameras all over the Bottoms, but the killer still managed to position the body underneath the hanging tree undetected. I know how you feel about defending Dr. Hall, but she'll understand. Little Rock has other good lawyers who can defend her. We're up against a real professional who is either ready to kill you next or is doing a great job at misdirection."

As if on cue, our waiter appeared with more coffee and our

breakfast plates. My presence in Little Rock was no longer just about Jana. Someone was planning to kill me, someone capable of killing four men without leaving a clue to his identity or motives. It seemed unlikely a change in location would dissuade him.

And, like Jana, I had no idea why any of this this was happening.

"Well, let's eat," I said. "No sense in letting the eggs get cold."

We ate in silence for a while, giving me some time to think. I couldn't taste the food, so it wasn't long before I pushed back my plate.

"Almost thirty years ago, I left Little Rock because of threats, not to my life, but threats nonetheless. I'm not about to cut and run a second time. No more talk about leaving. Clovis, you've been with me through thick and thin. You and I will go over the possibilities of who might want revenge, but regardless of that, we have a client to defend."

Clovis smiled and shook his head. "Why am I not surprised?"

"Right." I grinned. "Case closed. Clovis, you need to take a break. We can talk after I've met with Fletcher." He nodded and left.

I asked Brian why Mike hadn't come to breakfast.

"After we left you last night, Mike said there was something he wanted to check out. I called him this morning to see if he wanted to join us, but got no answer. I assumed he was sleeping in or had already gone out."

"Shit," I said to myself. Good thing Maggie wasn't here.

"If Mike isn't back by the time we're through with Fletcher, his whereabouts become your top priority."

I expected Fletcher and his deputy to be on time, but they had arrived early and were already seated when I opened the door. The deputy, Ray Spears, wore a dark suit and tie and introduced himself with a firm handshake.

Reuben "Dawg" Fletcher wore jeans that looked like they'd seen better days, the waistband curled over his belt. He was sporting bright red suspenders over his faded white shirt. A W. C. Fields bright red nose dominated his face. I couldn't help but notice his boots looked like they'd never seen a lick of polish. His hair, or what was left, didn't seem to have been combed in some time. He wasn't actually chewing, but his teeth were that dirty yellow tobacco color.

Fletcher clearly worked as hard at his rough-edged, country image as his deputy did in appearing well-groomed. We sat down across from each other.

"Well, Mr. Patterson, you wanted this meeting. What can I do for you?" Fletcher began.

"For starters, I'd like to know if Dr. Hall is a formal target of your investigation. The press seems to think she's about to be indicted."

"Ain't nothin' I do is formal, but if you're asking if I've got your client in my sights, the answer is yes."

At that point Deputy Spears reached in his briefcase and handed me a letter. A quick glance told me that Dr. Hall was the target of the investigation: she'd been invited to testify before the grand jury.

Unless the circumstances were unusual, no defense lawyer would allow his client to appear. The grand jury process is weighted in favor of the prosecutor. Witnesses are particularly vulnerable because their lawyers aren't allowed to accompany them. A witness could easily waive his Fifth Amendment rights before he was even charged. There were about a dozen other reasons I would never let Dr. Hall appear before this grand jury, and Fletcher and his deputy knew that.

"Seems like you and Mr. Spears have been hard at work. What's the hurry?"

"The only time I ever liked being in Little Rock was when the Razorbacks played SEC opponents in War Memorial Stadium, but now the only game they play is against the Little Sisters of the Poor. I avoid this city like the plague. I didn't ask for this special prosecutor appointment, but when the governor begged, I had no choice. The sooner I get back home the better. On my per diem, I don't get to stay in swanky digs like this."

I ignored the swipe. "Well, I'd like to get home myself. Any chance you'll tell me what charges you intend to file against my client?"

"I suspect you already know, so let's not dance around and waste each other's time. You want to know if we can make a deal. The answer is yes. You and I have never crossed swords, but if you check, you'll learn I make one offer and one offer only. I'll give you one day to accept, or it's off the table and we go to the mats."

Fletcher had me at a terrible disadvantage. I had no idea what he thought Jana had done wrong, but I might as well hear what Fletcher wanted. Maybe it was a slap on the wrist for some bookkeeping mistake. I was getting tired of his country boy act.

"You have me at a disadvantage because I don't know how serious the charges are, but I'm willing to listen."

"Oh, you can bet your ass they're serious. Your client is looking at spending the rest of her life in prison, and Arkansas's prison for women is no country club—nothing at all like that Netflix movie. So, here's what I will accept. Your client pleads guilty to a felony. We can be flexible, but it's got to be a Class A felony. You and Ray can work out the details. Your doctor agrees to do two years in prison and four years of probation, and she surrenders her medical license."

Fletcher paused, and Ray whispered something in his ear. "Oh, yeah, I almost forgot. She turns over all the clinics' records in her possession. She'll get a hefty fine, but she's a rich doctor. That won't be any skin off her back. That's about it. You ready to draw up the paperwork?"

Fletcher grinned and leaned back, crossing his legs on the top of the table. He knew I was ready to tell him to go to hell, but couldn't without consulting my client. And there was this thing about the records again. I needed to buy some time.

"How do I slow down this train?" I asked. "I have to meet with my client to discuss her options, but a felony and hard time? Neither the state auditors nor the prosecutor's office found any wrongdoing. Doesn't that count for something? Your proposal is coming from left field."

"I don't give a damn about any state auditor's findings, and her crimes have nothing to do with bookkeeping. Ask your client. She knows what she did. And as for Pagano declining to prosecute, everyone knows he's never met a criminal he doesn't like. Hell, he was a public defender before he pretended to become a prosecutor. You've got 'til midnight, Mr. Patterson, not one second more. If I were you, I'd have a come-to-Jesus talk with your client. She's not the saint she'd have everyone believe. Ray, give Jack's boy your card so they can call you back."

I felt the blood rush to my face. "Mr. Fletcher, or Dawg, if you prefer, Brian isn't anyone's 'boy.' Please show him the respect he deserves." *So much for not losing my cool.*

"My, aren't we touchy," he laughed as he swung his legs down. "We'll expect your call."

29

Brian didn't say a word as we walked back to the lobby. I was so mad I could spit. Clovis was waiting with a smile which made me feel a little better. Paul had called Mike last night about the body discovered in the Fourche Bottoms. Mike told him he wanted to do a little investigating and would keep Paul informed.

"Mike told Paul to let you know he's okay and not to worry," Clovis said.

Brian smiled with relief, and I heard him whisper, "The hunter is now the hunted."

I let it go, only because we had bigger fish to fry. "Clovis, get in touch with whoever's watching Sam and Jana. Tell them I hate to spoil their fishing, but they need to come home. I owe it to her to convey Fletcher's offer."

"Brian, I don't much care for Reuben Fletcher. I don't trust him any further than I can throw him. See what you can find out about him. Call Janis Harold. I bet she knows someone who'll give you the goods on him. And..."

I stopped, acutely aware I had no idea where to go next. Events were overtaking me, and I needed time to think.

Little Rock doesn't have a beach, but it has something almost as good. Bolstered by a group of concerned citizens, thoughtful civic leaders had blocked an effort to extend a high traffic thruway along the Arkansas River to western Little Rock. Instead, they built a walking/jogging/biking path that connected the downtown park to a municipal golf course and parks along the river. The path crossed the Arkansas River by way of a pedestrian bridge at the lock and dam.

"Sorry, guys, but I need a break. Meet me back here in five minutes. We're going for a walk across the Big Dam Bridge."

Clovis groused that he wasn't dressed for a walk. I wasn't up to a power walk or a jog myself. A stroll across the river to clear my head was what I wanted. I changed into jeans, and we were about to get in Mike's car when Mimi appeared, seemingly from nowhere.

"Jack!" she squealed. "I hoped I might run into you again." She threw her arms around me and whispered, "I don't give up."

She pulled away and was through the hotel's revolving door before I could react.

Brian stared, his mouth hanging open, and Clovis laughed out loud.

"What?" I demanded. "I met her last night at the bar. Said she's a fan."

Fifteen minutes later we had parked the car and were walking onto this magnificent monument to a community's commitment to something other than uncontrolled development. The bridge wasn't crowded, just a few joggers and moms with strollers. When we reached its crest, I stopped to lean against the railing, overwhelmed by the sight of the free-flowing river on one side and the raucous rush of water on the other as it passed through the dam on its way to the Mississippi.

I could have stayed there all afternoon. But Clovis was antsy. We turned to retrace our footsteps.

I noticed an empty picnic table near our car and sat down, not yet ready to return to town. Brian brought us bottles of cold water from the car, and we sat in glum silence.

"Guys, we've got to be missing something. Jana's no criminal—I'm sure of it. So why this full-court press to get her clinics' records and send her to jail? What could those records contain that's so important? Let's check with the state medical board about the ethics involving a patient's records, and remind me to ask her about malpractice complaints."

Clovis's phone rang and after listening for a few seconds, he signed off with a "see you then."

"Sam and Dr. Hall are on their way home. We'll meet them at five," he said.

"Hell of a situation," I mused. "She has less than twenty-four hours to make a decision that will affect her life forever. If she pleads not guilty, she risks a long prison sentence. Even if she's not convicted, her reputation will have been destroyed. Or she can take the deal and spend two years in prison. If she survives prison, she'll have to deal with the collateral consequences of a felony conviction. Either way, her life will never be the same."

"How can Fletcher get away with this?" Clovis grumbled. "He hasn't had the job for a week, yet he's already drawn up charges and presented them to a grand jury. He refuses to tell you the charges, and gives your client less than a day to decide whether to plead guilty to a felony or go to trial. How can anyone think that's fair?"

"It isn't fair, but it happens more often than you'd think. And don't buy into this fiction that all this happened this week. I can't prove it, but I'd bet you dollars to donuts the health director knew Sam's office wouldn't prosecute. Someone has been developing a case against Jana for a long time. Fletcher has been on board from the onset, and when Kate Erwin announced the case was closed—wham bam, the governor appoints Dawg special prosecutor."

"Too bad we don't have any evidence to support your theory," Brian commented.

"It is, but I'm not sure it would matter. I could make a lot of noise, complain to the judge, but prosecutorial misconduct is low on everyone's list of worries. Folks figure if someone commits a crime, how the police and prosecutor pursue him isn't worth getting worked up over. I've raised the issue of the speed of this prosecution with the press, but I bet not one reporter has given it a second thought. It's all about the drama and the guilt—due process doesn't sell newspapers or increase ratings," I sighed.

We had almost the whole afternoon before we were to meet with Sam and Jana. Stella and Kate were still enjoying their girls' weekend with Micki, no interruptions allowed. Brian was feeling the effects of last night and said he could use a few hour's sleep. Ben, Marshall, and Helen Cole were all at church.

"I have an idea," I said, getting to my feet.

Clovis rolled his eyes. He knew what was coming.

"Brian, we'll drop you off at the hotel. Clovis and I are going to have lunch at City Park, in fact, a picnic—I know the perfect spot. The hotel can supply us with some sandwiches."

I thought Clovis would try to quash the idea, but he surprised me. "You sure you're ready?" he asked.

"I think so—it's time."

Little Rock's City Park was an oasis of green space on the outskirts of downtown. I had proposed to Angie beneath a tall oak tree there, and we used to come to this park every chance we had during college. After the Cole case, I stopped there on the way out of town, and returned after the Stewart case, only to face my near death. Clovis knew of its significance, and why after receiving this latest death threat I wanted to come back.

"Okay," he said. "But no wandering around."

The hotel packed a great lunch of deviled eggs, chicken salad sandwiches, veggie chips, and chocolate chip cookies. A chilled split of French Chablis was the perfect accompaniment. Clovis and I sat beneath the old tree like we didn't have a care in the world, enjoying our food and chatting about this and that.

After we'd finished our cookies I asked, "So, how do you know Jana? I don't mean to pry, just curious."

"No, it's okay. You and I have never talked about my life after the car wreck destroyed my football career. I was pretty messed up in the head. My whole life had been about football, and in an instant I had no future—worse, I had no dreams. The driver of the logging truck who ran me off the country road should have paid my medical bills, but he didn't have insurance, much less any money. You can't get blood from a turnip.

"The staff at the ER was great, but I couldn't pay for rehab. I came home to mend. I didn't have a penny to see a doctor. Ben introduced me to Dr. Hall, who introduced me to her husband, Judd Wilson. Dr. Hall made sure I got the medical treatment I needed, and her husband paid for my last year in school and set me up in business when I came home. We've become friends over the years. Nobody knows this story except Ben, Dr. Hall, and now you.

"I paid Mr. Wilson back, but I can never repay Jana. I'm not talking about the medical bills. I'm talking about the hours she spent convincing me there was more to life than football. But for her, I could have ended up like Mace. I'd do most anything to keep her from going to jail. For the life of me I can't understand why anyone wants to destroy her."

"Neither can I, but I'm beginning to think the answer is in the records everyone is so hot to get. They must contain information that's a threat to Brady Flowers or whoever's controlling him. Prosecuting Jana is the only way they think they can get them. I doubt she has any idea what they contain, but by the time Dawg gets through it won't matter what she knows. Our job is to find out what is so critical about those records before they destroy her."

"And if you manage to figure it out, then what?" Clovis asked.

"I haven't gotten that far." I laughed and finished my wine.

"Let's go back to the hotel so I can prepare. Our meeting with Jana and Sam won't be easy."

30

I SPENT MY TIME AFTER LUNCH outlining the questions I had for Jana. Brian reappeared, looking much better than he had earlier, and we left with Clovis and Jordan. Clovis told me that Paul had spoken with Mike several times this afternoon.

"Do you have any idea what he's up to?" I asked.

"No, for once I don't."

I noticed Brian's chin wiggling, but I let it wiggle. I had too much on my plate already.

Jana greeted us at the front door. Her stiff posture betrayed her anxiety. After a quick hello, Clovis and Jordan excused themselves to talk to the men who were guarding the premises.

"Sam's gone home to get clean clothes. He told me it was important to maintain attorney-client privilege." She remained in the half-open doorway.

That was a relief. I had dreaded telling Sam he couldn't be present.

"He told me to tell you he expects you to figure out a way to keep him informed."

I laughed, and she relaxed a little. She opened the door wider, and showed us into the little den off the kitchen. We all sat down, and I took a deep breath.

"I'm sorry to cut your fishing trip short, but I met with the special prosecutor this morning. He has offered you a plea deal, but it comes with a twenty-four-hour fuse, no bargaining allowed."

She caught her breath, eyes wide with shock. "Wow, you don't mince words."

"I'm sorry, Jana. Sometimes there's no way to soften the blow. Sugarcoating the facts won't make them any sweeter. I was afraid of this, but I didn't expect it to hit so fast."

"What am I supposed to have done that warrants an indictment?"

She asked the right question. "I still don't know. When I asked, he said I should talk to you, that you would know exactly what crimes you've committed."

"Well, sorry, but I don't."

"I didn't think you would. We'll spend time today trying to figure it out. But first, let me tell you what he proposes."

"How bad is it? Just tell me—I'll be okay."

"Damn bad. He wants you to plead guilty to a felony and serve two years in prison. He also wants you to surrender your medical license, serve a four year probation, pay a substantial fine, and turn over all of your patients' medical records."

Her face flushed with anger. "Such a deal. What do I get in return?" she asked.

"You don't go through a public trial, and you don't risk a much longer prison term. Fletcher claims you'll spend the rest of your life in prison if he takes you to trial. But let's not focus on his offer. We'll come back to it later."

She lifted her hand, palm out, and I stopped. After a few seconds of silence, she raised her head, smiled, and said, "No! Not no, but *hell* no!"

I returned her smile and said, "Okay, sounds like we'd better talk about his offer first."

She grinned. "You know that's not what I mean. The 'hell no' is to his offer. I will not plead guilty. I won't agree to go to prison, and no, I will not surrender my medical license. And what the hell is all this about my patients' medical records? We can talk all evening, but tell him no."

With that she stood up. What was she up to?

"Jack, you told me I face life in prison. Don't expect me to sit here and answer twenty questions without a drink. It's past five o'clock, and thanks to your candor I need a scotch. What can I get you? And don't give me that bullshit 'we have business to conduct' speech. The same goes for you, young man." She turned to Brian, who was hovering outside the door to the den.

Brian blushed and said, "Dr. Hall, my apologies. I didn't mean to eavesdrop. Let me fix the drinks. Do you like your scotch neat or on the rocks?"

"On the rocks would be nice, thank you." Brian left in a hurry, and I turned to look at Jana.

"I'm sorry for the outburst, Jack, but I'm angry. I'm also tired of fighting Brady Flowers and those other idiots. If they'd told me I had to leave Arkansas, I might have agreed. You went through a similar decision thirty years ago. But their 'offer' leaves me no choice. How could I knuckle under to such demands?"

"Jana, I'm sorry you're having to go through this, and you're right: it's a Hobson's choice. So, let's figure out how to beat the rap and let's start right now. Why do you think they want your records? Lacking any other information, I think they must be the key. Stella and Brian are going out to the warehouse tomorrow to see if they can organize and convert them into a searchable digital format."

"I did that a while back. The records in the warehouse are the original paper files. I digitized them for a research project I hoped to do one day."

"Hold it right there. Wait for Brian."

At that moment, he appeared with a tray of drinks—perfect timing. "Brian, Dr. Hall just told me that the records are already digitized. The files in the warehouse are the original paper files."

"All the records are on disks and a separate laptop I keep in my safe. The clinic's computer consultant suggested I should back everything up on an external drive or in the cloud months ago, but with all that's happened..." Her bravado had worn off a little.

Brian was almost bursting with excitement. "Do you mind if I borrow the discs and your computer for a few days? I'll make copies of everything and return the originals. That is, if it's okay with Jack. Stella and I are meeting tomorrow."

"Go ahead. The reason I spent the money to have everything scanned and saved was so it would be readily available for a research project. You can tell how much time I've spent on that—none. I bet the laptop is deader than a doornail. You'll find all the old patient records on it, but no financial records. All the financial records went to the Crockett firm. They took everything for the audit."

"Jana, this is very good news. We'd never have been able to make sense out of the files at the warehouse. Don't worry—they'll be safe and sound with us." I said.

She said to Brian, "I'll give you all the usernames and passwords you need to access the laptop and the files. I also use a secure app to store all my various passwords. Heaven help us if it ever goes down."

"That's great. This will save us tons of time," Brian said.

I asked, "Any idea why Brady wanted the records, or why Fletcher wants them now? He tried to pretend they were an afterthought, but I wasn't buying that. The issue has come up too often."

"I have no idea. Brady said that since state money was used to subsidize the clinics they belonged to the Health Department. What would anyone want with old patient records?"

"They told Kate Erwin they were looking for financial irregularities," I replied.

"I don't think so. Brady was most insistent that we turn over the patients' health records. He had no need for the financials. We delivered financial reports to the Health Department monthly as part of our contract. I didn't want to turn the health records over because of privacy concerns. If the state has a patient's health records, someone might get access to them by submitting a Freedom of Information request. I had no confidence the state would fight such a request. Many of our patients would never come to us if they thought their ailments could become public."

"Give me an example?" I asked.

"Victims of spousal abuse, patients with venereal disease, and AIDS patients come to mind."

"That makes sense. What type of research project were you considering?" I asked.

"It was a dream of mine. After all these years, I felt we had assembled enough data to determine if anything stood out regarding the health of poor people in Arkansas. For example, does our population have an unusual number of cancer incidents relative to the poor in other states? I hoped to pinpoint health trends that would enable us to better serve our patients. Doctors treat the immediate problems, but sometimes we need to step back to see if we are missing the cause of a disease rather than merely treating it."

"Who knew about your plans for research?" I asked.

"Judd did—he had good suggestions," she smiled. "He had the patience of Job. After his death, I put the project on the back burner, but about two years ago my energy level returned, and I talked to my staff, Brady, and others at the Health Department, even a few key members of the legislature. I hoped to get some additional funds to finance the project.

"Brady encouraged me to talk to him about my plans almost every time we went out. I thought we shared a real interest in what the study might discover. Turned out I was wrong. My problems with the Health Department and the legislature began right after I went public with the plans."

I don't much believe in coincidences, but I let it go for now.

Clovis stuck his head in the door and offered to get us all fried chicken for dinner. Sounded perfect. I told him to give me an hour, and we'd be ready to take a break.

"An hour?" she questioned.

"At least," I said pulling my legal pad from my briefcase. "We're only getting started. You and I haven't had any contact for the last thirty years—there's a lot about you I don't know. I'll be gentle and try to respect your feelings, but I must know everything, including stuff you think doesn't matter. Those insignificant details are the keys to convincing a jury to find you not guilty."

"You really think this will go to a jury trial?" Her eyes had widened, but her voice remained steady.

"I do."

31

I'D HOPED TO AVOID A TRIAL, but I knew refusing Fletcher's offer would back him into a corner. That meant an indictment. Despite his bluster, we'd have other chances to make a deal, but he would always hold most of the cards, no matter what we unearthed. Prosecutors don't win over ninety-five percent of the cases they take to trial for nothing. Our justice system is stacked in their favor, despite the legal fictions of "innocent until proven guilty" and "beyond a reasonable doubt."

That's why a prosecutor like Sam Pagano is so important to our criminal justice system. We need prosecutors who don't think their job is "lock everyone up and throw away the key." We need prosecutors who pride themselves on knowing when not to prosecute. We need prosecutors who temper the letter of the law with mercy. These attorneys serve their communities much better than the likes of Fletcher.

I spent the next hour learning as much I could about Jana's life: her marriages, her early medical practice, her first clinic, her battles with the legislature to fund clinics for the poor, and her disputes with the Health Department over every issue under the sun.

When we came to a logical breaking point I said, "Let's change horses." I asked Brian to step out for a minute.

"I need to know a little more about your personal life, your relationship with Brady Flowers."

She rolled her eyes, a silent "must we?" But she knew the answer. "Jack, before you pry into every aspect of my personal life, tell me why you refer to the prosecutor as Fletcher. Every newspaper reporter and lawyer I know calls him 'Dawg.' He makes a big deal about his name, telling everyone he meets to call him 'Dawg.' Yet you keep calling him Fletcher."

"That's why I do it. I will call him Fletcher or Reuben every chance I get. It's a little irritant. What's the saying? 'It isn't the mountain ahead that wears you out—it's the grain of sand in your shoe.' My biggest problem will be remembering to call you Dr. Hall in court, rather than Jana. Jury trials are theater, and how lawyers address people sends subtle messages."

The door to the den opened and Sam walked in. He tossed me an unapologetic smile and plopped himself on the couch next to my client. "Don't get bent out of shape, Jack. I won't interfere with your attorney-client conference, but Clovis is in the kitchen ringing the bell. Dinner's ready."

We needed a break, and with Sam in the room I couldn't ask about Flowers. I realized it was almost seven-thirty, time to call Fletcher. As the others helped themselves to chicken, I asked Brian to listen to the conversation. I didn't need a witness, but he might detect something in Fletcher's tone I might miss.

"Mr. Fletcher, this is Jack Patterson. You're on speaker with my associate Brian Hattoy. No one else is in the room. Is that okay?"

"Not a problem, and please call me Dawg, everybody does."

"I've spoken with my client—in fact, I'm at her home as we speak. Can we slow things down? Wouldn't it be wise to meet in a day or two to talk about the charges? She's not going anywhere—what's the rush? I don't know what she's allegedly done, nor does she. How can I explain your offer without knowing the charges?"

"She's lying. She knows. As for giving you more time, I can't do that. I told you—I'm already tired of Little Rock. I made you a generous offer. You don't need more time. I know you folks in DC like to talk and run up big fees, but that's not the way we do things in Arkansas. You can agree to my offer and work out the details of a plea with Ray, or you can refuse. If that's the case, you and Ray can meet tomorrow to determine the date and time for her arraignment."

I didn't respond, and Dawg filled the silence.

"Either way, I won't embarrass Dr. Hall. I won't arrest her at the Country Club or make her spend time in the county jail while she makes bail. But that's the extent of my goodwill. If you want a trial, fine. But there won't be another chance to cut a deal, and you'll discover I can be a real son-of-a-bitch."

"I appreciate your candor. But if you won't give me more time, and you won't give me a clearer picture of the charges, then my client refuses your offer. We'll see you in court."

I'd known it would come to this, but my stomach felt hollow. The weight of Jana Hall's future had fallen directly on my shoulders.

"You're a fool, Patterson, but it's your client's funeral."

The phone went dead.

I turned to Brian. "What do you think?"

"I think you showed remarkable restraint. What a jerk with his veiled threats about the Country Club and county jail. He's not about to do anything that would draw sympathy for Dr. Hall. I dread what he'll say in the indictment and at his press conference, but he's smart enough not to drag her off in chains. The optics are wrong."

"I agree. Let's get back to dinner. We've got a lot to accomplish, and little time to do it."

I filled my plate with fried chicken and fixings and joined the others at the kitchen table. Brian and I ate in silence for a few minutes, enjoying the easy chatter.

"I hate to interrupt," I said, "but it's getting late and we have work to do. I spoke with Fletcher, and I can tell you it was not a pleasant experience."

Conversation ceased. Jana poured wine for everyone before we went into the den, giving me time to gather my thoughts. I wished Maggie were here, but she wasn't, and that was that. I had already asked Brian to take notes. I spoke directly to Jana.

"There was no give on his timeline or the charges. In his words, take the deal or go to trial."

Jana gulped, and Sam looked confused. I told him about Fletcher's offer and his face darkened with anger.

"Since he left me no room to maneuver, I told him Jana rejected his offer. I expect to hear from his deputy, Ray Spears, tomorrow about the date and time for the arraignment. He promised not to arrest her at some public venue or play games, but assured me that from now on he will be a son-of-a-bitch."

Jana said, "I like it better when you aren't so matter of fact."

"You won't like what I have to say next either, so let's get it on the table. You and Sam have two choices. Either Sam leaves tonight and you agree to curtail your time together for the next six months, or Fletcher will do everything he can to make the most out of your past and current relationships. Hell, he will anyway, but it won't be as bad if you're not seeing Sam."

"Who did you say is the son-of-a bitch?" she asked. Clovis's mouth dropped open.

Sam intervened. "Jana, that's not fair. It's not Jack's fault, and you know it. We'll face this together; screw Fletcher and screw the press. Kate made the decision not to prosecute. I can handle whatever crap they throw."

"What about you, Jana?" I asked. "As your lawyer, I have to tell you that being associated with Sam will hurt your case. I can't say how much, but it will hurt."

"Are you going to cut and run if I don't agree to ditch Sam?" Her anger was palpable. Even Sam looked shocked. I couldn't fault her emotions, but it was time to dial them down.

"Of course not. If you decide you want my former roommate hanging around, I'll turn it to our advantage." I grinned, and she melted.

"Oh, Jack, I'm sorry. I need you both because the truth is I'm scared to death. You've got a terrible bedside manner, but I need a great lawyer and I need Sam." She reached out for his hand, and Sam blushed.

"Well, okay. I guess that's settled. Sam, I don't trust Fletcher further than I can throw him, so expect to find the press waiting at the front door tomorrow morning. You know how to deal with them: just don't be surprised."

"Thanks. Now it's my turn," Sam said. "I intend to resign as the district's prosecutor tomorrow. It looks to me like you could use some help since Micki isn't available, and if I don't know my way around a courtroom by now, I'm in the wrong profession."

God knows his help would have been welcome, but I knew it

wouldn't work. As Brian had said, the optics were wrong.

"Please don't. Fletcher will find a hundred ways to prevent you from participating. I wouldn't put it past him to call you as a witness or to make you a target of his investigation, alleging you obstructed justice when the case was in your office. He knows I'm at a disadvantage without a local counsel. Why would he let you anywhere near the courtroom?

"Besides, I have other plans for you. I've got an idea, and I need a prosecutor who will keep an open mind."

32

"OKAY, TELL ME what you want me to do," Sam replied.

"We'll get to that in a minute. Just keep an open mind." I turned to Jana before he could object. "Jana, does the computer on your desk contain the clinics' financial records?"

She looked confused. "No, I told you earlier, the financial files are with the Crockett firm. I only use the iMac for emails and to pay my personal bills."

"Is there anything on the iMac you don't want anyone else to see?"

"What are you implying?" she asked, frowning.

"I'm not implying anything. I'm talking about personal pictures of you and Judd, notes you might have written to friends, that kind of thing."

"Jack, this is *terra incognita* for her. Tell her why you're asking," Sam interrupted.

He was right. I was moving too fast, forgetting that Jana was new to this side of the legal system.

"I'm sorry. It won't be long before state troopers who work for Fletcher appear at your door with a search warrant. They'll cart off your computers and any other records you have. They'll search every drawer and closet in your house. If there's anything on your computer, your phone, or in a box hidden in a closet that you don't want them to take, I want to deal with it now."

"They can search my house, take my belongings?" she asked in disbelief.

"Ask Sam," I said, tired of being the bad guy.

"They can. All they need is a judge who's willing to sign a search warrant. It wouldn't take much to convince a judge you might destroy evidence."

"I'm not concerned about anything on the iMac, and I don't have anything kinky hidden in my closets, but all my contacts are on my phone. When will I get it back?"

"After the trial, if you're lucky," I said.

"That can't be legal." She looked at Sam, hoping for a different opinion.

"Sorry, but a prosecutor can do most anything."

"Jana, I know this is hard to believe and hard to deal with," I said. "But it will happen, it happened to the Stewarts and countless other people. The state police will come with a warrant that allows them to search your home and remove whatever the prosecutor deems to be evidence. But they will have to get a warrant. We have time to duplicate anything on your computer or phone you don't want to lose. To save time, we'll copy everything. Give Clovis your phone, laptop, iMac, and any disks or flash drives you've got. At some point, we'll have to turn them over to Fletcher, but by then we will have copied the contents. You'll be able to access all your files, and Stella will have changed out your SIM card to a new phone. Meanwhile, Fletcher will get a nice little surprise when he shows up."

"Well, what if there's stuff I don't want you to copy? Stuff I want erased?" Her voice had risen. "Brian, please get me another glass of wine. I can't deal with this, it's too much."

She fled the room, and Brian quickly followed. Clovis wavered, but soon went after them.

My head dropped front-forward down onto the table. I felt like shit.

"You know she isn't as upset as she puts on," Sam said.

"Why not? I would be. So far I've only been the bearer of bad news."

"Come on, this isn't the time for a pity party. This isn't your first time around the block."

Maybe for him, I thought. *For me, it always feels like the first time.*

"I get the sense you have an idea what he's after." Sam persisted. "I can keep a secret."

I smiled. "My friend, keeping a secret from a woman, any woman, is nigh unto impossible.

He laughed. "You've got that right. If Jana asked, I would tell her. Do you really think Dawg will get a search warrant? He can get everything in discovery."

"I know, but the only constant in this prosecution has been their determination to get the patient records. I feel sure they'll take possession of the paper files in the warehouse. And I'm pretty sure they'll go after Jana's computers as well. I mean, why not?"

"What's so important about the damned records?" Sam asked. "We're not talking about wealthy patients with secrets to hide."

"I don't know, but I sure hope Jana can help us figure it out."

"You think we're looking at an early morning knock on the door?"

"Yep, probably about the same time the newspaper is delivered. Fletcher told me he could be a real SOB. He also doesn't want me to do what we're about to do. So be ready."

A pre-dawn raid is a tool hard-ass prosecutors use purely to intimidate. The sleepy target wakes up to find troopers standing at the door, accompanied by a deputy prosecutor. It's meant to frighten the target and make the judge, the jury pool, and the press think the target has something to hide.

"This is going to be tough on her," he sighed.

"Well, maybe it won't happen after all. But you need to be ready."

We both turned when the door opened. Jana walked in as if she didn't have a care in the world.

"Clovis said he'd join us soon. I gave him my phone and told him they could remove the computer and any other hardware they found in my desk. Can I fill your glass before you give me more bad news?" Jana said.

"Let me do it," Sam said, leaving with both our glasses.

She sat down next to me on the sofa and said, "Jack, I owe you an apology."

"I don't think so—my bedside manner clearly needs an overhaul."

"Yes, it does. But then I don't imagine you need it very often."

Wow—another zinger. Well, that's how it sounded to me. It took me a second, but I let it go.

"I asked Clovis when Fletcher would serve the search warrant. He didn't mince words. He said first thing tomorrow morning.

"So now I understand why you asked about Sam, and why you asked about what was on my computer. What I don't understand, Jack, is why I had to ask Clovis? Why didn't you tell me about an early morning raid?"

I didn't have a good answer and was relieved when Sam came from the kitchen carrying two glasses of wine, Clovis and Brian in tow. After a few minutes of idle chatter, I brought us back to business.

"Let's talk about tomorrow. Sam, if Fletcher or the state troopers come calling at dawn, or any other time, I want you to call me. Clovis and I can be here in fifteen minutes. Jana, don't engage in any way. Ask for a copy of the warrant and stand back. Don't even confirm your identity. No matter what they do or say, and despite how much you want to object, no confrontation. Sam, if you're staying, you know what to do."

She sighed and whispered, "I can't believe this is happening."

"I know, and I'm sorry. I wish there were some other way to deal with the situation, but there isn't."

She squared her shoulders and smiled. "It's okay. You can't change it, and I have to learn how to deal with it. What happens next?"

"Well, Fletcher's assistant will call me to schedule a time for you to appear in court and enter a plea. After that formality, I hope we'll get a little breathing room. We'll have two primary goals: first, to dissect every charge and decide how to defend against it, and second, we need to figure out what's in those patient records that has everyone so worked up. Jana, I'd like for you to work with Brian and Stella on that issue."

"Sure, but what are we looking for?" she asked.

"You told the legislature and Brady Flowers you wanted to examine the records, looking for health trends that significantly impacted the state's poorest residents, looking for anything that stood out about Arkansas's poor."

"You're asking us to find a needle in a haystack," Brian commented, shaking his head in disbelief.

"Well, yes, but it won't be that easy." No one laughed.

"Okay—we're all tired. We've done enough tonight. Sam, are you..."

"Yes, I'm staying, and I know what to do. If the bastards show, we'll give them coffee. Speaking of, do you mind disposing of the trash on your way back to the hotel?"

I smiled and said, "Happy to do so." Jana looked puzzled.

"Why would you take away the trash? The city picks it up at the street every Wednesday."

I left the response to Sam. "Because a devious prosecutor who wants to imply you are destroying evidence will go through your trash. Even if there are no documents, he'll inventory every empty beer, wine, or scotch bottle in your recycling bin and give an exaggerated inventory of the booze to the press and somehow get it in front of a judge and jury. If Fletcher's boys show tomorrow morning, they'll find an empty trash can and an empty recycling bin."

Clovis jumped up. "Jordan and I will do it. Y'all say your goodbyes. Morning comes early."

Brian followed them out, and I turned to Jana. "I can't emphasize how hard this will be. But you will survive: they can't eat you. Things will happen that make little sense. Ask questions. Don't ignore something because you think it's too insignificant. I will never be too busy to talk. You have a great asset in Sam. He can explain the process, but because of the privilege there will be things you can't tell him. It will drive him crazy, but he'll get over it."

To my relief, Sam nodded in agreement.

"Jana, right now I can't begin to predict how this mess will turn out, but I can assure you of one thing: I will do everything in my power to makes sure it turns out in your favor."

Total silence. It seemed as if someone had punched the mute button. I waited, and finally Jana responded.

"Well, your bedside manner has improved. Thank you, Jack. I have one question. I know you haven't deposited the check I gave you. Do I need to worry Fletcher will seize my bank account?"

"Good thinking—if he had any evidence you profited from the clinics, he might try. Sometimes prosecutors try to lock up an accused's assets so they can't hire a lawyer, even if there is no evidence of profiteering. But your lawyer is here to stay, and since the clinics were a financial drain rather than a source of income, we can win that battle."

Clovis opened the door and said, "Time for us to give Sam and Jana some shuteye."

As we walked out Jana cried, "Wow, my kitchen is spotless! You guys are welcome anytime."

It was a nice attempt to lighten up a difficult evening.

Clovis and Jordan dropped us off at the hotel, assuring us they'd be ready to roll whenever Fletcher showed up. Brian was ready to turn in, but I needed to unwind.

The bar was quiet, almost empty—after all it was a Sunday evening. I ordered a glass of wine and found a secluded corner table. I was relieved to see no sign of Mimi Stephens.

Jana's mood swings and barely concealed hostility were unnerving, and I couldn't very well ask for Sam to explain. I'd tried to maintain a positive attitude, but the prospect of an indictment and a trial frightened me. The odds are always with the prosecution, and Fletcher was more than confident. He was downright cocky. His refusal to tell me about the charges meant he had something on Jana yet to see the light of day.

Right now I missed Micki and Maggie. We would come up with ideas, bounce them around, toss them out, and then come up with a few more. But I sure didn't want Maggie in Little Rock when there was a revenge-seeking nut on the loose. Micki's strength as a partner was her candor. Sam could help me with the criminal process, but Micki could cut to the chase like no one else I knew.

Thinking about Micki and Maggie reminded me that I hadn't called Beth since she left Little Rock.

"Dad!" Her surprise was obvious. "What are you doing up so late?"

"I've spent all evening with Dr. Hall. She's about to be indicted, and when that happens I won't have time for much else. I have a favor to ask of you and Jeff."

"Sure—what can we do to help?"

"There seems to be a lot of sudden interest in her clinics' patient files. She wanted to use them to study specific medical issues that face Arkansas's poor, but she never had the time to start the project. If Stella sent you the records, would you and Jeff have time to take a look? It's a long shot, but I'll pay you for your time. In fact, I need to pay you so whatever you find will be work-product."

"We'll charge you a dollar. How does that sound? It'll give me something to do now that exams are over, and something for Jeff and I to do other than watch the Cardinals lose to the Cubs."

I thanked her and told her Stella would be in touch. We spent the next half hour catching up. Plans were in full swing for the late fall wedding in Charleston. I expected Beth to complain about her future mother-in-law, but no, they were getting along fine. She reminded me she would need money for deposits. I told her I'd send a check right away. Her request reminded me to check in with Red Shaw tomorrow. I didn't want to lose my best client due to neglect. It also reminded me to deposit the check Jana had given me in case Fletcher tried to seize her bank account. I didn't need it, but she might.

I had finished my wine and asked for the check when I saw Mimi approaching my table with a glass of wine in each hand. She was wearing a sweater and jeans, her wavy hair pulled back in a twist. She was shorter than I remembered, no taller than five-foot four.

"You bought me a drink last night, so I owe you. Besides, no one should drink alone."

She put the wine on the table and sat down. She had an engaging manner, and the small talk flowed easily. It helped that she knew everything about me. She had called herself a "fan"—a new experience for me. She didn't hesitate when I asked where she was from. She grew up a military brat, moving from base to base every couple of years, and graduated from Trinity University in San Antonio. She lived in Dallas and was in town to meet with a client.

I was both puzzled and intrigued. The aggressiveness she'd shown the other night had disappeared. The vamp had turned into the girl next door. After we finished our drinks, she stood and extended her hand.

"Thank you, Jack. I enjoyed our conversation. I'll be here on business for a few more days. I know you're busy, but if you find yourself free and want to share a meal, send me a text."

She reached into her handbag, handed me her card, and was gone before I could stand or say goodbye.

I was ready to turn in. It had been a full day, and tomorrow was likely to be even busier. But maybe Maggie was wrong—maybe every woman I met in Little Rock wasn't out to kill me.

33

WHENEVER I HAVE TO BE UP at a certain time, I wake up every hour on the hour, worried I'll oversleep. I gave up on going back to sleep around five-thirty, shaved, and got in the shower. Minutes later, I heard my phone ringing. Sopping wet, I grabbed it before it transferred the call to voicemail.

"As predicted, Fletcher and his team are at Dr. Hall's with a search warrant." Brian sounded annoyed.

"I'll be down as soon as I can."

I threw on yesterday's jeans and rushed down to find Brian and Clovis waiting next to Jordan's Suburban.

"Sam called. He told me to tell you Fletcher is not a happy camper," Clovis said.

"Well, isn't that just too damned bad."

******

When we made the turn onto River Ridge, we could see the flashing lights of state police cars and satellite TV trucks parked in Jana's driveway. Reporters had set up a bank of microphones outside the front door. It came as no surprise that Fletcher had leaked his dawn raid to the media, but we had a surprise of our own.

"Brian, tell the reporters they have five minutes to move their trucks and themselves from Dr. Hall's property. You know what to do if they refuse. Clovis and I will go straight into the house. Join us when you can."

Five or six troopers were standing on the porch outside the

wide-open front door. The largest one blocked the entryway.

"Sorry, but you can't come in. A court-ordered search is underway."

"Trooper, my name is Jack Patterson. I am Dr. Hall's attorney. If you deny me access for even one second, I will sue you for violating my client's civil rights, and I will have your badge. Do yourself a favor: step aside."

He took one look at Clovis, who seemed to have grown taller on the spot, and moved. Clovis thanked him and followed me in. Several more troopers were milling around in the entryway, and I could hear loud voices in the kitchen.

"Honey, I'm asking you for the last time: where is your computer and your cell phone?" Dawg barked.

"On advice of counsel I decline to answer your question." Jana was wearing scrubs, and she and Sam were sitting at the kitchen table drinking coffee. A copy of the morning paper lay on the table.

"If you don't answer, I'm going—"

"You're going to what, Fletcher?" I interrupted.

He whirled around. "How'd you get here so soon?"

"My driver knows a shortcut. What is happening here? Who invited the press, and what's behind this dawn raid nonsense? One of your troopers told me a court-ordered search is underway."

"I'm concerned evidence could be destroyed. Normal procedure, and you know it," he answered, thumbs hooked confidently in his suspenders.

"May I see the warrant?"

Sam handed it to me. Sure enough, it allowed Fletcher to search the premises and to take possession of Jana's computers, other electronic devices, files, and business records. I wondered what Fletcher had told the judge to get such a broad warrant.

"Patterson, you tell this little woman to tell me where her computers, phone, and files are, or I'll charge her with obstruction," Fletcher blustered.

"Mr. Fletcher. Never refer to my client as 'this little woman' again. Her name is Dr. Hall, and I expect you to show her the respect she has earned. As I'm sure you heard, on my advice she will not answer your questions."

"The location of her computers and files isn't protected by the Fifth Amendment. She has to tell me where they are."

"I disagree, and I've instructed her not to answer any question you may pose."

He was flustered, and I wasn't ready to let him off the hook.

"I will tell you, however, that if those items exist, she wouldn't keep them with her underwear or nightgowns. Tell your troopers to quit fondling her clothes and get the hell out of her bedroom."

His face turned bright red. "You will regret your smart-ass attitude, Patterson. My men have the legal right to search every inch of the premises."

"I guess you think that includes asking the press to join them?"

"I don't know who invited the press."

Just then a trooper appeared at the door. He'd removed his hat and was scratching his head. "Dawg, we got a problem. Some guy told the press they have to get off Dr. Hall's property or they'll be arrested for trespassing. He said a tow truck is on its way. Problem is, if they move there's nowhere to hold your press conference."

Fletcher knew he'd been caught red-handed. Sam chose that moment to flash a big grin.

Fletcher shouted, "What are you grinning at, Pagano? What's the district's prosecutor doing here, anyway? No wonder everyone is saying he and this woman are in bed together."

Fletcher seemed pleased with himself until he saw Sam's face.

"Trooper, I think you and Mr. Fletcher might want to leave the room. Otherwise you'll have to get between him and me. I've been a friend of Dr. Hall's for thirty years. Her home was invaded, and she was frightened. Her sister stayed with her for a short time, but now she's alone. I volunteered to stay in the guest bedroom for a few days. Be careful what you insinuate, Dawg. You're not the only one with a nasty bite, and right now, you're in *my* backyard." Sam was clearly ready for most anything.

They stared at each other like two schoolyard punks. I wasn't sure what would happen when suddenly another trooper broke in on the scene.

"Dawg, we can't find a thing—no files, no computers, no cell phone. Heck, we can't even find a cell phone charger."

"Did you check the trash?" Fletcher asked.

"Yep. The only thing in the trash is this morning's coffee grounds. We're also having trouble at the warehouse. Somebody changed the locks. We're trying to get a hold of the manager."

Fletcher whipped around to face me. "Is this your doing? I warned you. You don't know who you're dealing with, Patterson."

"Oh, but I do. You told me, and if this raid and the presence of the press are any indication, I'd say you're living up to your reputation. Now that your search is complete, I'm sure my client would be grateful if you left so she can get dressed."

Fletcher looked like he was about to burst. Brian and Jordan walked outside so they could listen to Fletcher's press conference if there was one. One thing was clear: it wouldn't be on Jana's lawn. The satellite trucks and reporters had moved as soon as the tow truck arrived.

Fletcher and his men left in a huff, and I joined Sam and Jana at the kitchen table. Clovis left to debrief the two men who had guarded the house overnight.

"I sure hope Dawg took his blood pressure meds," I said.

Sam poured me a cup of coffee and said, "You made an enemy today. Dawg Fletcher doesn't like to be outwitted or embarrassed. You did both. The press won't be happy either. You know the old saw: 'never quarrel with people who buy ink by the barrel?'"

"Well, you know I live to make the press happy. I was more worried the trooper might have to separate you two. Weren't you taking a chance?" I asked.

"As I told Fletcher, I stayed in Jana's guest room last night. I asked the two men guarding the house to check on me on the hour. I have two witnesses to the fact I slept alone. We'll see what Dawg says to the press. Although I'd never sue the jerk, maybe my threat will keep his head out of the gutter." He reached across the table to take Jana's hand. She hadn't said a word.

"Good thinking, Sam. Now the real work begins. Nothing else will come this easy," I said.

Fletcher had his press conference. He told them that his office had received a tip that precipitated the early morning, court-approved search. When asked what he had found, he told the press grand jury secrecy prevented him from revealing the results. What a crock. Unless a trooper put a pair of Jana's panties in his pocket, they hadn't taken a thing.

I told Jana that Brian and Stella would return her laptop and files to her as soon as possible.

"Jack, I was going to use those records for research. Why would anyone care?" she asked.

"Jana, I don't know. This is your world, not mine. It may be a coincidence, but this ruckus began after you told the legislature and Flowers you were looking for trends or anomalies. I think someone got bent out of shape over what you proposed and has been trying to get those records ever since."

She glanced at her watch, and we took the hint. Pre-dawn confrontations leave me starving, so I suggested we stop for breakfast. The classic dives I'd known in my childhood were gone, but Clovis said he knew the perfect place. I told Brian to ask Paul and Mike to meet us.

Jordan drove us out to the industrial district to what looked like an old Toddle House, red plastic booths and bar stools. The sign above the door advertised "Bill's Good Eats." It wasn't busy—apparently we'd missed the early morning rush. We commandeered a table for six in the back. The cook manning the grills was a short, wiry fellow. He worked in silence, frying eggs, flipping pancakes, and turning hash browns with ease. Every few minutes he'd raise a hand and a waitress would come fetch someone's breakfast.

I knew Clovis had chosen well when our waitress brought us a basket of biscuits with butter and honey. Betty had seen better days, and I found myself fascinated with the long scar that ran from her ear to the top of her cheek. She couldn't have been friendlier, she got our orders right, and no one had to ask for refills. Clovis recommended the pancakes with a side of sausage, but I opted for two fried eggs with a side of country ham and redeye gravy. Paul and Big Mike joined us and before long we were too busy eating to talk shop.

When Betty brought me the bill, my mouth dropped. Bill couldn't make any money at these prices. I paid her with cash and handed her a large, well-earned tip.

She poured us more coffee and said, "You boys take all the time you need. The lunch crowd won't come in 'til around eleven."

I turned to Clovis. "How'd you discover this place? Maybe not now, but..."

"Later," he said with a grin.

"So Mike, where on earth have you been? If Paul hadn't heard from you, I was ready to send out the National Guard."

"Sorry to worry you. I tried to get inside the head of the man behind the threats, how he might have gotten get past the sheriff's lookouts. I went to the Fourche Bottoms and Paul and I went bar hopping, but this guy is good—so far, no clues. But give me time—I'll figure him out."

I had tried not to think about my would-be assassin. Mike's confidence was reassuring.

"Thanks, Mike, I appreciate it. Can I offer a suggestion?" I asked. "Four men were there the evening they hanged me. All of them are dead."

Mike nodded, and Clovis looked thoughtful.

"You might want to to expand your search. You've been looking for a man. I've been the target of an assassin three times, and each time the bad guy turned out to be a woman. You weren't on board, but ask Paul about Brenda, Moira, and the Greek Midge."

"The Greek Midge?" Mike asked, brows raised.

"The Greek Midge," Clovis affirmed. "Paul can tell you all about her. Paul, Jack makes a good point. Try to find the whereabouts of Brenda and Tina Lalas. We know what happened to Moira, but check to see if she had associates. At least it's a start."

Paul and Mike left, promising to keep us informed.

"You know, Jack, we've been friends for a long time," Clovis said thoughtfully. "Been through thick and thin, yet you continue to surprise me. You're smack in the middle of dealing with Jana's issues, and I think maybe you've ignored the threats. But somewhere in the back of your mind, you're trying to figure out who wants to kill you."

"Well, when someone leaves a note on a dead body that says 'you're next,' it's hard to ignore," I countered. "You know, it could be more than one person. Moira had that creepy associate, and how did someone sabotage our plane and kill somebody in the Fourche at the same time?"

We were about to leave when Betty touched my arm. "Do you have a second, Mr. Patterson?"

From the look on her face I thought there might have been a mistake on the bill. I nodded.

"I saw on the news this morning that you're Dr. Hall's lawyer. Is that right?"

"Yes, it is."

"Well, she saved my life in more ways than one. See this?" She pointed to the scar on her face.

"I do, and I'm so sorry. Whatever happened must have been awful."

"Don't be. Dr. Hall saved my life—she also got me in rehab and helped me get my life back together. My name's Betty Worley, and I would do anything for her."

A light bulb went on in my brain. "Thanks, Betty, I'll keep you in mind. And I'll tell her you asked about her."

"Thank you, and I'm serious. I'd do anything for her. So would Bill." She motioned to the man behind the counter.

"Don't worry, you'll hear from me again."

My phone chirped as we were leaving Bill's. I saw a text from Kate Erwin suggesting we meet at the restaurant in the Armitage at 6:30 p.m.

Jordan asked, "Where to, boss?"

"Why don't you drop me off at the hotel—I have to pick up my laptop and call Red Shaw. Then you can run Brian out to Stella's. I should be at Tucker Bowie's office for most of the day, unless I hear from Ray Spears. That good with you, Clovis?"

"I'll have one of Paul's men escort you to Tucker's. I've got a client that needs a little attention. Jordan can drop me off at my office, but I can be back downtown in five minutes if you need me."

I spent the rest of the morning on the phone with Red and Gina. I didn't hear a word from Spears, which was a little worrisome, but definitely good for me. This move to San Antonio was complicated and required my attention. With Brian focused on health records and Maggie in Europe, I sure didn't want Red to think I was taking on too much.

When we'd finished our business, Red asked, "You feeling okay?"

"Pretty good, a little sore, but nothing to worry about," I replied.

"Glad to hear it. Lucy tells me there's been a series of gruesome murders in Little Rock. Makes DC sound safe. Anything I can do to help?"

"No, Red, but thanks. I've got plenty of people watching my back."

"You can never have too many people watching your back." He laughed, and the phone clicked off.

He was so right. I noticed a voicemail from a number I didn't recognize. I was ready to delete the robocall, but instead heard the voice of Ray Spears. I quickly punched in the number he left.

"This is Jack Patterson, returning your call."

"Glad to hear from you. I gotta tell you, if it were up to Dawg, his promises about treating Dr. Hall with respect during the process would be off the table. I hear he almost came to blows with Pagano. Not sure which dog I'd bet on in that fight." Ray sounded pleased with his attempt at humor.

I ignored the bait.

"Anyway. I've arranged for your client to appear before Judge Purdom at ten o'clock, this Thursday. Why don't we meet Wednesday afternoon at our office, say two o'clock? At that point, I'll give you a copy of the indictment, and we can discuss the logistics of getting your client in and out of the courthouse."

"I can't see the charges before Wednesday?" I asked.

"I'm telling you, if it were up to Dawg, you wouldn't see them until we walked into the courtroom, but cooler heads carried the day."

"Are you going to ask her to post bail?"

"That issue is up to the judge, but we won't ask for it and will support your request to waive bail. We will ask her to deposit her passport with the court."

"I appreciate that. Anything else?" I asked.

"We'll ask for this case be expedited. I'll give you a preliminary discovery request on Wednesday. It will come as no surprise we want her computers, her cell phone, and any patient records in her or your possession."

"You're right, it doesn't come as a surprise. It is difficult for me to respond to your request since I don't know the nature of the charges."

"Oh, Mr. Patterson, if you're not running a good bluff, you'd better have a serious talk with your client. Contrary to what Dawg said, the deal he offered is on the table until we walk into the courtroom. If your client pleads guilty, we'll stick to our original offer. Two years is a good deal. So don't wait too long."

There it was again: talk to your client, she knows what she's done. What could she have done that she hadn't told me? What in the hell did Jana know that I didn't?

34

We hung up, and I called Sam to tell him about my conversation with Spears and to get the lowdown on Judge Purdom, but I got his voicemail. Opening my laptop depressed me. My inbox was full of messages—clients, lawyers, and a ton of reporters who wanted me to comment on this morning's raid. Too bad I couldn't turn the press calls over to Maggie. I closed both the computer and my eyes, wondering if I needed to rethink my next move.

I opened my eyes at the sound of Tucker's voice. "You look like a man who needs a friend and a very strong drink."

Tucker and I met on the baseball field in high school and became reacquainted when I came back for the Cole case. He ran a very successful insurance agency, one of those people who is everybody's friend. I've never heard a single person say anything negative about Tucker. It occurred to me there weren't many people I could say that about.

We were soon on the way to his club. Paul's men were welcome to follow, but Tucker insisted on driving his Ford 4X4. He told me he loved to park beside the nicest Mercedes in the club's parking lot, knowing the old truck's presence drove Little Rock's old guard crazy. I should introduce Tucker to Larry's mom.

Soon we were in one of the last bastions of male chauvinism—a country club men's grill. Tucker was in charge. He stopped to greet every table with a joke or a little news, otherwise known as gossip. Tucker ordered for us both: bean soup, a cheeseburger with onion rings, and a vodka tonic. I waved away the vodka and asked for a beer.

"Thanks for lending me your office. I'll try not to get it fire-bombed," I joked. Tucker had taken heat for giving me an office during Woody's case.

"No worries. You're representing Jana Hall, not Woody Cole. Please tell me she's not in any real trouble. I'd do about anything for that woman."

"You're the second person today who's said those exact words. Why?"

Tucker waited until the waiter had brought him a fresh drink. "I bet half the members of this club employ someone who has worked for their family for decades. Nowadays, they pay them a decent wage, but don't give a rat's ass if they have to get health care at free clinics. When I was growing up, our housekeeper did more than the cleaning—she raised my sister and me. She kept us out of trouble, and we loved her. After mother passed, I brought her on full-time at the agency to clean the office and do whatever odd jobs she could.

"I've bailed her sons out of jail, paid her rent more often than I'd like to think, and helped her grandchildren get into better schools...."

I interrupted. "Sounds like you've done the right thing for someone you love."

"Thanks, but that's not the point. I want you to understand how special Bobbye Taylor is and why I would do anything for Dr. Hall. One day, Bobbye asked to leave work early. She hadn't been feeling well and had an appointment with Dr. Hall. She was proud Dr. Hall would see her.

"Something in her voice was worrisome. I told her I had to call on a client near the clinic and would give her a lift. I went in with her and sat down which embarrassed her no end. The waiting room was overflowing, and I figured we'd be there a while. But the nurse called her name in a matter of minutes. I figured I had plenty of time to return a few emails while I waited. To my surprise, it wasn't long before the nurse called me in.

"The bad news was that Bobbye had cancer. Dr. Hall said she needed surgery and the sooner the better, but it would be expensive—could I help? Dr. Hall would find a surgeon to do the surgery gratis, but even with the clinic's discount the hospital costs were substantial.

I told her that Bobbye was on our insurance plan—cost wouldn't be a problem.

"Well, Dr. Hall's jaw hit the floor. She told me another doctor assumed she didn't have the means to pay her medical bills and had referred Bobbye to the East End clinic. 'She cleans homes, she won't have insurance,' the doctor's office had told Jana. They hadn't even bothered to ask Bobbye."

"I'm afraid your story isn't that unusual," I said.

"No, but Dr. Hall called the referring doctor in my presence and gave him the what for. Then she called a surgeon at UAMS and asked her to see Bobbye as a personal favor. It didn't hurt for the surgeon to hear Bobbye had insurance. The bottom line is Bobbye is doing well. Jana came to the hospital every day after the surgery, and every member of the staff treated Bobbye like a queen because she was one of Dr. Hall's patients."

The waiter brought our food, and we dug in. Say what you want about country clubs, they always deliver on the basic food groups. The onion rings were absolute perfection. The second beer helped lighten my mood as did Tucker's recounting of what had happened to many of our old friends. One classmate who had majored in shop and the smoking area was now a successful Broadway producer, and to the surprise of several of our female classmates, our star running back had recently come out of the closet.

After we'd finished lunch and run out of stories, Tucker told me he wanted to pick up an afternoon golf game. He joked that he did more business on the golf course than he did in his office. I thanked him again and hopped into the car with my bodyguards. Either the beer or the onion rings had made me drowsy, and I was ready for a nap.

I noticed Mimi Stephens at the bar when I walked through the hotel lobby, but decided it would be a mistake to join her. I needed some sleep before I met with Kate Erwin tonight. I wondered what Mimi was doing in the bar at this hour, but decided it was none of my business and headed toward the elevator.

I couldn't have been asleep more than a few minutes when I heard my phone vibrating on the night stand. I picked it up, surprised to see it was already four o'clock.

"Hello," I answered, my voice groggy.

"Did I wake you up?" Jana asked.

"I guess I was more tired than I thought."

"I wondered when all the pressure would catch up with you. You need to listen to your body and take it easier. You're no spring chicken, you know."

"Hah—you and I are the same age," I responded. "But I'm glad you called. I spoke with Fletcher's deputy, and we have a date with the judge on Thursday morning."

"Good, that gives me a little time. Stella sent me a few of my patients' records. I spent the afternoon going through them, but I've just gotten started. I'd like to work on them without distractions. Why don't you bring sandwiches from Ben's tomorrow around lunchtime? We can talk then."

"Sounds great, but don't you want to know what's going on?"

"No, I don't."

We hung up, and I called Brian.

"I hear you're making progress," I began.

"Stella is a whiz, but you already know that. Whoever digitized those records did a first-rate job. They've all been scanned and put in a searchable format. Stella has loaned Dr. Hall a computer for the time being, and I've been to the Apple Store to get her a new phone, laptop, and iMac. Stella is downloading everything right now so soon Dr. Hall will have new equipment that mirrors her old stuff."

"Perfect. I'm meeting Kate Erwin in two hours. You're on your own tonight. Let's meet tomorrow, early. We have an arraignment on Thursday morning, so you and I will have to set aside the record search for a few days."

"The game is on?"

"Yep. Lace up your shoulder pads and snap on your headgear."

"Got it, Coach." Brian laughed and hung up. I punched in Sam's number. He picked up right away.

"I hear Dawg set the arraignment."

"You must have already spoken with Jana. Yes, Thursday morning at ten o'clock. The judge is a Judge Purdom. Know anything about him?"

"Oh jeez, we couldn't have received a worse draw. He's a former prosecutor with the U.S. Attorney's office in northwest Arkansas, a real hard-ass. Do you know anything about the charges?"

"Not a thing. I won't get the indictment until Wednesday afternoon. We'll have less than twenty-four hours to go over the charges with Jana and decide on a plea. Do you have time tomorrow to talk about what to expect from Judge Purdom? I meet Jana at noon."

"I'll make time. I'll come by Tucker's around ten o'clock if that's good."

"Perfect, and thanks."

"No, I'm the one who's grateful. To some extent, my future, as well as Jana's, is in your hands."

"Sounds like you kids are moving at lightning speed," I kidded.

"Sometimes you wake up and realize how much you've missed and how little time is left. The 'take it slow' route doesn't make sense to either of us anymore."

35

I SPENT THE REST OF THE AFTERNOON answering emails and catching up on other business. I looked forward to seeing Kate, to enjoying a good dinner with an intelligent woman that involved no romance, just welcome conversation. I had already asked the hostess to give me a quiet table, and she escorted me to the perfect banquette in the back corner of the restaurant.

I ordered a glass of wine rather than a cocktail and thought about the coming week. I saw Kate walking toward the table and stood to greet her. She extended her hand politely, but looked uncomfortable.

The waiter came to take her drink order and Kate responded, "Water, please."

I raised my eyebrows, and she blushed.

"I'm sorry. I know this dinner was supposed to be partly social, but I can only stay for a few minutes."

"Why the change? What's going on?" I asked, trying not to telegraph any irritation.

She looked me straight in the eye, no more blushing. "I am the lead prosecutor for four murders that occurred in the Fourche Bottoms, a place you know well. If you didn't have airtight alibis, you would be the primary suspect, and as the police chief reminded me this afternoon, your possible involvement is still an issue."

"My involvement? What does that mean? Do you think I was involved?" I asked.

"No, of course not. Do you think I'd be here right now if I thought you were involved in any way?"

She looked even more uncomfortable, and I realized what had happened.

"Don't say another word. Somehow the police chief found out you and I were meeting, and your ability to remain impartial in the investigation was called into question."

"That's a polite way to put it," she said.

"In fact, I can think of at least one person who would love to cast doubt on my innocence and leak to the press that I am a suspect."

She nodded.

"Okay, I'll make this easy for you.When you're asked about this meeting you can say that we met in a public place where you questioned me about the murders. I told you I had no involvement in the shootings, don't know the identity of any of the victims except Mace, and am willing to take a lie detector test. That won't do me any good, but it should keep you in the clear."

"Thanks, Jack. Micki told me you'd understand."

"You spoke with Micki?"

"Yes, I called her the moment I finished meeting with the chief. I knew she would be discreet and give me good advice."

That she could get advice from Micki when I couldn't was hard to take.

"Kate, I want to say something off the record. You will catch the person who committed the Fourche killings, and it won't be me. When you do, I would like for us to have a nice dinner and a good conversation. Do we have a deal?"

"Off the record, Mr. Patterson, it's a date."

She smiled and rose, as did I, our conversation ending with a formal handshake. It was no one's fault, but I felt cheated. And I'd learned something equally disheartening—the opposition's sphere of influence was broader than I had known.

I don't enjoy eating in a restaurant alone, but I had no choice other than room service, which sounded even more depressing. I reached into my pocket for my phone, but took a breath and left it there. Surely I could enjoy a nice dinner without either human or digital company. Over a filet with black peppercorn sauce and a nice glass of Zinfandel, I plotted out a strategy for the next few days.

An idea was percolating in my brain, and the quiet of the restaurant provided the perfect incubator.

After dinner I decided to find a table in the bar. I wasn't tired, and the thought of an early night in my hotel room was more than I could deal with. The hostess led me to a quiet table away from a noisy birthday celebration.

An attractive woman in a green dress caught my eye, and I was reminded of Mimi. Her card was still in my jacket pocket, so I texted her, hoping she might still be interested. I waited, but she didn't respond. It was probably for the best.

The waiter brought me a glass of port, and I was soon lost in thought. Beth would have called it a pity party. I was jolted out of my funk by the insistent vibrating of my phone.

I didn't recognize the number, but the message made my skin crawl. I called Clovis immediately.

"Clovis, get here right now. I'll call Sam. Someone has kidnapped Kate Erwin."

I had difficulty getting the last sentence out of my mouth.

"What? How do you know?" Clovis asked.

"I just got a text from an unknown number."

"Read it."

"If you want to see Kate Erwin alive, do as I say. Go to your favorite oak tree in City Park at midnight tonight and wait for instructions. Make no mistake, if Jones or any of his men go anywhere near the park, the woman will die. Come alone and don't be late."

"I'm on my way. Don't worry, I'll call Sam. And for heaven's sakes, get out of that bar. Go to your room and stay there."

I paid my bill and left. I imagined every eye in the bar was watching me, every person in the lobby. I couldn't help but feel guilty—I would soon be safe and sound in my comfy hotel room. I had no idea where Kate was or even if she was alive.

I didn't have long to wait. Clovis and Paul appeared at the same time. Sam was on his way. I handed my phone to Paul who tried to get a trace on the last number.

"Jack, walk me through your day until you got the text." Clovis took charge, and I responded to his matter-of-fact tone.

I described lunch with Tucker, taking a nap, talking with various clients on the phone. I told him about meeting Kate, but Clovis stopped me.

"Let's wait until Sam gets here. Have you spoken with anyone other than Kate tonight?"

"I texted Mimi Stephens a few minutes before I got the text," I said. I wasn't thrilled about revealing my text to Mimi, but no one even raised an eyebrow. Paul gave Clovis a knowing look, and he didn't even ask how she responded. I was about to ask why when Sam barged into the room.

"You okay, Jack?" Sam asked. "Has anyone called the police?"

Clovis responded, "Not yet. I thought we should consult with you before deciding on a course of action."

"What do you mean 'a course of action'?" I interrupted. "I'm going to the park at midnight, and that's that. Whoever sent that text wants me, not her."

Sam cleared his throat and asked, "Weren't the two of you supposed to have dinner tonight?"

"We were, and we almost did." I told them about Kate's encounter with the police chief and her fear that even a drink could be compromising.

Sam sighed. "She was right to be cautious, and I'll bet my grandma's walker that someone influential got to the chief. No one in the world thinks you're involved in the Fourche murders other than that your hanging was the catalyst."

"Listen, Sam," I said. "You do what you want, but I'm going to the park tonight, alone. If you won't give me a car, I'll take an Uber. There's no way I can let some asshole murder Kate because I turned chicken. I think there's a good chance he'll let her go. It's simple: she's the bait, I'm the trophy. Call the police or not, but I don't want a soul near that park." You could have heard the proverbial pin drop.

He cleared his throat and said quietly, "Jack, you know they won't let her go. She may already be dead."

"Why would they kill her when they want me?" I almost shouted.

"Don't lose your temper, Jack. It's not helpful. I'm only being realistic."

"Take your realism somewhere else. We've got less than three hours to figure out how I can walk into that park alive and get out the same way with Kate. To complicate things, I bet the only thing I find at that tree are instructions to go elsewhere. But one thing is certain."

"What's that?" Clovis asked.

"Kate's kidnapper and the person who murdered four men in the Fourche Bottoms must be one and the same and must know the history of that tree. If we can figure out who he is, we might be able to figure out how to keep me alive."

Clovis stared at me. At that moment, we were the only two people in the room. He sighed, shoving his fingers through his hair from front to back in frustration.

"Well, why don't you work on the who, while the rest of us come up with the plan to keep you alive."

36

Clovis and Paul huddled up in the bedroom. Sam and I sat on the sofa trying to figure out who knew me well enough to know about the tree's history. For the life of me, I couldn't come up with anyone who knew about Angie's and my affection for the tree except a few close friends.

By eleven, I couldn't stand it any longer.

"I don't want to be late. Is one of you going to drive me or what?"

Clovis spoke. "You know if you go alone, you'll be dead before you reach that tree."

"Gosh, thanks for the optimism. If you've got a better plan, now's the time to tell me."

"Okay, don't get your whiskers in a jigger. Jordan will drop you off at the parking lot and drive off at ten minutes 'til midnight."

"The text said if anyone came with me, he would kill Kate. Clovis, I know you—whatever your plan, just stay away."

Sam spoke up before Clovis could answer. "Jack, there's no sense in both of you getting killed. It makes much more sense for you to stay away while we try to rescue Kate."

I looked at the man I knew better than almost anyone else in the world. "If it were you, could you cool your heels in a hotel room and let law enforcement try to save Kate?"

"No, I guess not." He sighed and turned his back. It occurred to me they thought I was about to die.

"You know, I have every intention of having dinner with Kate again, so I'd really like to know what you intend to do."

Clovis told me of the plans to man the perimeter of the park. He hoped I would get instructions to go to a different location. If the kidnapper sent me all over town, he might make a mistake. Jordan would be waiting for my text. He also handed me a phone with everyone's numbers already programmed into it.

The phone would serve as a microphone. Clovis and crew could listen to whatever my kidnapper or I might say. Clovis said it worked much better than a wire. He showed me how to use the phone so I didn't accidentally turn it off. If Kate wasn't alive I was to scream, "You bastard!" and Clovis and his men would crash the park.

"You know, Jack, I'd rather do this another way."

"I know. But whoever won't go away until we face him."

Clovis smiled—during the Stewart case we had gotten into the habit of referring to the unknown bad guy as "whoever." I was sick of dealing with whoevers.

"Clovis, I couldn't live with myself if he killed Kate because I opted to protect my ass. Kate's bad enough, but next time it could be Maggie or Beth. It ends tonight. Whatever happens, you make sure our kidnapper doesn't get away. You got it?"

"I've got it."

I knew Clovis had a plan, but I also knew he didn't want to tell me what it was. I'd trusted him before, and would again. It's an odd feeling, knowing that in a couple of hours you were likely to be dead.

"Where's Jordan? I don't want to be late for my own funeral."

Clovis frowned in irritation, but Sam punched me on the shoulder and said, "Go get 'em, Jack."

The trip to the park didn't take long, and Jordan didn't say a word. The full moon bathed the trees in a soft glow. I noticed that the gate was unlocked.

I stepped out of the Tahoe and said, "Jordan, it's okay. It's time for you to leave. You'll know if I need you."

"I guess it would be pointless to tell you to be careful," he said.

I smiled. "It would."

I watched him drive away and walked across the parking lot. Angie's tree was about three hundred yards into the park. I was about halfway there when a dark figure emerged from behind a tree. It was

Mimi Stephens, pointing her handgun at me.

"Hello, Jack. Didn't your mother teach you not to go out this late at night?"

"Well, she tried. She also told me to beware of beautiful women carrying handguns. I never would have figured you for a murderer."

She didn't respond, and I didn't move. Handguns make me nervous. I held my arms up as she walked around behind me. I waited for the jolt, but she jammed the gun into my back and said, "Walk."

I walked, wondering how I might stall for time.

"I'll hand it to you, I really thought you enjoyed my company."

"Stop with the jokes. Keep walking," she whispered pushing the gun into my ribs again.

As we approached Angie's tree, I could see Kate slumped on the ground against the trunk, duct tape secure over her mouth. A blindfold covered her eyes. I shivered with relief—she wouldn't have needed the tape or the blindfold if she were dead.

A sudden shout from about thirty feet away interrupted my thoughts. I whirled toward the voice that shouted, "Who's there? Who in the hell are you?"

A form emerged through the half-light. As he edged closer I saw a man dressed in camouflage and also wielding a gun.

"Did you really think Patterson was going to show?" Mimi asked with disdain. "You misread his affection for Ms. Erwin, so I brought him to you." She pointed her gun at my head, pushing me forward with her free hand.

I objected, but she jammed the gun into my ribs and whispered, "Just be quiet." She was so close I could smell her perfume.

"Who are you?" the man asked, frustrated by Mimi's presence. I wondered which of the two was going to shoot me.

"A friend of your sister's."

"Friends? My sister had no friends," he snorted.

"Your sister died underneath this very tree three years ago at the hand of Clovis Jones. That's why you lured Patterson here. You plotted revenge on the man you blame for her death."

"Who are you? And how do you know who I am?"

Mimi's gun was no longer digging into my ribs, and she had

somehow slipped in front of me.

"I told you, I knew your sister. I also know you murdered four other men and left their bodies in the Fourche Bottoms. Was that part of your plan or a separate contract?"

"What's it to you? Get out of my way or I'll shoot you, too. Like I said, my sister had no friends. Now move!"

"I can't do that," Mimi answered.

At this point we were at a Mexican standoff. Neither of them seemed inclined to back off. For a long second I thought about running, but knew it wouldn't work. This scene had to play itself out.

"Why the hell not? If you knew my sister, you know he deserves to die. Now move—this is your last chance."

"Like I said, I can't do that. If I were you, I'd drop your firearm and put your hands over your head before you get killed."

The man smiled. "Who's gonna kill me, little woman? You?"

"No, that's not my style. But I wonder if you've noticed the two red dots on your chest."

The man looked down and saw the two red dots on him, right over his heart. His face curled in anger, but he dropped his gun and went to to his knees.

"Face down. Spread your arms and feet," she shouted.

I could hear sirens in the background. I didn't know whose side Mimi was on, but she seemed more interested in the man who was lying on the ground than she was in me. When he failed to respond, she kicked him in the vicinity of his balls.

"I said spread your feet!" she shouted.

I ran toward Kate and tore her blindfold off. Her eyes were unfocused, and she didn't say a word. I carefully peeled away the duct tape.

"Kate. Kate, talk," I said, giving her a little shake. Her only response was a feeble groan, but it was enough.

I reached for the cell phone serving as my makeshift microphone and spoke into it. "Clovis, get here quick and bring an ambulance."

I heard nothing in response so I yelled. "Clovis!"

"The ambulance will be here any minute, Jack."

I threw the phone down and whirled around to see Clovis, Sam, and Paul. Mimi had the man in handcuffs, her gun still trained at his head.

I tried to regain my composure, but to my intense irritation, I couldn't quit shaking and felt light-headed. Sam pulled me down beside the tree and we waited for the police to arrive. They tossed me a blanket, and between its warmth and two long swallows from the flask Paul handed me, I felt more or less myself.

The paramedics treated Kate gently—I can't say the same for the man in camouflage. Sam barked orders to the police and directed others to secure the crime scene. I watched in silence as the medics whisked Kate away and the police stuffed the bad guy into a patrol car and sped away.

Clovis and Mimi walked over to join me, and I stood up. She removed her baseball cap, undid her ponytail, and shook her hair loose. At that moment I had never seen a more beautiful woman, and it had nothing to do with her looks.

"Jack, meet Miriam 'Mimi' Stephens, Chief Detective for Interpol," he said.

She extended her hand, and I carefully shook it.

"Somebody want to tell me what's going on?" I looked at Clovis.

"The man who murdered those men and was ready to kill you is Dmitri Stalinski," he answered. "He is, or was, Moira's half-brother, an international assassin in his own right. He's been on Interpol's radar for some time. His image was flagged when he came into the country, and he was traced to Little Rock. Interpol dispatched Mimi here—she and Paul have been working together since."

Mimi added, "I apologize for misleading you, but we suspected Dmitri had you under surveillance, so I had to pretend to be one of your groupies. It wasn't a total act—I am a big fan. After all, you helped capture the Greek Midge."

"Mimi, you can mislead me anytime," I continued. "But I can't say the same for Clovis. I assume the snipers are with Interpol."

"Oh, no, they're not mine. Big Mike and Paul have been on Dmitri's scent for the last several days. Clovis had a hunch he would try to lure you to the park where Clovis killed Moira, and Mike and Brian had already scoped out the perfect spots to wait. We were lucky his hunch proved correct."

"Mike and Brian? I know they're both veterans of the Iraq War, but I never knew they were trained as snipers. Where are they? And, Paul, you were working with Interpol?"

He grinned and said, "Well, we all gotta make a living somehow."

Clovis continued. "Mike and Brian are still in their perches, making sure Stalinski didn't bring backup."

I looked up to the trees and shouted, "Thanks, fellows."

"You'll have plenty of time to thank them. Mike did a brilliant job tracking Stalinski. When Brian insisted on providing backup, Mike said, and I quote, 'no one could have better backup than Master Sergeant Hattoy.'"

Sam walked up and said, "Kate will be fine. She was drugged, but otherwise unharmed except for a few bruises where he grabbed her.

"Mike phoned that Kate was alive when Stalinski brought her to the park. He and Brian weren't about to let anything happen to her once she was in their sights, but the only way to capture Stalinski alive was to play it out. You were predictable. We knew you would insist on going to the park alone, and that Mimi's appearance would come as a total surprise.

"Sorry to keep you in the dark, but if you'd known Mimi was Interpol, you might have blown the whole mission. Your inclination would have been to protect her, and that could have proved fatal."

I didn't like it, but I knew he was right. I also didn't like being in the dark all this time. But once again, Clovis knew exactly what he was doing.

I turned to Mimi. "'Thank you' or 'good job' seems a bit inadequate. I have your card—let's have that dinner if you're actually going to be in town for a few days."

She gave Clovis a sideways glance. "Sorry, but Sam and I need to spend the next few days grilling Stalinski. We know someone hired him to kill the four men in the Fourche. Maybe now we can find out who and why. After that I'll take him to Brussels. Don't worry, his part in all this has ended."

"You'll be here at least a few days—isn't there…?"

She shook her head and said, "How about this: if you find yourself in Brussels, please look me up. Right now, this girl has work to do."

37

Everyone but Sam was waiting when I came down for breakfast. Clovis looked exhausted, but the others were full of energy, still on a high from the evening's activities. I felt great, truly glad to be alive.

"Well, I'm glad that's over," I began. "Mike and Brian, I can't thank you enough. But next time you decide to return to your military roots, could you give me a heads-up instead of scaring the shit out of me?"

Clovis had no information about Stalinski's interrogation. He assumed Sam would fill us in when he arrived. I said something about getting back to normal, but Clovis would have none of it—he wasn't willing to lighten up on my protection. If someone had hired Stalinski to kill me, they could hire someone else to finish the job. I couldn't argue with his logic—the possibility of another killer on the loose was sobering.

We were busy with breakfast when Sam walked in and pulled up a chair. He was unshaven and his eyes were heavy—he must have been up all night. We waited in silence while he ordered a full breakfast and doctored his coffee.

Micki was with Kate at the hospital—she was doing well. She would spend the next few days at Micki's. He added that visitors were unwelcome.

I didn't like it, but I got the message. The perception that Kate and I were close had almost cost Kate her life. Sam told us that Stalinski was in the hospital under police guard. Unless there was a break in the interrogation, an Interpol jet would take Mimi and Stalinski back to Brussels sometime in the next forty-eight hours.

I asked, "Does Mimi have any idea who paid him to murder Mace and his crew? Does she think my murder was another contract or an act of revenge?"

"She's sure he had a contract to kill Mace and the others, but doesn't have a clue who hired him or why. He landed in Miami and came directly here."

I changed the subject. "Okay, now that we've solved the mystery of the Fourche Bottoms, it's time to turn our attention back to Dr. Jana Hall. Clovis, I want you to tighten her security. Someone has to be behind all the unwanted attention she's received, someone with deep pockets."

"Why would anyone go to such lengths to discredit her?" Sam asked. He'd eaten every scrap of his breakfast and signaled the server to remove his plate.

"I sound like a broken record, but I think the answer lies in the files and records of her patients. Fletcher could hit us with something unexpected, but for now that's all we've got. Brian, I need you to put your paralegal hat back on and work with Stella and Jana. I'll check in with Beth. I need to tell her about last night before she hears about it through the Maggie-grapevine.

"Sam, if you have any time to spare, I need to pick your brain about our judge."

"Give me twenty-four hours to sleep and work out a few details with Interpol and my time is yours."

"Do you think I could have a few minutes with Mimi before she leaves?"

Sam smiled. "You don't give up, do you?"

He was right, but that wasn't the main reason why I wanted to see her. I chose to ignore their grins. "I know what you're thinking, but the reason I want to talk with her is to understand the process of how one hires a Stalinski. If we understand the method, maybe we can figure out who was behind his hiring and why. Sure it's a long shot, but it's better than nothing, which is what we have so far."

I faced a table of skeptical faces.

"Okay, maybe I also want to find out how to reach her if I'm ever in Brussels."

Sam promised he would arrange a meeting before she left town. I glanced at my watch. "Brian, why don't you and Stella meet us at Jana's, say twelve-thirty?"

"Sounds good! I've checked in with Rose—everything's cool in DC. You might want to check in with Uncle Red. He's probably heard about last night, too."

"Good idea," I agreed, but wondered how on earth Red could already have heard about last night.

Clovis spoke up. "When we finish, I need five minutes of your time."

"Sure," I responded, wondering what Clovis wanted to say out of earshot.

We lingered a while over coffee, listening to Mike and Paul explain how they had picked up Stalinski's trail and how they had come up with a plan they hoped would keep me alive last night.

I wanted someone to figure out who had hired Stalinski, and I thought Mike could be that person. He seemed to relish the assignment when I laid it out in front of the others. Anything had to be more exciting than hanging out in trees.

"Any restraints on how I gather the information?" he asked.

Sam scowled, but I cut him off.

"Since you're not working for law enforcement, neither the Fourth Amendment nor Miranda rights apply, but if you do anything illegal, don't get caught." Mike laughed, and Sam relaxed.

The party broke up, but Clovis hung back.

"I thought you'd want to know the fellows in St. Louis are still on full alert. They've promised to keep Beth and Jeff safe."

"Thanks. You know I worry."

"I do," he said with a small smile. "And another thing. I know you're dying to see Kate Erwin, but she's not out of the woods yet. We got Stalinski, but whoever's behind all this could easily hire another assassin. And that person will know you'll do most anything to save her life. Kate is a smart person—I'm sure she's already seen the trap."

"Well, it is what it is. Don't worry about it. In fact, you're right, but for the wrong reason."

"How do you mean?" he asked.

"Sam is too close to Jana. I need a prosecutor who has no reason to listen to anyone, who'll go after the bad guys and bring them to justice. If Kate and I are viewed as something we aren't, her motives will be suspect."

"You looking into the future?"

"That's what I do, and if I'm right, we'll need to do more than defend an injustice, we'll need to go after one."

38

THE BREAKFAST CROWD HAD DWINDLED, so the staff didn't mind that Clovis and I lingered over another cup of coffee.

"I don't understand why the Health Department is so determined to see Jana discredited and prosecuted. They've already closed her clinics and can probably get her to return the records. Why the rush to prosecute?" I asked.

"It's got to be hard for you to plan a defense without knowing the charges. But whatever the special prosecutor is cooking up must be razor thin, given the auditors' and Kate's inability to find any wrongdoing. What are you worried about?"

"Prosecutors are always confident, but Fletcher and Spears are downright cocksure. They keep saying 'talk to your client.' Unless she's a very good liar, Jana has no idea what she did wrong. Fletcher could come up with dirt on a twelve-year-old if he's so inclined. So, yes, I am worried."

"What can I do to help?"

"You've got your hands full keeping us safe. But now that you mention it, I have at least one project, maybe two, you could take on."

Clovis rolled his eyes, and over another cup of coffee I explained that I needed to know more about Jana's primary adversaries, Brady Flowers and the chairperson of the Senate Appropriations Committee. It was time to take the offensive.

It felt good to toss ideas and theories back and forth with Clovis, but I had other clients who needed my attention, none more demanding than Red Shaw. I took the elevator back to my room.

"You damn fool, one of these days you'll get yourself killed. Then who will I get to negotiate with those San Antonio hotshots?" Red began.

"You'll find someone half as good as me for twice the cost," I laughed.

"Well, that won't do me any good. It's time you left and came back to civilization."

"If you think DC is civilization, you aren't as smart as I thought. Ask Lucy how quickly you can end up sweeping the Capitol steps instead of owning them."

He laughed. "You have a point."

We got down to business, and he seemed surprised I was on top of the issues regarding the move and ready to discuss strategy. The hours I'd spent late at night studying the issues had paid off. For me it was a relief to think about something other than what had happened last night.

When we finally wound down, I asked, "Has Lucy heard any more about the prosecution of Dr. Hall?"

"I don't know—she hasn't mentioned it."

"Red, tell her to keep out of it. Things are about to get ugly. When I sling mud, I don't want to get her dirty," I said.

"You, slinging mud? She won't believe a word."

"I'm serious, Red. Tell her to be careful. I don't know who's behind all this, but I will find out. When you send a hit man after me, you better make sure he does the job, because I'm coming after you."

"Whoa—you're really pissed off."

"You're damned right I am. Wouldn't you be?" I growled, trying to sound like a tough guy.

My big-talk with Red was just that. I hoped Lucy would signal the big money in Arkansas that if they were supporting this crusade against Jana, they were backing the wrong horse.

It was later than I realized, so I called Ben's to order sandwiches before meeting everyone at Jana's. I looked forward to spending a few minutes with my old friend—I needed a good "settlin'" as my grandmother used to say.

When I opened the screen door, I found Ben sitting at his usual corner table, a cold Budweiser in his hand. I sat down and he pushed a second can in my direction.

"I hear there was a disturbance at City Park last night. You know anything about it?" His chin was wiggling.

"Heard the same thing myself. Funny how word gets around. Any idea what went down?" I grinned.

"I heard some damn fool walked straight into an ambush. Now, who'd be in the park after midnight?" Ben took a pull on his beer.

"I have no idea, but he must be one lucky son of a gun." I was happy to play along.

"You've almost gotten yourself killed twice in what—less than two weeks? No more small talk, Jack. What's going on?"

"Ben, I don't know. It looks like the first time was for revenge, and I guess maybe the second time was, too. But I'm beginning to think both events could be Jana-related. I've got Clovis, Brian, and Big Mike working on it, but so far we've drawn a blank. I need a break. Are you up for a little undercover work?"

"I've already told you how I feel about Dr. Hall. What do you have in mind?"

"Well, given how far Dawg Fletcher's belly hangs over his belt, I bet that sooner or later he'll bring his boys around here for barbeque. When he does, tell him ribs and beer are on the house. Don't worry, I'll pay the bill. Make nice and keep your ears open. You know what they say, 'loose lips sink ships.'"

"You are one sneaky so and so, Jack Patterson, suggesting I eavesdrop on one of my customers. Who do you think I am?"

"I think you're a good friend of Dr. Hall who might hear something that could keep her out of prison. But I'll understand if what I'm asking violates the pitmaster's code of privacy."

He burst out laughing.

"HIPAA for my customers, that's a new one. Someday I'll tell you about a friend of mine who has more money than is good for him, but waits tables and tends bar at the Country Club. Why? Because he listens to his customers talk about takeovers and corporate mergers over their cocktails and martinis. Rich people don't think nuthin' about talking in front of the help. If Fletcher and his staff are stupid enough to talk about their case in a public restaurant, their standards are in question, not mine.

"Ben Jr. will come up with a flyer that'll get them in the restaurant. Probably nothing will come of it except a healthy tab, but you're right. Who knows what a man who tells folks to call him 'Dawg' will say after a few beers and a belly full of ribs?"

"Thanks, Ben. I'm just fishing, putting a lot of lines in the water, hoping something will bite."

"That ain't the way you fish, Jack. I thought I taught you better. It's not about the number of lines in the water. It's where you fish and what's your bait."

The waitress appeared with several sacks of sandwiches, ribs, and all the fixins to take to Jana's. I thanked Ben and hopped into the Suburban, his words ringing in my ears.

It's where you fish and what's your bait.

39

When Jordan and I pulled into Jana's driveway, we found not only Jana and Sam, but also Clovis, Stella, and Brian waiting. Good thing I'd ordered double. I waited until we'd finished lunch before I asked Sam about Judge Purdom.

"Judge William 'Wild Bill' Purdom has no business being on the bench," Sam stated bluntly. "He's never met a business, corporation, or rich executive he doesn't like. He promised to reduce the influence of trial lawyers on the courts, and corporate America filled his campaign coffers with so much money that his competition for the bench dropped like flies. He's also lazy and dumb as a post."

Jana asked, "Why do you call him 'Wild Bill'?"

"Because he carries a six-shooter at all times—under his robes when court is in session, otherwise displayed in a holster for anyone to see. He wears a Stetson, cowboy boots, and that gun everywhere. The man's a caution against open carry laws. He scares the hell out of me."

Great, I thought. *Big guns and a bigger ego, and the brains to support neither.*

"Jana's an attractive woman of means, which he'll like," Sam continued. "But she's a doctor who works with poor people, which he won't. He's no nonsense and short tempered in the courtroom. Unless you're with one of the major law firms, he'll cut you off at the knees in a heartbeat.

"Here's something else: a prosecutor isn't supposed to know which judge he's drawn until the morning of the arraignment. We're still a few days away, and Fletcher's already crowed that Judge Purdom will hear the case. Looks like Fletcher has bypassed the random draw of judges—that doesn't bode well."

"No, it doesn't," I agreed. "Sam, since I can't keep you from knowing everything about the defense, I have another job for you."

"Put me in the game, Coach." He smiled at Jana.

"Fletcher is a real asshole. You know the man. He's already in the driver's seat, but I bet he's got a bag full of dirty tricks. What can I expect? For example, he promised not to seek bail and said he would urge the court to release Jana on her own recognizance."

Jana interrupted. "You told me Fletcher promised no games. Now you think he'll go back on his word?"

"Jana, I don't know. But we need to be prepared if he does, or if he somehow goes around the system." I felt like a heel, but she had to be aware of the possibilities.

"Sam, I also want you to be thinking about a media strategy. I bet Fletcher's got at least a couple of reporters in his back pocket. We could use a strategy to combat his tainting of the jury pool."

"I thought you didn't believe in talking to the press during a pending case."

"I don't, but that doesn't mean I shouldn't have a strategy."

We finished lunch, and Brian and Jordan offered to clean up while we continued our conversation in Jana's den.

"Okay, tell me where we are with the health records," I began.

Brian was looking for any criminal activity that might turn up in the records while Jana searched for unusual patterns of diseases. It was a good start, but it could take weeks or months to find anything significant, and we only had until the end of the week. I encouraged them to keep at it, but doubted they could accomplish much in such a short time.

Sam had gone over almost every detail of the arraignment process with Jana. She seemed resigned but nervous. Who wouldn't be?

I asked about Mimi, and Sam told me she had agreed to meet me this evening at the hotel bar before she left. He and Jana excused themselves and our meeting broke up.

I gave Clovis a wink and a nod, and he and Stella joined me in the kitchen.

"Stella, as usual, your work is top-notch. I've got a couple of other avenues for you to explore, but if you feel uncomfortable, let me know."

She laughed. "Jack, I've broken more privacy laws than the NSA on your behalf. What's up?"

"Well, first, I want you to do another sweep to make sure our conversations and emails remain private."

"That's easy, and even legal. I can check everyone's hardware within the next few hours," she replied.

"Including Sam's."

She raised her eyebrows. "If you say so."

"I do."

"What else?"

"Well, I want to track the cell phone calls of a certain public official. Can you do that without breaking the law? And without his knowledge."

"Are you worried about Sam?" Clovis interrupted.

"No, I'm not worried about Sam." I smiled. "I have an idea that Fletcher may be getting orders from a third party, perhaps the governor."

Clovis allowed himself a low whistle.

"Bugging a cell phone is a piece of cake," Stella replied. "The Feds do it all the time. The trick is not getting caught. And you'll need a subpoena to get the information into evidence. Can you pull that off?"

"If you find what I think you will, I'll get the subpoena."

Clovis asked, "Do you realize what you're suggesting?"

"I do."

"God help us!" he responded, pushing his chair back with a laugh. "If you don't need me, I think I'll take a break."

After Clovis left the room, I asked Stella a question. Her response was immediate.

"No way, not possible." She was adamant, but I knew I had planted the seed in her mind.

I glanced at my watch. I needed to clean up before I met Mimi, but I thought we had time for a quick detour. Motioning to Brian, I asked Jordan if he would mind driving us through the East End. I wanted to see Jana's old clinic.

As a result of either antipathy toward immigrants in the North or Jim Crow laws in the South, most American towns and cities are divided geographically by ethnicity, economics, or both. The "haves" don't live next door to the "have-nots." Who hasn't heard of "the wrong side of the tracks"?

In Little Rock, the East End is east of Interstate 30 and south of the Arkansas River, clear to Granite Mountain. Almost all of its residential inhabitants are African American. Many of the old housing projects have been torn down, and the airport has claimed several pockets of homes, but the recent economic upturn clearly missed this part of town. I couldn't believe we were only a few minutes from the popular River Market and the Clinton Presidential Library. As we drove down Ninth Street, I saw a couple of corner stores and a few homes that were still occupied, but mostly abandoned warehouses and junkyards protected by concertina wire.

We pulled into the parking lot of the clinic, and my heart sank. I knew it would be closed, but the heavy chains across the doors were a depressing sight. I saw a dilapidated basketball court next to the building. Weeds grew up through the concrete and the hoops had no nets, but a few kids were shooting baskets and talking trash.

Jordan objected when I opened the Suburban door, but I hopped out and Brian followed. In a matter of minutes, we were surrounded by a bunch of hostile teenagers.

The tallest of them held a ball inches from my face and demanded, "What you doing here, old man?"

I didn't back down. "I'm Dr. Jana Hall's lawyer. She asked me to check on the clinic. Is that a problem for you?" Jordan had joined Brian.

"Dr. Hall? You're her lawyer?" He tossed the ball to a younger kid on the fringe.

"I am," I answered.

"Well, then maybe you'll tell us. . . ." he began, but was immediately interrupted by other insistent voices.

"What's going on? How is she? When will the clinic reopen? Why does she need a lawyer?"

I realized that these kids and their families had no idea why the clinic had closed. They only knew that chains and locked doors kept them from their only realistic source of healthcare.

I raised an arm to calm them down and said, "Look, guys, I can't tell you the whole thing, but I can tell you that Dr. Hall is in trouble and needs your help."

"What you think we can do? We're just kids with nothin' much to do but shoot hoops." The little kid with the ball kicked it down the court in frustration.

"You can tell me about the clinic," I said firmly. "Did you ever go there? What did Dr. Hall's clinic mean to you and your family?"

Brian and I sat down on a bench near the court and the kids jostled for attention, all talking at once. Word got out, and before long we were hearing stories from young mothers carrying babies as well as the grandmothers who helped take care of them all. They all wanted us to know what Jana and her clinic meant to this neighborhood.

Jordan had relaxed and was taking videos on his iPhone. Brian was taking notes and gathering contact information. Some stories brought me to tears, and I wasn't alone.

It was almost dusk when I had to shut down the conversation. The young man who'd met me with such initial hostility tugged on my shirt sleeve.

"Please tell Dr. Hall we'll do whatever we can to help." I thanked him and he added, "And ask her to please come back and open up her clinic. We need her."

I was pleased to see that Jordan had caught the last exchange on video. I wanted Jana to be able to see and hear these kids when she was overwhelmed by the dark days I knew lay ahead.

Jordan pulled away and we rode back in silence. The stories had touched us all.

As we reached the hotel, Brian asked, "Jack, why would anyone want to close that clinic? I don't get it."

"Brian, that's what we're about to find out."

Jordan murmured, "Count me in to do whatever it takes."

I smiled and asked him to send Stella his videos. Besides giving a copy to Jana, I thought they might come in handy with a jury.

I barely had time to wash up and change shirts before I met Mimi.

When I walked into the crowded bar, I spotted her sitting by herself at a corner table. She had pulled her hair back in a tight ponytail and was wearing a dark blue suit and no makeup. I also noticed the bulge of a firearm under her jacket. It was quite a different look for the woman who I'd first seen in a slinky green dress.

I approached the table, but she didn't get up. It would have been awkward to do anything other than say hello and extend my hand, although I wanted to give a big hug to the woman who saved my life.

I took the chair across from her and asked if she wanted anything to drink.

"No, thank you. I've already ordered a Diet Coke. I'm on duty, and my plane leaves tonight."

I couldn't help but feel disappointed. I had hoped that drinks would lead to dinner, but no such luck. I heard a note of hostility in her voice that I didn't understand. Her early flirting must have been completely an act.

The waiter arrived with her Diet Coke, and I asked for a glass of the house Pinot Noir.

"Jack, I only have a little time. Do you need something specific?"

Again, the hostility. "Well, besides saying thank you over and over, I'd like to know how someone goes about hiring a hitman like Stalinski."

"Why? Is there someone you want taken out?" Her voice betrayed a hint of amusment.

"No, but if I know how someone like Stalinski gets hired, it might give me some insight into the person who hired him and maybe why. I take it you can't do a Google search for a hit man?"

"Not unless you want the FBI knocking on your door. No, the principal probably went through an agent. Most of the good professionals like Stalinski have agents who act as intermediaries to avoid any contact between the principal and the hit man. Or woman, as the case may be."

"But how does one find an intermediary?"

"It's a dirty secret, Jack, but it's all by word of mouth among fixers for people with immense wealth or access to it, like CEOs of international companies. These fixers make sure their clients aren't exposed to the little inconveniences the rest of the world must endure. You've seen movies about fixers who work for companies to make sure the CEO's mistress doesn't tell all, or the CEO's wayward son doesn't go to jail when he's caught for a DWI. You've seen *Michael Clayton,* haven't you?

"Well, take that character in the movie to a higher level—the ultimate risk manager. The fixers I'm talking about do whatever is necessary for their clients or employers, including arranging for inconvenient people to be blackmailed or murdered. They're the ones who know the agents for the Stalinskis and Moiras of this world."

I took a deep breath. "Think Stalinski will roll on his agent or whoever hired him?" I questioned.

"Unlikely. First, his life wouldn't be worth a plug nickel if he did, and second, Stalinski doesn't have any idea who hired him. We don't even think he was hired to kill you. We believe he was here for another reason—the murder of Mace and his crew, and that simply gave him the opportunity to seek revenge. But we aren't sure."

"That's not very reassuring," I said.

"No, it's not. That's why Clovis is still so nervous. We think revenge was Stalinski's motive, but he could have been fulfilling a contract. Watch your back, Jack."

"Why doesn't anyone go after these agents and fixers?"

"Remember for whom they work and what they do. They are very good at making sure their clients are never implicated in wrongdoing. They also know how to take care of themselves. Now and then one of them or one of their clients get reckless, but it's rare."

I had learned a lot, but I wasn't sure how helpful it was. I made one last attempt.

"Any chance I can convince you to stay another day and have dinner tonight?"

She at least smiled.

"I would like that. I really would. You seem like a decent fellow, someone I might like to get to know, but right now there's about a ninety percent chance that someone in this bar is watching every move you and I make. Why do you think I'm wearing this God-awful blue suit with my hair pulled so tight it's giving me a headache? I look awful with no lipstick or makeup. I'm surprised you're still interested.

"Trust me—until I get Stalinski to Brussels, and we get whatever information we can out of him, this meeting needs to look like a total pain in the ass."

"Don't you think you're a little paranoid?" I protested.

"Probably, but it's based on experience."

"Will I ever get to give you proper thanks or see you outside business?"

"There are direct flights from Dulles to Brussels every day."

She stood, extended her hand, looked quickly around the bar, and said in a clear voice, "Good luck Mr. Patterson. I hope I've answered all your questions."

40

I WOKE UP HUNGRY AS A BEAR and anxious about the impending appointment with Fletcher's deputy, Ray Spears. We would finally learn the details of the charges against Jana. I checked my phone and found a text informing me that the ten o'clock meeting had been rescheduled for two o'clock. The late notice was irritating, but I was also relieved. Now we would have plenty of time to plan the day's events. I texted the change to Sam, asking if he had time for lunch.

Clovis and Brian were waiting. I told myself that I would need extra energy today, justifying a breakfast of raspberry-walnut pancakes and country sausage. Brian seemed satisfied with a granola and yogurt combination, while Clovis sipped on black coffee.

I told them about the change in schedule and asked for a progress report. Clovis said nothing. I looked to Brian.

"Both Dr. Hall and I worked on the patients' files after you left. I found no evidence of criminal conduct, and she found nothing remotely unusual. Stella told me to tell you she has the files well organized and will spend the day working on the new projects you gave her."

"Tell Dr. Hall to shift her focus away from the Little Rock clinic for the next few days and concentrate on the other three clinics," I responded. "Spears is supposed to tell me what she'll be charged with at our meeting this afternoon. I had hoped to get ahead of the game if you spotted anything amiss, but it was always a long shot. Until we get the indictment and analyze the charges, I've got a different project in mind. You game?" I asked Brian.

"Of course," he answered.

"Stella is using her considerable skills to gain access to the cell phone records of certain public officials such as Brady Flowers and Fletcher. In case she's unsuccessful, there's another way to skin this cat: the Freedom of Information Act. You'll need to be creative. I don't want to set off any alarms, and using the FOIA is a public process."

"You want me to ask for the cell phone records of Brady Flowers and Fletcher without setting off alarms?" His mouth dropped open, and I caught the wisp of a memory—my grandmother's warning about flies.

"Yes, and not just those two. I've made a list of public officials whose cell phone records I want for the last six months." I handed him a page from my yellow pad.

He looked at my list in disbelief and handed it to Clovis. "What are you looking for, Jack?" Clovis asked.

"A common denominator, one person who's had recent conversations with Brady, Fletcher, and the others. Last night, Mimi gave me a rundown on fixers and how they operate. I think we're looking for a high-level fixer, a kind of risk manager."

"Do you think public officials would take calls from that kind of person on an official cell phone? Or even their personal phone for that matter?"

"Clovis, neither you nor I would be so foolish—you're in the business and you've taught me better. But think about it—why would any of those folks worry about calls from someone they know, someone they trust? Didn't several college basketball coaches lose their jobs because they used their school cell phone to call and text women who weren't their spouses? The Freedom of Information Act is a great tool because public officials seldom stop to think the act applies to them. I want to use every tool we have to our advantage, and Arkansas has one of the broadest sunshine legislation in the country.

"Anything we learn from Stella's cyber snooping will be helpful, but it won't be admissible in court. I want to use FOIA if Brian can manage it quietly. If neither works, I can think of at least one other way to get the information we need."

"And that would be…?" Brian asked.

"A subpoena," I answered.

"Jack, there's no way Purdom will issue the subpoena you want in Dr. Hall's case. He's not about to let you go fishing into Fletcher's records just because he's prosecuting her," Clovis responded. "Mind if I work with Brian, and we coordinate with Stella? I have a few thoughts."

"I was counting on it," I said, smiling.

Our conversation turned to logistics and who would join me for the Spears meeting. I had counted on Brian's company, but now I wanted him to work on the projects I'd given him. We decided Jordan would drive and Clovis would come to the special prosecutor's office. I trusted his level head and figured I might need him to run interference with the press.

I returned to my room to catch up with my other life. Over the years I've learned to compartmentalize, but an indictment or a major court appearance is hard to put in a box. It was impossible to concentrate on anything else.

Fortunately I'd made a few random notes while we were talking. I decided to call Tucker Bowie first, but he was out so I left a message. I tried to reach Beth, but again had to be content with a message. I turned to my computer. Maggie had emailed that she and Walter would be back in the states soon. Next on the list was Rose, our office assistant. I told her I wouldn't be available for a few days, and no, I wasn't sure how long I'd be away. I spent the rest of the morning responding to emails from lawyers and clients, asking to reschedule meetings and calls.

Time got away from me, and before I knew it Sam texted that he was waiting in the lobby. We'd already decided to eat elsewhere. Clovis had told me that Micki was meeting Brady Flowers for lunch in the main dining room. I was tempted to sneak a peek, but decided the last thing I needed right now was to piss off Micki.

We walked up Main Street to the Soul Fish Café and ordered hushpuppies and fried catfish. Sam was fidgety and out of sorts. I told him to relax—things would work out.

"That's easy for you to say. I tell you, Jack, I'm not sure I can spend one more day as a prosecutor. Seeing the reality of the other side of the judicial system tears me up. I can't help but worry that Jana might end up in prison. This case has opened my eyes to the pain I cause every day."

"You don't cause the pain," I responded. "But the pain is real. Jana's situation has given you insight into the misery of those close to the offender. Don't resign. Use what you have learned to do things differently. Think of it as an opportunity."

"That's horseshit! Some bastard is trying to destroy Jana. I don't want to think of it as an opportunity—I want to punch him in the nose."

Sam was in no mood to be lectured, and I didn't blame him. Who was I to preach to Sam Pagano?

"Okay, I can't say I blame you. But please don't resign, because I might need you to be the district's prosecutor."

"You going to ket me know what you have in mind?" he asked, still irritated.

"I'd rather not, because I hope I never need you. But please don't resign, and don't let Kate resign either. Let's leave it at that."

He played with his silverware. I was surprised to see his face suddenly change, slipping into his politician's mask. I turned to see a man in a well-cut, dark suit approaching our table, hand already extended. He appeared to be about forty-five, fair hair beginning to thin, with the tanned face of a golfer or tennis player. He walked with an easy gait, and I guessed he could be a lawyer or a bank exec.

"Hey, Sam, good to see you," he said with an easy smile. Sam stood to shake his hand. Turning to me, the man said, "And this must be the famous Jack Patterson."

Sam took the initiative. "Jack, this is Roy Pence. He's a friend of Kristine, Kristine White."

Without missing a beat, Roy gave me a friendly pat on the shoulder, said he was late for a meeting, and walked toward the front door.

Looking amused, Sam said, "Looks like your secret's out. Roy Pence moved here a few years ago. I'm not sure what he does, but he sure knows the right people, got himself appointed to a couple of local boards, and is at every political event regardless of party. Kristine was always trying to get us to socialize, but he's not my type—a little too slick for my taste. He ended up supporting my opponent, but every time I run into him he acts like I'm his best friend."

The server appeared with enormous plates of catfish and hushpuppies, along with the requisite green beans and french fries. The fish was hot and crispy, almost as good as the hole-in-the-wall places I remembered going to as a kid.

"Did you give any thought to what tricks you might play if you were an unethical prosecutor?" I asked between mouthfuls.

"I did. You've already brought up one possibility—Fletcher could go back on his word regarding bail," Sam replied.

"I'll raise that issue with Spears, but I don't think he will. Fletcher made a big deal about it the first time." *But we should prepare Jana for that possibility anyway,* I thought glumly.

"I feel sure Fletcher will leak the indictment to the press, and give the specifics to a couple of select reporters—off the record, of course," Sam continued. "The press will compare Jana to Jack the Ripper or worse. We've already talked about it. I think she'll be okay."

"I hope so, but it will be tough for both of you. For all I know, they could charge her with swimming in the reservoir. There's bound to be a lag between the indictment and whatever we say to counter the charges. Don't either one of you watch TV or listen to the news. Turn the news off."

"We'll be okay. I'm more worried about Judge Purdom. I'd bet my last dollar that that he and Fletcher have already had a few *ex parte* conversations. You'll face a hostile bench tomorrow."

"That seems to be par for the course in Little Rock," I laughed. "Tell you what—let me deal with Fletcher and the judge. I've had plenty of experience with prosecutorial overreach and judicial hostility. You make sure Jana's prepared for the indignities of the booking process. I sure hope the bailiff won't get carried away. Tonight will be tough enough. Jana doesn't think she's ever broken the law. She will be devastated when she reads the indictment. I'm counting on you to be upbeat and to keep her focused."

Sam seemed relieved, "Don't worry, we'll be able to rebut whatever Fletcher has dreamed up. Jana Hall is not a criminal. Of that I am sure."

The busboy came to clear our plates, and the server brought us the quintessential Southern diner dessert: banana pudding. As we dug in, it occurred to me that Sam was about to get a rude awakening.

41

I COULD HEAR MY CELL PHONE VIBRATING before I opened the door to my hotel room. Why did I continue to leave it behind? The text from Clovis said he would pick me up in less than an hour, and I saw that Beth had called. I punched in her number immediately, not bothering to listen to her message.

"Beth, I'm sorry—I was having lunch with Sam when you called. Did Jeff find anything?" I felt sure he hadn't.

"Well, actually, he did. In fact, he's been working on it around the clock. Can he call Dr. Hall to explain what he's found?"

"Of course!" I gave her Jana's number. "What did he find?"

"I honestly can't tell you. He tried to explain, but he left me at first base with medical jargon. Listen Dad, I've got a class in a few minutes, and I want to text him Dr. Hall's number. Let's talk soon."

The brevity of our conversation wasn't surprising—that Jeff had found something irregular was. I texted Jana to expect Jeff's call, daring to think we might have caught a break.

I donned a coat and tie. Unnecessary, but I admit my lawyer's uniform gave me a certain confidence. I packed up my laptop, cell phone, and trusty yellow legal pad in the old briefcase Angie had given me years ago. Clovis was waiting in the lobby. His sport coat concealed a shoulder holster and weapon—a tie would have been superfluous.

"You clean up pretty well," he kidded. "How was lunch?"

"The catfish was terrific, but Sam couldn't have been more nervous if he were the defendant," I answered.

"You okay?" he asked as we walked into the sunlight.

"I'll feel a lot better when I know what we're up against."

"Think so?" he said as he opened the door to the Suburban. Sally was in in the driver's seat—Jordan sat next to her. Clovis followed me into the back seat.

"Extra precaution?" I asked, wondering if I'd ever sit in the front seat of a car again.

"Mimi called from Brussels as soon as they landed. Stalinski remains silent, but information gleaned from websites monitored by Interpol suggests there's a search on for someone to complete a contract in Little Rock."

"Great," I muttered.

I had thought about asking Maggie to come to Little Rock now that Stalinski had been caught, but with the possibility of a new killer on the loose, not a chance. We rode in silence, well aware the next twenty-four hours would be as tough as they come.

A nondescript five-story building in west Little Rock housed the special prosecutor's office. We tried to be nonchalant, but getting into the building wasn't easy. Security freaked when Clovis pulled out his firearm before he went through the scanner. He ended up checking the gun much like a hat—they gave him a numbered claim check. They scanned my briefcase several times, and we were subjected to wand searches.

Security led us to an empty, no-frills conference room—no coffee, no water, and no pastries. We were left to cool our heels for a good long time. I was about to walk out when Spears strode in, followed by a fellow he introduced as Baldwin. Clovis and I both rose.

"Sorry to keep you waiting," Spears said. I noticed he'd brought nothing with him, not even a legal pad, nor had Baldwin.

"No problem." I answered. "What have you got for me?"

Spears looked puzzled. "For you? I thought you would be ready to talk about the plea deal. Am I wrong?"

"You are. Both the state's auditors and the Pulaski County Prosecutor's Office have exonerated Dr. Hall. I don't know why you think she committed a crime. Until I've seen an indictment, I can't recommend that she plead guilty to a parking ticket, much less to a felony and two years in jail."

"Does that mean we need to arrest your client before the arraignment?"

"I didn't say that. She will appear tomorrow at ten. But you said you would give me a copy of the indictment this afternoon, and that after I went over it with my client, there would be an opportunity to discuss a plea. Has that changed?"

"Somewhat. The plea offer is good until the arraignment, but we are still polishing the indictment. I don't have it. I can give you an idea of the charges against your client, but Dawg has said no one gets a copy until tomorrow."

"What changed?"

"Well, playing cute at Dr. Hall's home didn't help. We know you have her computers and copies of the clinics' records. If you turn those over we might be more accommodating. But the real reason is the more we investigate, the more expansive the indictment becomes."

I ignored the threat to expand the charges. "There was no reason for an early morning raid. The items you want will be produced during discovery. What's the rush?"

"The records belong to the Department of Health. Until you return the originals and all copies, there will be no cooperation."

"Understood. I'll talk to my client." We were all still standing, and he looked uncomfortable. Baldwin hadn't made a peep.

The silence lingered, and I said, "Um, perhaps we should sit down?"

Spears started, pulled out a chair, and said, "I'm sorry."

I waited until everyone was comfortable before continuing. "Thank you. What can you tell me about the indictment?"

"Dr. Hall was the supervising physician at the Little Rock clinic. She either performed every major procedure, or supervised the doctors and nurses who performed the procedures or treated the diseases. She performed abortions that violated state law. The East End clinic treated patients for diseases or injuries, but failed in some instances to notify law enforcement as required by law. Minors received treatments without parental consent. Each of these offenses carries a maximum penalty of ten years. When you remind her of these crimes, she will surely realize she should take the deal." He had worked himself into quite a little fervor. Baldwin nodded like a silent parrot over his shoulder.

Such charges had nothing to do with record keeping or anything the Health Department had asked the state auditors or Sam's office to examine. Someone had gone through every patient's file looking for a crime committed by a nurse or doctor. As the supervising doctor, they could charge Jana as a conspirator for each illegal procedure or treatment.

"Will you charge other doctors or employees as well?" I asked, trying to remain calm.

"I'm glad you asked," Spears answered. "For the time being, we've limited the charges to Dr. Hall, but you never know—Dawg could change his mind. It's something for your client to consider. If she returns all the files and pleads guilty, I think we'll feel our office has done its job. It would be up to the local prosecutor to proceed against anyone else. But, like I said, you never know."

Great. Jana rolls over or Fletcher goes after her friends and colleagues. Another version of 'spill the beans, whether you have them or not, or we'll charge your wife and kids.' The squeeze was on.

"Could you give me a draft of the indictment as it stands now? If Dr. Hall can see the names of the patients, we can identify the circumstances and the treatments. At that point, she can make an informed decision."

"Sorry. Dawg is adamant. No one sees the indictment until it's final—won't be until tomorrow."

I'd bet my mother's favorite cat that select members of the press were already poring over it.

Spears continued, "Nothing in the indictment should surprise Dr. Hall. She'll remember the abortions and the minors."

I was about ready to smack him, but felt a nudge from Clovis and gained control. I had one more question before we could leave.

"Okay, since the situation has changed, I take it you will ask Dr. Hall to post bond. How much do you have in mind?"

"Oh, no. Dawg gave his word. We have no intention of asking her to post bond," Spears replied, giving Baldwin a sideways glance.

"Anything else we should know?" I asked. This guy was about as trustworthy as a snake.

"Well, yes. Judge Purdom's clerk has asked us to meet in his chambers at nine-thirty. The judge wants to make sure everything goes smoothly in open court. He's a stickler for no surprises."

Clovis produced the claim check for his gun and holster, and we left the building in silence. At least there were no reporters waiting outside. He knew me well enough not to interrupt as I gathered my thoughts on the way to Jana's.

The outlook wasn't good. Jana faced charges for allegedly criminal events at the Little Rock clinic, and if she didn't take the fall, her colleagues would be charged. Without the specifics of the charges, I had no idea whether any actual criminal conduct had occurred, but I knew that with a team of prosecutors and law enforcement agents poring over the records, no doctor was immune from prosecution.

That said, had Jana violated the law? I couldn't imagine Jana skirting Arkansas's abortion laws, but then again politicians are always trying to push the envelope regarding a woman's right to privacy. I had no idea what was legal and what wasn't these days. What if what was best for the patient conflicted with the law?

A second problem was Spears's reference to conspiracy. What if another doctor or nurse had done something illegal? Because Jana was the supervising physician, she could get caught up in the net prosecutors call conspiracy. Criminal conspiracy doesn't take much to prove: one predicate act and implied consent. These days if someone helps an old lady across the street a creative prosecutor could construe it as a conspiracy to commit jaywalking. One thing was certain: the case against Jana had nothing to do with sloppy record keeping in Mena, Arkansas.

Sam's car was the only one in the driveway when we pulled up. Maybe Fletcher hadn't leaked the indictment after all. I was about to hop out of the car when Clovis stopped me.

"Stay here for a few minutes, Jack." I noticed Jordan had pulled out his weapon. He remained in the car while Clovis walked toward the house.

"What's going on?" I asked Jordan.

"Mimi's warning has Clovis on edge. He's not taking any chances."

I was sick and tired of all this protection. Then again, I was still alive because of Clovis's diligence. *I should be be more patient.*

Clovis returned with the "all clear." Jana, Sam, Stella, and Brian were sitting at the kitchen table when we walked in. I wasted no time in giving them the bad news.

"I don't have the indictment. Fletcher reneged, refused to turn it over. Spears said the charges are evolving as they review more records, but he did give me a summary."

No one seemed surprised or offered a response, so I continued.

"The alleged crimes fall into three categories. First, they say abortions were performed in violation of state law. Second, they claim the Little Rock clinic treated certain injuries and diseases that weren't properly reported to law enforcement. Third, they allege that minors were treated without parental consent. I'm sure there are explanations for each instance, but we are flying blind until we can identify the specific patients. Jana, he said you performed the abortions. Let's begin there."

Sam reacted in frustration. "Jana must have treated thousands of patients. It's unfair to ask her to remember every patient she ever treated."

Jana placed her hand on top of his and asked, "How would they present such a charge in court?"

"I don't know a lot about Arkansas abortion law except that it's very restrictive, but both Brian and I are about to become experts. My guess is they would introduce into evidence the medical records of the abortion and ask the patient to testify about her treatment."

"So the name of the patient would become public?" she persisted.

"Not at first. They would probably use an alias in the indictment, but once an individual patient testifies, I don't see how we could protect her privacy. What are you worried about? If Fletcher zeroes in on specific cases, we'll simply explain what happened in each case. I take it you performed abortions?"

"Only twice, and yes, I'd do them again."

"Sounds like you know where Fletcher is headed," I suggested.

"I've been thinking of little else. Fletcher told you I knew what I did. I've been racking my brain to think what I might have done wrong at the Little Rock clinic. It came to me as I focused my attention on the patients' records. You knew what was coming, didn't you, Jack?"

"No, but I knew they had to have more than billing errors."

"Right. Well, let's talk about the two abortions first. I don't normally perform abortions, and the clinic doctors are very careful to obey the law when they are necessary. No doctor enjoys the procedure, which is almost always one of last resort. But twice in the last twenty years we have faced the dilemma every doctor dreads: violate the law, or watch a patient die." Brian handed her a glass of water, and she paused to take a few sips.

"I'll try not to get too technical. When a woman gets pregnant certain hormone levels rise. If at the same time she suffers from a growing cancer, those hormones will cause the cancer cells to grow much more rapidly. Without an abortion, the patient will die of cancer long before the baby comes to term."

Sam interrupted. "So, you had to abort the pregnancy to save the patient's life. No jury would convict you. I can't believe Fletcher would try."

Jana smiled at him. "As it happened, neither of these women came to us until much later than allowed by Arkansas law. They were both young, professional women who knew they had cancer and understood the complications presented by pregnancy. Their time was up—they were out of options. I was certain these women wouldn't live unless I broke the law. I couldn't ask one of my doctors to take the risk, so I did."

It was a lot to take in. Not for the first time I wondered why the government pushed itself into personal decisions. Never mind the moral issues surrounding unwanted pregnancies and unwanted children. Surely such difficult decisions should be made by those affected: the patient, her physician, and her family.

Yes, a jury would have a hard time convicting Jana, but something told me there was more to the story. I waited for the other shoe to drop.

"Both women are alive and in good health, their cancer in remission. But here's the problem. Both women grew up in strict religious households. One was a Catholic, and the other's family belonged to a dogmatic conservative sect. At the time they became pregnant, neither woman was married. Their choice to end their pregnancies was hard enough. I promised each of them I would never tell a soul about their abortions."

Sam was on his feet—he couldn't help himself. "Jana, circumstances have changed. They'll understand. Once they know you need their help, they're bound to understand."

She gave him a look that would have curdled milk, and he sank back into his chair. "Jack, I told them what I was doing was illegal. I'm not sure they understood the legalities, but I'm sure they understood what I promised. I will take Fletcher's deal unless you can assure me they won't have to testify."

42

No one said a word—even Sam looked defeated. Jana's motives were commendable, but I couldn't let her quit without a fight. I had to buy time.

"Jana, I understand how much you care about your patients. You're right to protect their privacy. Until I see the actual indictment, understand the charges, and do a great deal of research, I can't give you good advice. Please give me a chance. Please don't quit. Your work was important, your clinics were important, and they can be again. The rights of your patients are equally as important. Don't give up on any of them."

I cleared my throat and continued. "Please don't plead guilty tomorrow. Fletcher won't withdraw his plea offer—nothing would make him happier than to avoid a trial. Give me time to figure out how to protect both you and your patients. I believe in you—don't give up on me."

Sam raised his eyebrows, and Clovis got up to fool with the coffee maker.

"Jack, I have no intention of giving up on you, but I will not go back on my promise. If you can't keep the identity of those patients out of the public record, I will go to jail. I didn't save their lives to have an asshole like Fletcher destroy them."

"I hear you loud and clear."

"Well, I don't," said Sam. "There's no way those two women want you to go to jail."

"You're right." Jana faced him. "Those women would probably do anything for me. I'm not naïve, Sam. I know what happens in prison.

I have plans for my future. But how could I enjoy that life if I threw those women under the bus? I took an oath to do no harm. That includes violating a patient's right to privacy."

Sam remained silent.

She continued, "I understand the concern about treating minors without parental consent. But think about our clinics. We treated parents who could barely rub two nickels together, much less get their kids vaccinated. We treated young women who are sex slaves, children who don't know who or where their parents are, and women and children who are victims of family abuse. We treated the everyday illnesses of people who live on the streets, or in places worse than an underpass or a temporary shelter, places well-meaning people don't talk about in their fundraising letters.

"I instructed my doctors and staff to report to the authorities when required unless such a report would put the patient at risk. The same goes for parental consent. We got it when we could, but sometimes that's either impossible or dangerous. When a crack-addicted mother's boyfriend rapes and beats a young girl, who would you ask to sign the form consenting to treatment?

"The indictment won't accuse us of giving a flu shot to a minor from west Little Rock without her mother's permission. Each case will involve a situation that most folks don't want to know about. It's not unusual for a young girl in the East End to contract a sexually transmitted disease from her stepfather or her mother's boyfriend. What do you think happens to the child or the mother if we report this to the authorities? And guess what? These girls aren't always black or immigrant or poor. Sometimes they're middle class white kids caught in a situation they can't handle. They're terrified, and they have nowhere else to go. I thank God for the relatives, teachers, and social workers who point them in our direction. At our clinics, we put the patient first. Reporting and consent forms are secondary."

Sam looked up. "But you didn't personally treat these kids, right?"

"That's true, but we still have the confidentiality issue. I can't let either a patient or a physician go through the ordeal of having to explain in public why we didn't get the consent or report the disease to authorities," Jana said.

"I hate to make matters worse," I interrupted. "Even if Jana wasn't the physician of record, she supervised the clinic. She insisted that her doctors put the patient first. Spears mentioned several conspiracy counts. He threatened to indict staff and other doctors if Jana doesn't agree to the plea."

"No!" Jana exclaimed, her eyes filling with tears. "That does it. I can't let that happen."

I sensed I was about to lose control of the situation.

"Jana, listen to me," I said. "I won't let that happen, I promise. Prosecutors make threats all the time. They'll threaten to indict spouses, children, even the family dog if it will get their target to cooperate or plead guilty. Trust me—I know what I'm doing. Doesn't a doctor tell the patient the worst before they lay out the treatment plan? Now that I've laid out the worst, let's talk about the treatment."

Jana smiled for the first time. "Okay, Doc, but let's take a little break first. I'll be back in a few minutes. Sam, why don't you get us something to drink? Jack's treatment might call for a little scotch."

I gave Stella a quick glance, and she followed Jana from the room.

After Clovis and Sam left, Brian turned to me and said, "Can't identify the patients, and can't implicate the doctors or the staff. You're going into the ring with both hands tied behind your back."

"Right on all counts," I admitted. "I didn't expect the client confidentiality issue, but first thing's first. We need to get through the arraignment without Jana pleading guilty, and then you and I will hit the books. It's tempting to think success depends on our innate abilities. But any lawyer worth their salt knows the solution to most problems exists in two hundred years of case law. A little luck helps, too."

Clovis and Sam returned with a tray of drinks, and Jana and Stella followed. I waited until they settled down.

"Jana, the press will be outside your door tomorrow morning. Clovis's people will help you run their gauntlet. Please don't say a word no matter what they say. Sam, that goes for you, too. Someone will surely try to push your buttons. Ignore them."

"Jack, I've held maybe a hundred more press conferences than you. I know how to deal with the press."

"I know, but humor me. Those press conferences were part of your job. This time you're a spectator in a case aginst someone you care about. It's different," I replied.

"I hear you, and will behave," he replied with a scowl. "The sheriff has arranged for Jana to sign the paperwork and go through the booking process before arraignment. We should be able to walk out of the courtroom after the proceedings."

"I hope so," I replied. "But don't get too confident. I have a feeling Fletcher has a few cards he hasn't played. Don't plan anything for the rest of the day. We'll reconvene at Tucker's after court and lay out a plan for the next month. Jana, you will be frustrated by how long the process takes. I can't see a trial before late fall or next year. We'll have plenty of time to figure out the state's underlying motivation."

"It won't take long if I plead guilty. Two years isn't forever. The clinics are already closed," she sighed.

"Don't talk like that," Sam said.

I interrupted. "Jana, I've promised that I'll figure out a way to avoid breaching doctor-patient confidences or exposing your colleagues. Right now, the only goal is to make it through tomorrow. Let's not get caught up looking too far ahead.

"Speaking of tomorrow. Sam, I take it you'll be in the courtroom?"

"Wild horses couldn't keep me away," he answered.

"Good. But do me a favor. If anyone asks why you're there, I want you to say you're on official business and leave it at that."

"I thought you didn't want me speaking to the press."

"I don't. But if either Fletcher or the court should ask, your answer should be 'official business.' In fact, it would be helpful if Kate Erwin spoke for the office."

"Kate? I'm sure she'll be glad to come, but what's going on in that devious mind of yours?" He looked unhappy, and I could tell Jana wanted an explanation.

"Nothing to get worried about. Look, we're all tired and tomorrow will be a big day, so have a good dinner and get a good night's sleep. Jana, have you heard from Jeff?"

"Yes, he called earlier this morning. He said he didn't have time to explain, but he had asked Stella to email him files from the Delta clinic. His heart's in the right place, but I doubt he found anything."

43

I NEVER SLEEP WELL the night before a court appearance. I toss and turn, envisioning outlandish courtroom possibilities. Tonight my outlandish worries were actually realistic: a judge who carried a six-shooter under his robe, a skittish client, and whatever tricks Fletcher might be ready to play.

Clovis and I met in the coffee shop early the next morning. For once, we were both content with coffee and toast.

"Nervous?" he asked.

"I shouldn't be, but I am. It's only an arraignment. I have a bad feeling about today."

He nodded in agreement, adding that Sam and Jana were on their way to the courthouse to get the preliminaries out of the way. Sam had a bit of good news: no reporters at Jana's this morning. I knew we wouldn't be so lucky at the courthouse. I noticed there was no mention of either the indictment or arraignment in the morning paper.

We avoided any more discussion about the case, choosing instead to discuss the wisdom of the Lobos' drafting the Razorbacks' offensive left tackle in the first round of the NFL draft. I ran upstairs to change into my courtroom uniform, a dark but well-worn suit. A lawyer who looks too well-dressed can turn off a judge or juror.

Within a matter of minutes, Brian and I were climbing the weathered marble steps up to the third floor of the Pulaski County Courthouse. As is my habit, I was early, and we found Judge Purdom's courtroom empty. We waited near the door, enjoying the atmosphere of the old building. It wasn't long before a very short woman approached carrying a tray of glasses and a water pitcher. I jumped up to help her with the heavy doors.

"You must be Mr. Patterson?" she asked as she put the tray down on a table.

"I am."

She extended her hand. "Well, thank you. I'm Candy Polk, the court reporter. The judge should be along shortly. Anything I can do for you?"

I smiled. "No, I like to get to court early. It gives me a few minutes to get comfortable with the surroundings."

She returned the smile. "Don't get too comfortable—Judge Purdom runs a tight ship. Can I give you some advice?"

"Sure—I'm the new kid on the block," I responded.

"Judge Purdom is old school. Make sure you ask permission to approach the bench, stand when he enters the courtroom, and don't sit down until he gives you permission. After he tells everyone to be seated, make sure you remain in your chair, even when you question witnesses or answer his questions."

"Thanks," I said. "I'll try to remember." I introduced her to Brian.

"Nice to meet you," she said. "I know Mr. Patterson is licensed in Arkansas. The judge has already checked the status of his license. Mr. Patterson will have to move your admission before you can speak to the court or examine a witness."

"I'm not a lawyer. I'm a paralegal," Brian responded.

"Oh dear," she said.

"What's wrong?" I asked.

"Well, it's a good thing you told me. Judge Purdom doesn't allow non-lawyers to sit inside the rail. He would have a hissy fit."

I was tempted to object to Purdom's old-fashioned ways, but I decided not to argue.

"Brian will sit on the front row. Can he hand me documents?"

"Well, yes, that should work. Just remember to ask permission. It's a good rule of thumb to always ask permission first. I'll give you the high sign when you cross the line." She winked and left the room.

Brian moved his papers to the row right behind the short rail that separates the lawyer's tables from the gallery.

"It's probably not a good idea to join you in chambers," he deadpanned.

"Probably not," I agreed.

I wondered if I might have responded differently if he had been Maggie. After I left DOJ, I hadn't tried a case without Maggie sitting beside me.

We continued to talk about nothing. I could see he was nervous, and now, so was I. It was almost ten o'clock—where was Fletcher? I was fuming when I saw the door open a crack. Candy's face appeared, followed by a wagging finger. I told Brian to sit tight and obeyed her summons.

The judge's chambers were an expansive set of rooms connected by tall doors. I couldn't help but notice an old-fashioned coat rack standing behind the judge's desk. Hanging from the rack was a belt that held a pearl-handled six-shooter in a leather holster. Each loop on the belt held a bullet, like the ones bandits carried in bad Westerns. The bathroom door was wide open, and I could see a tall dark-haired woman applying red lipstick. I wondered when John Wayne would show.

Dawg Fletcher and Ray Spears were sitting at a table in the corner of the room with a man in a cowboy hat who I figured had to be Judge Purdom. He was sure no John Wayne. Fletcher was smoking a cigar, looking like he'd just brought the herd home.

"Join us, Mr. Patterson. Pay no attention to Doris, she's primping."

So now the woman in the bathroom had a name. I would later find out that Doris served the judge not only as his clerk, but also in a personal capacity. Sam would warn me not to get on her bad side.

I took the empty chair at the table and waited. We might have been old friends about to deal a hand of poker.

Purdom spoke with a drawl. "I expect this morning to be straightforward. I'll ask if you waive the reading of the indictment, you'll say yes. I'll ask how your client pleads to the charges, you'll say guilty. I'll ask your client a few questions about whether she understands the consequences, she'll say she does. Then I'll release her into your custody until sentencing."

Fletcher and Spears were grinning. The wagons had circled, and per the script, the Indians would lose. Trying to curb my temper, I turned to Purdom.

"Your Honor, there's been a misunderstanding. I have yet to see the indictment. I can't waive its reading until I've seen it."

Fletcher interrupted. "Sorry—I guess your boy forgot to pick it up." He shoved a multi-page document across the table. I ignored him.

"My client is not about to enter a plea of guilty to charges she hasn't seen. Whatever the charges, my client will plead not guilty."

Judge Purdom shot Fletcher a glance and said, "Well, you can't instruct your client if you haven't read the indictment. That's understandable. Take your time, read the charges, and if there are no surprises, we can proceed as I outlined."

"Judge, I will read the pleading as you suggest, and if there are no surprises, I'll waive its reading in open court. But let me be clear about one thing: surprise or no surprise, Dr. Hall will plead not guilty."

I didn't like hearing him mutter, "Then your client's a damn fool."

"Pardon me, Judge. I didn't catch what you said."

"I didn't say a damn thing," he growled, then shouted, "Candy, get your ass in here. This conversation is going on the record."

Candy came hustling into the room with her steno machine. She barely had time to sit down before Purdom began.

"We are in chambers in the matter of the State of Arkansas versus Dr. Jana Hall, case number 2019-73. Representing the state are Reuben Fletcher and Raymond Spears. Representing Dr. Hall is Jack Patterson from Washington, DC. Mr. Fletcher has presented Mr. Patterson with a grand jury indictment alleging that his client committed various crimes against the state of Arkansas. I will afford Mr. Patterson all the time he needs to review the indictment and decide whether his client desires to waive its reading in open court."

He gave me a dirty look.

"That's it for now, Candy. The next thing I have to say to Mr. Patterson is off the record." She rose and hurried out, tossing me what I hoped was a sympathetic smile as she closed the door. Purdom turned his glare on me.

"Mr. Patterson, the court knows of your shenanigans in the Cole and Stewart cases. Your reputation for disrespecting courtroom decorum precedes you. Let me assure you I won't stand for any such antics in my courtroom. Do you understand?"

I didn't, but answered, "Yes, Your Honor."

"Good. I guess you've got your own reasons for representing Dr. Hall, but if I were you I'd try to convince her not to waste this court's time or yours."

I took a deep breath. Fletcher's smarmy grin made it obvious that he and Purdom were in cahoots. Wondering what the next scene would bring, I plucked the indictment from the table and returned to the courtroom.

I handed the sheaf of papers to Brian, who was trying to calm an obviously angry Sam. "See if there are any surprises in this."

I turned to Sam. "What's wrong? Where's Jana?"

"We went through the fingerprinting, filled out the forms, everything. We were in the sheriff's office. A sergeant had just brought us coffee when the court's bailiff and two troopers barged in and insisted that Jana come with them. I wanted to pitch a fit, but I knew better. Jana was scared to death, but she left with them. Problem is, I have no idea where they took her. I've been all over the courthouse, and no one's talking."

Brian was reading the indictment, and I noticed that Kate Erwin was sitting next to him. She looked more than a little uncomfortable.

"Hello, Kate. Good to see you."

She rose. "You want to tell me why I'm here?"

"Our little get-together in chambers was unusual, to say the least. I'll tell you what happened when I can, but for now I want Fletcher and his toadies to see us huddling as if we're up to no good." Fletcher, Spears, and several assistants were taking their places in the courtroom.

"Are we up to no good?" Kate asked with a grin.

"We are the last chance good has."

44

"OYEZ, OYEZ, this honorable court is now in session, the Honorable Judge William Purdom presiding. Draw near and give attention, for the court is now in session. God save the United States and this honorable court!" Making this statement was every bailiff's proudest moment.

Purdom strode into the courtroom wearing his robes, but without his cowboy hat. The bulge at his waist left us with no doubt that he was packing. I stood at the defense counsel table by my lonesome. Jana was nowhere to be seen.

"Gentlemen, please be seated," Purdom began. "We are here on the matter of the State of Arkansas versus Dr. Jana Hall. Bailiff, bring in the defendant."

The bailiff opened a side door and two large men escorted Jana to the table where I sat. My heart turned over. They had dressed her in a bright orange jumpsuit, her ankles and wrists were shackled, and she wore prison issue flip-flops. Someone had washed her hair, and it remained wet and uncombed. I rose to object, but sat down when I caught Candy's silent warning.

"Permission to address the court, Your Honor."

"Yes, Mr. Patterson."

"Your Honor, I must object. Dr. Hall is a respected member of this community. She reported this morning of her own free will in civilian clothing. She has not yet been arraigned. Why is she restrained and dressed in prison clothing?"

"Mr. Patterson, you're not from these parts," he noted with exaggerated patience. "I've allowed too many criminals to appear in this court unrestrained and in street clothes only to find they presented a danger to court personnel. I've adopted a policy that at their first appearance, all criminals are searched, outfitted in jumpsuits, and restrained until I've evaluated their risk."

"May I inquire why she was given a shower?"

"You'd be surprised how many criminals have lice. My policy requires criminals to shower with lice-killing shampoo before they appear in my courtroom. I look after my court personnel. You have a problem with that, Mr. Patterson?"

I ignored his question. "Your Honor, with all due respect, please quit treating and referring to my client as a criminal. She was not arrested and has not been arraigned, much less found guilty." I struggled to maintain my composure.

Purdom turned a dark glare of annoyance on me.

Sensing the judge was about to blow his lines, Fletcher spoke.

"Your Honor, the prosecution has no objection to the removal of Dr. Hall's restraints."

Taking the hint, Judge Purdom responded, "That decision is mine to make, counselor, but given my observation of her demeanor I will instruct the bailiff to remove her restraints. For future appearances in this courtroom the defendant may dress in civilian attire. Bailiff!"

The bailiff made a big display out of pulling out his keys and slowly removing Jana's handcuffs and leg irons. She remained silent, dealing with the circumstances surprisingly well. I couldn't say the same for Sam, who looked truly miserable. Brian attempted to hand me his notes, but I waved him away.

The bailiff finally completed his task and led Jana to the defense table. She sank into the chair next to me, visibly trembling.

Judge Purdom asked, "Satisfied, counsel?"

"Thank you, Your Honor." I hoped my disdain wasn't too obvious. "Your Honor, I notice there are several photographers present in the courtroom. May I inquire about the court's policy regarding cameras in the courtroom? Pictures of my client in shackles and a prison jumpsuit will taint a potential jury pool."

"You may inquire. This court believes in public justice and cameras in the courtroom. The press is welcome, and they are free to take pictures of anything that interests them, as long as they stay behind the rail and don't interfere with a proceeding. Once we have a jury, the rules will change, but for now they remain."

Fletcher added, "For the record, the prosecution has no objection to cameras in the courtroom."

I bet they didn't. The image presented to the public in the local papers and on TV would be that of a guilty woman: a woman with wet, unkempt hair, dressed in an orange jumpsuit.

"Thank you, Mr. Fletcher. Mr. Patterson if you object to cameras in the courtroom, you may file a motion. I will take it up in due course. Now are there any further preliminaries before we get to the business at hand?"

Fletcher began to rise, but sat down quickly at the judge's frown.

"Your Honor, I see that Prosecuting Attorney Pagano and his chief deputy are in the courtroom. The governor appointed me as special prosecutor in this case after their office refused to bring charges against Ms. Hall. Mr. Patterson has already raised their reluctance to indict as evidence of her innocence. Mr. Patterson is already engaging in trickery."

His remarks came as a surprise to the judge, who looked flustered.

Kate's firm voice was a welcome surprise. "Your Honor, may I stand and address Mr. Fletcher's concerns?"

"You may."

"Mr. Pagano is not here in any official capacity today, but rather to offer emotional support to an old friend. However, I am here in my official capacity and as part of an ongoing investigation."

Kate smiled easily and a few cameras flashed.

Fletcher's reaction was both audible and predictable. "What the hell?"

Purdom maintained his composure. "Young lady, I think you need to explain yourself. What ongoing investigation?"

"With all due respect, I am not at liberty to discuss the investigation. But as an officer of this court, I can tell you an investigation is pending and that my presence here today is part of that investigation."

Her response satisfied neither the judge nor Fletcher. The press was stirring.

"Your Honor, if I may?" I asked.

"Go ahead," he replied.

"If Mr. Fletcher has concerns about anyone's presence in the courtroom, he is within his rights to file a motion before any evidentiary hearing or trial. Today's arraignment is not such a proceeding. Why don't we proceed with the arraignment? Your Honor will then know how to best deal with these other issues."

Purdom glanced at Fletcher who nodded in agreement.

"You make a good point, Mr. Patterson. We'll go forward with the reading of the indictment."

"Judge, my client waives the reading of the indictment."

"Is your client prepared to enter a plea?"

"She is. Dr. Jana Hall pleads not guilty."

Purdom again glanced at Fletcher. They could well have been teenagers flirting at a high school dance.

"Okay, let the record reflect that the accused has entered a plea of not guilty to the charges. When we conclude, we will meet in chambers to go over preliminary matters such as a trial date, discovery, and any motions either party may wish to file."

Purdom was so eager to get back to chambers I worried he would forget to release Jana.

"Your Honor, I ask that Dr. Hall be released on her own recognizance."

I half expected Fletcher to go back on his word, but he didn't. "Your Honor, the prosecution has no objection as long as she deposits her passport with the clerk."

My relief was short-lived.

"The decision on bail is not yours to make Mr. Fletcher," said the judge with a scowl. "I'm not inclined to let criminals loose on the streets. Bail should be an exception rather than the rule. But if the prosecution doesn't think she's a flight risk, bail is set at five-hundred thousand dollars."

"Your Honor, that amount is beyond excessive," I protested.

Purdom responded with an evil grin.

"If you think bail is excessive, you may file a motion. But this court takes judicial notice that the defendant is a person of means. The prosecution may not be worried she is a flight risk, but I am. Until you file your motion and we have a hearing, the amount is five-hundred thousand dollars."

Purdom and Fletcher had obviously rehearsed this scene. Fletcher appears to be reasonable, but behind the scenes conspires with the judge to impose an exorbitant bail. And *he* had accused *me* of tricks. I was about to lose it when I felt Jana's shaking hand reach for mine under the table. I took a deep breath, hoping my backup would appear before it was too late.

Purdom watched us for a few seconds and then rose to leave. As everyone rose with him, a voice called out from the rear of the room.

"Your Honor, I take it that a surety bond written by St. Paul will be sufficient?"

45

THE JUDGE STOPPED in mid-step and bellowed, "Who the hell are you?"

"My name is Tucker Bowie, and I possess binding authority with St. Paul Fire and Casualty up to ten million dollars. I think your clerk will find my paperwork in order." He walked forward with a confident grin.

Fletcher sat down with a thud.

The judge demanded, "Who is paying the premium for such a bond, and how did you get here so fast?"

"Well, legally that information is between my client and me, but I see no harm in telling you. When I spoke with Mr. Patterson yesterday—he's been a friend for many years—he said the prosecution had assured him his client would be released without bond. But he asked if I could write one in case the situation were to change. I'm certain his client can pay the premium, and I'm ready to write the bond right now.

"As for how I got here so fast, the golf course is closed today for a junior tournament. I had nothing better to do, so I came to watch." Tucker gave me a wink.

"Bailiff." The man jumped at Purdom's tone. "Take the defendant and Mr. Bowie to the clerk. If his paperwork is in order, you may release her. Mr. Fletcher and Mr. Patterson, I want to see you both in chambers—now."

I wanted to join Tucker and Jana as they followed the bailiff, but I felt a subtle nudge from Brian. Glad I had enlisted Tucker, I followed Fletcher to chambers.

The judge removed his robes, hung up his six-shooter, and

motioned for us to sit at the same round table. We were back to scene one.

"All right," he began. "Let's get to it. I thought Ms. Hall would have the good sense to plead guilty, but since she's being poorly advised, that's not in the offing. So, we're looking at a trial of how many days?" He looked at Fletcher.

"Three days max, unless you let Patterson confuse the issue with a bunch of stories about what a good doctor Dr. Hall was."

That was exactly what I had planned to do, but I kept quiet.

"Well, that won't happen. Reputation evidence is relevant only in sentencing. This case will be about what happened at her clinic and whether or not she broke the law. From my reading of the indictment, this is a records case. The files will confirm the age of the patients at the time of treatment and what treatment was administered. You'll call the patient to confirm the treatment, and that's it. How soon can you get the records to Mr. Patterson? I won't stand for delays."

"He already has the records, Your Honor. That's an issue we'd like to address. Dr. Hall and Mr. Patterson possess records that we need, records that belong to the state of Arkansas," Fletcher said.

"Get me whatever you need, and I'll sign it," the judge said.

Here came the train down the track. I might as well have been sitting outside with Brian.

"May I speak?" I asked, already knowing the answer.

"No," the judge replied. "You may file written objections to any order I enter, and I'll rule in a timely fashion. But I see no problem with your client returning the state's property. It's not like they'll destroy anything."

Like hell they wouldn't, I thought. At this point, I'd had enough.

"Judge Purdom, I ask for this conversation to be on the record."

"I'll decide when conversations should be on the record, not you. I'm trying to figure out how soon we can get this case to trial." He looked at Fletcher. "Three days, huh?"

"Maybe two," Fletcher answered.

"I think I can squeeze it in at the end of the month. How about May twenty-fourth and twenty-fifth? Can you exchange documents by then?"

Fletcher grinned. "No problem. We'll have the relevant documents to Mr. Patterson before trial. If we find anything relevant in the records he turns over, we'll notify him. I'm in as big a hurry to return home as you are to get this case off your docket."

Surely they were bluffing. I tried for a delay.

"Judge, I didn't get a copy of the indictment until an hour ago. Now you want me to go to trial in less than four weeks? I won't have time to file motions or interview witnesses. I suggest you schedule a trial this fall."

"May twenty-fourth it is." He didn't even look at me.

"What if I want a preliminary hearing?" I didn't want a preliminary hearing, because then the prosecution would call the women who had undergone abortions as witnesses. But the judge didn't know that.

"If you ask for a preliminary hearing, I'll deny your request. You are dealing with a grand jury indictment, Mr. Patterson. Arkansas law doesn't afford the opportunity for a preliminary hearing when the indictment comes from a grand jury. Your lack of understanding of Arkansas law concerns this court."

He glanced at Fletcher who tried not to react. I waited for the next blow to fall.

Purdom handed me a short document. "This explains how I go about jury selection. In a nutshell, I ask the *voir dire* questions. Lawyers try to use *voir dire* as an early opening statement. I don't like that, so I prevent it from happening. You will get the names of the potential jurors the day before the trial. That cuts down on rich criminals running down the backgrounds of potential jurors to intimidate them. Questions?"

I wanted to ask how many rich criminals had been in his courtroom. Most of the criminal defendants I knew were dirt poor and represented by public defenders who didn't have the time or resources to investigate potential jurors.

Fletcher spoke before I could answer. "Judge, one more thing. Jury nullification is a real danger here, and it begins with calling the defendant Dr. Hall."

Jury nullification is not a favorite of the courts. It results when a lawyer argues that their client may have violated the law, but the law was unfair or out of date. Or he might argue that his client had a clear, over-riding reason to break the law. Jury nullification has had some recent success in marijuana possession cases. Many jurors believe marijuana has medical benefits and that its use should be legal. The defense tries to fashion an argument that encourages jurors to ignore the law and find their client not guilty.

I had already decided jury nullification might be our only chance. Fletcher wasn't stupid. He had prejudiced the judge against my strategy before I used it, employing his own strategy of "judge" nullification.

"There will be no jury nullification in my court room," Purdom blustered. "Don't even think about it, Patterson, or you'll be sleeping under the jail."

I didn't bother to respond. I was tired of being told to file a motion.

Purdom actually smiled, and I knew another hammer was about to drop, more likely an anvil.

"Let's recap. We have a trial date, and Dawg, I mean Prosecutor Fletcher, will get me the paperwork we've discussed, and you will deliver to him the medical records in your client's possession. Do either of you have anything to add before I make one last suggestion?"

"I think that's it," Fletcher answered, swinging his legs down from the table.

"Mr. Patterson, the court is concerned about your apparent lack of understanding of Arkansas law and procedure. I worry you could offer ineffective counsel to your client. I know you are licensed in Arkansas and have handled a case in this state's court, but in that case you had the benefit of an experienced Arkansas criminal defense counsel, Ms. Lawrence.

"We will go to trial in a little over three weeks. The last thing I want is for the state to go through the time and expense of a trial only to have a conviction reversed because of your ineptitude. I want you to bring in another Arkansas lawyer as lead counsel. You're free to sit inside the rail and offer advice, but let someone else sit first chair and carry the load."

His intent was clear: bring on a new lead counsel or he would remove me. Purdom was prepared to throw me off the case "in the interest of justice." Someone had thought through this strategy very carefully, and I didn't think it was Fletcher. Purdom waited for me to respond.

"Judge, I respect your concern, but with such a quick trial setting it would be difficult to find a competent attorney who would be acceptable to Dr. Hall and who could get up to speed in time, even if I sat second chair." Maybe I could at least get the case postponed.

"Well, I can see how that might present a problem, but I've been told that another law firm represented Ms. Hall before you came to town. When her lawyers realized they had a serious conflict, they advised her to hire Les Butterman. I'm sure Les would take her case and allow you to consult.

How on earth did the judge know anything about Jana's former law firm or their attempt to foist Les on her?

"Judge, I appreciate your efforts to be sure Dr. Hall has adequate representation, but from what she's said, I doubt she would agree to hiring Les. Moreover, I don't think we would work well together. Perhaps you can suggest someone else?"

Purdom didn't blink an eye. "Dr. Hall should be relieved to have a competent attorney working on her behalf. I'm sure Les will have no problem working with you. But if it's a problem for you, you have a good reason to withdraw."

Fletcher's smile was insolent. I wanted to knock him into the middle of next week. Who in the hell, judge or no judge, had the right to tell me I wasn't qualified or should withdraw? Defending Jana would be tough enough in an impartial court environment, but in this kangaroo court, we didn't stand a chance. Ignoring his court reporter's advice, I rose, ready to do battle. I hesitated when I heard a commotion at the doors. I tried to see what was happening, but a bailiff wielding a thick cudgel blocked my view.

Shoving the surprised bailiff aside, Micki Lawrence spoke directly to Purdom.

"Judge, there's no reason for Jack to withdraw or to engage co-counsel. He already has one."

46

Micki apologized for being late and walked over to stand by my side.

Fletcher quickly covered his surprise and said, "Judge, I believe you know Micki Lawrence. She is well qualified to serve as co-counsel, but I believe she has a conflict. She represents the Health Department in another matter."

Micki gave the judge a quick nod before turning to speak directly to Fletcher.

"Just how did you know I had a contract with the Health Department, since that information has nothing to do with your investigation? What you don't know is that yesterday afternoon that contract came to an end. I never met with anyone connected with the contract until yesterday, and I have now returned the retainer. I was not privy to any confidential information, and as soon as I learned what the director expected of me, I walked away from the contract. If you don't believe me, check with Mr. Flowers."

Fletcher turned to Purdom and said, "Judge, I'm sure Ms. Lawrence is telling the truth, but someone should check with Mr. Flowers."

Micki responded before Purdom could say a word. "You do that, and if you're even thinking I shouldn't represent Dr. Hall, file a written motion, like the judge told Jack." She gave me a wink.

I don't know what made me happier, knowing Micki and I would once again join forces, or how brutally she was handling Fletcher.

I wondered how she knew what had happened in chambers. Only one person knew besides the three of us. I hoped Candy wouldn't lose her job.

Micki continued. "Judge, your clerk told me we have a trial date in three weeks. So if you're through, we'd like to leave. We have a case to prepare. May we be excused?"

A dazed Purdom said nothing. Micki's appearance had taken him off-script. Fletcher was quicker. "When can we expect to receive the clinics' records?"

"Not until I've received and had time to review the court order. If you have a copy with you, please deliver it to Ms. Lawrence's office. She'll know where to find me," I said, relishing my sudden change of status. It was my turn to grin.

I couldn't wait to hear what had caused my good fortune. Micki Lawrence would be a damn sight better co-counsel than Butterman, better than anyone else I could think of.

Clovis and Brian met up with us as we left chambers. Micki asked us to give her a minute—she needed to thank Candy. I looked for Jana, but Clovis told me she had asked to be taken home. Who could blame her for wanting to change into her own clothes and take some time for herself after such cruel treatment? Sam and Kate had returned to their office.

Micki soon joined us, and I suggested we meet Sam and Kate at some place public for lunch.

"I'm all in for lunch. But why do we need Kate and Sam, and why in a public place? You have a lot to tell me about the case, and I want to tell you about my meeting with Flowers. Are you holding out on me already, Jack? You know how I feel about keeping me in the dark."

"Hey, you only signed on as co-counsel fifteen minutes ago," I laughed. "No, I'm not keeping you in the dark. I haven't had a moment to tell you anything. Trust me, by the end of the day you'll know everything."

"Right. I've heard you say 'trust me' before," she said with a twinkle in her eyes.

I ignored her dig and told Clovis he was in charge of logistics, which included dodging the press and their bank of microphones in the courthouse's large rotunda. He led us to a service elevator that went to the basement, then we walked up a flight of stairs and outside to a waiting Suburban. We had taken advantage of this escape route during Woody Cole's case.

Brian offered to return to the courthouse to see if Fletcher was talking to the press. He'd meet us for lunch. I suggested the bar at the Armitage for lunch, but Micki squashed my suggestion, commenting that she'd had quite enough of that hotel. I knew she would explain in her own good time. Clovis suggested Doe's again, a favorite of lawyers, lobbyists, and reporters who relished a long lunch of steak and tamales.

We agreed to meet at one-thirty to let the crowd die down. The car would drop me by the hotel to change clothes and then take Micki to her office. Clovis would contact Sam and Kate and call Jana to schedule a convenient time for us to meet at her house.

I used the time before lunch to return a few calls. I assured a doubtful Red that I would be ready for our meeting with the NFL although I had no idea how I could pull it off. Now that Micki was available, I considered letting her take over. I hadn't done Jana much good.

"Enough with the self-doubts, Jack," I said to myself. It was too late to back out now.

Clovis had reserved a private room at Doe's. Everyone would see us sitting together, but no one could listen to our conversation.

"Perfect," I said to Clovis as we walked into the restaurant.

When we were settled, I looked to Brian. "Tell us about Fletcher's press conference."

"It was ugly. He all but accused Dr. Hall of running a health clinic for the underworld. He claimed the crimes in the indictment were the tip of the iceberg, and as soon as they recovered 'stolen' medical records, more charges would be brought. He said illegal abortions, treatment of prostitutes, and supplying illegal drugs were commonplace at the clinics and were all paid for with taxpayer money. Fletcher called it a 'criminal enterprise of monumental proportions.'

"Even worse, he said that unless Dr. Hall pleads guilty, returns all the clinics' records, and closes the clinics for good, he will have no choice but to call every victim and coworker to the witness stand to expose her 'contract with the devil.'"

"'Contract with the devil'—he said that?" Sam asked.

"He did, and he quoted a few Bible verses I'm not familiar with, maybe because he made them up."

I remembered Fletcher telling the judge he could try the case in two days. Yet he had told the press he would call witness after witness unless Jana pled guilty. I wondered if he knew Jana didn't want her coworkers or patients involved. Or was it a bluff, a bluff Jana would never let us call.

Brian ended by offering to get a video of the press conference. If he couldn't, he would write up a summary.

I asked, "Micki, are you ready to tell us what happened yesterday? Thank you for saving my butt this morning and for joining another lost cause, by the way."

Micki smiled. "An assistant called on Monday to say Director Flowers wanted to discuss my work for the Health Department. She asked if I could meet him for lunch at Crittenden's yesterday. I agreed.

"We met for lunch, and butter wouldn't melt in his mouth. He told me I was absolutely his first choice for the job, and that my work on the obesity project would lead to similar work. He said the Health Department was in constant need of outside counsel for specific projects.

"I tried to clarify my responsibilities for the obesity project, but he had a smooth way of avoiding specifics. No alarm bells went off until about halfway through lunch. The waiter appeared with two glasses of wine, and he insisted that I join him in a toast to celebrate our working together.

"We finished the meal and, none the wiser about what my work would entail, I told him I needed to get back to the office. That's when he dropped the bomb. He suggested we discuss the details of the project upstairs in a room he kept for private meetings. He said, 'You enjoyed the wine, didn't you? Well, I have a bottle on ice upstairs. I think you'll find working with me rewarding in more ways than you were expecting.' I told him that under no circumstance would I go upstairs to discuss business or anything else. I should have slapped him then and there.

"He had the gall to say, 'Micki don't be foolish, and don't pretend to be offended. We're both adults. You know how things work in the real world. I'm in a position to throw a lot of lucrative work your way, and you're a woman I'd like to get to know. You scratch my back, and I'll scratch yours. So, don't be foolish—join me upstairs. I promise you won't regret one moment.'

"He stood up and offered his hand. I rose and took it, reaching for my wine glass with the other. He said, 'Leave it, we have plenty upstairs.' I let go of his hand, grabbed his belt, and pulled his trousers out away from his midriff. He thought I was being suggestive until the cold wine hit his Johnson. I emptied the entire glass and walked away.

"'Bitch!' he called after me in a loud voice.

"I turned and said to the entire room. 'Don't worry—Mr. Flowers is just upset. He has a problem with bladder control. Waiter, I think he needs your help.'

"I raced back to the office, read my retainer agreement, and consulted with friends about my ethical responsibilities. I decided that if I returned the money, I was free to help defend Dr. Hall. I must warn you, Jack, I am pissed off with that bastard in particular, and with men in general. I almost made Larry sleep by himself last night." She smiled, then added, "Almost."

Micki was back.

47

MICKI'S STORY BLEW ME AWAY. I didn't think that kind of thing went on anymore, but in many ways I live a sheltered life. It does, despite the #MeToo movement and the public downfall of several well-known men. It will continue as long as some men believe they have an innate power over women or the right to demean and abuse those who cannot defend themselves. Whoever said "Power corrupts, and absolute power corrupts absolutely" was right on the money.

Micki interrupted my musings. "Here's another little nugget: when I went back to thank Candy, I could see into the judge's chambers. Purdom and Fletcher were on a speakerphone. I caught a few expletives before Fletcher slammed the door shut. I don't think they saw me, I sure hope not. I asked Candy who was on the other end of the conversation. She glanced at the closed door and whispered, 'A Mr. Roy Pence—he's called the judge several times. I have no idea who he is, but you'd think the judge was talking to the president. As soon as you left chambers, the judge hollered to get him on the phone. Whoever he is, you could hear he's hopping mad.'"

"That woman is a treasure."

The name seemed familiar, and I saw Sam's eyes light up. "Roy Pence. Jack, you met him at the Soul Fish Café."

I remembered him—Sam had described him as "Kristine's friend" and Sam had said he knew all the right people and attended every political gathering. I wondered but put my thoughts on hold and turned back to Micki. "Did Candy give you Pence's phone number?"

Micki smiled and handed me a slip of paper. Maybe a bit more of luck had come our way.

"Consider this my first contribution to the effort. Now why don't you explain why you asked Kate and Sam to lunch and why you wanted us to meet at a public venue?"

"Micki, we've got two problems to overcome before we can devise a strategy to defend Jana. The first is that she refuses to implicate any of her coworkers or embarrass her patients. She told me she'd rather plead guilty than risk charges against her colleagues or the possibility her patients might be forced to testify."

"Shades of Woody Cole," Micki murmured.

The Woody Cole case was the first case Micki and I worked on together, and Woody had refused to cooperate in his defense. He wanted to plead guilty and receive the death penalty.

"Exactly. But the second problem is tougher. It's obvious that the judge and Fletcher are in bed together. No matter what type of creative defense we're able to craft, they have no intention of letting us get away with anything out of the ordinary. For example, I think Jana's case might be a perfect opportunity to argue for jury nullification, but not with this judge."

Micki gave it a little thought. "I hadn't thought about that possibility. Do you think it could work?"

"Well, if Jana continues to insist on protecting her colleagues and patients, we might throw Fletcher a curve. We would admit that Jana had committed the specific charges, but try to convince the jury they weren't criminal. Given her reputation, a local jury might admire her so much they wouldn't convict her of a crime. It's a reach, but sometimes it works. Juries in a few communities have refused to convict someone who uses marijuana for medical reasons, regardless of the law."

"There's no way either Purdom or Fletcher will let you get away with that kind of argument. The judge will have you behind bars the moment you try." Sam's blunt statement was sobering.

"I agree. Fletcher brought up the strategy to the judge in chambers, and Purdom shot it dead. He might as well have used one of his pistols."

"Sounds like we're back to square one," Micki said.

"Thanks to you, not quite. This slip of paper and Roy Pence could be our first break. We need to discover everything we can about him and his connection to the judge and Fletcher."

"Jack, we have three weeks to prepare a defense. We don't have the time or the manpower to chase wild geese." Micki frowned.

"I know we have very little time, but humor me."

Kate Erwin interrupted before Micki had a chance at a rejoinder. "I'm not sure I should hear this. Are you trying to draw me into your client's defense? I'm sure I should have no part in it. Our office didn't find a reason to prosecute Dr. Hall, but that doesn't mean we are free to help you defend her. I'm still a prosecutor working for the state, which means if I must take sides, I should support Fletcher."

It was time for me to tell her why I had invited her to lunch. I glanced at Clovis, who closed the door to the room.

"Kate, you're right. I will do my best not to include you in any discussions about defense strategy, but your invitation to the courtroom this morning and now to lunch has nothing to do with Jana's defense. You and Sam are in charge of the murder investigation of the four men in Fourche Bottoms and the attack on me. It is in that context that I asked you to join us."

"You know we've already caught the murderer. That case is closed," Kate pointed out.

"Is it?" I asked.

"Well, we still have no idea who hired Stalinski or whether he tried to kill you on his own, but we probably never will. Last time I talked to Mimi, she said Stalinski isn't talking."

"What if the phone number Micki just gave me turns out to be a number Stalinski called while he was in town?" I asked.

"Whoever he called, Stalinski would have used a phone that couldn't be traced. We know that the only way to contact him was through an intermediary. No one called him directly." She didn't budge.

"What if Stalinski and Pence called the identical number, the intermediary?" I asked.

"If that were the case you'd have Mimi on the next plane to Little Rock. Is that a possibility?" she asked.

"Well, I don't know yet," I admitted. "I only got the phone number a few minutes ago. We don't know much about Roy Pence, what he does, or why he was on the phone with Fletcher and the judge, but I'll find out. If I find a connection between Pence and the Fourche murders, would you like to know about it?"

Sam interrupted. "You're not suggesting there's a connection between the Fourche murders and Jana's case, are you? Mace Cooper and Stalinski were out for personal revenge: Mace for a thirty-year-old whipping you gave him, and Stalinski because his stepsister died trying to kill you. Stalinski killed Mace and the others because he wanted to be the man who ended your life."

"No, you don't know that. Stalinski intimated to Mimi that he was fulfilling a contract when he killed those four men. You think revenge was his motivation, but what if he had another motive? What if someone hired him to kill Mace, the others, and me?"

"Well, I guess he could have had a different motive for the four, but it's a hard sell to think he had anything to do with Jana or her case. Do you have any proof, any evidence that links the two, other than your fertile imagination?" Sam asked.

"No, but I'm asking you to keep an open mind, and I'm asking your office to respond to whatever I discover. As Micki keeps reminding me, we are running out of time."

"You asked me to keep an open mind once before, and it served justice well. So I'll keep an open mind, but remember, we don't operate on speculation or conjecture. We need facts—simple, hard facts."

"No, I need more," Kate interrupted, rising abruptly. "My job complicates my life enough without jumping through hoops chasing wild-ass theories. You want my advice? Make a deal before Dr. Hall ends up spending the rest of her life in prison. If she doesn't want to implicate her staff or her patients, she needs to cut her losses. Sorry, Sam. You know I tell it like it is, and it's time to go. You and I have a budget meeting in thirty minutes."

Kate's tirade left us in silence. She walked out of the room, and Sam followed. No hugs or handshakes on the way out. I waited until she closed the door before I turned to Micki.

"What was that about?"

"She's confused. Who wouldn't be? She's used to black and white—you've introduced her to gray. And you *are* trying to lure her into helping Dr. Hall. Her workplace ethics conflict with her feelings for Sam, and now you. After all, you did save her life. Jack, I warned her that any involvement with you would make things complicated."

"Look, I'm sorry to have complicated her life," I responded in irritation. "We're talking about Jana Hall's life, too. But we may need Kate. So, what can I do?"

"Don't worry, she'll come around. If we need her, she'll be there. But why would we need her? What is going on in that brain of yours? The question is—why has the state of Arkansas gone after Dr. Hall with such a vengeance, and how do we defend her?"

48

We decided Micki would take the lead in distracting Fletcher and the judge. With the help of her two interns, Sarah and Trey, she would file various motions and other paperwork designed to convince Fletcher we were prepared to go to trial. Brian would work with Jana to discover what was in the medical records. Clovis and Stella would focus on the identity of Roy Pence and his connection with Fletcher, the judge, and Brady Flowers.

The mention of Flowers brought an immediate, angry scowl to Micki's face. "What does that bastard have to do with anything?" she asked.

"He may be a candidate for your all-time least favorite client, but he is the head of the Health Department. And I think he may have gotten a little big for his britches."

"What do you mean?" Micki asked.

"Micki, you're one of the best lawyers I know. But it's hard to understand why the Health Department hired you as their counsel for an obesity study. It seems too convenient."

"I understand exactly why I was hired—that asshole Flowers wanted in my pants."

"Or maybe someone wanted to make sure you couldn't represent Jana?" I suggested. "Think about it. If Jana needed a real criminal lawyer, not those corporate types at the Crockett firm, who would she call? You and Jack Lassiter are the most likely choices. I did a little checking. Jack's firm has a conflict, as do two other lawyers Jack recommended. Think it's a coincidence every criminal defense lawyer worth his salt has a Health Department contract right now?"

"You talked to Jack?"

"I did. At the same time you were hired for the obesity study, his firm was engaged to handle Medicaid audit work. Brady Flowers locked them up with a nice retainer. Sound familiar?"

"So why did Flowers make a fool of himself trying to get me in the sack?"

"He tried the same thing with Jana, hoping to use their personal relationship to get the clinics' medical records. He had no luck with her either. I've never met the man, but he seems to have an exaggerated sense of his prowess. Or maybe his ego impedes his judgment, hardly a unique phenomenon."

"That much is certain," Micki laughed.

"Micki, if we find a connection between Flowers and Pence, we'll finally have something we can sink our teeth into."

"And what if it turns out Pence is just a friend of the judge, doesn't know Brady from Adam?" she asked. "We're up a creek without a paddle."

"Have a little patience," I said. "We haven't even pushed off from shore. Give it a chance."

"And what will you be doing while we're off on your wild goose chase?"

"I haven't given you a wild goose to chase. I expect you to prepare for a trial in three weeks."

"Hah! Sure glad we've got plenty of time. What about the fact that Dr. Hall wants to plead guilty?" Micki asked.

"That's where we're headed next, to convince her to trust us while we uncover what's behind this rush to judgment."

She didn't give up. "You avoided the question. What are you doing while we follow your instructions?"

"For the next few days I'll be in San Antonio, pretending to be concentrating on another client, the Los Angeles Lobos." I smiled, wishing there were a better way to spill the beans.

"Please tell me you're kidding," she said softly, and I knew I was in trouble.

"Micki, I scheduled this trip weeks ago, long before any of this happened. It's my real job, remember? I'm prepared to cancel, but my absence could serve as a diversion. I want everyone to think I've turned Jana's defense over to you, that I'm out of the picture. In fact, while I'm out of town, I want you to contact Fletcher and suggest I've left you holding the bag."

"Is it a diversion, or are you ready to bag this case, and her? I can't say I blame you, looks damn tough from where I sit." Her tone was hard as nails.

I took a deep breath, trying to contain my anger. "Do you really think I would walk away from a friend or from you? From any client for that matter?"

Micki lowered her eyes. "Sorry, I know you wouldn't. But I came on board as your partner, and now you're leaving me for football?"

"I'm sorry, but it's not football—it's a financial transaction. Red trusts me. He needs me, and he deserves the same loyalty as Jana. Micki, I really do I believe my absence will work in her favor. I want Fletcher, the judge, and everyone outside our circle to think I've gone AWOL. Hey, it worked before."

"Billy Hopper was a different circumstance, and you know it," she responded with a frown.

"Well, I hope the situation changes, but right now it's what I've got. Let's go see Jana."

"Before we go, what about Sam? What about Kate? Will you tell them your absence is a diversion?" Micki asked.

"I haven't had time to think about it. What do you think?"

"Sam, yes. Kate's a tough call."

"Why?"

"There are no secrets between Sam and Jana. She needs him, no matter how it compromises confidentiality and strategy. The moment you tell her you'll be in San Antonio, she'll tell Sam."

"I agree. What about Kate?"

"If she thinks you aren't involved, she'll revert to the old Kate, which will be a good thing. That is, if you show up again."

"Don't worry, I'll show up. And my guess is we will need her. I say we include Sam, but tell him to leave Kate out of the loop. On another topic, how's it going with Larry's mother?" I asked.

"Not so good."

"I told you I'd help, and I will."

"I don't know what you can do, but if you pull off that miracle, I'll forget about San Antonio."

"Deal," I responded.

"Tell me the truth, Jack. Is Jana's case the one we can't win? You know, all those years ago when Debbie was an addict and a prostitute, Jana not only treated her, but gave her good advice and helped her recover. She's so excited that we're defending her, but I worry this case won't end well."

"Debbie was a victim of the sex trade, not a prostitute. But to answer your question, we'll find a way. There's got to be more to this than an overzealous prosecutor and a horny state official. We have to unearth the motive and bring it to light. It's good to have you back, Micki Lawrence."

At some point, Brian and Clovis had tactfully moved to the other end of the table. Clovis caught me off-guard when he spoke.

"Jack, it's time to go. Dr. Hall is waiting, and Jordan has the car running."

"Give me a minute," I responded, turning to Micki.

"There's a downside to letting everyone think I'm off the case. You and Larry will be in greater danger if someone has hired another assassin."

"What about you? You'll be alone in San Antonio," Clovis said.

"Big Mike will be with me. I want him as my conduit back to you. I'll be in meetings most of the time. He can double as protection."

"You've planned this out well. Don't worry about Micki and Larry. As for Brian, I trust him to take care of himself, but I'll have his back," Clovis said. "Do you really think the murders in the Fourche Bottoms relate to Dr. Hall's case?"

"I do."

"Do you have any evidence at all?" Micki questioned.

"Not a lick, just a hunch. We have three weeks to turn my sow's ear into a silk purse."

49

SAM WAS WITH JANA when we arrived, no surprise. I was glad to see Stella sitting with them at the kitchen table. She told me that Jeff was in eastern Arkansas running tests and asking questions. She didn't elaborate, and I made a mental note to follow up. After a few moments of light conversation, I laid out our strategy, including the fact that I needed to spend a few days in San Antonio starting tomorrow.

Before Jana could react, Sam snarled, "What the hell!? Micki takes over Jana's defense, Jana and Brian spend night and day searching for some medical needle in a haystack, and Clovis and Stella try to run down scuttlebutt on Roy Pence, a man perfectly acceptable to most everyone in Little Rock. All while you go play big dog in San Antonio? What's gotten into you? You afraid Fletcher's gonna get the best of you?"

You could have cut the air with a knife. I took a deep breath, but before I could reply, Jana turned to Sam.

"Sam, you know better than that. You apologize to Jack this minute or I'll show you the door. Jack has been here for me from day one. You're scared and frustrated you can't fix this mess, and you're taking it out on him. Remember, if I'd had my way, I would have pled guilty today. Confidence in Jack is the only reason I'm not spending tonight in jail. And, despite your assurances I wouldn't have to post bail, Jack's the one who made sure I didn't."

She glared at Sam who squirmed in his chair. "Jack, how much do I owe Tucker?"

"The bond wasn't cheap, but Tucker waived his commission and negotiated a reduced premium with the carrier. He told me he'd get around to sending you a bill, but he's not worried about payment. He was glad to help," I said, relieved by the unexpected change of subject. But she wasn't finished.

"Come on, Sam, apologize to Jack. I have more than a few questions, and if you've got the bullhead, you should just leave." Sam's heart wasn't in an apology. He mouthed the words until Jana gave him a dirty look.

"Okay, I apologize, I know you won't walk out, but I'll be damned if I understand your plan."

"Sam, right now the deck is totally stacked against Jana—we need a break. Micki and Brian are capable of working out the courtroom strategy without me. Maybe if I leave, the bad guys will get careless, make a mistake.

"And Jana, I know you have questions—fire away."

"Okay, you think the medical records contain information that someone wants to remain secret. But I've searched *ad nauseam*, and I don't see anything unusual."

"What did Jeff tell you he found?" I asked.

"He's been focusing on eastern Arkansas. He thinks the numbers for certain diseases were higher than the norm. But that can't be the case."

"Why not?"

"For certain diseases, the clinic is required to report every instance to the Arkansas Health Department. If the Health Department sees anything unusual in the numbers, they are required to pass the information on to the National Center for Disease Control in Atlanta. If the numbers concern the CDC, they'll send a team of experts to investigate. Nothing like that has happened."

"Is it possible that the state didn't pass on the information?"

"It's unlikely," she said.

"But possible," I responded. "Any idea what Jeff found?"

"He found an unusual number of patients diagnosed with Alzheimer's, Parkinson's, and multiple sclerosis. Suicide rates among poor farm and migrant workers were also high. Finally, many children had symptoms that would indicate arsenic poisoning if I didn't know better. If Jeff's findings are correct, a red flag should have been raised, and the state and the CDC should have noticed. Neither the state nor the CDC expressed any concern, so Jeff's findings must have been erroneous."

"What did you mean 'if I didn't know better'?"

"The FDA banned arsenic from pesticides back in the early eighties."

A newly interested Sam interrupted. "Why do you assume Jeff was wrong? If his findings are correct, should your staff have noticed the excessive numbers?"

Jana smiled. "Good question. The answer is no. The individual doctors and nurses at the Delta clinic were overwhelmed by patients with all kinds of ailments. These people are dirt poor, and many are migrants or undocumented immigrants who have never had the benefit of even basic health care. My staff treated them for the flu, pneumonia, STIs, broken limbs, liver disease, cancers—you name it, they saw it. They were front-line docs, trying to heal and cure. They had neither the time nor the capacity to notice trends. That's why we gave the Health Department monthly reports—it's their job to watch for trends and anomalies."

"Does anyone know what Jeff is doing in the Delta?" I asked.

"He wanted to see the situation for himself. He wanted to talk to folks, see where they live, and conduct soil and water sampling," Stella answered.

"Clovis, find out where Jeff is and send your best person to get him out of there."

"I'm on it," he replied and bolted from the room.

"You don't think Jeff is in any danger, do you?" Jana asked in alarm.

Ignoring Jana, I turned to Sam. "Who can I talk to about farming in the Delta? Someone I can trust."

"Remember Tag Wingfield from Stuttgart? His family owns thousands of acres of farmland. He managed my campaign last year. He's a great guy, as honest as the day is long."

"Of course I remember him. He was my shortstop in college, saved my ass turning double plays. I haven't heard from him since, but see if he'd be willing to have an off-the-record conversation in the next couple of days."

"I'll call him this afternoon. He asks about you all the time."

I returned to Jana's question. "Do I think Jeff is in any danger? Yes, I do, and the sooner he's back in Little Rock, the better I'll feel."

"Why the sudden concern?" Sam asked.

"Remember a couple years ago when Jana testified before the House Health and Human Services Committee? She told them she wanted to study the records from the health clinics to determine if there was something unique about the diseases found among the state's poorest residents. Think about it. The committee had barely adjourned before Flowers initiated a process that would defund the clinics, transfer their records to the state, and discredit Jana.

"We learned a lot at the arraignment today, but one stands out. The state already has the patients' records—otherwise they couldn't have indicted Jana. The judge said it's a records case, and Fletcher threatened to expand the indictment as they continue to go through the records. He also said he would give us all the relevant records prior to the trial. Sam, they don't need the records—they already have them.

"The fact is, Jana, they don't want *you* to have those records. They don't care what made your patients sick, and they don't want you to conduct a study. They want to destroy your credibility. And they're damn close to pulling it off.

"Now, out of the blue, a young doctor from Barnes Hospital shows up asking questions and taking soil samples. What do you think, Sam? Is Jeff in any danger?"

"Jeff needs to go home." Tears welled up in Jana's eyes—she looked defeated.

"It's too late for that. Jana, it's not your fault—Jeff is exactly where he wants to be," I answered. "Besides, maybe he found out why Flowers is so determined to get the clinics' records out of your hands. There has to be a reason for this monumental effort to destroy you and your career. Until now, the only hint of a lead we've had is this guy Roy Pence, and we know zip about him except that he's made himself perfectly acceptable to Little Rock's finest."

Sam gave me a long look. I knew I was pushing, but I was tired of dealing with his temper and his suspicions. Friend or not, it was time for him to get with the program. Fortunately, Jana burst out laughing, and Sam gave me a little salute. We moved on, but that was about it.

Clovis had slipped back into the room—he looked a good deal more relaxed. "Jeff's okay. Paul found him in a barbecue joint in DeValls Bluff. He agreed to keep eating until Paul gets there. He wants to finish whatever he's doing in the Delta, so I told Paul to stay with him."

I breathed a sigh of relief.

"Brian, Stella, and Clovis, find out all you can about this Mr. Pence. I want to know where he comes from, where he was born, where he went to school, where he's worked, and what flavor ice cream he likes. Not a stone goes unturned, not even a pebble. Got it? Here's the number Candy gave Micki. Get a record of all the phone calls that went to or from that number. Sam, how would I find out how many times Judge Purdom or Fletcher called that number?"

"Well, you could file a FOIA request with the county clerk and get a record of the calls made on the phone in his chambers, but it would take forever and wouldn't cover their personal cell phones. Not to mention it would give the game away. Kate could subpoena the information, but she won't without probable cause, and all we have is a hunch," he answered.

"There must be some way to find out whether Pence, Purdom, and Fletcher are in regular communication. And we need to find out if Micki's buddy Brady Flowers has been part of the conversation."

Micki spoke up. "Jack, let me work on this. You don't have time to get into the weeds, and I think I know how to get Kate involved. Almost nothing would make me happier than to discover Flowers is up to his neck in this conspiracy."

Sam offered, "I can talk to Robbie Staley, the county clerk. She might have a few ideas. She's definitely not a fan of Purdom."

"Now we're getting somewhere. Clovis, I bet one of your guys can find at least one person at the Health Department who doesn't like working for Flowers. See if you can find out who pulls Brady's strings.

"Micki, let's file a few motions. Purdom said he would deny a motion for a preliminary hearing. File one anyway, same for the *voir dire*. I want to overwhelm Fletcher's staff with motions, convince them we're ready to go to trial. Maybe if you wear them out, the judge and

Fletcher will feel the need to meet more often. Think Candy might keep a record of the meetings and phone calls?"

"That can be arranged." Micki's tone made me glad she was on my side.

Brian raised the question that no one had asked.

"What happens if Roy Pence is a dead end? What if he turns out to be a random friend of Purdom with no connections to Dr. Hall or the Fourche killings?"

"We'll cross that bridge if we come to it. Who is this guy anyway? He didn't just drop in from Mars."

"Maybe their bookie?" Jana suggested.

Her cool wisecrack broke the tension and we all relaxed. I was about to ask Micki about the subpoenas when Jordan poked his head through the door.

"Debbie called. Fletcher's deputy arrived with the court order to turn over all the medical records. She scanned it and emailed it to Micki."

Micki opened her laptop and read the order.

I asked. "How bad is it?"

"Damn bad."

50

THE ORDER REQUIRED Dr. Hall and her attorneys turn over every single medical record—originals and copies—in her possession and in whatever format someone kept them. We could not keep a single copy. If we needed to see any record that related to the specific charges against Dr. Hall, we would be given access at an unspecified time before trial.

It also required us to turn over any copies of reports sent to the Health Department concerning certain diseases. We were to deliver Jana's computers to the special prosecutor's office for purging of any information about the clinics' or patients' medical records. This part of the order could have been a huge pain in the ass, requiring Jana to duplicate all of her personal information, bank records, personal emails, etc. Fortunately, Stella and I had foreseen the potential breadth of the order, and she had already set up a duplicate system containing no medical records on a separate computer. Jana would never see her original computer again.

It was no surprise that Jana didn't feel the sense of satisfaction I did. "You live your life trying to be a good person, trying to give back to your community. You think you enjoy some semblance of personal privacy. Then one day you lose it. Every aspect of your life is an open book to an asshole prosecutor, dissected by state police flunkies, and you are powerless to stop it. Whatever happens, whether the verdict is innocent or guilty, my whole life will have been on display to the public, grist for easy gossip."

She shoved her hands through her hair in frustration. Sam

reached over to console her, but she shook him off. “No, don’t. I’ll be okay. It’s just, well, it’s a lot to deal with.”

“Jana, you’ve got every right to feel frustrated,” I said, pushing my chair back from the table. “Let’s take a little break, get something to drink. Are there any cookies around here?”

That got a laugh, and we rose to stretch and get a breath of air. By the time we reconvened, Jana had regained her usual composure.

“I’m sorry I lost it. Stella, thank you for backing up my computer. I can’t imagine losing my personal information.”

Stella smiled. “Fletcher telegraphed his pitch with his early morning raid. Jack knew he wouldn’t give up, we just got there ahead of him. The timing of the court order is a problem. It will be tough to turn over what they’ve asked for by noon. And what about Jeff’s computer? I bet he saved whatever he found in the Delta on his personal laptop.

I had finished reading the order. “Well, maybe Jeff’s computer can wait.”

“What do you mean?” Stella looked confused.

“The court order refers to records in the possession of Dr. Hall and her attorneys. It doesn’t say, ‘those records subject to their control or in the hands of independent contractors.’ It could be sloppy drafting or an oversight, but the way I read it, the order it doesn’t include Jeff’s computer.”

“You know good and well that won’t be the way Fletcher or the judge interpret the order,” Micki said.

“I do, but for the time being, we’ll go with my interpretation.”

“Fine—but don’t blame me when your ass winds up in jail,” Micki smiled.

“I’ll take the risk. We’ll give Fletcher all the records we have. Jeff and Stella will keep any records that are currently in their possession.”

Micki raised an eyebrow, but let it go. We spent the rest of the afternoon outlining a schedule and delegating tasks.

Jana suggested we all go out to dinner, but I declined, explaining my absence would reinforce the impression that I had bowed out of the case. If Micki and I had drinks at the hotel bar, it would be natural to assume I was handing off the representation.

Jana asked, "How long will you be gone?"

"Only a few days. I'm sorry, please trust me."

She smiled and said, "I do, even though Sam doesn't."

I turned to face him.

"Look, Sam, if I'm right, Jana won't have to plead guilty, and you and Kate will have plenty to keep you busy. So cut me some slack, watch over Jana, and have a little patience."

He didn't respond, and I gave up.

As we were riding back to the hotel, Micki asked, "What's with all these visual deceptions? Do you really think our adversaries will think you've bowed out?"

"Well, probably not, but we can keep them guessing."

"And you seem to have forgotten that I have no desire to be anywhere near the Armitage," she pointed out.

"No, I remember, but humor me this once," I begged, well aware how many times I'd used that phrase in the past. She gave me a dirty look, but let it go.

Jordan dropped us at the front door, and I found a table for two in the rear of the bar. Micki stopped at least a half a dozen tables to shake hands or greet lawyers she knew before joining me.

"Okay, every lawyer in town will know we were here together. We've accomplished the visual you wanted. Now what do you want to talk about that you don't want the others to hear?" she asked after we had ordered drinks.

"Very perceptive," I said, smiling. "I'm convinced that with Purdom in Fletcher's pocket, he will convict Jana and send her to prison for God knows how long. An appeals court might overturn a verdict if we present a perfect defense, but Fletcher and whoever is pulling his strings will have still won."

"Why? I don't understand," she responded.

"Because I don't think this charade is about Jana going to prison, but rather a need to discredit her. Over the years Jana has become not only a symbol of the plight of the very poor in Arkansas, but also a model of how to provide essential health care services for them. If Kate had indicted Jana for financial misdoings at the clinics, Fletcher wouldn't have been necessary. A special prosecutor was someone's backup plan. Branding her a felon would do the trick. I bet if I went to Fletcher and offered to plead her guilty to a felony, we could get Jana off on probation."

"Why is destroying her credibility so important?" she asked.

The waiter brought our drinks, giving me a moment to gather my thoughts.

"Micki, a few years ago Jana told the state legislature that if they continued to fund the clinics, she could use the data to identify the cause of certain diseases that targeted Arkansas's poor. Someone heard that testimony and decided to stop her. Brady Flowers convinced the legislature to defund and close the clinics, but getting the records proved to be more difficult. Once they think they have the records, they might back off a little."

"You alluded to this earlier. So you want me to buy time while you try to discover the why and who?" she asked.

"More than that. While I'm gone, I want you to find out what kind of deal Fletcher is willing to make. If he thinks all the medical records are safely tucked away, he might agree to let Jana plead guilty without incurring jail time. We may decide to fight the charges all the way to the Supreme Court, but Jana must know all her options. I don't like it, but we need to keep the door open."

"What happens if you discover why and who is behind all this? You still have Fletcher and the judge to overcome. I bet they've already figured out how to prevent you from introducing anything that exonerates Dr. Hall."

"If that happens, I'll need Kate. But let's not get ahead of ourselves. For the time being, you focus on convincing Fletcher you've taken over the defense and want to make a deal."

Micki smiled and said, "God, it's fun to watch how your mind works. Any other orders before you fly off to San Antonio?"

"Only one. I want you to file a FOIA request asking the Health Department to produce any and all of the clinics' records in their possesion."

"Fat chance of that. And to what end?" she asked.

"Those records are at the core of the attack on Jana. The bad guys will destroy them as soon as they can, but a FOIA request isn't something they can easily ignore. I hope Fletcher will ask you to withdraw the request as part of any plea deal. If he does, we'll know we're on the right track."

"Jack Patterson, you can be one devious son-of-a-bitch."

51

I SPENT THE EVENING trying to read briefing books about the Lobos' potential move to San Antonio. Despite my efforts to concentrate, I couldn't help thinking about Jana. I had tried to be optimistic, but in truth I had nothing to work with—Fletcher held all the cards. I couldn't let Red down, but how could I abandon Jana? Either way, I felt downright shitty.

For the next three days, I went from one meeting to another. Red was pleased with my knowledge of the situation—I credited Gina's briefing books. We threw San Antonio and the NFL for a loop by questioning them about how the city would assimilate the players and the staff into the community. They were expecting questions about tax benefits and infrastructure issues such as a new stadium, but we asked about the city's commitment to affordable housing, charitable organizations, and its support of ethnic communities.

I'd like to take credit for the strategy, but it was Gina's. It kept the city leaders off balance. They were ready to go toe-to-toe on tax subsidies, but Gina threw them curve balls about public education and the availability of arts and sciences venues. Every time they brought up the preferred location for the stadium, I raised concerns about the safety of the city's drinking water.

After three days, the city caved on almost everything we needed in the way of tax subsidies and infrastructure. They were ready to do almost anything to avoid another question about the EPA's latest evaluation of the city's sewer system or the city's lack of public transportation.

Red offered to drop me off in Little Rock on his way back to DC, and I accepted. Clovis's people had found more than a few disgruntled Health Department employees, but so far no one had volunteered information about falsifying reports to the CDC. Stella had hacked into Pence's computer and phone records, but had found nothing fishy so far. Jeff and Brian got the soil samples they needed without getting shot, but were waiting on the test results.

Micki had better luck. Fletcher had met with her when she delivered the medical reports and Jana's computers. She played frustrated by my absence and asked about a plea. Fletcher told her he would be open to a discussion after he had reviewed the medical records and verified that her compliance met with the court order. Meanwhile, Sarah and Trey had been preparing motions for her signature. She had moved for a preliminary hearing, a motion to let defense counsel conduct *voir dire* of the jury, a motion for a continuance, and a motion to dismiss the indictment asserting that Fletcher had exceeded his authority.

They would file the FOIA requests this afternoon. Purdom would deny every motion, but we hoped Fletcher would agree to a plea deal if Micki withdrew the FOIA requests.

Clovis was waiting when we touched down at Hodges Air Center.

"Welcome home," he said as I hopped into the car. "There's been a change in plans. I've canceled your hotel room here in Little Rock and booked you on a flight to St. Louis this afternoon. I've also booked a room at a hotel near Beth's home in St. Louis."

I spoke in a panic, "What's wrong? Has something happened to Beth?"

"No, sorry to scare you. The travel arrangements are a diversion. Micki wants the team to stay at her house. It'll be like the old days. Well, not quite: we'll have Larry's company."

"Hey, I like Larry. There's a lot more to him than meets the eye," I responded. "Staying at Micki's makes sense. Has anything happened?"

"I don't want to cut in front, but Judge Purdom has scheduled a hearing for tomorrow morning. Word is he'll rule on the motions Micki filed and lay down parameters for the trial. Fletcher has called Micki and offered to meet after the hearing to discuss a plea deal."

"Purdom will deny every motion, and Fletcher gets to bargain from a position of strength," I responded, thinking out loud.

"That's the way it looks."

"Well, let's get this show on the road."

We reached Micki's ranch just before two o'clock. Micki gave me a few minutes to get settled before she called us into her living area. Everyone was present: Sam and Jana, Brian, Stella, Clovis, Jeff, and Micki. I asked Larry to join us, and after a nod from Micki he chose a chair near the kitchen door. Big Mike had begged off—he wanted to meet with Paul about increased security for the compound.

Micki took charge. "Jack, sit back and listen. I know you're ready to hand out more orders, but let me give you the full picture first. The situation has become somewhat complex. Much of what we have discovered would be inadmissible in court because of the, shall we say, *unusual* methods Stella employed, but I'm sure you can figure out how to use it. Let's begin with Jeff."

Beth had introduced me to Jeff when they were both at Davidson. He was the catcher for the baseball team and looked like Johnny Bench with his stocky chest and big forearms. After years of medical school and long hours of internships and residencies, he had lost his catcher's build and young face. He was now a grown man who exuded a physician's confidence.

"After an analysis of the Delta clinic's medical records, I can confirm that the clinic treated an unusual number of farm and migrant workers suffering from Alzheimer's, Parkinson's, and multiple sclerosis. Many of the children treated presented with symptoms that a reasonable doctor would once have attributed to arsenic poisoning.

"The FDA banned the use of arsenic in pesticides in the eighties, so I thought maybe the problem was an improper use of MSMA."

He stopped when he saw Micki's frown.

"Sorry," he smiled. "That's monosodium methanearsonate, an organic arsenical that's been approved for use on cotton. I suspected that MSMA had gotten into the water table from the cotton fields, but that's not what I found.

"With the help of Google, I was able to pinpoint where each patient lived at the time of treatment. I decided to inspect the various farms in the area to get soil samples and to find out what crops were grown where. I found no problems in either the soil or water in the cotton fields, but in the rice and soybean fields the levels of arsenic were off the charts. I found other chemicals in the soil that I couldn't identify. I've sent the samples to a lab at Barnes in St. Louis for a more thorough identification. Arsenic and other chemicals have also crept into water tables in the rice and bean fields.

"I wanted to check out the homes of the farm workers, especially the migrant workers who lived in trailers. I managed to scrounge up an official-looking uniform and was able pose as a county inspector." He paused to enjoy our chuckles and murmurs of appreciation.

"The water from the faucets and showers had similar levels of arsenic and contained the same unidentified chemicals I'd found in the fields. It's a wonder that everyone who lives in those trailers isn't sick as a dog."

I interrupted. "Did you talk to any actual farmers?"

"Most of those fields are owned by corporate farming operations. The on-site managers were not interested in discussing arsenic. I left one farm at gun point.

"Here's the puzzle. The required reports from the Delta clinic to the state's Health Department clearly depicted the number of Alzheimer's, Parkinson's, and MS cases. There is no doubt in my mind that red flags and alarm bells should have gone off, and the state should have notified the CDC. But they didn't. Nothing unusual has been reported from Arkansas to the CDC in years."

"What do you think is causing the high levels of arsenic?" I asked.

"I don't know. No manufacturer of pesticides would dare take the risk of using arsenic."

I looked to Sam. "When are we scheduled to meet with Tag?"

"Tomorrow. You're having lunch with Tag at the Buffalo Grill after the hearing."

Micki interrupted, "Jack, if you don't quit asking questions, we'll be here all day. It's Stella's turn."

Stella looked a little nervous, a most unusual occurrence. "Jack, please don't ask how I discovered what I did. You won't be able to use any of it in court. Fletcher has been in regular contact with Roy Pence for months, long before the governor appointed him special prosecutor. Since the appointment, Fletcher has been in regular contact with Judge Purdom, and the two of them have had at least five three-way conference calls with Pence."

"Well, that's a can of worms," I noted.

"More than just worms," she said, frowning. "The real snake in the grass is Brady Flowers. He's had any number of conversations with Pence over the last couple of years on both the Health Department's landline and his cell phone. The traffic has picked up in the last few months. I have a complete record of the days and times."

"Any possibility Pence called Stalinski?" I asked.

"Hard to say, Stalinski used a burn phone while he was here, and Pence called a burn phone during that time, but I can't determine the number he called. Pence called a number I think belonged to Mace Cooper while Mace was alive, but I need to verify that number before I'm sure. I'm working on it. On several occasions Pence called the same international number. Mimi is trying to track down who he called."

"Good work, Stella," I responded. "And don't worry—sometimes the end result does justify the means.

"Okay, who's next?"

52

BRIAN REPORTED that Pence had rented an office on the twelfth floor of the old Worthen Bank building and was a registered lobbyist for an amorphous organization called The Agricultural and Chemical Trust. Its published address was the same as Pence's office, but Brian found no filing at the courthouse or the Secretary of State's office describing its beneficiaries or terms. The Trust maintained a bank account at Larry's family's bank, Bradford Bank and Trust.

Larry had no current connection with the family bank, and said he'd never heard of either the Trust or Roy Pence.

Jana noted that she and Brian had confirmed Jeff's findings, adding, "I'm disappointed in myself. I should have done the analysis I promised the legislature when I had the chance."

"Don't be so hard on yourself, Jana. You had your hands full. And if you had, you might not be alive to tell the tale. A little digging might result in interesting trends at the other clinics," I said.

"What do you mean? The other three clinics served more urban populations, not rural areas growing rice, beans, or cotton."

"Your clinics treated the poor, a population almost invisible to luckier folks. Without a determined state Health Department, an aggressive EPA, or an informed CDC, unscrupulous people will cut corners. That's why city water pipes are full of lead, air is full of pollutants from refineries and power plants, and companies dump raw sewage into our lakes and streams. Those same people need cheap labor to do work no one else will do, but they don't give a rat's ass about the health of their workers. In fact, they are considered expendable." I knew I was on a high horse, but it felt pretty good.

Micki brought me back down to earth. "Jack, your outrage won't do Jana one bit of good. Stick with the business at hand."

Clovis was next. "Brady Flowers has put the fear of God in his employees: it's either his way or the highway. I've heard rumors that women who want to keep their job learn how to keep the boss happy, if you get my drift, but they're only rumors.

"We also learned that Flowers is a control freak. No reports or findings are forwarded or published without his personal review and approval. The few employees who agreed to speak say this process has created a bottleneck."

"So if a report is supposed to go to the CDC, Flowers has to review it and approve it first?" I asked.

Clovis answered, "That's about the size of it. He keeps all pending matters locked in a file cabinet in his office. Employees learn not to ask whether a certain report has gone out. An inquiring mind results in a quick transfer to Arkansas's version of Siberia."

Micki asked, "What about the legislature? They audit most departments at least every other year."

"They haven't audited the Health Department since Flowers became its head. The legislature audits the department's programs and the recipients of its grants, but not the operations of the department itself. The scuttlebutt is that the chairwoman of the Appropriations Committee and Flowers have a close relationship. It also doesn't hurt that the chairwoman's husband, Jonas, works for the Health Department in a cushy job that requires constant travel to the four corners of the state."

"Well, well, how convenient." I commented, trying to keep a straight face.

Micki said, "Okay, Jack, we get the point—my turn. I have filed the motions you and I discussed. Fletcher's responses and briefs were due yesterday, but I've gotten nothing. Purdom has called a hearing for tomorrow. I'm sure he'll deny every single motion. Fletcher wants to meet after the hearing, but if you're in the courtroom, he might cancel."

"Let's make sure he doesn't. Have you prepared the Freedom of Information requests for the medical records?"

"I have."

"Make sure they're filed before the hearing. Fletcher will want those requests withdrawn. The filing is important to get his best offer."

Jana interrupted in a sharp voice. "Offer? What offer? What are you talking about, Jack?"

It was time to tell Jana and Sam about my backup plan.

"Jana, you told me you'll plead guilty before you let the prosecution force your patients to testify or go public with their health issues. I've taken you at your word. I've developed a strategy to end this case before it goes to trial, but it's somewhat of a long shot."

"I haven't changed my mind. I won't violate my patients' confidences, nor will I put my staff in jeopardy. There will be no trial. So what is all this about a plea?" she demanded.

"Micki and I believe that given enough pressure, Fletcher may relent on his determination to send you to prison. After we issue FOIA requests for the clinics' medical records, we think he'll offer you a single felony charge with no jail time in exchange for our dropping the FOIA requests."

"It's all about the medical records isn't it?" she asked.

"It has to be. They've been after those records since day one, and they're determined to brand you as a felon so you have no credibility."

"So, you withdraw the FOIA requests, and I get a get-out-of-jail-free card?"

"That's about it."

"Okay. Do I have any part in the decision to withdraw the FOIA requests?"

"You do, but if you don't allow me to withdraw them, you face almost certain conviction and, with this judge, a lengthy prison sentence."

"When do I have to decide? Do Sam and I have time to talk about it?"

"You do. Micki and I will need your decision after the hearing tomorrow morning."

"You'll have it."

It was Sam's turn to act surprised. "Jana, if Jack can get you off without serving time, you need to jump at the chance. A conviction without jail time is like a slap on the wrist."

Sam obviously knew better, but I let his statement pass. A felony conviction has serious consequences that would remain with Jana for the rest of her life. A felony is its own life sentence.

"You and I will discuss it, darling. But not now." Her firm tone ended the conversation. I wished I could be a fly on the wall when that discussion occurred.

Jana turned to me. "Do you need me any longer? This has been a lot to take in—I'd like to go home and think it over for a while. Sam can tell me anything I need to know when he comes over tonight. I'll see the rest of you tomorrow."

I made no objection, and she rose to leave. Sam jumped up and walked outside with her. Clovis told us not to worry—Paul would drive her home, and he had assigned several men to watch her house.

As soon as the door closed, Micki asked, "Jack, do you think she might not allow us to withdraw the FOIA requests?"

"I don't think so, but this case brings a new surprise every day. We'll just have to wait and see. Speaking of tomorrow, did you prepare the other motion we talked about?"

"You mean that damned fool idea you had in San Antonio?"

"That's the one."

"I did, but let's be clear. You want to ask the judge to instruct the jury that if they feel Jana acted in the best interest of her patients, they can ignore the law and find her not guilty. I've heard of jury nullification, but you want the judge to instruct the jury it's okay. Are you crazy? How long do you think it will take for Purdom to deny your request?"

"About a heartbeat, but that's not the point. I want both Fletcher and the judge to think I'll do everything possible to argue jury nullification."

"Why? Another diversion?"

"Only partly. As you know, I have a reputation for outlandish courtroom antics. I want them to worry about what I might do during the trial. I want them to be so worried they place a call to Pence after our hearing."

"You can't wiretap their phones. That's where I draw the line."

Micki and I might as well have been alone in the room. Her voice had risen and the others were listening intently.

"Why on earth would I want to bug their phones? That wouldn't be fair," I answered with a grin. Stella let out a whoop and everyone relaxed.

Micki shook her head. "Sometimes I don't want to know what's going on in that brain of yours. When Sam returns, let's talk about how we can get access to the phone records and the files in Flower's office. We have lots to accomplish, and we are running out of time."

53

Sam returned a few minutes later, shaking his head in disbelief. He said they had agreed to talk again tonight, but Jana was seriously thinking about refusing any deal with Fletcher.

"Micki, let's make sure we file the FOIA requests tomorrow morning before the hearing. Clovis, ask one of your men to let us know if shredders show up at the Health Department or Fletcher's office. Stella, what phone company records do we need?"

"For Pence, it's all Verizon. For the courthouse, Fletcher, and the Health Department, it's AT&T," she answered.

"Micki, we'll need subpoenas for the phone records. Clovis, have them served right after her meeting with Fletcher."

Micki frowned. "Purdom isn't about to let you subpoena phone records, and if he does, Fletcher will move to quash them."

"Micki, we need subpoenas for more than the phone records. I want to subpoena Pence and Flowers as witnesses. I also want a subpoena *duces tecum* for all the files in Flowers's file cabinet as well as his personal bank records."

"Are you trying to get yourself killed? What are you going to say when Purdom asks how their testimony can be relevant?"

"I'll say Flowers harassed the prosecuting attorney's office for months, and I want the jury to hear why."

"Purdom will never let that into evidence," Sam said.

I could tell Brian had a question, but was reluctant to interrupt. "What's on your mind, Brian?"

He looked embarrassed but spoke up. "I don't understand.

You're issuing subpoenas for a trial that won't happen? Maggie told me to expect the unexpected, but I'm having trouble following your thinking."

Micki chuckled. "Brian, you hit the nail on the head. Why are we going to all this trouble if Jana won't allow a trial to go forward?"

I responded. "I hope the FOIA requests will bring about a plea deal Jana can accept. That seems to be the most realistic solution without going to trial. She's thrown a wrench in the works by suggesting she might not take such a deal, but maybe I can talk some sense into her. I damn sure will try."

"So will I. I can't bear the thought of Jana in prison for a day, much less for years. But I have to warn you—Jana is headstrong and rarely changes her mind," Sam said.

"I know it's a long shot, but I also hope to talk her out of pleading guilty to protect her patients," I said.

"Not much chance of that," Micki countered. "I tried while you were away and got nowhere."

"Me, too," added Sam.

"Which brings us back to Brian's question: why are we busting our butts to prepare for a trial that won't happen? It's a good question. I know the chances are slim, but I hope all the various motions, subpoenas, FOIA requests, and my courtroom tactics will force the opposition into a mistake. They don't know the case won't go to trial.

"If they think I might introduce jury nullification into the proceedings, force Pence or Flowers to testify, or subject the health clinics' medical records to public scrutiny, they might slip up. I have no idea what form such an error might take, and if it isn't forthcoming, we'll have to adjust on the fly."

Brian responded, "Okay, but the judge is a puppet, and Fletcher pulls his strings. He'll surely deny every motion Micki has filed. I don't see Fletcher leaving the courtroom worried about much of anything. What am I missing?"

Micki giggled. "I like this guy, Jack. He says what I want to say, but nicer."

I smiled. "I may fall flat on my face tomorrow, but something tells me to push the envelope as far as I can and see what happens. Besides, does anyone have a better idea?"

Their silence was just becoming uncomfortable when Micki replied.

"Well, I sure don't. And if Maggie were here, she would remind us that she trusts Jack's instincts more than most people's certainties."

Sam nodded his head and said, "I hate to admit it, but she's right."

We had been going at it for a long while and were all tired and on edge, so Micki called a break. Clovis had ordered pizza. It wasn't Theo's in New Orleans, but it was good enough.

I pulled Jeff aside. "Jeff, your findings may have given us the break we need—thank you. I have another favor to ask."

"You're welcome, happy to help. What else can I do?"

"You might want to know what I'm asking before you agree," I suggested. "I want to list you as an expert witness. As you know, a trial is unlikely, but I want them to wonder why you're here, what you know."

"I'm not sure what kind of expert I might be, but I'll do my best."

"Thanks." I had poured myself a glass of wine when Stella walked over holding a beer and balancing pizza on a paper plate. I pulled up a chair, and we sat down.

"Stella, you've done terrific work," I said. "Any chance Verizon or AT&T will turn over the phone records without a fight?"

"Nope, not even with a subpoena. Folks expect their carriers to protect their privacy."

"Okay, be thinking about how we might give them some incentive to cooperate."

Stella asked, "Have you looked at the notebook I gave you?"

"Not yet. I'll scan it tonight," I said, although I didn't look forward to looking at what I imagined would be a list of phone numbers.

"You might find page seventy-three of interest," she commented as Clovis came to join us.

I heard her, but it didn't sink in. I was tired and ready to call it a day. No one objected. I remembered to ask Micki to subpoena Pence's bank records and to remind Clovis to check in with the people in St. Louis watching Beth. I found Sam in the kitchen and gave him a couple of suggestions about how to convince Jana to go along with our plans tomorrow.

He started to respond, but thought better of it and left. Clovis and Stella weren't far behind him, and Jeff and Brian soon wished us goodnight. I wasn't all that comfortable sitting by the fire while Micki snuggled against Larry on the big sofa. I told them I had to catch up on some reading and settled into a comfortable chair in my bedroom with Stella's book of phone numbers.

I turned to page seventy-three as she had suggested. It contained a list of a series of phone calls to a number in Little Rock. Stella had noted that the dates of these calls coincided with the week the governor had appointed a special prosecutor. Then I realized who Pence had called.

I said to myself, "Well, I'll be damned."

I also checked the date of the overseas call. As I expected, it took place the day the papers ran with the story about the hanging.

I wanted to share my newfound knowledge with Micki, but decided against it. Let Micki and Larry have a night to themselves. If I was right, none of us would sleep much for the next few days.

54

When we arrived at the courthouse, I sat on a bench while Micki went to see what she could learn from Candy. Brian and Jeff went directly to the courtroom to save a few places behind the rail. Clovis reported that Sam and Jana were on their way, and that he had heard from the people looking after Beth. All was quiet in St. Louis.

I had told no one that Mimi had called me early this morning.

"Sam called me last night with the phone information, but he wouldn't tell me what to do with it. You told him I would know what to do."

"Well, don't you?"

"The number does me no good unless somebody calls it." She sounded frustrated.

"Exactly," I said.

"Don't be coy, Jack."

"Listen, I'm not being coy, only careful. I don't know European Union law. If I suggest you take a certain action, for all I know I might be committing a crime. I asked Sam to tell you what Stella discovered—the rest is up to you."

"Fair enough, but at least tell me if Pence or anyone else might call this number again."

"I think someone will call that number before the sun sets, but I could be wrong."

"Okay, I'll take it from here. Be careful, Jack."

Micki rejoined me in the hallway. She had learned nothing from Candy except that the judge was on the phone and was not to be disturbed. So Micki and I went into the courtroom to set up shop at the counsel's table. Jana and Sam soon joined us. Sam's frown told me he'd been unsuccessful in influencing Jana's decision to plead guilty.

Jana spoke before I could even say good morning. "Is there a place we can talk, Jack? No offense, Micki, but I'd like this conversation to be private."

I told her we had about fifteen minutes, and she said that would be more than enough time. We stepped outside and found a bench in the waiting area.

She took a deep breath. "I appreciate everything you have done and are trying to do, but I've decided I want to end this process. Sam doesn't agree, but it's not his decision to make. I want to plead guilty, and I refuse to let you back off on the FOIA requests. I want to know what is making my patients sick. If you withdrew the FOIA requests and the clinics' records were destroyed, I couldn't live with myself.

"Sam asked if I've thought about what would happen to our life together. I want that very much, but I couldn't live with myself, much less Sam, if I sold my soul. I know what a felony conviction will mean for us, but at least I'll know I didn't sell out."

I saw the resolve in her eyes, and knew I needed to buy time.

"Jana, I knew this would be your decision, and I respect it."

"I hoped you would understand. But you'll need all your skills to help Sam understand." She tried to stifle a sniff and pulled a tissue from her handbag.

"It's okay, Jana, but I need one thing from you. You say you want to understand who and what is making your patients sick—well, so do I. But I need time. I won't let this case get anywhere close to trial, but to accomplish what you and I both want, I need time. I need you to let me act as if I have every intention of going to trial. You may think I'm spinning my wheels, but I do have a plan."

"Give me one good reason to delay, not just a 'trust me.'"

"I can give you three. We're still waiting for the lab results from the soil samples. You can continue to analyze the records in Jeff's possession. And as long as you don't plead guilty, you have another day with Sam. You might not have many more days with him after you plead guilty, so why not enjoy those you do have?"

She smiled. "I never knew you were such a romantic."

I didn't either, but I would use any trick in the book to gain more time.

"Okay, Jack," she said. "I'll play my part, but I'm not about to let you talk me into a trial or withdrawing the FOIA requests. Don't waste your breath."

"You have my word," I said.

She relaxed and asked, "Okay, what next? What will happen this morning?"

"I intend to piss off both the judge and the prosecutor, and hopefully get closer to finding out who and what is behind this prosecution." I rose and took her arm. "Time to go—you don't want to be late for the show."

******

"Oyez, oyez, the court is in session, the Honorable Judge Purdom presiding," proclaimed the bailiff.

Purdom rushed into the courtroom, his gun belt and firearm in plain view. He sat down, glanced toward Fletcher and his entourage of deputy prosecutors, and smiled. He turned to our table, gave a nod to Micki, then fixed me with a frown.

"Mr. Patterson. I see you are back. I had hoped you would return to DC."

"Wouldn't miss this hearing for the world, your Honor."

He frowned again and said, "We'll see about that. Several motions are pending before this court. I'm prepared to rule."

Micki spoke. "Your Honor, aren't you going to hear oral argument before you decide?"

"I am not. Your motions were well-briefed, Ms. Lawrence. I see no need for oral argument."

Micki answered, "Very well, Your Honor. On another issue, and I assume it's an oversight, I haven't received the prosecution's response to any of my motions."

"Your motions pertain to how I will conduct the trial. I don't believe they called for a response from the prosecution."

Fletcher didn't even try to hide a satisfied smirk.

The judge read from his notes. "I deny your motion for a continuance. This is a documents case that will require little testimony. Trial will begin in two weeks. Your motion to conduct *voir dire* is denied. You know better than to ask, Ms. Lawrence. You've been in my courtroom many times."

"Doesn't hurt a girl to try," Micki flirted. Nothing else had worked.

Purdom smiled. "I guess you have a point. Denied. Your motion for a preliminary hearing is denied. I already advised Mr. Patterson not to bother, but I guess he hasn't been around to tell you."

So, Purdom knew I'd been out of town—interesting.

"This last motion came in this morning. I see the fingerprints of Mr. Patterson on this one. Mr. Fletcher, has the prosecution seen this motion for a jury instruction?"

"We have Your Honor, and we oppose it."

"May I speak, Your Honor?" I asked.

"No, you may not. Your brief was sufficient. Motion denied. Let me make myself clear. If you even *hint* at the subject of jury nullification again in my courtroom, I will hold you in contempt and refer your conduct to the supreme court's committee on professional responsibility for disbarment. I will not put up with that kind of conduct in my courtroom. Do you understand, Mr. Patterson?"

"I hear you loud and clear, Your Honor."

Judge Purdom's face turned brick red, and for a second I thought he might pull out his pistol. "I didn't ask you if you *heard* me, counsel. I asked if you *understand* me? Do you?"

I paused, but gave in. "Yes, sir, I do understand, Your Honor," I said, returning his glare with one of my own.

The silence was broken when a young man in a dark suit slipped into the courtroom, whispered to Fletcher, and left.

The judge rapped his gavel on the desk and said, "If there are no further issues, this trial will begin in two weeks."

Fletcher spoke from his seat. "Your Honor, my associate just told me that defense counsel has submitted a Freedom of Information request to the Health Department for the clinics' medical records. He also told me that defense counsel has listed a Dr. Jeff Fields on his witness list. I'm concerned this FOIA request is an attempt to circumvent the court's order that the defendant turn over the medical records. The use of an expert witness is an attempt to introduce opinion testimony to excuse Dr. Hall's conduct, a back-handed attempt to get around this court's admonition concerning jury nullification."

"May I respond, Your Honor?"

I knew Purdom wanted to tell me to shut up, but he had no choice but to say what he did. "Go ahead, Mr. Patterson, but make it brief."

"Regarding Dr. Fields, if the prosecution would like to verify his credentials, I will support their motion for a continuance until they can depose him."

He wasn't about let me get away with that trick. "I don't think his qualifications are the issue. As I've said, this is a documents case, and I will not allow you to introduce expert testimony that Dr. Hall's conduct was medically acceptable. The law is the law, no matter what some 'expert' might say. You may proffer Dr. Fields's testimony, but I will not let a jury hear anything he has to say. Don't even think about bringing him into the courtroom."

He'd given me an issue on appeal—too bad we'd never have a trial.

"Your Honor, as for the FOIA request, the law gives me the right to make such a request. I am not trying to get around this court's order. But as you have said, this is a documents case, and at this point I don't have access to the patients' records which the prosecution intends to introduce to prosecute my client. Mr. Fletcher has said he will provide me copies at some point, but the FOIA request serves two purposes. It ensures I will get all the records I need in plenty of time and gives me access to any other records that may be exculpatory.

"Your Honor, surely neither you nor the prosecutor want to deny me access to exculpatory evidence."

We had gone off script, and neither the judge nor Fletcher knew what to do. They would likely figure out how to force me to withdraw the FOIA requests, but for now they were stymied.

"Your Honor, you asked if there were any further issues. I have one more procedural issue. You ordered me not to introduce any expert testimony, but my co-counsel tells me that several witnesses to the actual procedures at issue are not cooperative. I need to issue subpoenas, and ask your permission to work with the clerk to get them out."

I was well aware that none of Jana's patients or staff wanted to be witnesses. I was counting on the fact that Fletcher's people had experienced the same reluctance, so he would suspect nothing strange in my request to issue subpoenas for reluctant witnesses. The judge looked to Fletcher, who appeared to be still flustered over the FOIA request. Purdom cleared his throat and Fletcher nodded his assent.

The judge said, "I will allow both the prosecution and the defense to brief me on the issue of the FOIA requests, and after due consideration I will rule. As to trial subpoenas, I'll allow counsel latitude in issuing subpoenas. If the prosecution has any problems with your subpoenas, I'm sure they will move to quash. Otherwise, work with the county clerk. The trial is fast approaching."

55

WE ALL ROSE, and as soon as Purdom left the room, Micki walked over to the prosecution's table to ask Fletcher when they could meet. Fletcher was still confused, and Micki had to repeat her request. He recovered and told her curtly that any meeting would have to wait until the afternoon. She pressed him for a definite time, and they agreed on two o'clock. We suspected he needed guidance from Pence on how to handle our FOIA requests. That gave me plenty of time to talk with Jana.

I had suggested that we meet at Micki's office after the hearing. We managed to avoid the press and within thirty minutes everyone was in Micki's conference room.

"Jana, Micki will meet with Fletcher this afternoon. He'll want us to withdraw the FOIA requests and he'll want you to plead guilty. In exchange for your guilty plea, he will support our request for no prison time."

"I told you I won't accept such a deal. I want you to fight to keep the medical records. My patients deserve to know what is making them sick."

"I understand your position, but I still want Micki to meet with Fletcher. I want her to push Fletcher to agree that if the judge won't accept his recommendation for no prison, the deal is off. She won't make a big stink about withdrawing the FOIA requests, but she'll be firm on the issue of prison."

"You think Fletcher and the judge might have worked up a bait and switch?" Micki interrupted. "Fletcher recommends no prison, but the judge won't go along. Fletcher gets to keep his end of the bargain, but gets what he's wanted all along."

"He won't be the first prosecutor to play that game. He promises leniency and blames the judge when the defendant gets screwed," I agreed.

"Should I be offended?" Sam asked, the first sign of humor he'd shown in days.

Micki smiled. "No Sam, you've always kept your word when your office made a plea deal. But it's a well-known tactic, and Jack has every right to be suspicious." She turned back to me. "How do you want me to leave it with Fletcher?"

"Tell him you have to clear everything with the client, but that the deal looks good. Then hightail it back here. We'll give Jana one more time to rethink her position, but if she stays firm, I'll call Fletcher and tell him the deal is off."

"I've told you over and over—I won't change my mind!" Jana exclaimed.

"Seems to me you're in a mighty big hurry to go to prison," Micki responded sharply. "Jack asked for time. Give him a chance to do his job."

Jana seemed ready to reply in kind, but instead sat down rather abruptly.

"And why should you get to give Fletcher the good news?" Micki asked, turning to me.

I paused, wondering if I should tell them what I expected. *Oh, what the hell.*

"Because when we refuse the deal and subpoena Pence and Flowers, someone will decide it's time to get rid of me once and for all. I want to distance you as much as I can from that possibility."

"Then why on earth do you want to subpoena the records, Pence, and Flowers? Jana has already decided there will be no deal and no trial—she's determined to plead guilty. Why make yourself a target?" Micki asked, and Jana and Brian nodded in agreement.

"For the same reason Jana is refusing to accept Fletcher's deal. I want to know who's behind her prosecution and why. I want to know why those folks in the Delta got sick. Unless I push hard, Jana will go to jail and we'll never know. When we issue those subpoenas, two things will happen. Fletcher will move to quash the subpoenas. He doesn't care whether or not Jana's guilty. He's controlled by either Flowers or Pence. Plus it's an ego thing with him."

"And Judge Purdom will grant his motion," Micki said, using a tone reserved for five-year-olds.

"Right. He's in Fletcher's pocket. If Pence and Flowers are the bad guys, they'll worry about what I know, and will hire someone like Stalinski to...well, to take me out."

"Sam, put a stop to this. I can handle prison, but I can't handle Jack risking his life!" Jana exclaimed.

Sam didn't respond, and Jana cried, "Sam, do something!"

I looked at Sam, and like when we were schoolboys, I knew what he was thinking. He turned to Jana and spoke.

"I will do something, Jana, but you won't like it. Jack has been right to encourage me to sit this one out. He's right that my judgment is clouded by my love for you. He offers good counsel and is an even better friend, but it's time I did what I should have done in the first place—take the political heat and go back to work. If Jack's instincts are right, a murderer is about to get off scot-free, and poor people in the Delta will continue to get sick and die."

"Sam, if you get any further involved in this case it could mean your career," Micki warned.

"Let's see—Jana will plead guilty to a crime she didn't commit and go to prison to protect her patients. Jack's ready to risk his life to bait a hit man. But *I'm* supposed to worry about my political career?

"Jack, after Micki meets with Fletcher and you issue your subpoenas, I want you to come to my office with every bit of evidence you have, admissible or not. Kate and I will be waiting."

Micki hadn't given up. "Sam, we have no hard or admissible evidence, just supposition and Jack's instincts."

Sam smiled. "Weren't you the one who said we should trust Jack's instincts?"

Micki shrugged, and Sam took Jana's hand.

"Come on Jana, let's get you home. I've got a full afternoon ahead of me."

The die was cast. Sam and Jana left, and I went back to giving orders.

"Brian and Stella, try to assemble everything you have into a format I can give to Sam and Kate this afternoon."

"Everything?" Stella asked nervously.

"The phone records, the medical records, the summary reports you made for me, yes, everything. Don't worry about where it came from—I'll deal with that if need be."

Micki warned, "Fletcher and the judge will have a cow when they discover you gave Sam a copy of the medical records."

I smiled. "Yes, they will, but I think they will have met their match in an energized Sam Pagano. Jeff, the same goes for you. I want you to give Sam whatever you've got. And see if you can try to light a fire under that lab. We need their results. If you need help, ask Brian.

"Micki, you've got plenty on your plate. Meeting with Fletcher and getting the subpoenas out and served won't be easy. I'll text you after I've had lunch with Tag Wingfield.

"Clovis, are your people ready to serve the subpoenas? And do you mind calling Sam? He's probably forgotten about lunch."

"Is that all, counselor?" Micki asked, her voice sharp with both irritation and anxiety.

Before I could reply, Clovis stepped in.

"We've got it covered, Jack. Time to go." His voice was reassuring. I hoped I exuded the same confidence.

On our way to lunch he said, "Sam texted to say he would meet us at the Buffalo Grill in a few. He hadn't forgotten."

I had a sudden thought and called Micki.

"I'm an idiot," I began.

"You'll get no argument from me, partner. Except you're the one having a burger with an old baseball buddy, while I'm struggling to get all your subpoenas ready. Who's the idiot?"

"The subpoenas are why I'm calling. Make sure we ask for Pence's and Flowers's computers and any electronic devices, like an Amazon Echo. We also need to subpoena Google or Yahoo or whoever to get their emails and do a social media search. Pence may not be on Facebook, but I bet Flowers is."

"Stella's way ahead of you. She's sent me the precise language we should use for the subpoenas. If Flowers is dumb enough to have an Echo and we can get it, no telling what we'll hear. Stella tells me that an Echo records every noise in a house or an apartment twenty-four hours a day. We're on top of things, Jack. Enjoy your lunch."

We pulled into the parking lot and I spotted Tag Wingfield, my old shortstop for the Stafford State Cardinals, waiting outside the Buffalo Grill with Sam. Would have known him anywhere.

He was about average height, maybe five foot ten, and as wiry as they come. He had a rifle arm when we were in college, and very few balls got past him. Nobody on the team worked harder to improve. I don't think he ever committed an error when I pitched, and he turned a lot of decent hits into routine outs. He had aged well—his hair was grey but still full, and years of working in the sun had given him a permanent tan.

We greeted each other with hugs and firm handshakes, picked up a pitcher of cold beer at the bar and found a table in the back. He was happy to tell me all about his twin girls, who both now lived in San Francisco and had formed a partnership to produce documentary films.

We all ordered grilled turkey sandwiches with fries. I don't know why they're so good, but take my word for it, they are. After we'd caught up on our kids, Tag got straight to the point.

"Sam says you've got questions about farming. Can't imagine why or if I can help, but fire away."

"You've probably read that I represent Dr. Jana Hall. She ran a clinic in the Delta for years. I don't know…?"

He stopped me. "Sure I know Jana. Haven't seen her in a while, but I used to send all my workers to her clinic. That clinic improved the quality of health care in the Delta by about a hundred percent. She's easy on the eyes, too, as I remember. What does she have to do with farming?"

"Well, she treated several patients at the Delta clinic who had symptoms of arsenic poisoning. I thought you might know what caused it. Or maybe you know if there's a farmer in your parts who might try to get around the ban on arsenic in pesticides. We know that a variation of arsenic can be used on cotton, but soil samples indicate it might have been used on beans and rice."

Tag's toned changed. "No farmer I know would dare use arsenic anywhere near his beans or rice. If he did, the EPA would be the least of his problems. His neighbors would beat the shit out of him and run him out of town on a rail. Took us years to get that poison out of our soil and water."

That was no help at all, but he had more to say. "But I know that a bunch of the corporate farms use a new product called ZEIT. It's a combination pesticide and herbicide. The distributor claimed it would increase the yield by twenty percent plus and promised that it was safe. Safe for people, safe for pets, safe for birds, safe for everyone. The salesman came by my farm and tried to convince me to try it, even left me a sample."

"What's in it? Could it contain arsenic?"

"Not a chance. The EPA would be all over any product that contains arsenic. Besides it had all the usual approvals from the Department of Agriculture and the Health Department."

"The feds or the state?" Sam asked.

"Hell, I don't know. I don't have time for salesmen. He dropped off a bunch of literature and the sample, but I knew I wouldn't use the stuff. He called a few times, but I never returned his calls. You know, I'm fine. I don't need to increase my margins like those corporate farms."

His smug expression made me smile. "Why do you think the problem might be ZEIT? If the government approved it and it increases yields, it's gotta be okay, right? C'mon, Tag, why didn't you try it?"

"Easy—the ducks."

"The ducks? Are you telling me that ducks who landed and fed on the fields that used ZEIT died?"

"No, nothing like that. But ducks stick to a flight pattern. They come back to the same fields to rest and feed every year. The year after the big boys started using ZEIT, ducks stopped landing in their fields, wouldn't go near 'em. It's been great for me. I get my limit every morning, but some of the private clubs that hunt the corporate farms are mighty unhappy.

"You want to know the real reason I don't use ZEIT? It's the ducks. I'm not about to jeopardize duck season for a few more beans."

We all laughed, and Tag said we should come down for a duck hunt this fall. We'd find plenty of ducks on his property.

"Ducks," I thought to myself. In the Cole case, a duck club's log had provided vital evidence. Now once again, Arkansas's obsession with duck hunting could provide the break we needed.

"Tag, any chance you still have the paperwork that salesman gave you?" I asked as we stood to leave.

"I doubt it, but I do have the sample he left. Haven't had time to empty the shed where I put the barrel."

"Think one of my guys could take a sample?"

"Hell, you can have the whole damn barrel. It's not doing me any good."

56

I CALLED JEFF as soon as Clovis and I left the parking lot. He and Paul would meet Tag at his farm this afternoon. Better yet, he expected to get the lab results from Barnes today. Before Micki left to meet Fletcher, she asked her interns to research ZEIT, its manufacturer, and the results of any environmental testing. She also asked them to prepare FOIA requests and subpoenas for every government agency that approved its use. ZEIT might turn out to be a red herring, but it was the only lead we had so far.

Micki's meeting with Fletcher had been short and sweet. If we would withdraw the FOIA requests and Jana agreed to plead guilty, he would support no prison time. Otherwise, he would go to trial and seek a maximum prison sentence. He wasn't willing to vacate the agreement if the judge wouldn't go along with no prison. He told Micki he'd never had a judge refuse to go along with his recommendation. I bet not, at least, not this judge.

"I'm on the way to your office—see you there. We'll get the subpoenas out the door, then I'll call Fletcher. Our lunch with Tag was pretty interesting. I'm not holding my breath, but we may have had a breakthrough."

"I won't hold mine either. And don't forget to call Jana. I think she should take the deal. She's done so much good for one person. Why not be with someone you love and let someone else fight the battles?" Micki asked.

"Sounds like someone is ready for time away from the trenches."

"You don't know the half of it," she said.

"I'll call Jana right now. See you later."

Jana's response was, "No deal, not even close. That bastard wants the medical records and a felony plea, and can't even guarantee that the judge won't send me away for who knows how long. I'd have been better off sleeping with Brady Flowers. At least my eyes could have been closed while I was being fucked."

I wondered if Jana had been in the scotch a little early. Who could blame her? I told her I would call Fletcher and say thanks, but no thanks.

Mongo was manning the reception desk at Micki's office. I told him I needed a little privacy and walked into her office.

I settled into the comfortable chair she kept in the corner and called Fletcher, expecting to be shunted to various screeners. He answered after a decorous couple of rings.

"Jack Patterson. I was expecting Micki to make the call. You ready put this loser behind you and head back to DC?"

"You know, Dawg, I would like to go home, but I can't do that. Your deal stinks and you know it."

He paused for just a few seconds, then drawled, "Well, Jack, we don't always get what we want, do we? What can I do to sweeten my offer so you can swallow it?"

"How about drop the charges and go back to Fort Smith?"

"Naw, can't do that, funny man. Maybe your client doesn't understand the seriousness of her situation. I hope you told her what a good deal she's getting, considering the crimes she committed."

I chose not to rise to the bait. "Fletcher, I'll give you one more chance. Drop the charges and go home. I'll do what you aren't willing to do for Dr. Hall: I'll guarantee you won't go to prison."

I heard a few choice words before he muted the line. After a few seconds, an angry Fletcher pushed back. "What in the hell are you talking about? Are you threatening me?"

"No, I'm not the prosecutor, you are. I'm telling you I know what and who is behind this prosecution, and unless you drop the case, I won't be responsible for what happens next."

This time he took a little longer to reply, but the message was the same.

"Listen, you little East Coast snot, go straight to hell. I'll see you in court."

"I take it you're refusing my offer?"

"You can take it any way you want. I feel sorry for your client. She's about to go to jail for long time because her lawyer is an incompetent asshole. You be sure to tell her that."

I noted the time. It was two forty-seven p.m. If my instincts were right, Fletcher was calling Pence right about now. I called Stella to give her a heads up.

Micki walked into her office at that moment. "Was that Fletcher? How'd he take it?

"Not well. I don't think he'll invite me to his next tailgate."

She laughed and said, "Clovis's people are serving the subpoenas. Are you sure you know what you're doing?"

"I am. Well, no, I'm not," I replied. "But it's done, and we're going with it. So let's get packed up. We'll be with Sam and Kate for the rest of the afternoon."

"Did you get the reaction you wanted from Fletcher? I told you before, he doesn't understand subtlety," Micki said, smirking.

"When I suggested he could either drop the case or go to prison, I think he got my drift."

"What!? You told him what?"

"Well, you told me Dawg isn't into subtlety."

"Sure wish I could have been part of that conversation!" she said, laughing.

"It had its moments." I grinned. "And you might get your chance. It won't be long before we hear from a very angry prosecutor and his puppet judge."

"Okay, so we've had a feel-good moment," she said. "After we give Sam and Kate all our evidence, what comes next? We have to prepare for an imaginary trial, and we represent a client who insists on pleading guilty no matter what we do. You've stirred things up, and we may yet discover what's making people sick. You've made both the judge and the prosecutor madder than two wet hens, but how does that help keep Jana out of prison?"

"Well, I guess that's the sixty-four thousand dollar question."

Micki threw up her hands and reminded me we had work to do. I hadn't heard a word from Jeff—I had hoped he'd have the lab report before we met with Sam and Kate. Micki turned her attention to organizing her interns' research and all the documentation Stella and Brian had accumulated.

I left Micki to it, figuring she could use some peace and quiet. Clovis was waiting in the small conference room. I filled him in on my conversation with Fletcher. He threw his head back and ran his fingers through his hair in frustration.

"Jack, are you trying to get yourself killed? When will you stop playing chicken with people with no scruples?"

"I'm sorry, Clovis, but what other choice do I have? As it stands now, I can't win this case the normal way. I've got enough information to make them worry, but not enough to stop them. I have to resort to a bluff, try to make them think I know more than I do. I'm going to subpoena the manufacturer of ZEIT for their toxicity studies, as well as the CDC and the EPA. I bet neither of them has ever even heard of ZEIT."

"Won't it take some time for them to respond?" he asked.

"Yes, Clovis, I guess it will at that. At least a week or two," I replied, thinking of Jana and Sam.

"Well, that's all fine and good. But when we serve the subpoenas to the CDC and the EPA, there will be no going back. Once you alert the feds, the manufacturer will have no choice but to pull out all the stops to fend off an investigation. That includes eliminating the biggest thorn in their side, one Jack Patterson."

"Don't think I haven't thought about that once or twice. I'm counting on you to keep me alive until this mess plays out."

"How long you think that will take? A week, a month? Seems like I end up playing that role every time you come to town."

"I'd say I'll be out of the woods tomorrow, or I'll need to rethink the whole thing."

"What happens tomorrow?"

I had no idea how to answer his question. Too many pieces were still outside the puzzle.

57

THE FIRST BREAK CAME FROM JEFF. Barnes had identified the chemicals in the soil and water samples and confirmed that the samples contained high levels of arsenic. Except for arsenic, the same chemicals were listed in a brochure published by ZEIT that Jeff and Paul found next to the five-gallon barrel of ZEIT in Tag's shed. Barnes was now testing the contents of the barrel.

It seemed obvious that the folks who had developed ZEIT had added arsenic to the chemical make-up of the pesticide/herbicide without listing it as an ingredient. Sarah and Trey were all over the Internet trying to run down the manufacturer. The chore was proving more difficult than it should have been. The brochure listed a distributor, a company in Rapid City, South Dakota, called ZEIT Supply, Inc., but they couldn't find any reference to the manufacturer or developer.

I encouraged them to keep looking, and as soon as Micki was ready we left we left to meet with Kate and Sam at at the county courthouse.

Sam began with a caveat.

"I've explained to Kate that I'm no longer on leave, but she's talked sense into me. I am privy to information that you may have obtained by questionable means. So your chore today is to convince Kate, not me, that our office should open an investigation. If she thinks there is probable cause we will move forward. But please, please, don't allude to evidence that could taint our investigation."

Micki took a light approach. "You know, my usual role is to convince you not to prosecute. I don't think I've ever tried to convince a prosecutor to go forward with an investigation." She paused and was rewarded with laughter. "I'll try, but you've already made it tough. Are you asking me not to allude to any of Stella's evidence?"

Kate replied. "Yes, that's correct. I know Sam would like us to jump in and investigate this Pence character, but unless you have evidence of criminal activity, there is nothing we can do. This office correctly investigates crimes, not people. And we cannot act with the taint of ill-gotten evidence."

"Kate, we've discovered that a product called ZEIT has been used as both an herbicide and pesticide on rice and bean fields in violation of both federal and state law. It has affected the health of local inhabitants for years. Do you consider that ill-gotten evidence?" Micki asked, trying but failing to maintain her composure.

"Has ZEIT been used on any fields in Pulaski or Perry County?" Kate asked in return.

"I don't know; we haven't yet investigated local farms. But it has poisoned people living in the Delta."

"Our jurisdiction doesn't extend to the Delta," Kate reminded her. "Do you have any proof that links Pence to ZEIT?"

"Not yet. But we have served subpoenas on both Pence and Flowers."

"Micki, if those subpoenas produce evidence of a crime, we'll jump right on it. But we'll need to cooperate with prosecutors in the affected counties."

Micki was frustrated, and Sam looked miserable, but we all knew Kate was right. We had a lot of theories and a good deal of inadmissible evidence, but without proof, neither Sam nor his office could do much of anything.

Kate filled the silence.

"Let me point out something else. You believe investigating Pence will help Dr. Hall, but it won't. Fletcher is determined to bring her to trial, and you can bet your bottom dollar that Purdom will quash your subpoenas before the end of the day."

"You're right on both points," I agreed. "But you're wrong about our motives. Micki and I aren't here to convince you to open an investigation."

Sam scowled, and Kate raised her eyebrows.

"We're here to offer our help with a current and open investigation: the conspiracy to murder me and the murder of Mace Cooper and four others."

Kate frowned. "That case is closed. Mace Cooper tried to kill you, and Stalinski killed Mace and the others."

"But you don't know who hired Stalinski, and the conspiracy to commit murder I'm talking about occurred only in the last hour."

On the way to Kate's office, Stella had texted me that Fletcher had called Pence's phone just minutes after I had told him there would be no plea deal. And minutes later, Pence had placed a call to the international number we suspected was the agent for a hit man.

"What are you talking about?" Sam asked.

"I'd rather not go into details, but when you call Mimi she will tell you that in the last hour someone in Little Rock called an overseas agent to put out a contract on me.

"Kate, Micki agreed not to taint this office with certain information. But if the person who placed that oversees call turns out to be Roy Pence, then I think you have sufficient information to investigate his role in both murder and attempted murder. You also might want to know that Fletcher and Judge Purdom spoke with Pence immediately after Jana's arraignment.

"I'm happy to say that information was obtained in a perfectly legitimate manner. The judge's clerk, Candy, volunteered the information to Micki. She can and will tell you how often the two spoke with Pence. I feel sure you can take it from there." I grinned.

Kate was relentless. "If Mimi can verify that Pence called an agent for a hit man, we will investigate and issue subpoenas that Judge Purdom can't quash, but an investigation will take time. Fletcher isn't going away, and if he's implicated, he'll turn Dr. Hall's trial over to a deputy. You might get a conviction overturned on appeal, but they will have destroyed Jana in the meantime."

Sam said, "Kate, Jack will never get the chance to appeal. Jana intends to plead guilty to protect the identity of her patients and staff. He's doing his best, but she's on edge, and I don't know how much longer he can keep her from jumping."

I wondered if Jana had told Sam about her suicide attempt.

Kate shook her head, seemingly unmoved, and I lost it.

"For God's sake, Kate! Have a heart! Yes, some of our evidence is inadmissible—yes, much of it is speculative. Yes, Purdom and Fletcher are in the driver's seat. But we have hard evidence that folks in the Delta are being poisoned on a daily basis. Who cares what county they live in? A doctor who brought health care to people who had none before is about to lose both her profession and her freedom on trumped-up charges. Quit thinking about protecting your job or the sanctity of the prosecutor's office and do what's right for those people who have no other protection."

I stopped, knowing I'd gone too far. Frustration was no excuse for my outburst. Kate's face had paled, but she said nothing. Neither did anyone else. After an awkward silence, Sam spoke.

"Jack, don't be so hard on Kate. She's in a tough position. She and I will call Mimi as soon as you and Micki leave. I think we're up a creek no matter what she says. If Pence didn't make the call, we're back to square one, and no one will try to kill you. If you're right, I hope Clovis and his guys are as good as he thinks. Either way, we're out of time to help Jana."

"Well, maybe not," I said.

Sam perked up. "What do you mean?"

I thought about it for a few seconds before I turned to Micki. "I'll explain on the way home, but I need you and Kate to step out of the room for a minute. I want to ask Sam for a favor."

"What happened to 'no secrets,' partner?"

"I'll explain, I promise."

Kate spoke to Sam. "I'll leave, but Sam, don't let him talk you into anything illegal. And for God's sake don't let him give you tainted evidence."

"I'm not happy," said Micki, failing to look unhappy.

She and Kate left, and Sam asked, "What's up?"

58

WE LEFT A FEW MINUTES LATER. Clovis's Tahoe had barely cleared the curb when Micki asked, "Well?"

"Well, you won't like it, but I asked Sam to call Kristine McElroy. I didn't want to deal with your questions in front of Kate."

"Kristine. Why in the world would you ask him to call Kristine?"

"I knew you wouldn't like it."

Before Kristine set her cap for the soon-to-be governor, she had her sights set on Sam. Maggie and Micki had conspired against that match-up. As an extra complication, Micki had represented two of Kristine's former husbands.

"Okay, you're right. I would have flown off the handle, but Kate knows all about Kristine and has the same opinion of her that I do. Kristine's nothing more than a gold digger, the most manipulative woman I've ever come across. Why did you ask Sam to call her, and why shouldn't Kate know?"

"I want Sam to ask Kristine to set up a meeting with the governor. I told him to call in a favor if he had to."

"Why? If she agrees to set the meeting, she'll sit in. She never leaves the man's side, and you'll have to go it alone. She doesn't think much of me, and the feeling is mutual. Why on earth do you want to meet with the governor?"

"I want him to fire the special prosecutor."

"Good lord, Jack! Why would he do that? Surely you don't think Kristine would agree to such an outlandish request. Someone, probably Fletcher, will accuse the governor of obstructing justice, and you could be charged with conspiracy. At a minimum, you'll be disbarred."

"Now you know why I wanted Kate to leave. She would have talked him out of making the call."

"And for good reason. What makes you think Kristine and the governor would even consider doing such a thing?"

"Maybe I'll make them an offer they can't refuse."

"So now you're the *consigliere* to the Godfather?"

"Something like that."

"You're nuts," she said under her breath and turned away to gaze out the window.

I had noticed Clovis watching us in the rear view mirror. Now he spoke up. "Jack, you and Micki need to take your phones off mute. Debbie says Fletcher called to let you know that the judge quashed all your subpoenas and stayed your FOIA requests. He's also scheduled a contempt hearing for tomorrow afternoon. The paperwork is on its way to Micki's office."

"That doesn't sound good," I laughed.

"A contempt hearing is never a good sign, especially when the judge is Purdom," Micki responded.

We settled into a strained silence. I was concerned that I hadn't heard from Sam about his calls to Kristine or Mimi. I did get a text from Jeff. The lab at Barnes had confirmed that the sample of ZEIT from the barrel in Tag's shed contained significant amounts of arsenic. It might not do Jana any good, but we had solved a puzzle she cared about.

I told Micki the news. "How will you use the information?" she asked.

"First, I'll ask Jana to reconsider her guilty plea. She'll refuse—her loyalty to her patients runs too deep. After that, we'll use the information however it best serves our client. At some point, I intend to turn the information over to the EPA, the CDC, and the Environmental Crimes Section of the Department of Justice.

"Micki, find an experienced class action lawyer who will partner with you in a lawsuit on behalf of the Delta clinic's patients. It won't break my heart to have the manufacturer of that poison pay out major bucks to the people in the Delta."

"Don't you want to be a part of the lawsuit?" she asked.

"No, I have zero experience with class actions. If the manufacturer doesn't turn out to be a bankrupt turnip, maybe you'll take care of me in my old age, but my focus has to be on Jana."

"And if you're held in contempt tomorrow? I wouldn't put it past Purdom to remove us as Jana's counsel for professional misconduct."

"Nor would I. But if he does, it guarantees the trial would have to be postponed. Remember, their goal is to get possession of all the medical records and to destroy Jana. How could we file a class action lawsuit against ZEIT's manufacturer if there are no medical records?"

"I hadn't thought about that," Micki admitted. "Every time we see a little light, someone closes the door."

Debbie greeted us at Micki's office with a stack of papers from Fletcher and the judge. She had already made copies.

The judge had scheduled the hearing for three-thirty tomorrow. Micki surmised he'd scheduled it late in the day so we'd have no time to file an appeal when he found us in contempt. We would go to jail for no telling how many days.

Micki said "we," but when I looked at the formal show cause order I saw that the charges were directed only at me. That was how they could get around a continuance. Put me away and leave Micki to prepare for trial alone. Even worse, Fletcher must have figured out we had copies of the medical records. The order demanded us to turn over all records or copies subject to our control, including any records in the possession of Jeff Fields or Stella Rice. The order also included everything Jeff had accumulated while in my employ, including soil, water samples, and any analyses of the samples.

Word of Jeff roaming the Delta had gotten out, and Fletcher was trying to prevent us from sending his work to anyone else. I thought about the possibility of Jeff sending the results to the EPA, but the wording of the order made that possibility a nonstarter.

As Micki so aptly put it, "You can flaunt court orders all you want, but sending your future son-in-law to jail for contempt is not in the cards."

She was right: we were up a creek without a paddle. And I hadn't heard a word from Sam about Kristine or Mimi.

Debbie offered to get fried chicken from Maddie's Place since we'd be up late preparing for tomorrow's hearing. *What's the point?* I wondered. Purdom would do whatever Fletcher wanted. I wondered if I would have to shower with lice shampoo. Should I warn Beth before the news appeared on the internet? Micki jolted me out of my funk, reminding me to call Jana, not a call I looked forward to.

Micki's conference room was empty, so I spent a few minutes there giving myself an "attitude adjustment" before I punched in Jana's number.

"Jack, tell me what's going on. Sam is late, and I should be doing something. How can I help?"

"Well, how about telling me you've changed your mind about pleading guilty?" I asked.

"Sorry, can't do that."

"What if I told you that arsenic poisoning was making your Delta patients sick? It was in a pesticide/herbicide called ZEIT. Jeff is running down the manufacturer."

"I hope the manufacturer gets what's coming to him, but it has nothing to do with my decision to protect my patients and my staff. You've got something else on your mind—out with it, Jack."

I spent the next ten minutes explaining the show cause order, the order quashing our subpoenas, and the order staying our Freedom of Information requests. I decided not to mention the contempt hearing.

"Please tell me you're going to fight them. Let me know if you need more money. You can't let them win, Jack."

"We don't need more money. And, yes, we will fight them, I promise you that."

I put the phone down feeling totally defeated. How could we have come so far, learned so much, and found no way to help Jana? It wasn't a question, it was a fact.

Micki poked her head through the door.

"You look like you just lost your best friend. The call to Jana couldn't have been that bad."

"It was tough, Micki. She has faith in us, thinks we can pull a rabbit out of a hat. Right now I feel like we're out of both rabbits and hats."

"C'mon, Jack. I now you're feeling low, but get a grip—you led us up this creek, you can't bail out now."

She was right, of course. I tried to sound more positive. "Okay, boss, give me a few minutes to regroup."

"Jack, you need more than a few minutes. I've asked Clovis to take you out to my place. You need time to recharge. Brian has already prepared responses to the crap Fletcher delivered and is working on a sort of fill-in-the-blank response to whatever Purdom hands down. These guys are fairly predictable. If we're in luck we can get the supreme court to overturn any order Purdom issues in a matter of days.

"And you're not the only one who's exhausted. We all need a break—I think even a little one will do the trick. Larry and I are going out for pizza. Brian, Jeff, and Paul have decided on sushi. Stella and Clovis are grilling at the ranch—I think it's some sort of surprise. We can all regroup after dinner. I promise we'll be ready for whatever tomorrow brings."

She was right, but I couldn't help feeling like the fifth wheel.

On the way to Micki's, I suggested that Clovis and Stella might prefer to enjoy a night on their own. Clovis rolled his eyes, and Stella said she hoped I would enjoy dinner.

We pulled up the long driveway of Micki's ranch, and I hopped out of the car as soon as Clovis stopped. I could I smell the charcoal grill and wondered who else was here. I walked quickly around to the patio and almost ran smack into Walter Matthews.

"About time you got here. Maggie and I had no idea when to put the steaks on."

"Walter? Maggie's here? Aren't you supposed to be in Europe?"

Maggie walked out from the kitchen and said, "I hear you're about to land yourself in jail again. Do you think I would miss that?"

I could hardly believe my eyes. After a long group hug, I stepped back, trying to make sense of their presence.

"I thought you were in Amsterdam. Walter, Little Rock isn't exactly a safe place these days, at least not—"

"Stop, Jack. Let me explain," Maggie interrupted. "Walter and I returned from Europe about the time you went to San Antonio. I've stayed in touch with Brian, and Micki sent me reports almost every day. When I heard about your latest court appearance, I knew it was time for us to come. Besides, I hear you're meeting with Kristine McElroy. Do you think I would let you near that she-wolf without me?"

"Well, it's not exactly set. And she's Kristine White now. Wait a minute. How do you know about Kristine? I only told Micki a few hours ago." I felt a tinge of annoyance at their subterfuge, but quickly let it go.

"In all this excitement, I forgot to tell you. Sam pulled it off. We're meeting with the governor and Kristine at ten o'clock tomorrow morning at the state capitol. Now go have a martini with your golfing buddy and make sure he doesn't overcook the steaks. I think he's missed you almost as much as I have. After dinner, you can explain how you plan to convince the governor and Kristine to fire the special prosecutor."

59

WALTER'S STEAKS WERE PERFECT, as usual. We talked about their trip, their new home, Beth and Jeff—anything but the situation at hand. After dinner, Clovis and Stella volunteered to deal with the dishes, and Maggie, Walter, and I settled down in front of the fireplace with brandy. I filled them in on the day's events, and they peppered me with questions. Going through the issues and our conclusions with them was exactly what I needed. In the end, they didn't give me good odds, but it was good to have had a dress rehearsal for tomorrow.

I took a few minutes during the lull between dinner and brandy to call Sam. He told me about his call to Kristine.

"I won't tell you how difficult it was to even make the call, or what I had to promise, but you have your meeting. Thirty minutes at ten o'clock tomorrow morning. I'm glad Maggie's here to go with you. Don't lose your temper, Jack. Kristine has that effect on people."

"Have you told Jana?"

"No, I haven't. I don't want to get her hopes up, and I'm sure Kristine will say no to whatever you ask unless it serves her purposes."

"What about Mimi? Have you heard from her?"

"Not yet—Brussels and Little Rock aren't exactly in the same time zone."

That wasn't much help, but at least I knew he hadn't forgotten.

Clovis and Stella joined us in the great room, and the others returned not long after. Larry and Micki chose our company, but after greeting Walter and Maggie, the guys decided to enjoy a last beer out on the patio. I was glad they could relax. Martin, Walter's head of security, had sent a few of his men to Little Rock to help Clovis, and they had taken over security for the evening. We were safer at Micki's than anywhere else I could think of, but no one was taking chances.

Walter and Maggie used the opportunity to discuss the latest plans for their new home with Larry. Stella and Clovis tried to look interested, but soon said goodnight.

I was only a few minutes behind them. Tomorrow would be crucial, and I always worked better after a good night's rest. I was asleep before my head hit the pillow.

Maggie and I left the ranch early the next morning. We wanted to look over Micki's response to the judge before we met with the governor and Kristine. We were greeted by the bubbly Debbie who gave us blueberry muffins hot from the oven. She'd made a fresh pot of coffee and the water for Maggie's tea was simmering in the kettle. Micki was in the shower. She'd already been on a three-mile run, and the two security guards on the front porch were sweating and trying to catch their breath. Micki set a wicked pace on her morning runs.

We had just sat down with coffee, tea, and muffins when she joined us, clad in her familiar office uniform—jeans, a plaid shirt, and boots. Except that this morning she was barefoot and toweling off her wet hair.

"Don't look shocked, Jack. My yoga instructor tells me to go barefoot around the office as often as I can. It's supposed to increase my balance."

Maggie and Micki embraced, and Micki asked, "Did you talk him out of seeing Kristine?"

Maggie laughed. "You know better."

I spoke up. "You did a great job on the responses to the judge's orders."

"Thanks, I wish Purdom would read what we busted our butts to prepare, but I'm not holding my breath. Mongo has gone to the courthouse to file everything and deliver copies to Fletcher and the judge. I take it you're dead set on meeting with Ms. White and her puppet husband."

"For the umpteenth time, do you have a better idea?"

"No, but I was hoping you might have had one of your shower

thoughts."

"There was no inspiration with me in the shower this morning," I countered.

"That's enough, you two," Maggie interrupted.

Micki and I laughed. Remembering the good moments we once had helped when times were tough. Today could be easily be a disaster.

The three of us discussed the logistics of the day. Micki tried to fill in the blank spaces for Maggie about what we expected to happen this afternoon. Maggie excused herself to make a phone call, and Micki and I were left with a few minutes to ourselves.

"Are you okay with our strategy? Maybe we should…"

"No second thoughts, Jack," she interrupted. "Just don't get thrown in jail this morning. You'll spoil Purdom's fun, and he might go after me."

Maggie returned and I caught her giving Micki a wink. When we got in the car I asked, "What was the wink about?"

"Nothing. Micki and I share a healthy dislike for Kristine. I wouldn't put anything past her. You know Micki thinks you run a risk of being charged with conspiracy to obstruct justice. Don't you worry Kristine might set you up?"

"I noticed you didn't answer my question. I'm the one who asked for today's meeting. Neither she nor the governor have any idea what I want. I didn't even tell Sam why I wanted to meet. If Kristine is suspicious and called Fletcher, all the better. I'll be careful, I promise. Pitching baseball taught me to never telegraph pitches or show your best stuff the first time around. You save your best pitch for when the game gets tight."

"You and your baseball analogies. I never have a clue what you mean," Maggie sighed.

"Of course you do."

I felt a sense of *deja vu* when I walked into the Capitol rotunda. It's a beautiful building modeled after the U.S. Capitol. I hadn't returned since Woody Cole shot the U.S. Senator from Arkansas beneath its dome. My legal career has never been the same. I wondered if today's meeting might be the last one of my career. If Micki was right about obstruction of justice, it could be.

The governor's office is on the second floor. The receptionist asked us to wait on a bench outside her office. To my surprise, she didn't keep us waiting long, and led us straight into the governor's private office. It was small, two chairs on one side of the desk, the governor's big chair on the other side. Another chair flanked the desk on the governor's left—Kristine's?

The governor and Kristine came in from a side door, and he offered me his hand. Kristine looked at Maggie and asked, "Have we met?"

They had, and Maggie responded, "We have, but not for more than a few minutes. We met over drinks at Brave New Restaurant. But there's no reason for you to remember."

Kristine had been about as friendly as a cobra that night, but Maggie's tone disguised her true feelings about the encounter. She also didn't mention that Kristine was Sam's date at the time.

The governor was friendlier, shaking her hand and inviting us to sit across from him. He said to Maggie, "I met your husband before I got into politics. It was an honor and a privilege."

Kristine looked at Maggie with open curiosity, but said nothing.

"What can I do for you folks today?" asked Governor White while looking straight at Maggie.

He had no idea who I was or why I was there. I couldn't say the same for Kristine, who was perched on the edge of her chair.

"Governor, I am the attorney for Dr. Jana Hall. I don't know if you remember, but you appointed a special prosecutor, Reuben Fletcher, to investigate certain allegations against her."

"Dawg Fletcher? Oh, yes, I remember something about that case. Whatever happened with that?"

I suspected the governor and Kristine both knew what had happened, but I went along with their memory lapse.

"Fletcher brought charges against Dr. Hall, and the judge has set her case for trial in two weeks."

"Well, Dawg doesn't let the grass grow, does he?" he chuckled. "So, what can I do for you? I hope you're not here to request a pardon."

"No, Governor, I'm not here for a pardon. I'm here to keep you from getting caught up in a serious miscarriage of justice, to prevent you from becoming embroiled in a major scandal, and to give you an opportunity to get out in front of a federal investigation into the poisoning of a large number of individuals in your state."

Obviously baffled, White frowned and looked to his wife, who spoke directly to him.

"Tony darling, Jack is famous for tactics and theatrics. He must be desperate, or he wouldn't be here asking for our help. Dawg must have his client dead to rights. I think we've heard enough." She gave me a wicked smile. "Forgive us if we don't show you the door."

"I'm not here to seek either a pardon or your assistance. I'm here to prevent you and your administration from spending the rest of your term answering questions about what role you had in a major cover-up and murder. It's your reputation and future at stake, not mine. If you choose to walk away, it will be the worst decision you've made in what will be a very short political career."

Maggie spoke up. "We have twenty-five more minutes on your calendar. Why not listen to what Jack has to say?"

Kristine gave Maggie a dirty look, but I could tell the governor was listening.

"Mrs. Matthews, is Mr. Patterson telling the truth?"

"He is."

Kristine had risen, visibly seething and ready to leave. The governor put out a hand to stop her.

"Kristine, please don't leave. I want to hear what Mr. Patterson has to say. You know I value your opinion. But Walter Matthews was one of my idols when I was a young man starting out in business. He owns one of the largest insurance companies in the world, and I follow what he has to say about the insurance industry and business in general, as do many people you know and respect.

"I've read articles about his marriage to Mrs. Matthews and what they are doing with their foundation. If she says we should hear Mr. Patterson out, it would be politic of us to listen."

Kristine stared at Maggie and returned to her chair. She would never be embarrassed that she didn't know who Maggie was, but Kristine was a woman who was impressed by money. I hoped I could finish my presentation before Maggie told Kristine what she actually thought of her.

"Whatever you say, dear," she murmured.

"You say Arkansans are being poisoned? Do you have proof?" the governor asked.

"We do. Turns out there is a pesticide/herbicide sold in Arkansas called ZEIT. When ZEIT was recently tested, it was found to contain a high concentration of arsenic. That fact has been omitted on all of ZEIT's labels and literature. The arsenic has seeped into the Delta's water table and soil, causing many farm workers and their families to become sick. I'm sure you know it's against the law to use arsenic in a pesticide on beans or rice."

Kristine jumped in. "What's this got to do with Tony? This is a matter for the Health Department. You should talk to Brady Flowers."

"Normally, I would agree, Mrs. White. But Mr. Flowers has known for some time that the arsenic is poisoning your constituents, and he hid it from the public and federal officials."

Kristine turned pale, and the governor's face darkened in anger.

"Do you have evidence that Flowers knew about ZEIT or is it just speculation?"

"I do have evidence, but let me give you some background first."

Kristine bit her lip, but said nothing.

"For years the state of Arkansas has funded medical clinics for the poor through a special appropriation. Every year the head of this program, my client Dr. Hall, appeared before the legislature to report on the clinics' work. Several years ago, she told the legislature she had accumulated enough data to do a complete study of the diseases affecting Arkansas's poor.

"That statement raised concerns in several quarters. The manufacturer of ZEIT knew a careful review of the Delta clinic's records would reveal that an unusual number of patients had become sick from arsenic poisoning. As director of the state's Health Department, Brady Flowers was charged with reviewing the clinics' medical records. Yearly reports sent to him from the Delta clinic clearly indicated that a good number of its patients had been exposed to high levels of arsenic.

"Instead of alerting the EPA and other state and federal agencies, Brady has been sitting on this information. The reports are locked in a safe in his office. Almost immediately after Dr. Hall's well-intended statement to the legislature, he developed a scheme to close the health clinics and take possession of all their records so the existence of arsenic in the Delta would never see the light of day. He also went on a campaign to destroy Dr. Hall's credibility so she could never be involved in health care again. The risk was too great.

"As you know, Flowers has been successful. All the clinics have been closed, and those tax dollars now fund an obesity study. Fletcher has obtained the records, and Dr. Hall has been charged with multiple felonies."

Kristine interrupted, "If you have evidence against Flowers you should give it to the authorities and the legislature. Tony just got elected. He wasn't involved in cutting funding to the clinics or anything else."

I looked at Tony. "Governor, whether you were in office or not, the Health Department is an agency under your control, Flowers is your health director, and you appointed Fletcher as special prosecutor. Let me finish, so you can see why I brought this problem to you."

He frowned at Kristine and gestured for me to continue.

"We have evidence that ties an attempted murder to Flowers and Fletcher."

"Murder!" Kristine exclaimed. "What murder? What kind of evidence?"

"A man named Roy Pence has been in constant contact with Flowers for the last few years. He grew up in St. Louis, spent his early career in public relations for a chemical manufacturer, then moved to DC where he worked as a lobbyist for the chemical industry. He moved to Little Rock about six years ago to head the American Chemical and Agricultural Trust, an organization whose membership includes the manufacturer of ZEIT. Pence has also taken part in more than fifteen phone calls with Fletcher since you appointed him special prosecutor."

"And I suppose you know what they talked about?" Kristine was beside herself. "Isn't wiretapping illegal? We should never have met with you. Tony, I think you should call the authorities and have Jack arrested."

Now the governor looked truly irritated, but I answered before he could intervene.

"No, I didn't tape or listen to their phone conversations. But I also know that Pence called an assassin's agent. The assassin, a man named Stalinski, tried to end my life. And I know that yesterday Pence placed another call to the same agent. I can only assume he wants to arrange for another assassin to complete the job."

"You...you...mean someone actually tried to kill you?" the governor asked.

"Yes, and I believe there will be another attempt soon. That's one reason I'm here. I don't take attempts on my life well."

"You should tell your friend Sam Pagano about these phone calls—if they really took place," Kristine hissed. Sam was right—she was trying to get me to lose my temper.

"He already knows, as does Interpol. That's why I came here to encourage you to take action before you get dragged into a murder investigation."

"I don't think I know anyone named Roy Pence. Do you, Kristine?" The governor looked at his wife who remained silent, but avoided eye contact with her husband. "And I still don't know what any of this has to do with me."

"Well, if Pence, Flowers, and Fletcher have conspired to commit murder or to hide the intentional poisoning of hundreds of Arkansans, the press and investigators will want to know what role, if any, you played in their scheme and what action you took when you learned of it."

"What can I do?"

I looked at him for a few seconds. This man had recently been elected governor of Arkansas. Could he really be so politically obtuse?

"If I were you, in an abundance of caution, I would order an independent audit of the Health Department, not their financials but their operations. If Flowers is clean, an audit will clear him. But if he's been hiding evidence of arsenic poisoning from the feds and other state regulatory agencies, you'll be ahead of the game."

"I guess I could call the chairwoman of the Appropriations Committee and see what she thinks," he said reluctantly.

"I wouldn't do that."

Kristine found her voice. "Why not?"

"We have credible evidence that she and Flowers are having an extramarital affair. She played a role in closing the clinics and pressuring the prosecutor to investigate Dr. Hall."

"There's no way Brady is sleeping with that woman!" Kristine blurted, turning bright red.

"You could be right—I don't have definitive proof of such an affair, but I do know she's not the first woman Flowers has seduced to get favors. We have proof that he has sexually harassed several of the Health Department's employees."

Kristine's hand flew to her throat with a little gasp and she turned away quickly.

Governor White asked, "You okay? Do you need water or something? Kristine?"

She waved him off, trying to compose herself. He sighed and turned back to me.

"Okay, Mr. Patterson. I appreciate your bringing this matter to my attention and will consider what you've suggested. I hope your assumption regarding an assassin proves to be incorrect."

My next request wouldn't be easy to sell either.

"Governor, I have another suggestion, in fact it's the other reason I'm here today. You should remove Fletcher as special prosecutor. In fact, now that you know Fletcher has been conspiring with Pence and Flowers, I don't see that you have a choice. Otherwise, questions about why you hired him and why you didn't fire him will hound you as long as you're in office."

Kristine had recoverd quickly. "So, that's your game. Fletcher is about to send your client to prison, and you don't have a defense. You want my husband to interfere with a pending criminal case, a classic case of obstruction of justice. What they say about you is right. You'll do anything to get a client off, even if it's unethical or criminal. I should report your request to Dawg this instant."

I knew I couldn't get to the governor without Kristine on board, and that seemed unlikely. Well, nothing ventured, nothing gained.

"Governor, before I address Kristine's concerns, would you object if I had a few minutes alone with her? I promised a friend to convey a message to her, and since our time is almost over, I wouldn't want her belief that I was requesting something improper to interfere with my promise."

He looked at her. I hoped my reference to a message might make her curious.

She surprised me. "All right—I think that's a good idea. I do need to cool down, and I might as well hear what you have to say before we conclude our meeting. And, Tony, you'll be able to spend a few minutes with Mrs. Matthews. Come on, Jack. My office is right outside."

I followed her out of the room obediently, less worried about leaving Maggie alone with the governor, and more worried about myself. Her office was small, but well-furnished. She perched herself on the corner of her desk and motioned me to take a chair. I remained standing, and she cut to the chase.

"Okay, Patterson, no more bullshit. Exactly what do you want? You know Tony would be crucified if he fired Fletcher. He could even be impeached. I know Sam didn't send any message. You've got something to say you don't want Tony to hear. So—out with it!"

"Okay, I'll be direct. Your husband said neither of you know a Roy Pence. But that's not correct, is it?"

"What are you talking about?"

"I'm talking about at least five conversations you had with Pence around the time your husband appointed Fletcher special prosecutor. I'm talking about the phone conversations you had with Brady Flowers. I can assure you I don't know what was said, but I can imagine. You want to know what I think?"

"No, I don't," she responded sharply.

"I'd like to think that your conversations with Flowers were about the Department of Health and had nothing to do with the decision to appoint Dawg Fletcher special prosecutor. I'd like to think that the conversations with Pence were about his substantial contributions to your husband's campaign deficit. Campaign contributions are public records. You might want to return those funds before Sam's investigation goes much further."

"Is that what you believe?"

"It's what I choose to believe. But I can tell you that federal investigators are about to descend on the state of Arkansas. They are going to come after you like a duck on a June bug unless your husband can find a way to disassociate himself from Pence, Fletcher, and Flowers. They will suspect that Flowers used his charms to convince you to ask your husband to remove Sam from the Hall investigation and to appoint Fletcher special prosecutor. They will conclude that Pence's substantial campaign contributions were a *quid pro quo* for following Flowers' suggestions.

"Investigators will surely dig into what else may have been said or promised, and either Pence or Flowers may agree to cooperate to get their sentences reduced. You and your husband will spend hundreds of thousands of dollars defending your conduct as a criminal investigation destroys your agenda and political future. It will become an investigation of your entire life."

I felt like a jerk, but that did it. Tears streaked down her cheeks and she gave a little sob. The last thing Kristine wanted was for criminal investigators to reopen an investigation into what happened to her first husband, who died in Mexico under suspicious circumstances. I let her cry for a minute before continuing.

"Kristine, none of this has to happen. Because I believe you and the governor were pawns in a terrible conspiracy, I'm willing to help. I suggest he fire Fletcher, put Flowers on leave, and order an audit of the Health Department. Such actions put you way ahead of the coming investigation and remove you both from involvement in any attempted murder investigation."

"But the phone calls still exist," she said, wiping away the tears.

"They do, but I think Sam, Interpol, and any other investigators will think those calls were innocent, just as I do. So far, my legal defense team are the only ones who know they exist. So it's possible they may never see the light of day."

"Are you blackmailing me, Jack?" Kristine asked with a flirty little smile.

"Of course not. I'm asking you to help me convince your husband to undo the damage that was done when he appointed Fletcher. We both know that Fletcher should never have been appointed. There was never any reason for Sam's office to stand down."

"Will you help with the press outrage if he fires the special prosecutor?"

"When Interpol arrests Pence, Fletcher, and Flowers, he'll look like a genius, but I promise to do whatever I can to support his decision, as will my client."

"One more thing. You don't have to answer, but is Flowers really having an affair with that cow?"

"Flowers can be charming, but underneath all that charm and good looks is one manipulative asshole. I want him to get what he's got coming."

"So do I, Jack, so do I," Kristine muttered. "Okay, tell me how to convince Tony to do what we both know needs to be done."

60

MAGGIE AND TONY WERE DEEP IN CONVERSATION when Kristine and I returned to his office. I know Maggie well. She wasn't faking it—she was genuinely engaged.

"Guess what, Kristine? Walter Matthews is here in Little Rock, and Maggie thinks we might have time to meet." Tony's tone of admiration was both heartening and a little creepy.

The last half hour had been tough for Kristine. Her open animosity had given way to confusion. She turned to stare at Maggie, probably wondering how in a matter of minutes "Mrs. Matthews" had become "Maggie" and what else Maggie and Tony had talked about. Come to think of it, so did I.

But she gathered herself and forged ahead.

"Oh, that's great. I'm sure you'll have a lot in common," she said, forcing a smile. "But, Tony, the more I've thought about it, the more I can see Jack's point. If it turns out there really is a connection between Fletcher and this Pence fellow—well, we had no idea, but it could be construed the wrong way. I also remember that Brady, er… Director Flowers, was more than pushy when he insisted that you appoint Fletcher to be special prosecutor. I know the chief justice thought you had no choice in the matter, but perhaps you should have gone with your own good instincts.

"You know, if Fletcher is removed, the case against Dr. Hall won't go away. It will go back to Pagano's office, and they can have someone independent go over the facts and the charges. But, given this new information, you will have done the right thing. Don't you think that's the safe approach?"

The governor looked doubtful, and she continued.

"Sweetheart, you ran on a platform of cleaning up state government. This is a good opportunity to fulfill your promise. An independent audit of the Health Department and a top to bottom review of its policies and procedures is the perfect place to start." Kristine was on a roll.

"What about Flowers? Do I boot him, too?" the governor asked. His tone managed to convey suspicion and irritation.

"No, but a respected attorney has brought to your attention multiple claims of sexual harassment against the man. He should be put on leave until there can be a full investigation. Every business in America has recognized that sexual harassment claims can't be ignored."

The corner of his mouth turned up slightly. I could see that the governor understood and appreciated his wife's good counsel. His voice took on an official tone.

"Mr. Patterson, I will remove Fletcher from his position by two o'clock today and return Dr. Hall's case to the district prosecutor for appropriate action. My general counsel won't be happy with the rush job, but he'll manage. I hope you can convince Sam Pagano to order an independent review of the charges against Dr. Hall. It might help with any uproar from the press.

"At the same time, I'll announce my decision to place Flowers on leave and to audit the Health Department. As soon as we finish this conversation, state troopers will escort Flowers from his office at the Health Department. I feel sure he'll object, but we can't risk the destruction of any records."

He turned to his wife. "I never did quite trust that man anyway. Seemed a little slick for my taste, but people I trusted said I should keep him on." Kristine dropped her eyes. "Take a look at our campaign contribution list. If Pence, Fletcher, or Flowers gave us money, tell Betsy to send it back."

He wasn't finished. "Mr. Patterson, Maggie, thank you for bringing this matter to my attention. I don't know how this business would have turned out, but it looks like we could have been toast, so thank you. And I wonder if I might ask you for a couple of favors?"

"Governor, I'm feeling pretty good right now, so ask away," I replied.

"I don't think Flowers will fight the sexual harassment charges. I've heard rumors, too." He glanced at Kristine again. "But if he does, I may need information to support your claims, although I understand the importance of protecting the victims. We'll find a balance, but I may need your help."

"You will have it," I said, although I believed as soon as word got out that Flowers had been put on leave, employees would come out of the woodwork to claim harassment. Men like Flowers never understand their behavior is wrong.

"Second, for some reason this meeting never made its way onto my calendar. As far as anyone knows, it never happened, and I'd like to keep it that way. I know people like Pagano will have to know the results of our conversation. I won't lie, but I don't plan to allude to it or speak of it unless I have to. Is that okay with you? Some lawyers are inclined to broadcast what a good job they've done."

"I'm not that lawyer," I said, meaning every word.

We shook hands, and Maggie promised to arrange a meeting with Walter. We left without another word to Kristine.

Mike and our driver were waiting at the curb. We slid into the back seat, and I gave Maggie a nudge. "You seemed to hit it off pretty well with the governor. What was that about meeting with Walter? You told me that you wouldn't let Walter within a mile of Kristine."

"And I still won't. I promised Tony a one-on-one meeting with Walter. Kristine will not be included. The governor is not a puppet or as naïve as people think. I feel sure he suspects Kristine may have been a victim of Flowers's charms, or vice versa, but he would never air their laundry in front of an audience. He might have surprised you, even if Kristine hadn't come on board. Speaking of, how did you get her to agree?"

I smiled. "Have you forgotten? We never met with the governor or Kristine."

Maggie gave me a dirty look. I gave her the highlights. She didn't know about the calls to Kristine from Pence and Flowers. Stella had pointed them out to me earlier in her book of phone records, and I asked her to keep them to herself. In response to Flowers's manipulations and Pence's campaign contributions, Kristine had probably played an aggressive role in Fletcher's appointment. Now she had to hope no one else discovered the same evidence.

I had worried that Kristine would alert Flowers and Pence to our meeting. That she didn't was a good sign she wasn't more involved than I suspected. I wouldn't want to be Flowers if he made the mistake of calling Kristine for help. The possibility that he was involved with a state senator had come as quite a shock to Kristine. *Hell hath no fury....*

Maggie asked, "Who will you call first with the good news? Micki, Sam, or Dr. Hall? This is cause for celebration."

"Not yet. No dancing in the end zone until the game is over. The order removing Fletcher hasn't been issued. The governor's general counsel and other aides may put up a stink or urge caution. Kristine may have second thoughts.

"Fletcher is bound to raise holy hell, and we'll have to be prepared for whatever he does. Besides, I face contempt charges. Our client may have caught a break, but I may still find myself in jail for a day or two. Purdom will be livid when he hears Fletcher has been fired.

"Jana has criminal charges hanging over her head, and Sam has to be careful how he handles her case when it's returned. There could be a hit man lurking out there, and we have nothing concrete to connect Pence to ZEIT or the attempt on my life."

"So we won a battle, but not the war," Maggie sighed.

"Something like that. If the governor sends Fletcher back to Fort Smith, we will have accomplished a lot, but we aren't ready to dance yet."

"Okay, what's next?" she asked.

"Ask everyone to meet us at Micki's office. If the governor does what he promised, we can watch his press conference from there. We need to prepare for the contempt hearing. Ask Jana and Sam to come if they can."

I called Micki to tell her to expect a crowd, and she offered to have sandwiches delivered for lunch. I gave her the high points of our meeting with the governor, including the likelihood that he would remove Fletcher this afternoon. Her reaction was not what I expected.

"Jack, that's great news for Jana, but it could be bad news for you.

Purdom will be pissed, and Fletcher will be after your hide."

"Well, I can't help that. And what's the worst thing that can happen? I spend a few nights in jail."

"That's what I'm worried about."

"Why? I've spent the night in your county jail before. It's not the Armitage, but it's not the end of the world."

"I'm afraid it could be. Hear me out. Why did Purdom charge you with contempt and not me? Where is the one place Clovis can't protect you? They've worked it all out. Purdom finds you in contempt, and you find yourself on your own in the county lockup, easy pickings for an assassin. Jails keep people in, they don't keep people out."

"Micki, nothing will happen," I said. "Have you shared your concerns with Sam? Last time I spent the night in jail he arranged for me to be in a suicide watch cell. There is nothing to worry about."

"As a matter of fact, I did call him," she replied.

"And…?"

"He said you should be worried."

"Well, that's not good. I wonder what he knows?"

61

Everyone was at Micki's by the time we arrived except Sam and Jana. Debbie was in her element, offering everyone sandwiches and cookies. Tony, Maggie's new best friend, called to tell her his press conference was scheduled for twelve-thirty, and the local news station would carry it.

I begged off explaining what had happened until Sam and Jana arrived. The grin on Maggie's face should have given us away, but the worried look on Micki's face forestalled any exuberance.

Micki and I spent a few minutes talking about the contempt hearing. Sam and Jana walked in just as Mongo announced that the governor was about to speak. I was surprised to see Kate Erwin follow Sam in. She didn't look comfortable, but she was here.

Tony looked in control as he stepped to the podium. Kristine was nowhere to be seen. He got to the point right away.

"When I ran for office, I promised the citizens of Arkansas a wholesale review of state government in order to eliminate waste and inefficiency. I am here to announce that I'm keeping my promise, beginning with our state's Department of Health. What could be more important than the health of our citizens? I have asked for an independent audit not only of its finances, but of its procedures, practices, and policies. The results will be made available to the public in their entirety, and I will hold open forums on how to correct any deficiencies. Acting Director Madeline Short, has assured me I'll have the full cooperation of the department.

"On another matter, I have made appointments to several state boards and commissions, judicial and prosecutorial vacancies, and other personnel matters. My aides are handing out a list of those appointments. Any questions?"

Several hands shot up, and he pointed to a woman in the second row.

"Governor, why the Health Department first?"

Tony chose to answer this question with a long and involved spiel about the importance of health programs for the state's children. I laughed, realizing he hoped most of the audience would tune him out. The next question wasn't so easy.

"Governor, you mentioned Acting Director Madeline Short. What happened to Brady Flowers?" asked a reporter.

"Credible allegations of sexual harassment have been made against Director Flowers, and I have placed him on leave without pay. There is no place for improper conduct in my administration, and these allegations will be fully investigated. It would be inappropriate for me to comment further."

He brushed aside follow-up questions with the ease of a practiced politician. It struck me that none of the reporters showed any surprise over the allegations against Flowers.

Clearly bored, a few reporters began to leave the room, and the governor called, "Last question, please." A veteran reporter from Fort Smith waved his hand, and Tony nodded.

"Governor, I see that you have ended the office of special prosecutor Reuben Fletcher. Isn't there a pending criminal matter against Dr. Jana Hall?"

The Governor was ready for this one. "Yes, I have terminated the office and thanked Mr. Fletcher for his service. That termination does not eliminate the pending criminal matter against Dr. Hall, which will be returned to the prosecuting attorney. It will, however, save the state the considerable expense of a special prosecutor. I intend to run a tight financial ship, and Mr. Fletcher's unlimited budget troubled my fiscal heart. Moreover, Mr. Fletcher's charge was to look at financial discrepancies at public health clinics operated by Dr. Hall, not to investigate her personally.

"I appreciate the service of Mr. Fletcher, but this administration intends to fulfill its duty as good steward of our citizens' tax dollars. Thank you for coming today."

Mongo turned the television off, and the room erupted in a combination of laughter and triumph. My own respect for Tony's political acumen went through the roof. But neither Sam nor Jana were laughing, and I called for quiet.

"Jana, I know you must be confused. Let me tell you where things stand."

"Thank you. What does all this mean? Is it over?"

"The governor has fired Dawg Fletcher. The charges against you have not been dropped, but will be returned to Sam's office. The governor hopes Sam will ask another prosecutor to investigate the charges. That decision is up to Sam and Kate. The good news is that the governor clearly thinks Fletcher overstepped his mandate and has sent him back to Fort Smith.

"Flowers has already been escorted from the Health Department building. He's going to need a very good lawyer—maybe Les Butterman is available. My bet is that the locked files in Flowers's office will reveal his complicity in hiding the effects of ZEIT on the Delta clinic's patients. Now for the bad news—"

"Wait a minute," Sam interrupted. "Don't we get to celebrate a little? From where I sit, things look a lot brighter. No more Fletcher is a big deal. No more Brady Flowers is a big deal. I have no idea how you pulled it off. I'm not sure I want to know, but you did. How on earth did you co-opt Kristine?"

"The credit belongs to Maggie. She knew how to deal with both Kristine and the governor. And I've learned not to underestimate Tony White."

Maggie ignored my compliment. "That reminds me—I need to remind Walter to call Tony."

"Tony?" Micki giggled.

"Yes, Tony. He's actually a bit of a dear," she replied. "Go on without me, I'll be back in a few."

The door closed and Sam repeated, "Tony?"

I shrugged my shoulders, "I told you she deserves the credit."

He shook his head and said, "That's all fine, well, and good, but your date with Judge Purdom approaches. Do you have any kind of strategy?"

"Well, no. I haven't had time to think about it. Purdom is bound to be pissed off about Fletcher's dismissal, and there's no telling what Pence has suggested."

Now that I did have time to think about it I felt uneasy. "Sam, I'll be safe spending a couple of nights in jail, won't I? I mean, that's what guards are for, right?"

Maggie returned before he could reply, followed by Mimi Stephens.

"I don't think a night in jail is in your future," she said. "At least, not this night."

62

EVERYONE BUT ME broke out into laughter. I was surprised to see her and puzzled by the inside joke.

Sam spoke up. "Now I get to fill you in. Turns out your instincts were right—Pence did call an agent in order to hire an assassin, and thanks to your phone call, Mimi obtained a warrant and was listening. The plan was simple: Purdom would make sure you spent the night in jail, and Pence would make sure you were dead before morning. When Micki worried you could be in serious danger in jail, she was dead on, pardon the pun.

"Mimi apprehended the foreign agent before he could hire anyone. She also called the FBI, and we've been working night and day with them preparing search warrants, subpoenas, and an arrest warrant for Pence. We don't yet have enough hard evidence to arrest Fletcher, Flowers, or Purdom, but it's only a matter of time."

Kate said, "The only bit of bad news is that we can't find Pence. His office is closed and his apartment empty. We do have his files and computers, and we'll soon have access to his bank accounts."

"Don't worry, Jack. We'll find Pence," Mimi interjected.

"All this is great, but I still have a hearing this afternoon with a very angry judge who carries a six-shooter. Maybe he'll carry out their plan on the spot," I said half in jest.

"Unfortunately neither Kate nor I can call off a contempt hearing," Sam said, shaking his head.

Maggie smiled. "You know, I don't think you should worry about that hearing."

"Okay, Maggie," I said. "You've already saved my bacon once today. What do you know that we don't?"

"While I was outside talking to Walter, I received a call from your friend, Judge Marshall Fitzgerald. Apparently Judge Purdom bypassed court procedures to make sure he was assigned to Dr. Hall's case, a serious breach of judicial ethics. Marshall, the senior member of the Pulaski County bench, and the Chief Justice of the Arkansas Supreme Court paid Judge Purdom a visit this morning. As a result, Purdom has stepped down from the case, and the contempt hearing has been postponed until the case can be assigned to a different judge."

Micki let out a shout.

"And how did Marshall know about Purdom and the contempt hearing?" I asked with a grin.

"Last night I called to let him know that Walter and I were in town and to see if he would have time for a quick visit. One thing led to another, and I told him about the pickle you were in. Of course, you know Marshall would never do anything improper."

This time I let everyone take a few minutes to celebrate.

"Okay, okay," I broke in finally. "This morning when Maggie asked if Fletcher's removal was cause for celebration, I told her it was too early. But with Purdom no longer in the picture and Pence on the run, I think barbeque at Micki's this afternoon is in order. We have lots of details to iron out, but with the contempt hearing postponed, we now have a free afternoon."

Micki put Debbie in charge of the arrangements. I pulled Mimi aside, thanked her, and asked her to join us. I admit my motive wasn't business related.

"Jack, I'd love to stay, but my boss wants me back in Brussels. The FBI is working with Sam, and when Pence is apprehended there will be the usual turf battle over who gets him first."

"So soon? I can't tell you how disappointed I am," I said sincerely.

"Don't give up yet, Jack. You'll hear from me before too long." She gave me a quick peck on the cheek and left the room.

Clovis walked over and said, "You lose another?"

"Looks like it."

"Too bad, I liked her. You ready to head out to Micki's?"

"Let me have a few words with Jana first."

I found her sitting alone in a corner while Micki, Sam, and Kate conferred. They had already worked out a plan to assign Jana's case to someone who would realize that every doctor in the state could be charged with a crime if someone looked hard enough. There are too many forms to fill out, prescriptions that can be second-guessed, and too much government interference in a patient-doctor relationship.

I sat down next to her and said, "I need to get back to DC before too long. Micki can handle things from here. Jana, I'm so sorry you've had to go through this ordeal, but now we have a good reason to stay in touch." I nodded toward Sam.

"I hope so, but you know your friend. A pretty blonde in a sports car is hard for him to resist," she pouted. I laughed, and she continued. "Jack, how can I ever thank you enough? I'm still not quite sure exactly what you did or how you did it. I owe you so much."

"Aw, shucks, ma'am," I drawled. "You don't owe me a thing, but I do have a small favor to ask."

I spent the next five minutes explaining how she could help a friend of mine. When I finished she laughed and said, "You know, Jack, you are a hopeless romantic. Of course I'll help."

Her response brought my warm sense of satisfaction full circle, and I told Clovis it was time to go. Gina Halep's unexpected phone call on the way out to Micki's brought an abrupt end to my complacency. She needed me in Los Angeles. The city was threatening to sue the Lobos even though the league had asked us to move and the two new LA teams wanted us out of the city. I tried to think of an excuse, but knew I would have to go. I was sure Micki could handle the clean-up of any loose ends here. Walter would want Maggie to return to DC with him, so I decided to take Brian with me.

Clovis and I took a detour on the way out to Micki's. I asked him to drive by Jana's shuttered clinic in the East End. I hoped it would be open the next time I came to Little Rock. By the time we reached Micki's, Debbie had managed to acquire a frozen margarita machine and Ben's cooker was smoking away.

Someone handed me a beer, and after a few high fives, I went to find Jeff. I knew he had a flight back to St. Louis early the next day.

"Jeff, I can't thank you enough. Your research and your perseverance cracked the case."

"Well, under different circumstances I know Dr. Hall would have come to the same conclusions. But I enjoyed the challenge, and her philosophy about health care, particularly for those who can't afford it, has given me pause to think about my own career path. It was time well spent."

We both raised our beers, and he said in a lighter tone, "Gosh, that barbecue smells good."

I could see he was itching to join Paul, Brian, and Big Mike, so I waved him away. Those four had formed an easy friendship, and I hoped it would last.

Sam walked by balancing a plate and two margaritas. "Hey, Jack, come get some food," he called.

Jana, who followed him with her own plate, stopped to whisper, "I've already made the initial call. This will be fun."

"Want to tell me how you plan to pull it off?" I asked.

"My lawyer has taught me the virtue of patience. Now it's your turn. But I promise to let you know how things pan out."

"Fair enough," I conceded.

I found Maggie and Walter sitting on the porch with Stella. I told them about Gina's call and that the Lobos' plane would pick Brian and me up tomorrow morning.

"Do you plan to meet with the governor while you're here?" I asked Walter.

"No time this trip, but I did have a nice phone chat with him this afternoon, seems like a decent guy. He wants to interest me in putting a new data center at an abandoned warehouse site here in Little Rock. Claims the area has plenty of qualified workers. If I can't get Stella to move to DC to head my IT department, maybe I can entice her with a data center of her own. Anyway, I'm bringing a team back to town in a few weeks to meet with him and the members of his development authority."

I turned to Maggie, but she forestalled my question with her answer. She knew what I was thinking.

"No, Jack, Kristine will not be part of those meetings. I've already spoken with Stella—she's got my back," she said.

Walter looked confused, and Maggie kissed him on the cheek. "It's a private joke," she explained with a smirk.

The barbecue did smell good. I got a plate and went to find Micki. We shared a few laughs at Fletcher's expense before I told her about the LA trip. She scowled—this wouldn't be the first time I'd left her to finish the game. Truth was we both knew she could handle the clean-up as well as or better than I could. I promised to come back if anything went haywire, one of the benefits of access to a private jet.

We all enjoyed the evening, but Brian and I slipped out before too long. Clovis had arranged for us to stay the night at the Armitage since we were to leave early the next morning.

When we arrived at the hotel, I was tired and begged off having a drink with Brian and Big Mike. Mike was a last minute addition to our traveling team courtesy of Maggie. She wasn't ready to forego our security detail until Pence was in custody.

I took the elevator to the third floor and puttered around my room a little. I was tired, but not quite ready for bed, a little keyed up from the day's events. I poured myself a scotch from the mini bar and decided to take a quick bath. I don't normally take baths, but a warm tub and a smooth glass of scotch sounded like the perfect way to end a long day.

The warm water did feel good. Too good, I realized when I found myself falling asleep. I toweled off and was halfway through the bathroom door when I realized that the bedroom was totally dark. I was sure I'd left the lights on. Was this it? Had Pence found a way to hire an assassin after all?

I tried to turn the bathroom lights back on, but my fingers couldn't find the switch. I wondered how it would happen—a bullet, a knife at my throat, or the time-honored blow to the head with a blunt instrument. I was about to make a dash for the door when I heard a familiar voice.

"I thought you'd never get out of that tub," said Mimi.

63

I ADMIT TO SLEEPING IN THE NEXT MORNING. When I sleepily reached across the bed to pull Mimi close, I found she was gone. I couldn't help wondering if I had dreamed the whole wonderful night.

A few days in LA turned out to be a whole week, followed by four more days in San Antonio. But the Lobos were closer to a move than I'd ever thought possible. Micki and Sam kept me in the loop on a daily basis, but they managed fine without me.

Kate found a prosecutor in Pope County who was willing to conduct an independent review of the evidence and charges against Jana. After his third meeting with Micki, he advised Sam to drop the charges, saying he had better things to do than go after a doctor who was saving lives.

To my surprise, the case received very little media attention, probably because the press was fixated on the continuing string of workplace harassment accusations against Brady Flowers. Those charges weren't his only problem. Investigators discovered that American Chemical and Agricultural Trust had made regular deposits into an account in his name at Bradford Bank and Trust. The locked file in his office contained dozens of original reports that should have gone to the CDC. These reports validated Jeff's findings and confirmed the unusual number of Alzheimer's, MS, and Parkinson's patients in the Delta. The FBI had turned over their findings to the Department of Justice. Sam was gleeful, but I knew how long it took the DOJ to bring a case.

Micki wasn't sitting on her hands. She brought in a Dallas law firm, a husband and wife team who've been successful in class action litigation.

They would use the data developed by Jeff to build a case against the American Chemical and Agricultural Trust and the large chemical company that had manufactured ZEIT. In response to press inquiries, the chemical company claimed that ZEIT's supplier had assured them that the compound would only be used on cotton and that the formula had been approved by the EPA and the state Department of Health. Micki thought the distributing company was a front.

I hoped the chemical company had deep pockets and that the families harmed would get at least some compensation. I also hoped the case would put much-needed money into Micki's coffers, but I was glad not to be involved. I had plenty on my own plate.

So far, the governor looks like the hero for his prompt reaction to the complaints against Flowers. No one seems to care that he fired Fletcher. It turns out the man has a gambling problem and has checked himself into the Betty Ford clinic. Who knew? I don't think he's seen the last of the FBI.

Judge Purdom announced his retirement the day after he met with Marshall and immediately left for Montana to "spend much-needed time with his family." Sam suspects he cut a deal with the FBI and DOJ to be a witness against Pence, Flowers, and Fletcher.

Brian, Mike, and I are on our way back to DC, but we'll stop in Little Rock for a couple of days. Jana is hosting a celebratory dinner for her defense team at the Little Rock Country Club. Walter and Maggie sent polite regrets, but everyone else accepted her invitation. I kidded Maggie that her absence had more to do with Kristine than it did with Walter's board meeting. She didn't deny it. Micki tells me Debbie is beside herself with excitement at the thought of dressing up.

A cocktail dress isn't Micki's style, but I have to say she turned more than a few heads when she and Larry entered the dining room. The two of them looked as happy as a pair of clams, and I knew why.

Jana had followed through on the favor I'd asked. We met for coffee, and she told me the story. Jana had called Larry's mother and invited her for tea. Mrs. Bradford, Penny, had bristled when Jana complimented Micki. Jana continued, telling Penny how much she owed Micki, that Micki would always have a special place in her heart. Then, ever so gently, Jana reminded Larry's mom how close Jana's husband Judd and Stan Bradford had been, and how much she had enjoyed getting to know Stan.

Mrs. Bradford was not her husband's first wife, and she had been poorly received by Little Rock's polite society. Judd took it upon himself to change polite society's attitude and for the most part had been successful.

Mrs. Bradford was no fool. She understood that Jana was reminding her of her own background and that people in glass houses shouldn't throw stones. Jana also invited Micki to events that Penny was sure to attend. She made a point of introducing Micki as "my personal lawyer" and told everyone how happy she was that Micki and Larry Bradford were a couple. Penny got the point and has since treated Micki and Larry better.

Jana said things would never be perfect. Penny's opinion would never change: in her eyes Larry still needed to quit fooling around with wood and go to work for the bank. But at least she no longer felt that Micki was beneath her son's station.

Over a second cup of coffee, I gave Jana an account of the money she'd given me. The largest share would go to Micki with a bonus to her interns, Sarah and Trey. Stella's fee, which would have been cheap at twice the price, had been paid, and there was money left over. I offered to send her a check, but she refused. I refused to keep the money, so we were at a stalemate. Jana suggested a nice check for Jeff and a bonus for Brian and Clovis, to which I agreed. We agreed to donate the remainder to Walter and Maggie's foundation.

When I greeted Micki at dinner, she gave me a kiss on cheek and whispered, "Jana says you're responsible for Mrs. Bradford's change of heart. She won't elaborate, but thank you."

The occasion was a terrific success. We reminisced, told jokes about each other, and drank too much wine. Sam announced he was leaving the prosecutor's office at the end of the month and the governor would appoint Kate as acting prosecutor. He and Jana had decided to take the next six months to travel to "bucket list" spots, both abroad and here in the States. When they returned, they would reopen Jana's East End clinic and form a legal clinic to serve the needs of East End residents.

It was almost too perfect, and I worried a little about Sam and Jana as a permanent couple. She was very independent, and as for Sam, I hoped he'd gotten over the allure of politics and blondes in sports cars. I wasn't sure which would be more dangerous.

Jana told me that Janis Harold had settled the claims of Judd's first wife and children for less than a month's worth of the Crockett firm's fees. The brother's case had been dismissed outright. The estate hadn't been closed yet because Janis had questioned the Crockett firm's fees which had already exceeded the maximum allowed under the state's probate law.

As usual, I was ready to leave before anyone else. I found Brian, and Jordan drove us back to the Armitage. A part of me hoped to find Mimi waiting in my bed, but no such luck. I slid under the covers, feeling good about the day.

I had drifted into that space between awake and asleep when I was jolted into the present by a sudden, strong light. Trying to focus, I rolled out of bed and was confronted by a man holding a Maglite in one hand and a gun in the other, both pointed directly at my forehead.

He was a few inches shorter than me. The Maglite hid his face, but I knew this was the man I'd met with Sam at lunch.

"Roy Pence, I believe." I tried to sound nonchalant.

He smiled. "Ever the clown, Jack. Well, no more jokes. You destroyed everything, and before I disappear into the sunset, you're gonna get what you deserve."

"Why?" I asked.

"What do you mean, why? You fucked up a great gig, that's why."

"No, that not what I meant. Why did you hire Stalinski to kill Mace and the others?"

"Mace worked for me, but he wanted revenge—he let his hatred overcome his judgment. When you survived the lynching, I knew he'd become reckless and I couldn't trust him. I had to get rid of him and his stupid friends who wouldn't keep their mouths shut. I hired Stalinski to eliminate them and any evidence that could link them to me. It was his idea to frame you for their murders, sabotage your plane, and kidnap Erwin. Too bad he wasn't as good as represented."

"What about ZEIT? What about the arsenic? Why?"

"For a bigshot lawyer who represents business you sure are naïve. It's all about money, yields, and profits. Who do you think is behind the chemical company—a bunch of preachers? Do you think the corporate farmers didn't know what was in ZEIT? Why do you think Brady Flowers sat on those reports? Why do you think Fletcher and Purdom went after your Dr. Hall? It always comes down to money, and no, none of it bothers me in the least. Those illegals and share croppers don't count for much. Shoot, they're a dime a dozen. If one of them dies, there's thousands more at the border waiting to take their place."

"But surely they don't deserve to be systematically poisoned," I responded in disbelief.

"Patterson, you really are a chump. No one really cares about the poor, except a few weaklings like your Dr. Hall. Most people are happy to let them to do their grunt work, pay them as little as possible, and keep them invisible."

Sadly, I knew he was right. But I didn't have to like it. *What the hell,* I thought. "You're disgusting!"

"I don't like you either, but I've got the gun and you don't, and that's the end of the story. Sorry, Jack, bleeding hearts like you always lose."

He laughed and raised the gun to fire. I heard a muffled noise, then a shot, but felt nothing. Pence's arm flew up—his gun went off, but the bullet hit the ceiling, and he fell to the floor. I looked up to see Brian walk quickly through the door that connected to his room, kick the gun away, and stand over Pence who now lay writing in pain on the floor.

I heard noises and screams in the hallway, but couldn't move.

"You okay, Jack?" Brian asked. "We only have a minute before all hell breaks loose. Put on a robe and pour yourself a stiff drink. Good thing Clovis booked us into adjoining rooms. It's a nice hotel, but these walls aren't very thick."

I still couldn't find my voice, but I managed to find a robe and pulled a little bottle of Brandy from the mini-fridge. It was only a matter of minutes before I saw Sam, Clovis, and Big Mike crash into the room, followed by the police and paramedics who carted Pence off, I assumed to a hospital.

I sat in a corner chair and nursed my brandy, listening to Brian explain that he'd heard what sounded like an argument coming from my room. He grabbed his gun from his suitcase and barged through the door just as Pence was about to kill me. It was pure luck that he shot first.

That's what he told the police, but I wasn't buying a word of. It wasn't pure luck that had saved my ass.

Sam convinced the police to keep their questions to a minimum, and we were soon moved to a fourth floor suite while the officers marked off my former room as a crime scene. Turning suddenly pale, Brian sank into a chair, and Mike handed him a drink.

Clovis asked again, for about the fourth time, if I was okay. I found I could speak and turned to Brian.

"Brian, what can I say? 'Thank you' seems a bit inadequate."

He had regained a little color, but said nothing.

Big Mike turned to me and said, "Didn't I tell you I'd rather have Master Sergeant Hattoy covering my ass than anyone else I know?"

"You did, but he's supposed to be my paralegal, not my bodyguard."

Now he looked truly embarrassed, and Clovis came to his rescue.

"Well, Jack you have a habit of really pissing people off. It takes an army to keep you safe."

After the laughter died down, Sam said, "Jack, I'll need a statement at some point, but Micki has already called to say if I don't let you go home tomorrow, she will personally remove my manhood. Is there anything else I should know tonight?"

"Yes. Pence hired Stalinski to kill Mace and then the others. He told me that Mace couldn't be trusted because of his hatred for me, and the others couldn't keep quiet.

"He also suggested that the corporations who own the big farms knew ZEIT contained arsenic, but chose to look the other way. It will be up to Micki to prove who drove the decision to add arsenic to the formula: the chemical company or the corporations."

A rush of adrenaline and a little booze kept me going, but I'd just about had it. I could hardly keep my eyes open.

Clovis got to his feet and said, "Okay, everyone, that's enough, time to go. Jack can give a statement in DC. Micki will discover who was responsible for the arsenic, and the bad guys will pay the price. Sam, you've got a bright future, both professionally and personally—try not to screw it up. Jana will reopen her clinics and hundreds of Arkansans will have better lives because of her dedication.

"Jack, my friend, it's time for you to go home."

Clovis was right, but his words had a peculiar ring. I'd left Little Rock more than twenty-five years ago and made the decision never to return. But I'd come home many times over the past five years, reconnected with old friends and made new ones. In many ways Little Rock was at least my second home. Yet when Clovis said, "it's time to go home" I felt a quick chill. I sensed finality in his words. Maybe I was still loopy from having escaped death once again, or maybe a chapter in my life was closing.

I collapsed onto the bed and fell asleep to his words "it's time for you to go home" echoing in my head.

Acknowledgements

LIKE ALL MY NOVELS, Suzy read, reread, and edited every draft of this book, and I am constantly grateful for all she brings to my books and life. My children and their spouses are a continual source of ideas, suggestions, and encouragement.

My sister Terry and the professionals at UAMS were a wonderful resource for the health issues raised in this book, especially the difficulties of providing quality health care to the poor in a rural state.

My deepest thanks and appreciation goes to the professionals at Beaufort Books. Eric Kampmann believed in me and the Jack Patterson series from day one. Managing Editor Megan Trank has been a constant in my literary career and a source of support whether it be editing, cover design, publicity, and the hundred other things necessary to turn a manuscript into a published novel. She is a true friend in every sense of the word. A special thanks to Michael Short for the cover design and Carly DaSilva and Georgia Larsen for their editing talents.

I am continually grateful to George and his family.